ROLLER GIRL

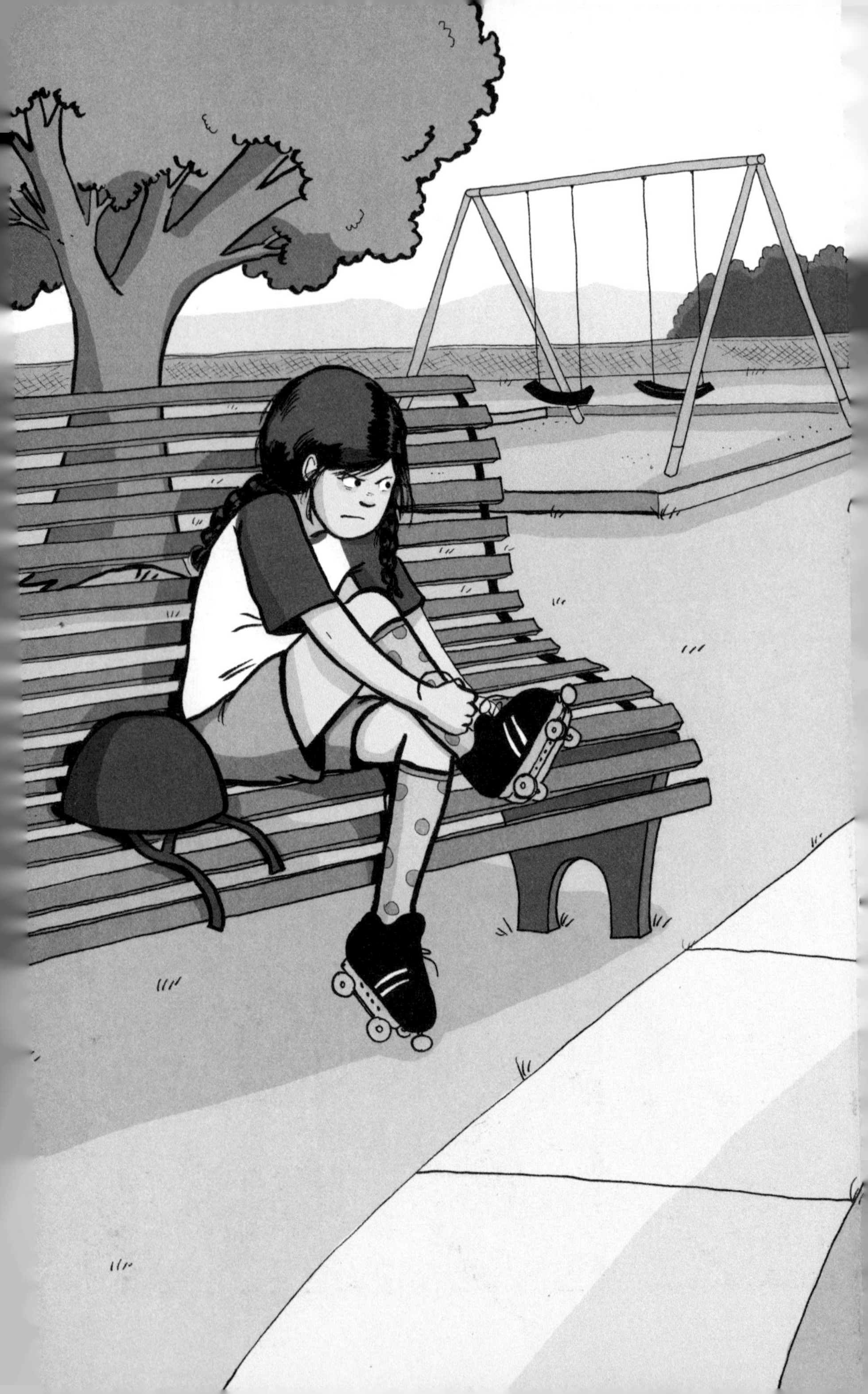

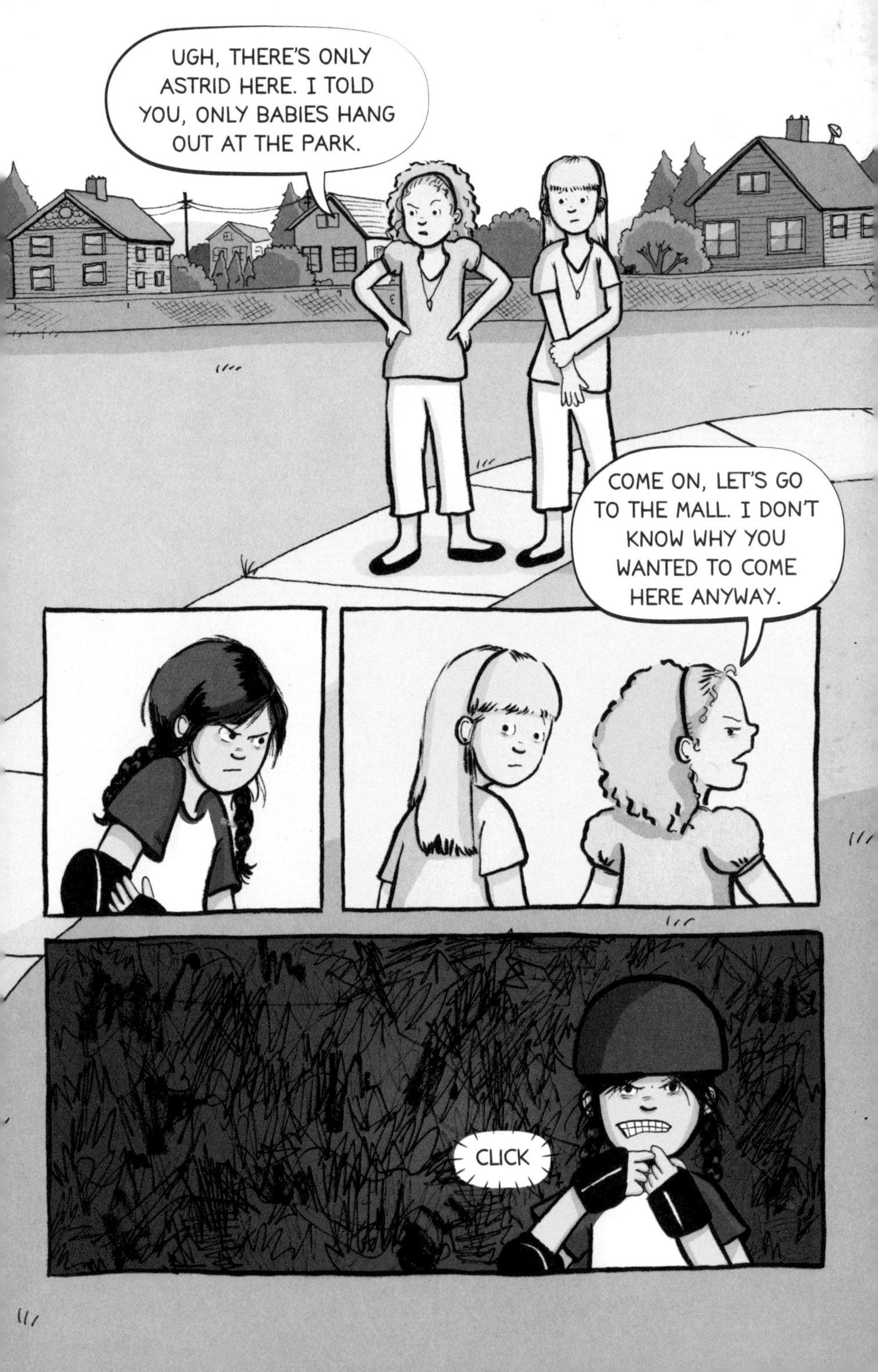
UGH, THERE'S ONLY ASTRID HERE. I TOLD YOU, ONLY BABIES HANG OUT AT THE PARK.
COME ON, LET'S GO TO THE MALL. I DON'T KNOW WHY YOU WANTED TO COME HERE ANYWAY.
CLICK

ROLLER GIRL

by Victoria Jamieson

Dial Books for Young Readers ❦ an imprint of Penguin Group (USA) LLC

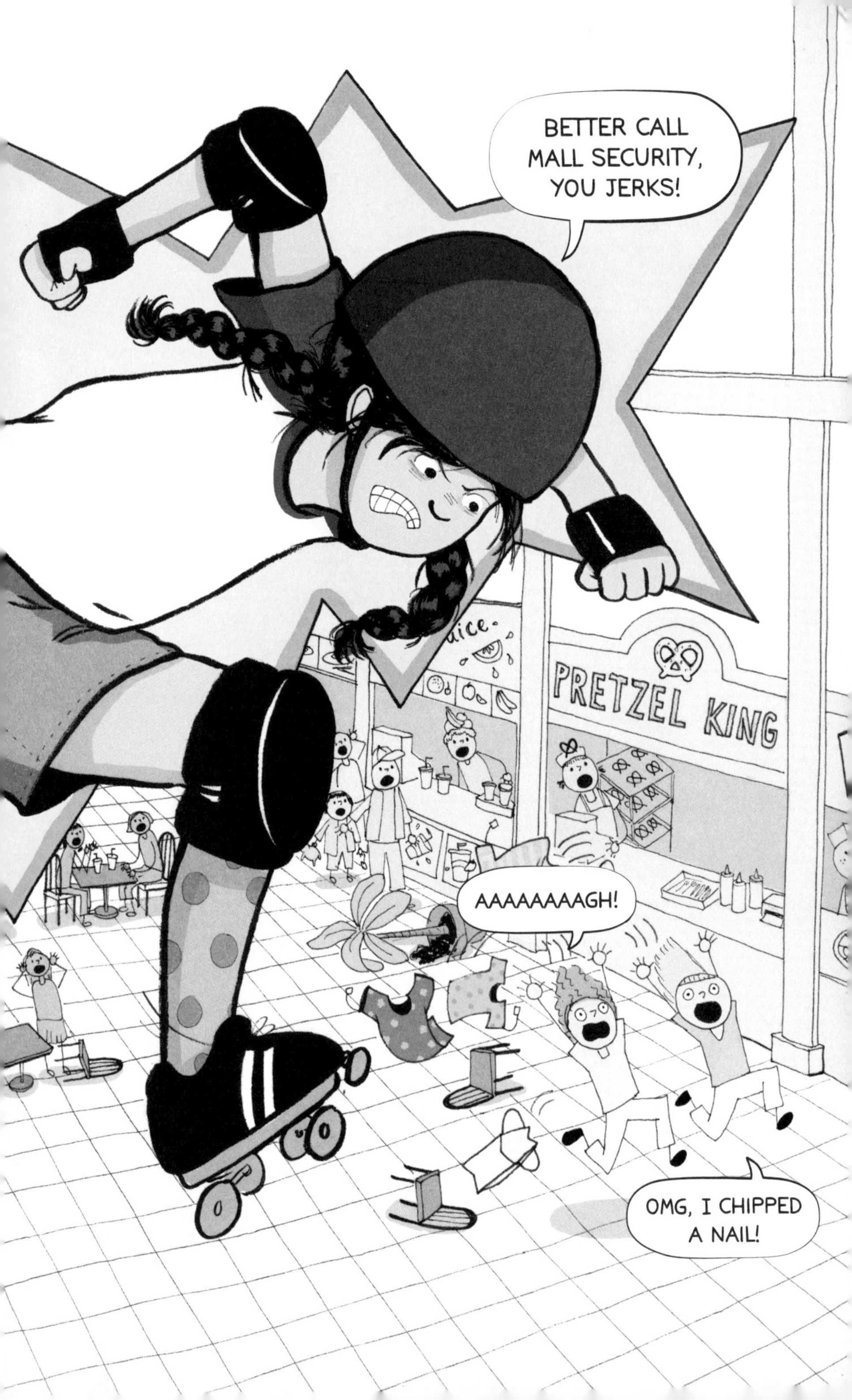

BETTER CALL MALL SECURITY, YOU JERKS!
PRETZEL KING
AAAAAAAAGH!
OMG, I CHIPPED A NAIL!

DIAL BOOKS FOR YOUNG READERS

PUBLISHED BY THE PENGUIN GROUP • PENGUIN GROUP (USA) LLC, 375 HUDSON STREET, NEW YORK, NY 10014

USA I CANADA I UK I IRELAND I AUSTRALIA I NEW ZEALAND I INDIA I SOUTH AFRICA I CHINA

PENGUIN.COM

A PENGUIN RANDOM HOUSE COMPANY

LIBRARY OF CONGRESS CATALOGING-IN-PUBLICATION DATA

JAMIESON, VICTORIA. • ROLLER GIRL / BY VICTORIA JAMIESON.

PAGES CM • SUMMARY: "A GRAPHIC NOVEL ADVENTURE ABOUT A GIRL WHO DISCOVERS ROLLER DERBY RIGHT AS SHE
AND HER BEST FRIEND ARE GROWING APART"— PROVIDED BY PUBLISHER.

ISBN 978-0-8037-4016-7 (PAPERBACK)   ISBN 978-0-525-42967-8 (HARDCOVER)

1. GRAPHIC NOVELS. [1. GRAPHIC NOVELS. 2. ROLLER DERBY— FICTION. 3. ROLLER SKATING— FICTION.

4. BEST FRIENDS— FICTION. 5. FRIENDSHIP— FICTION.] I. TITLE.

PZ7.7.J36RO 2015 741.5'973— DC23 2014011310

MANUFACTURED IN USA ON ACID-FREE PAPER • 10 9 8 7 6 5

DESIGNED BY VICTORIA JAMIESON AND JASON HENRY

THE ARTWORK FOR THIS BOOK WAS CREATED WITH INK AND COLORED DIGITALLY.

THE PUBLISHER DOES NOT HAVE ANY CONTROL OVER AND DOES NOT ASSUME ANY RESPONSIBILITY
FOR AUTHOR OR THIRD-PARTY WEBSITES OR THEIR CONTENT.

Many thanks to skaters around the world who let me borrow their derby names for some of my characters. This book is dedicated to them, and to all the skaters, officials, volunteers, and fans who bring roller derby to life. I'm so proud to be part of this incredible community.

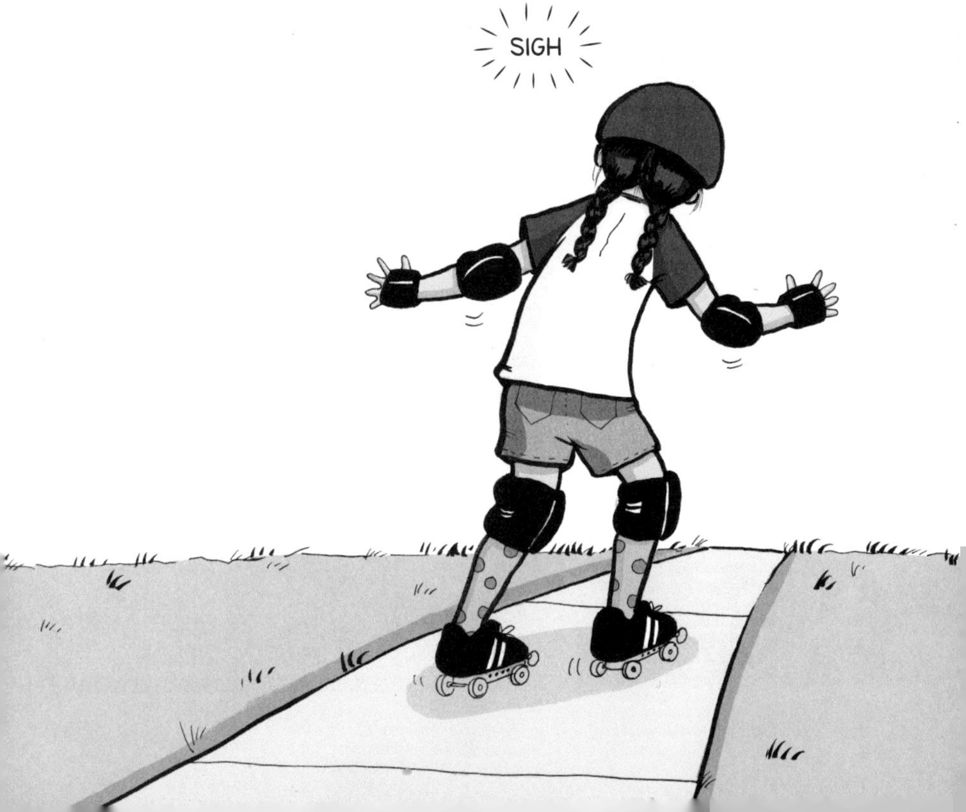
SIGH

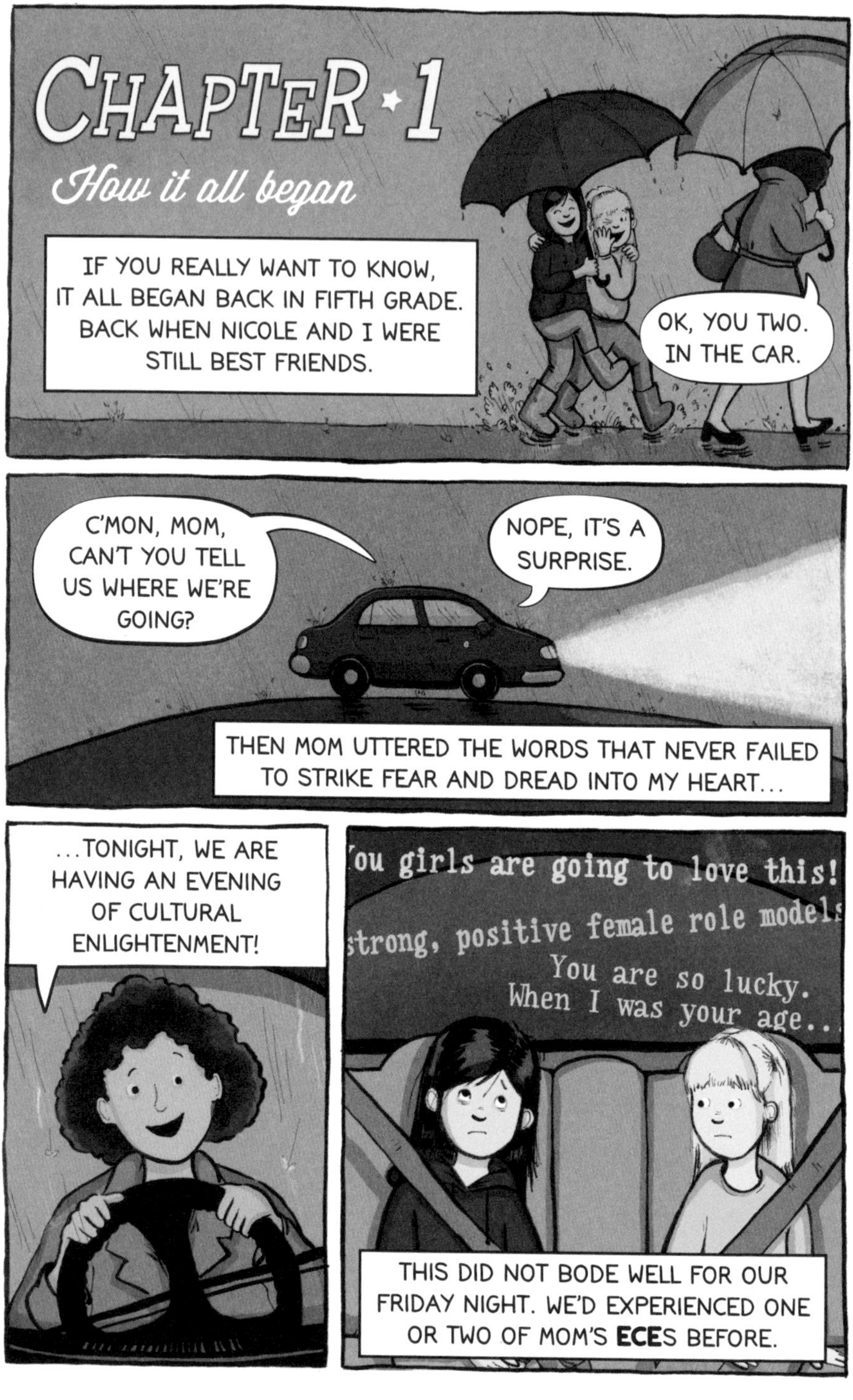
CHAPTER 1
How it all began
IF YOU REALLY WANT TO KNOW, IT ALL BEGAN BACK IN FIFTH GRADE. BACK WHEN NICOLE AND I WERE STILL BEST FRIENDS.
OK, YOU TWO. IN THE CAR.
C'MON, MOM, CAN'T YOU TELL US WHERE WE'RE GOING?
NOPE, IT'S A SURPRISE.
THEN MOM UTTERED THE WORDS THAT NEVER FAILED TO STRIKE FEAR AND DREAD INTO MY HEART...
...TONIGHT, WE ARE HAVING AN EVENING OF CULTURAL ENLIGHTENMENT!
ou girls are going to love this!
strong, positive female role model
You are so lucky.
When I was your age...
THIS DID NOT BODE WELL FOR OUR FRIDAY NIGHT. WE'D EXPERIENCED ONE OR TWO OF MOM'S **ECE**S BEFORE.

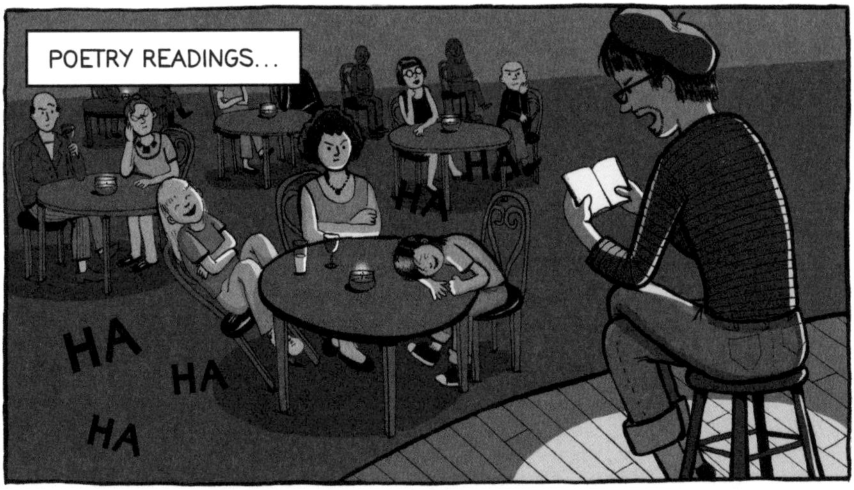
POETRY READINGS...
HA
HA
HA
HA
HA

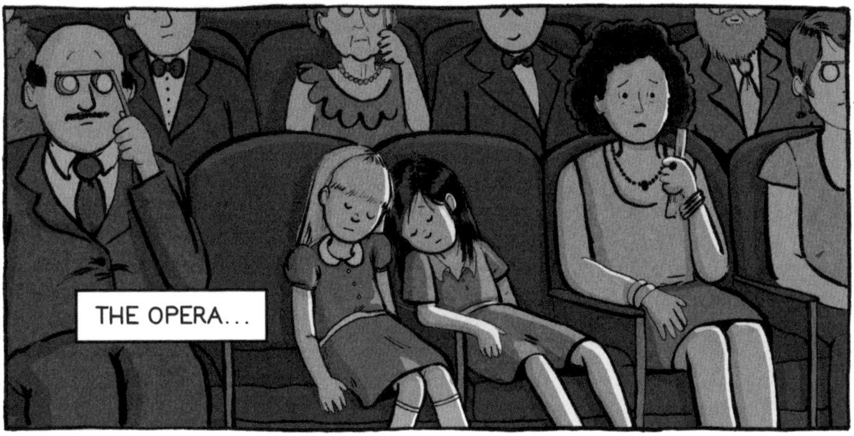
THE OPERA...

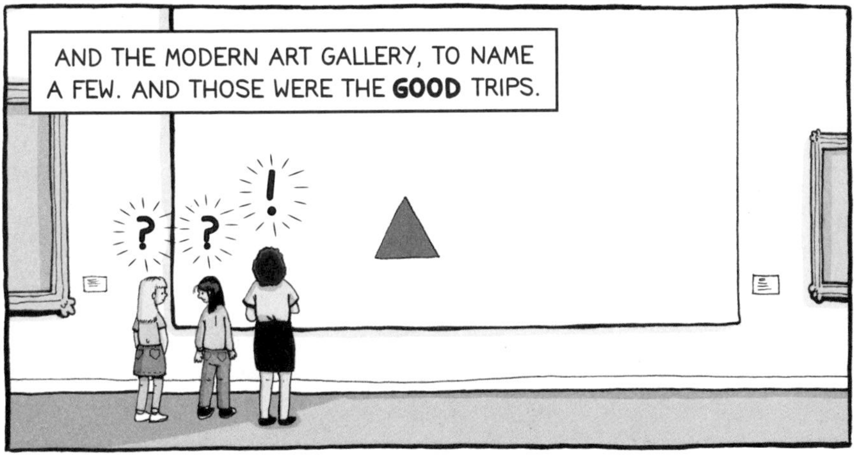
AND THE MODERN ART GALLERY, TO NAME A FEW. AND THOSE WERE THE **GOOD** TRIPS.
?
?
!

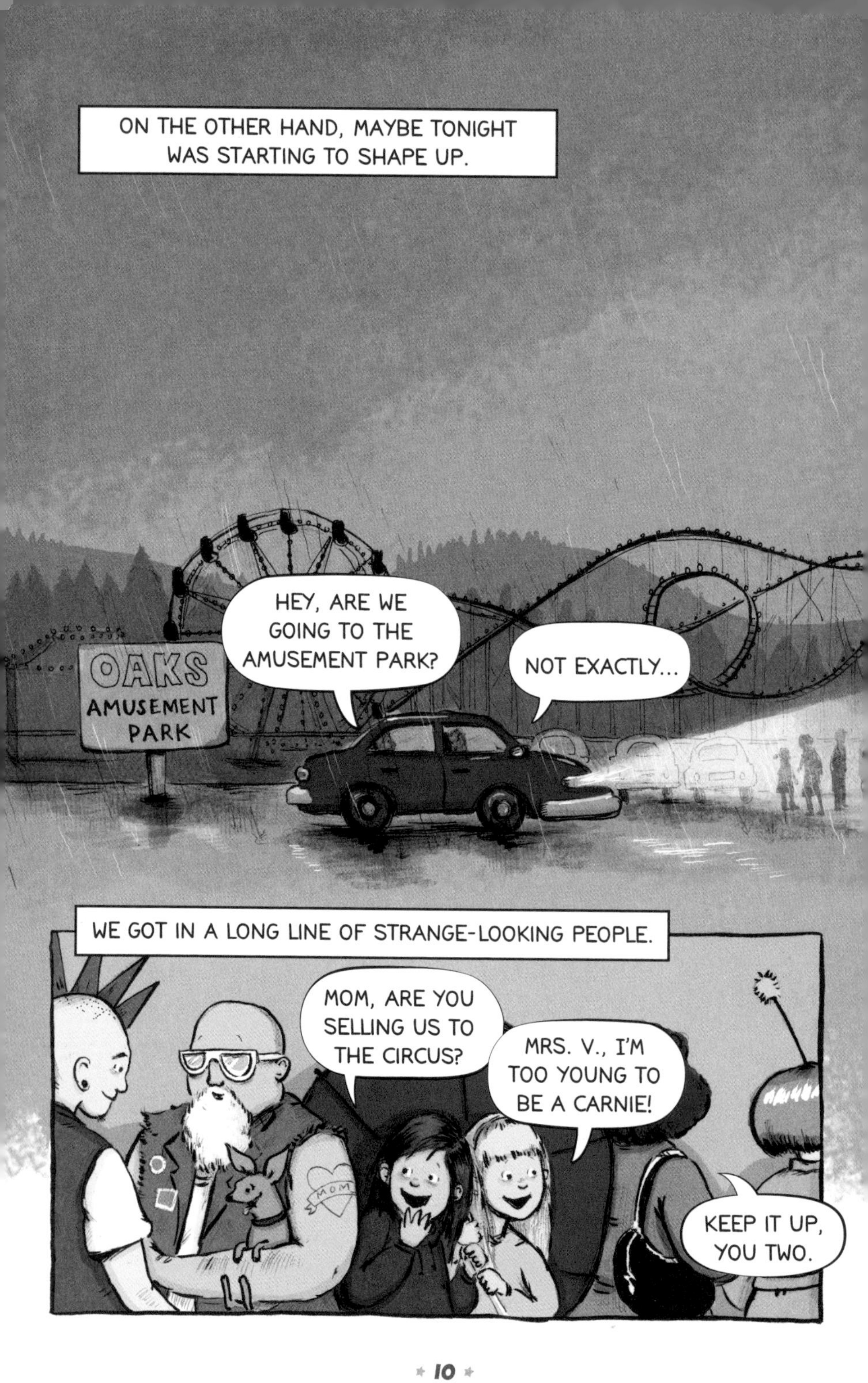
ON THE OTHER HAND, MAYBE TONIGHT WAS STARTING TO SHAPE UP.
OAKS AMUSEMENT PARK
HEY, ARE WE GOING TO THE AMUSEMENT PARK?
NOT EXACTLY...
WE GOT IN A LONG LINE OF STRANGE-LOOKING PEOPLE.
MOM, ARE YOU SELLING US TO THE CIRCUS?
MRS. V., I'M TOO YOUNG TO BE A CARNIE!
MOM
KEEP IT UP, YOU TWO.

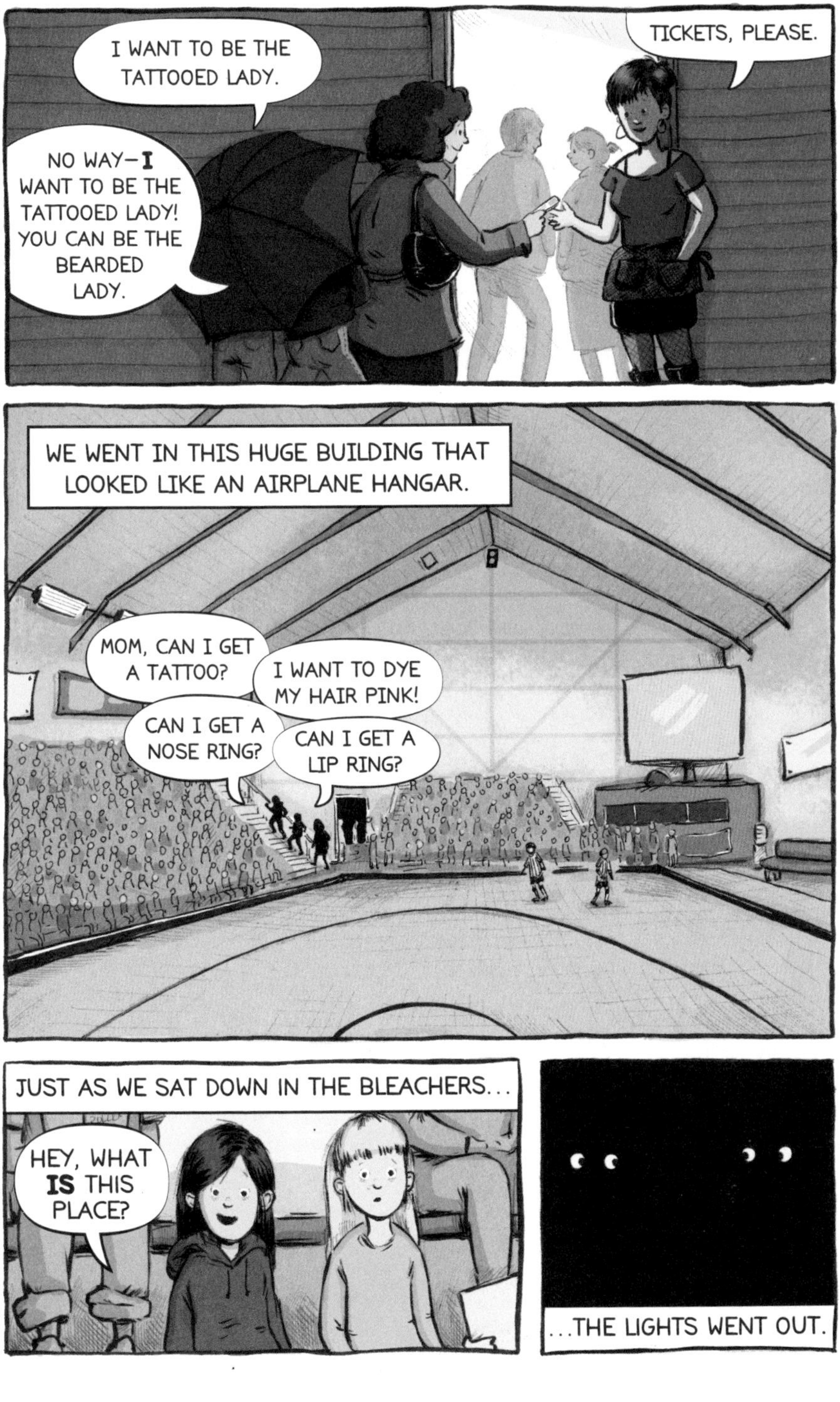
I WANT TO BE THE TATTOOED LADY.
TICKETS, PLEASE.
NO WAY—**I** WANT TO BE THE TATTOOED LADY! YOU CAN BE THE BEARDED LADY.
WE WENT IN THIS HUGE BUILDING THAT LOOKED LIKE AN AIRPLANE HANGAR.
MOM, CAN I GET A TATTOO?
I WANT TO DYE MY HAIR PINK!
CAN I GET A NOSE RING?
CAN I GET A LIP RING?
JUST AS WE SAT DOWN IN THE BLEACHERS...
HEY, WHAT **IS** THIS PLACE?
...THE LIGHTS WENT OUT.

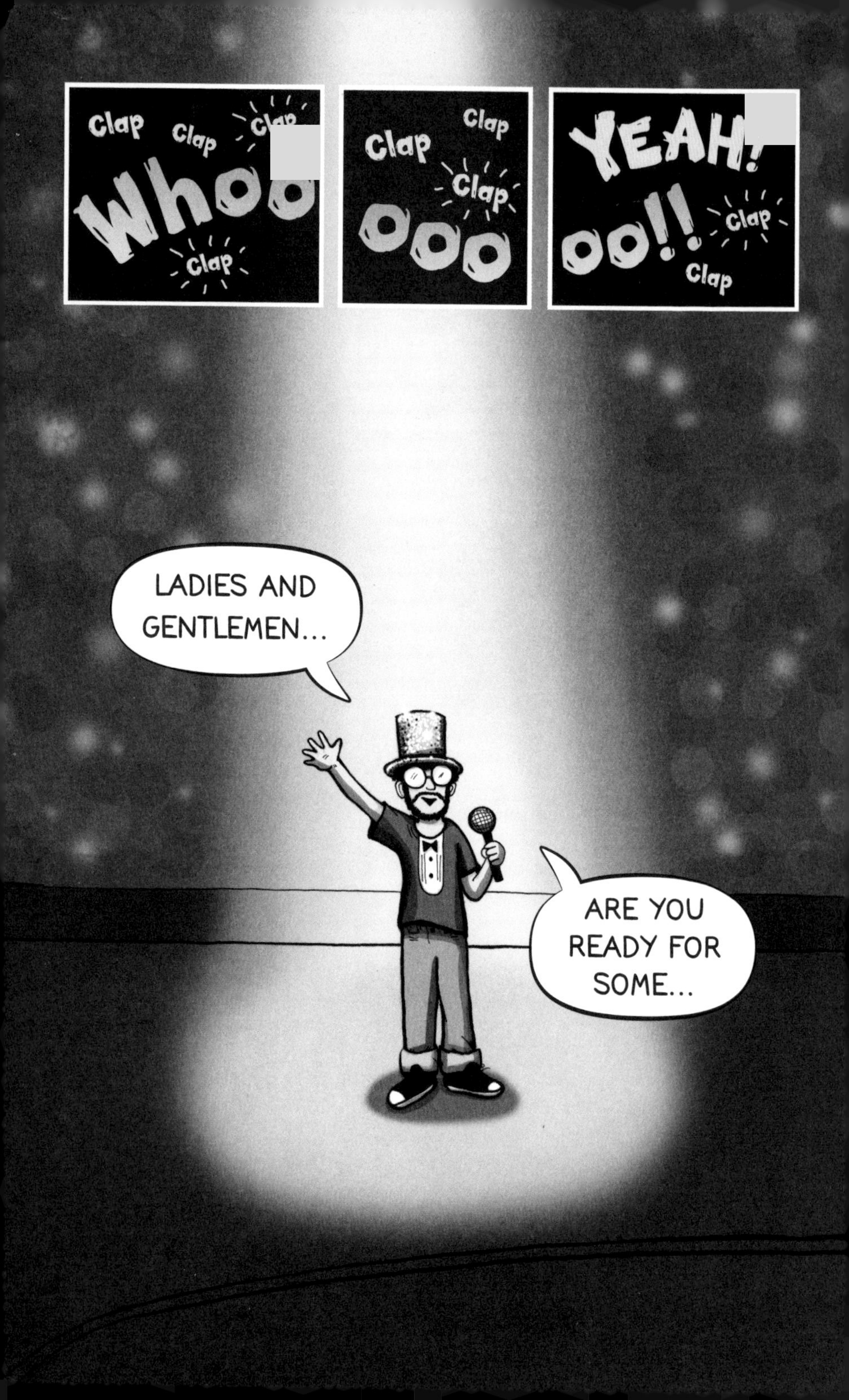

Clap
Clap
Whoo
Clap
Clap
Clap
Clap
OOO
YEAH!
OO!!
Clap
Clap
LADIES AND GENTLEMEN...
ARE YOU READY FOR SOME...

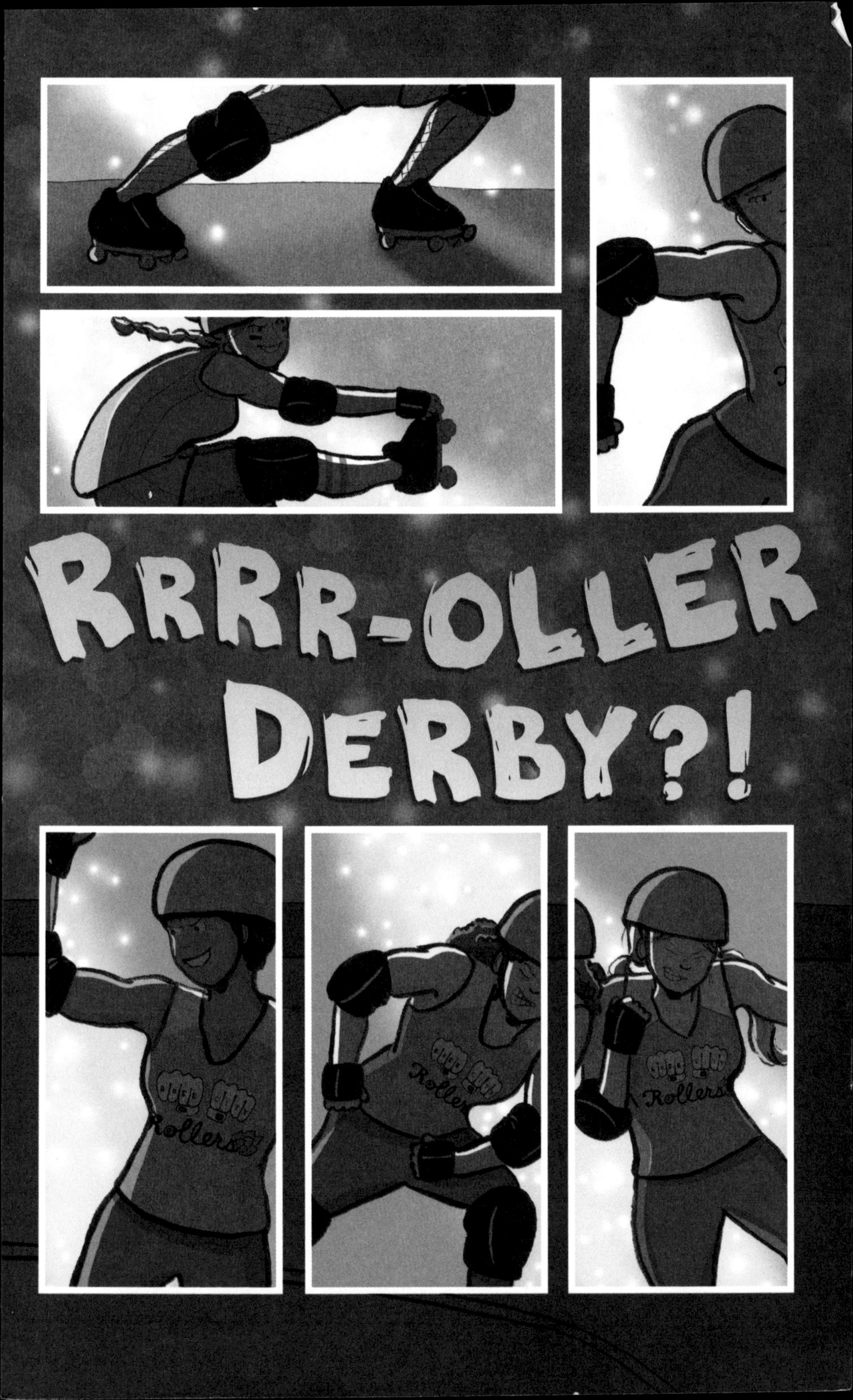
RRRR-OLLER
DERBY?!
Rollers
Rollers
Rollers

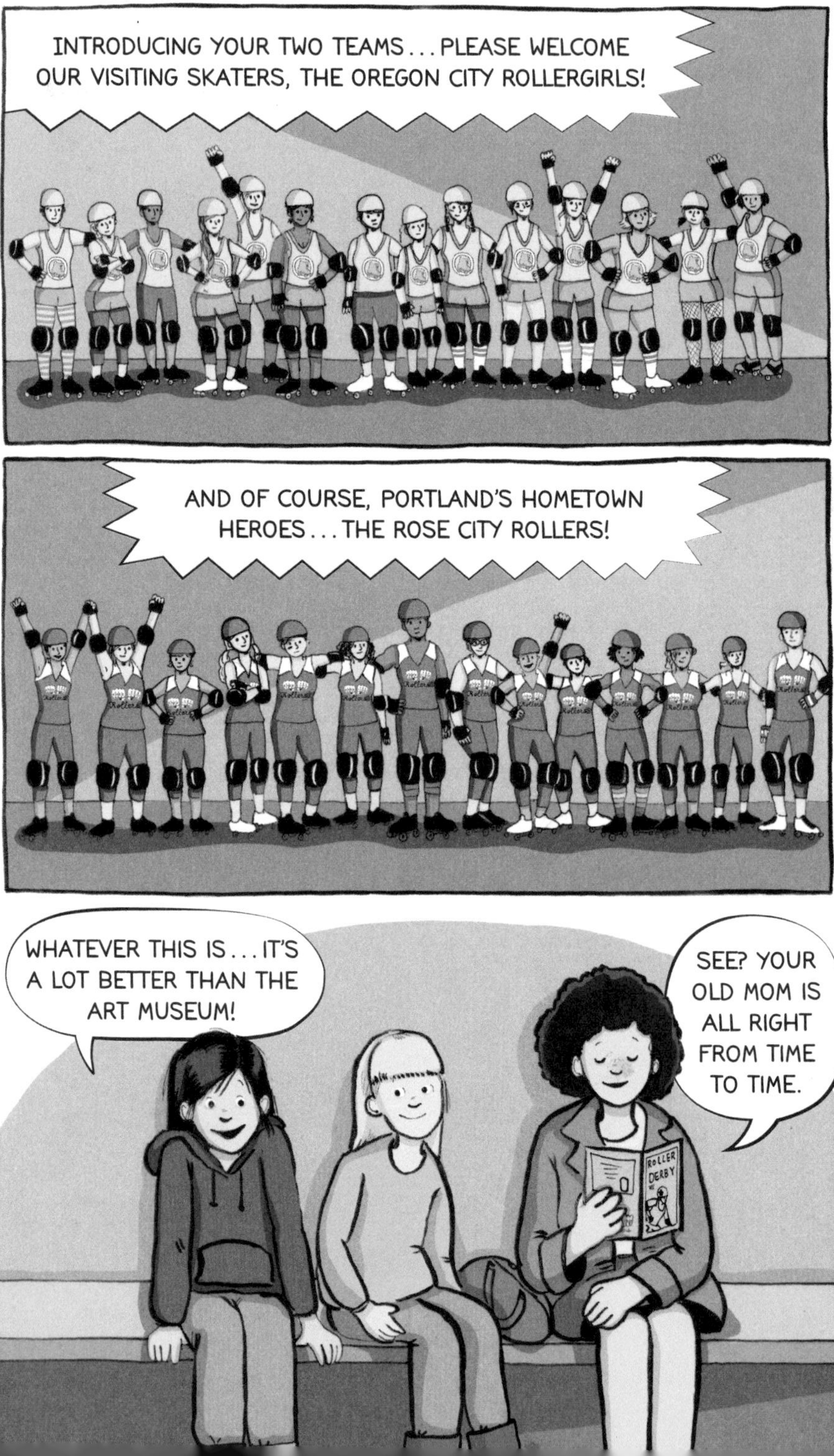
INTRODUCING YOUR TWO TEAMS... PLEASE WELCOME OUR VISITING SKATERS, THE OREGON CITY ROLLERGIRLS!
AND OF COURSE, PORTLAND'S HOMETOWN HEROES... THE ROSE CITY ROLLERS!
WHATEVER THIS IS... IT'S A LOT BETTER THAN THE ART MUSEUM!
SEE? YOUR OLD MOM IS ALL RIGHT FROM TIME TO TIME.
ROLLER DERBY

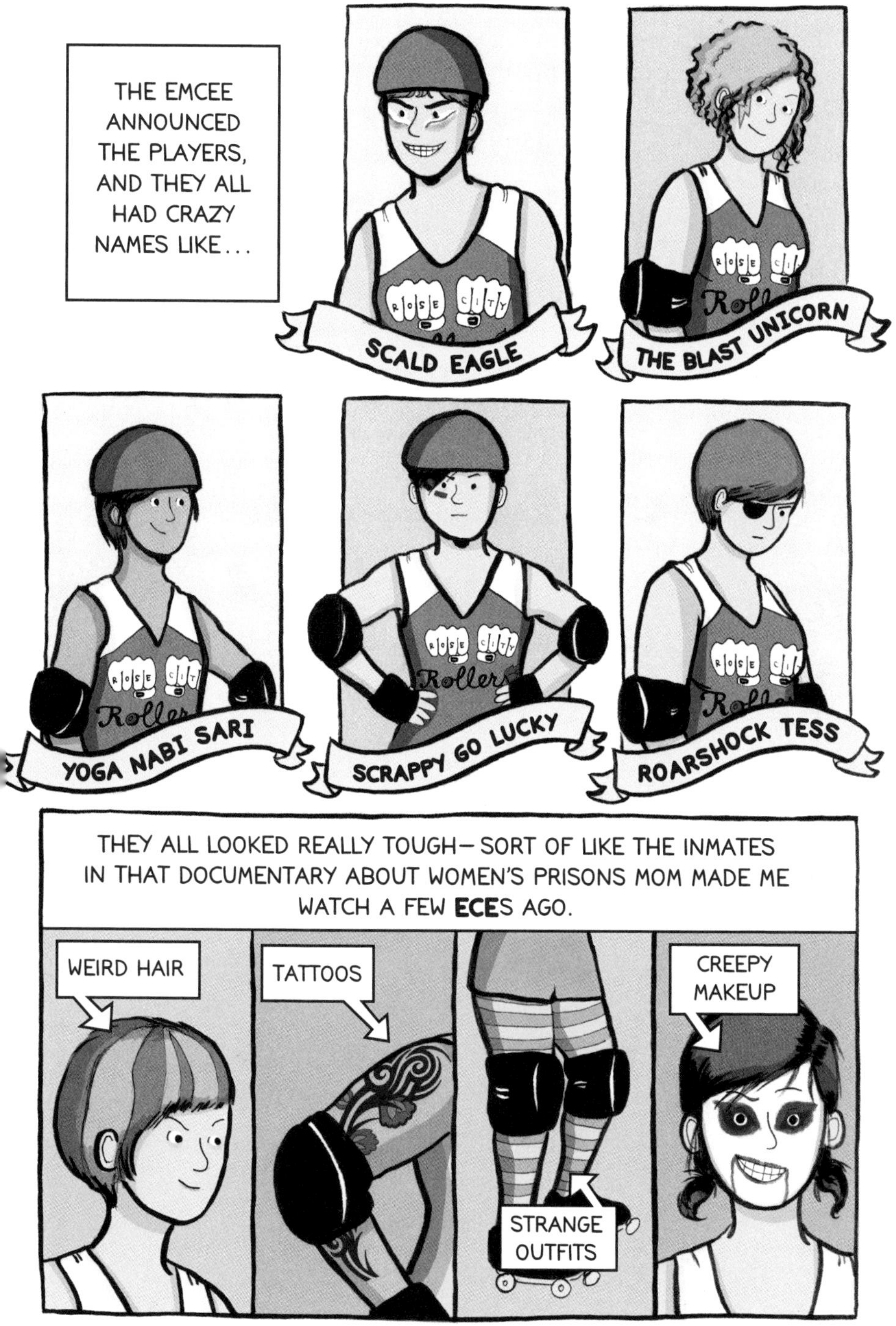
THE EMCEE ANNOUNCED THE PLAYERS, AND THEY ALL HAD CRAZY NAMES LIKE...
SCALD EAGLE
THE BLAST UNICORN
YOGA NABI SARI
SCRAPPY GO LUCKY
ROARSHOCK TESS
THEY ALL LOOKED REALLY TOUGH—SORT OF LIKE THE INMATES IN THAT DOCUMENTARY ABOUT WOMEN'S PRISONS MOM MADE ME WATCH A FEW **ECE**S AGO.
WEIRD HAIR
TATTOOS
STRANGE OUTFITS
CREEPY MAKEUP

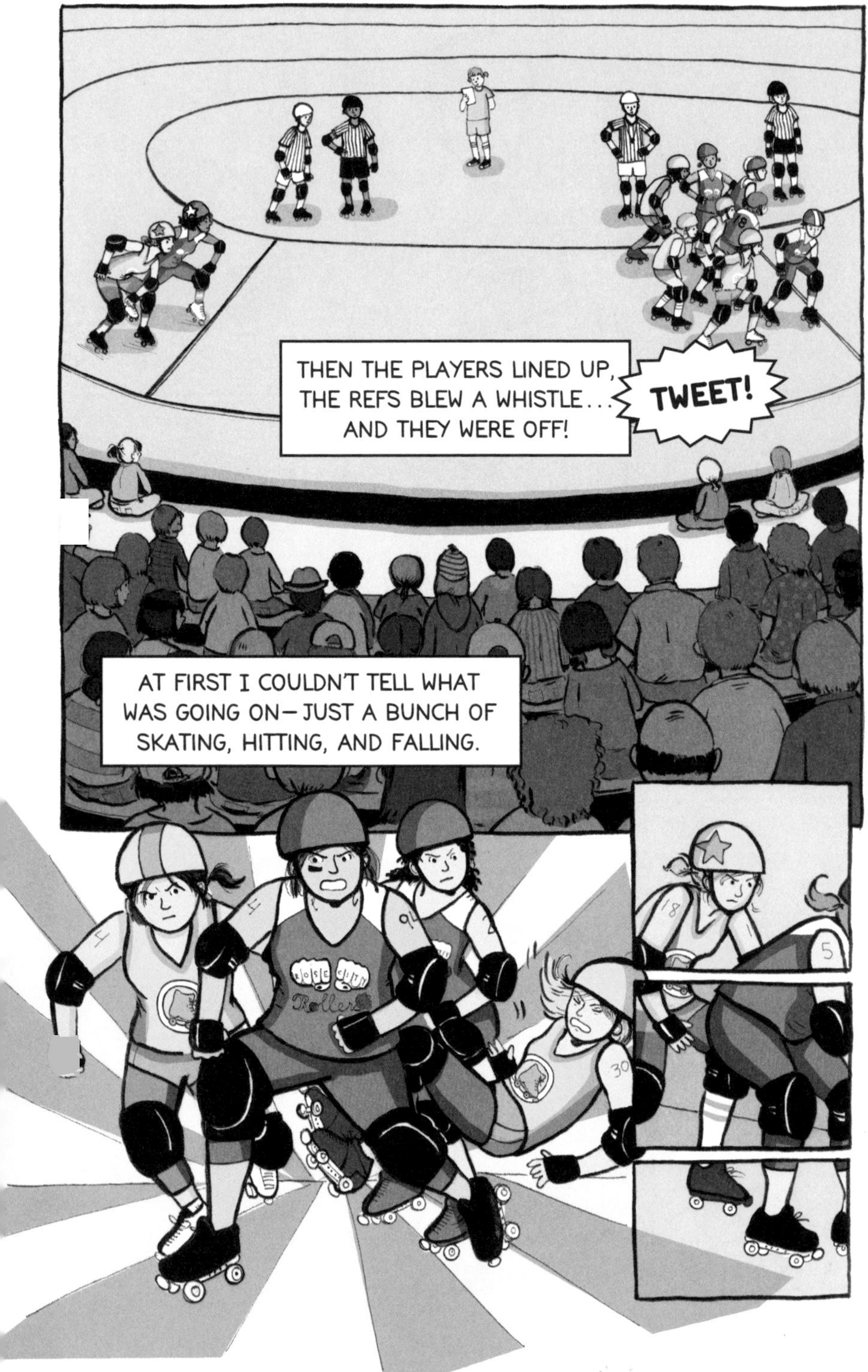
THEN THE PLAYERS LINED UP, THE REFS BLEW A WHISTLE... AND THEY WERE OFF!
TWEET!
AT FIRST I COULDN'T TELL WHAT WAS GOING ON—JUST A BUNCH OF SKATING, HITTING, AND FALLING.
ROSE CITY Rollers

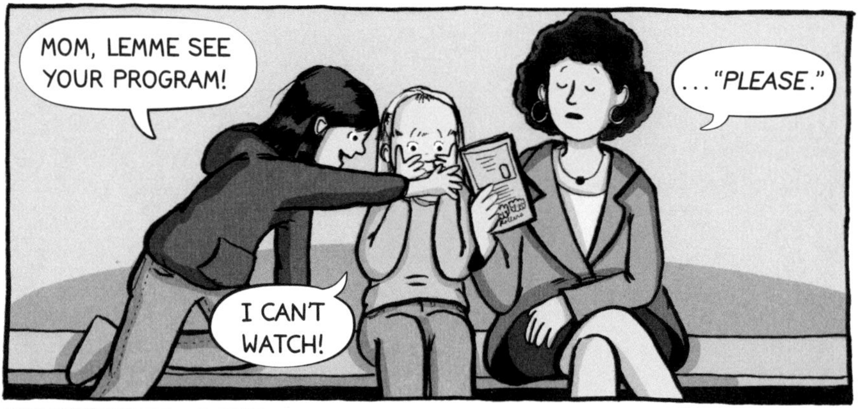
MOM, LEMME SEE YOUR PROGRAM!
I CAN'T WATCH!
. . . "PLEASE."

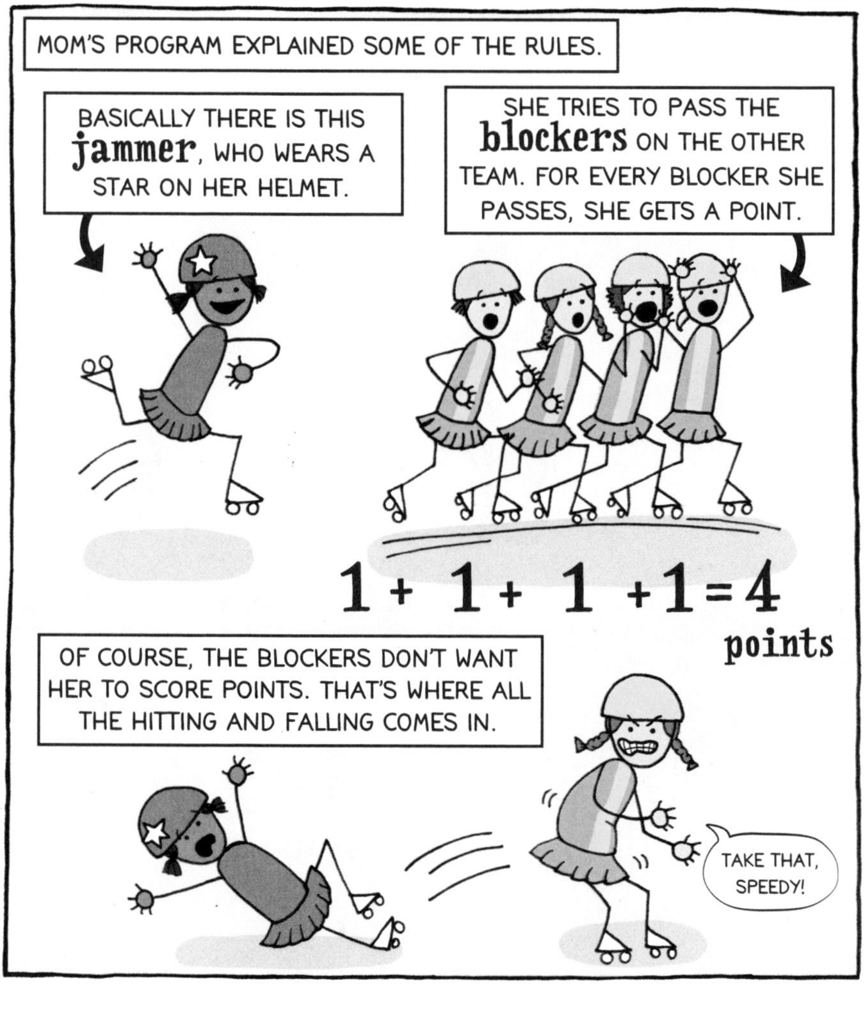
MOM'S PROGRAM EXPLAINED SOME OF THE RULES.
BASICALLY THERE IS THIS jammer, WHO WEARS A STAR ON HER HELMET.
SHE TRIES TO PASS THE blockers ON THE OTHER TEAM. FOR EVERY BLOCKER SHE PASSES, SHE GETS A POINT.
1 + 1 + 1 + 1 = 4
points
OF COURSE, THE BLOCKERS DON'T WANT HER TO SCORE POINTS. THAT'S WHERE ALL THE HITTING AND FALLING COMES IN.
TAKE THAT, SPEEDY!

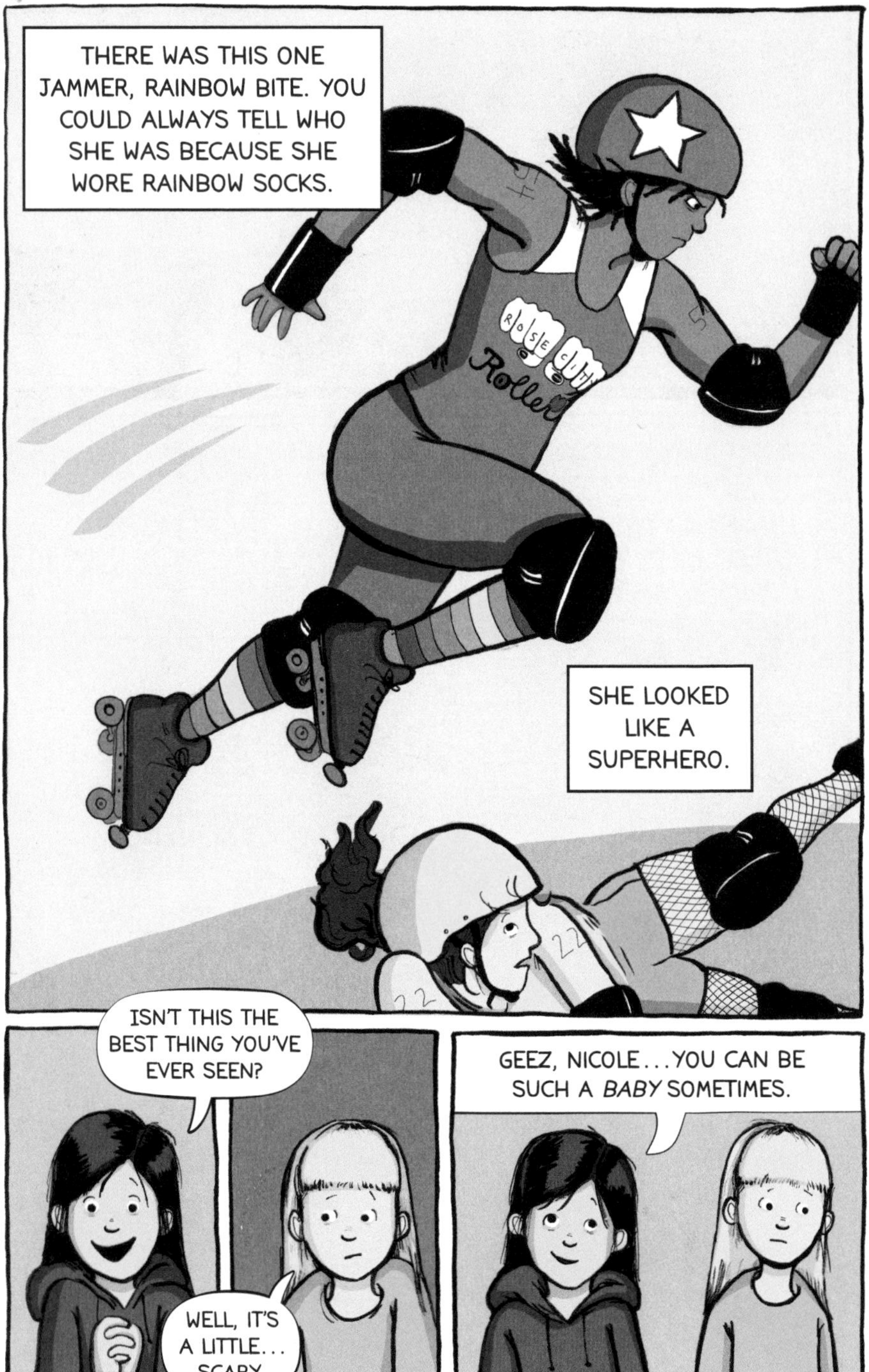
THERE WAS THIS ONE JAMMER, RAINBOW BITE. YOU COULD ALWAYS TELL WHO SHE WAS BECAUSE SHE WORE RAINBOW SOCKS.
ROSE CITY Rollers
SHE LOOKED LIKE A SUPERHERO.
ISN'T THIS THE BEST THING YOU'VE EVER SEEN?
WELL, IT'S A LITTLE... SCARY.
GEEZ, NICOLE...YOU CAN BE SUCH A *BABY* SOMETIMES.

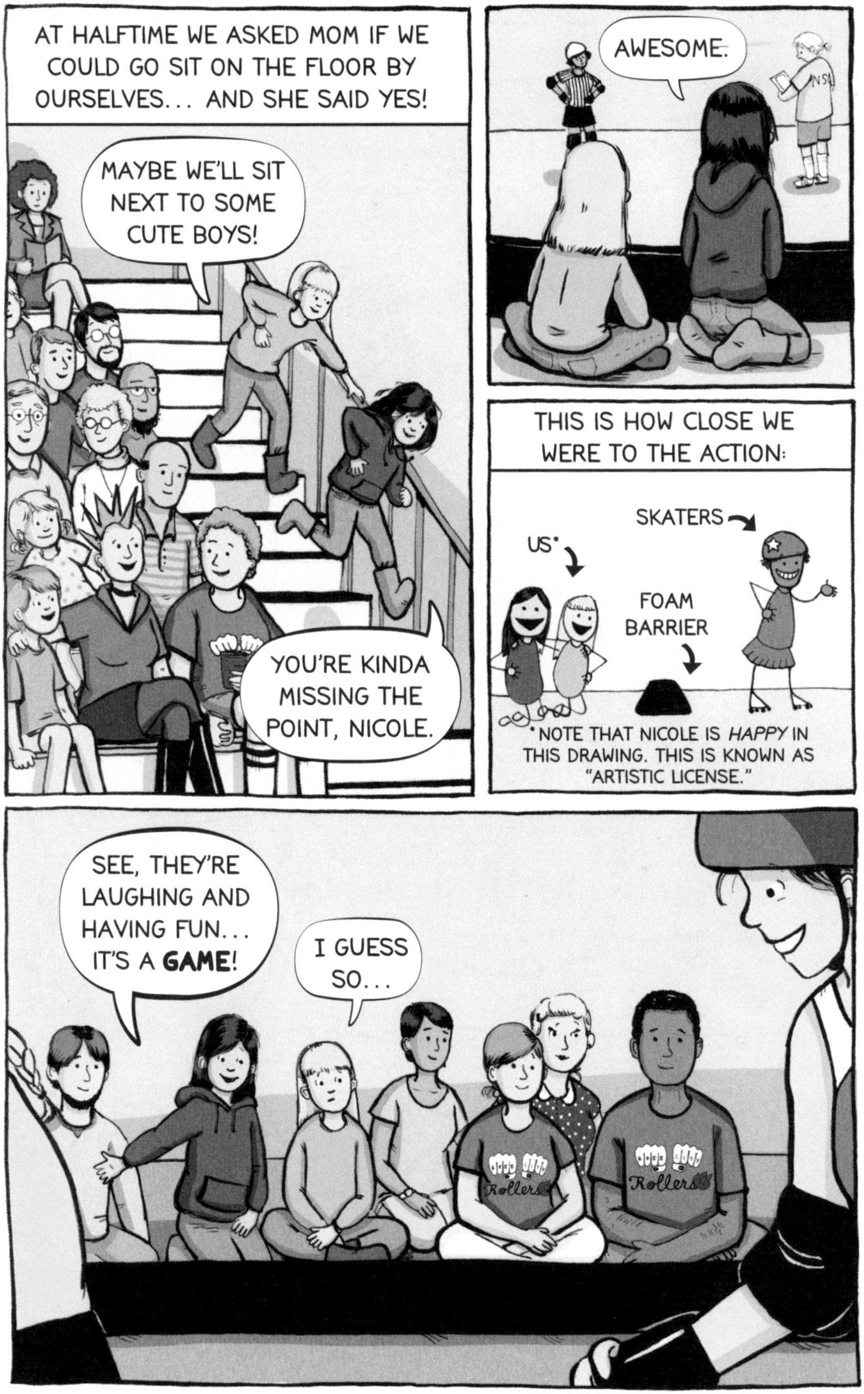
AT HALFTIME WE ASKED MOM IF WE COULD GO SIT ON THE FLOOR BY OURSELVES... AND SHE SAID YES!
MAYBE WE'LL SIT NEXT TO SOME CUTE BOYS!
YOU'RE KINDA MISSING THE POINT, NICOLE.
AWESOME.
THIS IS HOW CLOSE WE WERE TO THE ACTION:
SKATERS
US*
FOAM BARRIER
*NOTE THAT NICOLE IS *HAPPY* IN THIS DRAWING. THIS IS KNOWN AS "ARTISTIC LICENSE."
SEE, THEY'RE LAUGHING AND HAVING FUN... IT'S A **GAME**!
I GUESS SO...

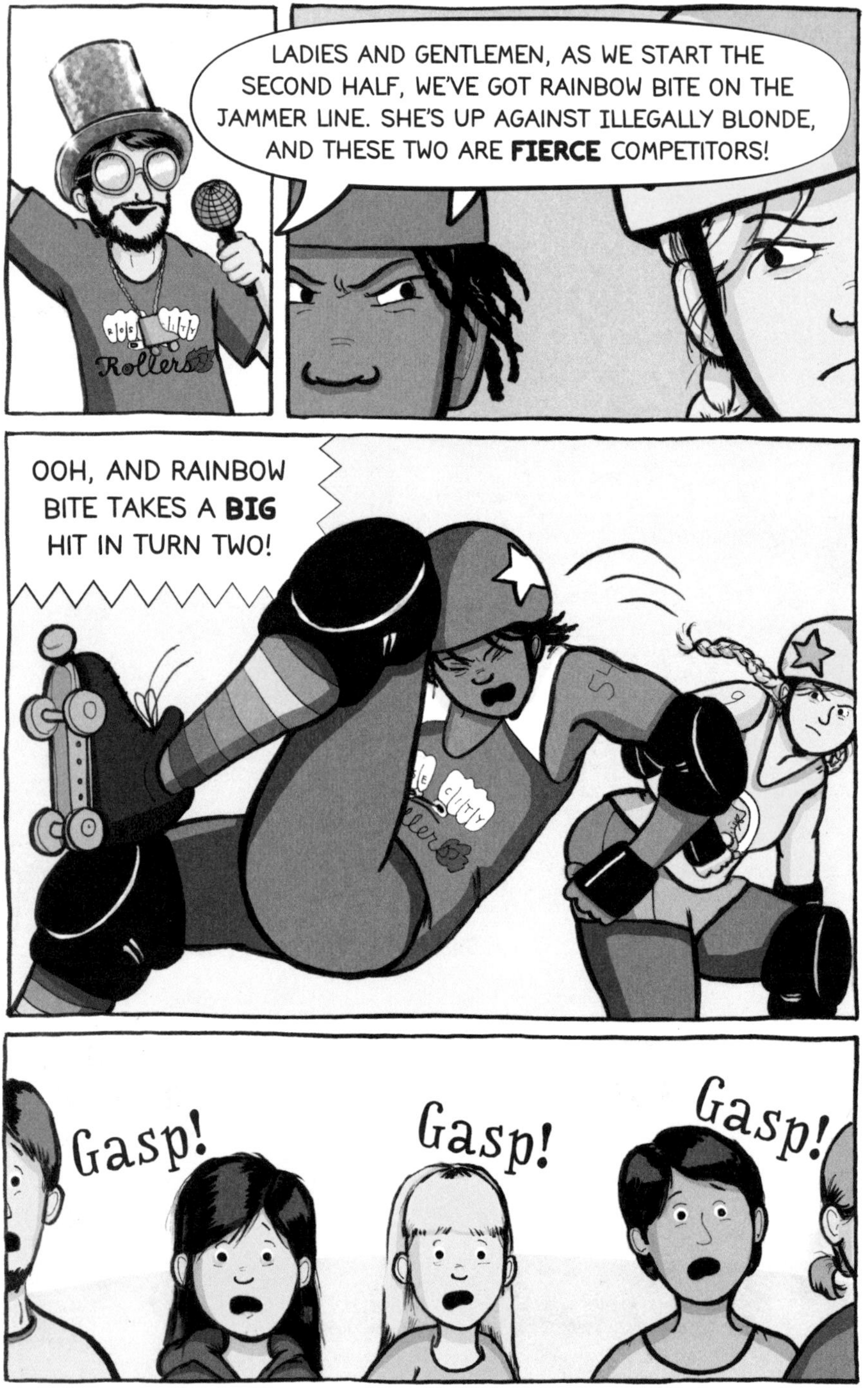
LADIES AND GENTLEMEN, AS WE START THE SECOND HALF, WE'VE GOT RAINBOW BITE ON THE JAMMER LINE. SHE'S UP AGAINST ILLEGALLY BLONDE, AND THESE TWO ARE **FIERCE** COMPETITORS!
OOH, AND RAINBOW BITE TAKES A **BIG** HIT IN TURN TWO!
Gasp!
Gasp!
Gasp!

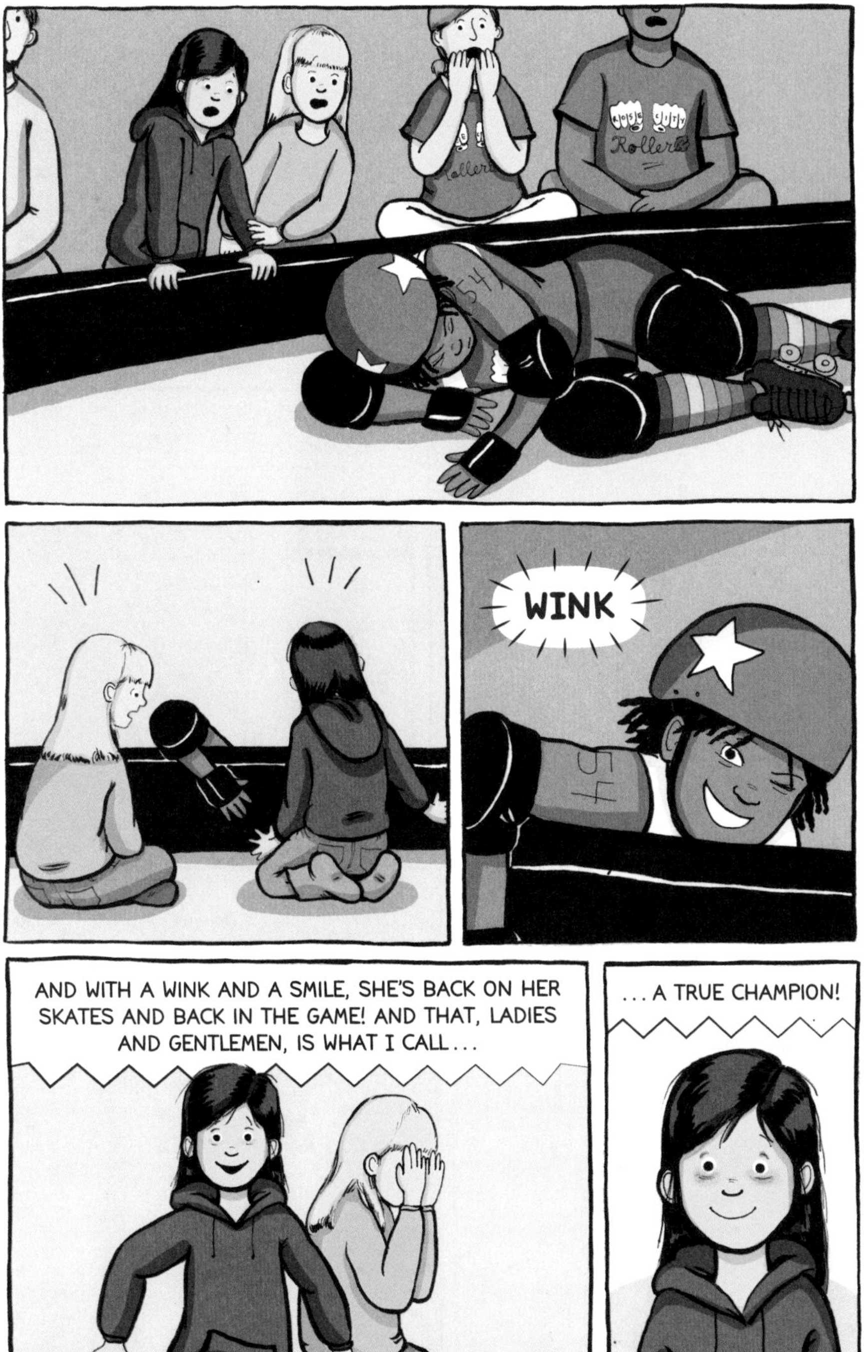

ROSE CITY Rollers
WINK
AND WITH A WINK AND A SMILE, SHE'S BACK ON HER SKATES AND BACK IN THE GAME! AND THAT, LADIES AND GENTLEMEN, IS WHAT I CALL...
...A TRUE CHAMPION!

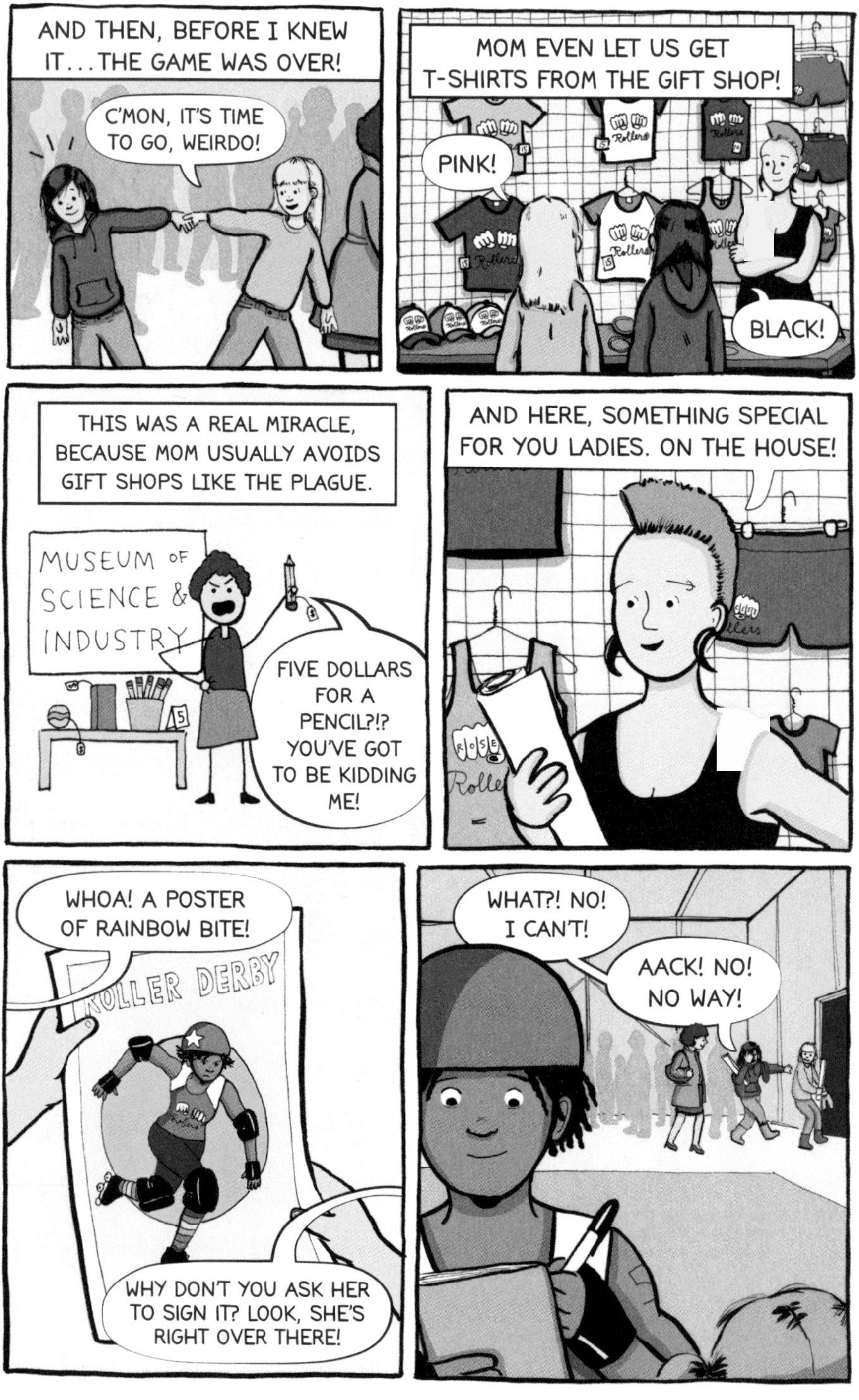
AND THEN, BEFORE I KNEW IT... THE GAME WAS OVER!
C'MON, IT'S TIME TO GO, WEIRDO!
MOM EVEN LET US GET T-SHIRTS FROM THE GIFT SHOP!
PINK!
BLACK!
THIS WAS A REAL MIRACLE, BECAUSE MOM USUALLY AVOIDS GIFT SHOPS LIKE THE PLAGUE.
MUSEUM OF SCIENCE & INDUSTRY
FIVE DOLLARS FOR A PENCIL?!? YOU'VE GOT TO BE KIDDING ME!
AND HERE, SOMETHING SPECIAL FOR YOU LADIES. ON THE HOUSE!
WHOA! A POSTER OF RAINBOW BITE!
ROLLER DERBY
WHY DON'T YOU ASK HER TO SIGN IT? LOOK, SHE'S RIGHT OVER THERE!
WHAT?! NO! I CAN'T!
AACK! NO! NO WAY!

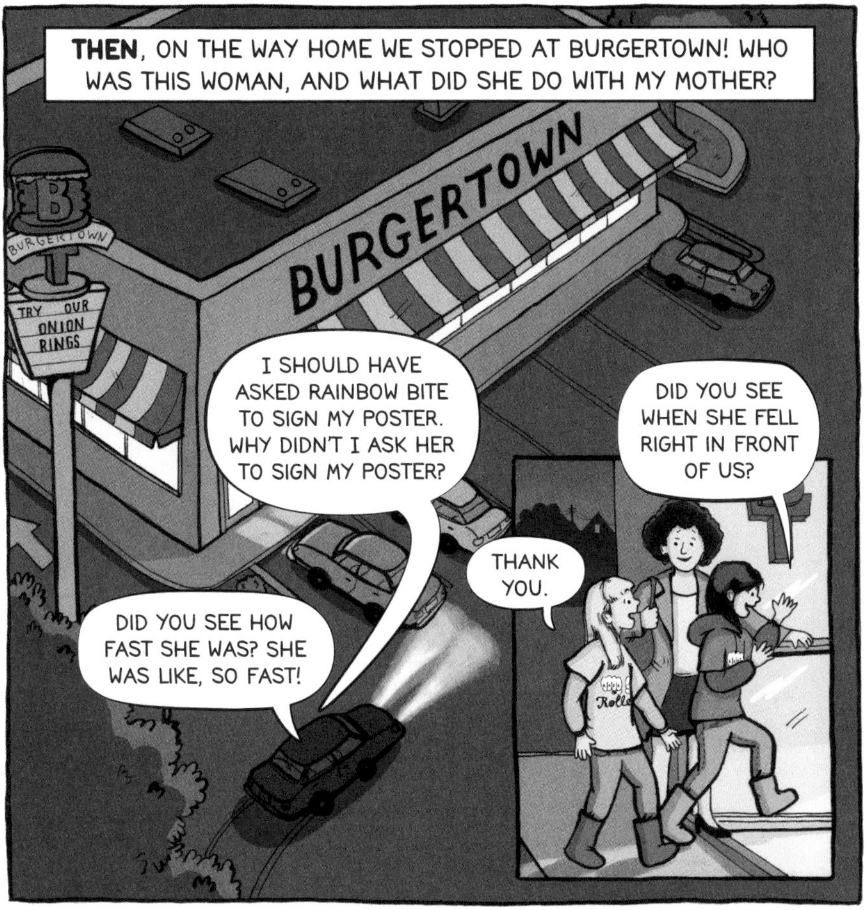
THEN, ON THE WAY HOME WE STOPPED AT BURGERTOWN! WHO WAS THIS WOMAN, AND WHAT DID SHE DO WITH MY MOTHER?
BURGERTOWN
BURGERTOWN
TRY OUR ONION RINGS
I SHOULD HAVE ASKED RAINBOW BITE TO SIGN MY POSTER. WHY DIDN'T I ASK HER TO SIGN MY POSTER?
DID YOU SEE WHEN SHE FELL RIGHT IN FRONT OF US?
THANK YOU.
DID YOU SEE HOW FAST SHE WAS? SHE WAS LIKE, SO FAST!

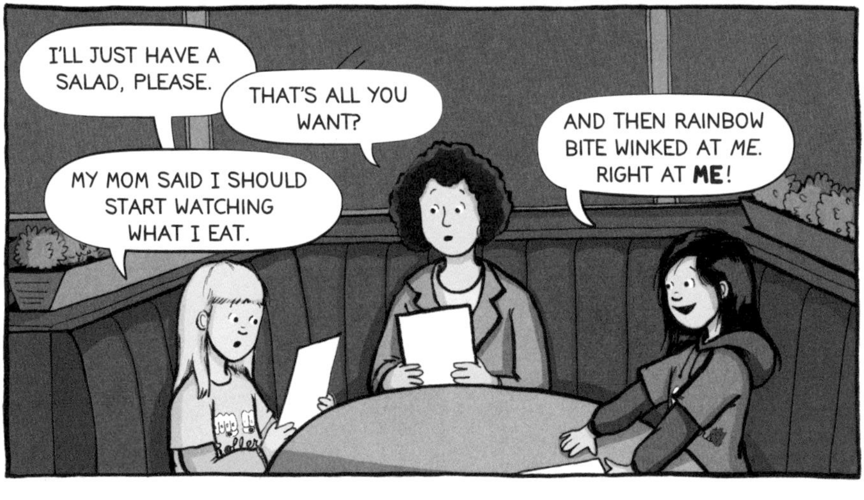
I'LL JUST HAVE A SALAD, PLEASE.
THAT'S ALL YOU WANT?
MY MOM SAID I SHOULD START WATCHING WHAT I EAT.
AND THEN RAINBOW BITE WINKED AT *ME*. RIGHT AT **ME**!

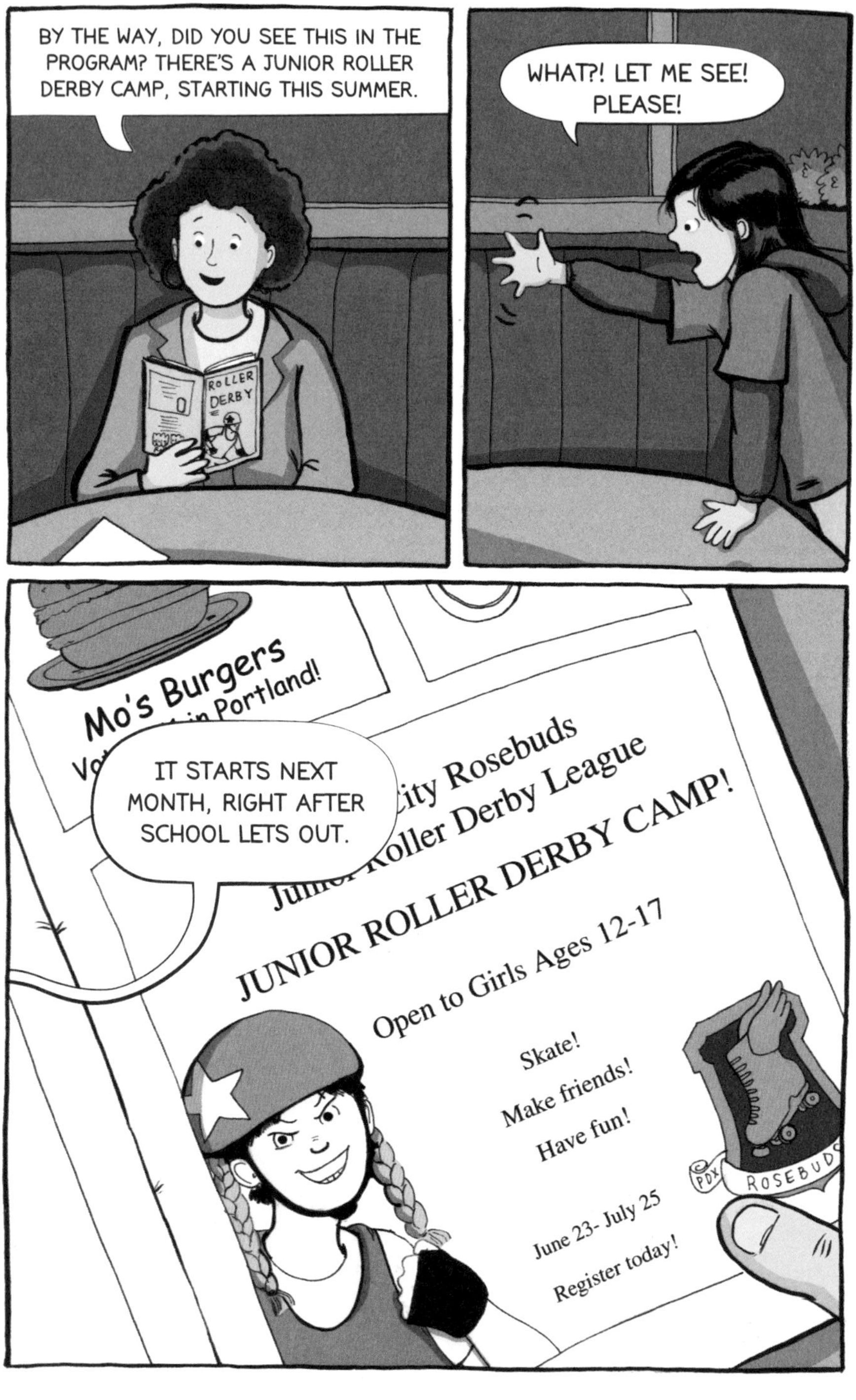
BY THE WAY, DID YOU SEE THIS IN THE PROGRAM? THERE'S A JUNIOR ROLLER DERBY CAMP, STARTING THIS SUMMER.
ROLLER DERBY
WHAT?! LET ME SEE! PLEASE!
Mo's Burgers
in Portland!
IT STARTS NEXT MONTH, RIGHT AFTER SCHOOL LETS OUT.
City Rosebuds
Roller Derby League
JUNIOR ROLLER DERBY CAMP!
Open to Girls Ages 12-17
Skate!
Make friends!
Have fun!
June 23- July 25
Register today!
PDX
ROSEBUDS

AND JUST LIKE THAT, MY FATE WAS DECIDED.
I WAS GOING TO BE A ROLLER GIRL.
ROSE CITY
Rollers

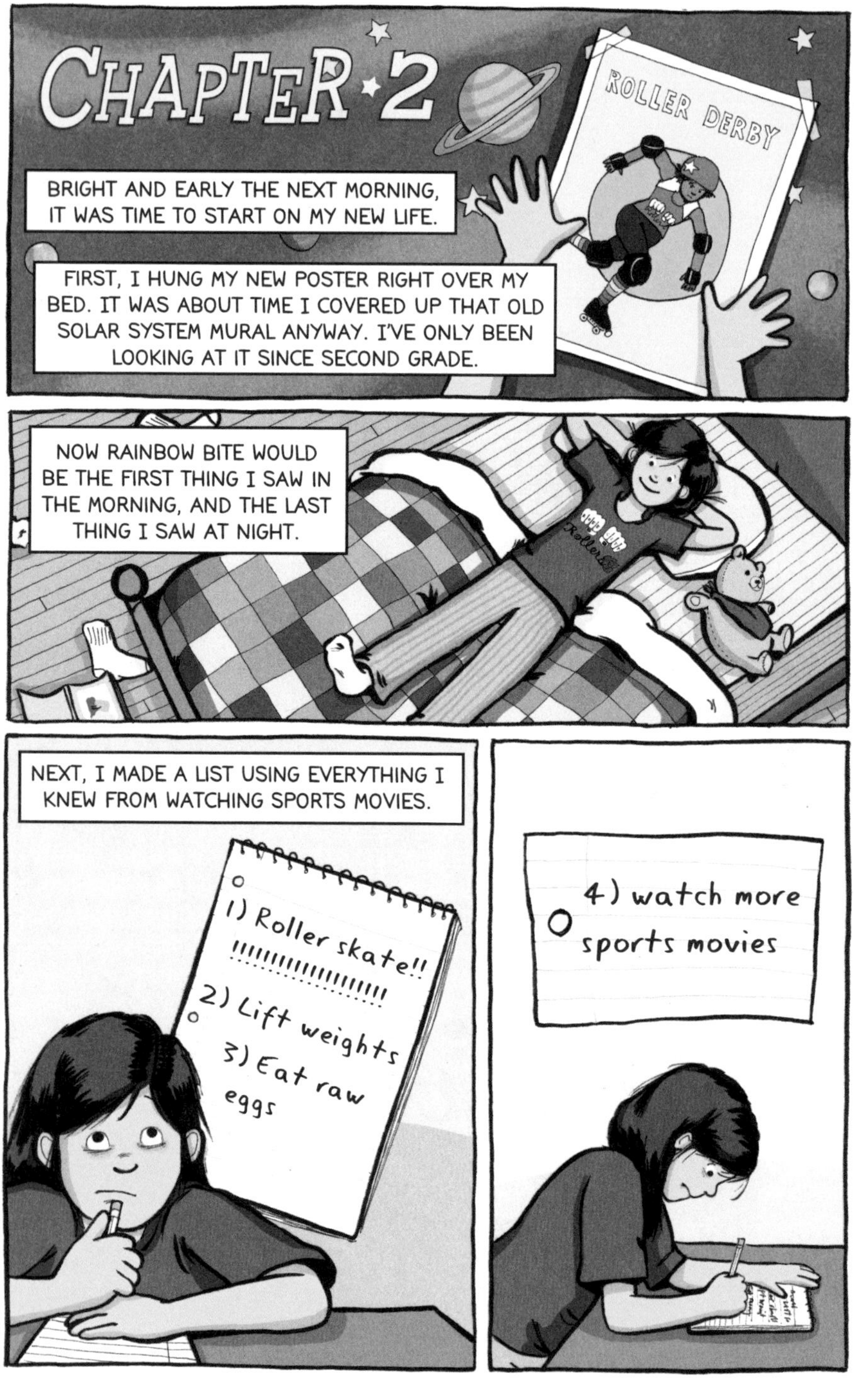

CHAPTER 2
ROLLER DERBY
BRIGHT AND EARLY THE NEXT MORNING, IT WAS TIME TO START ON MY NEW LIFE.
FIRST, I HUNG MY NEW POSTER RIGHT OVER MY BED. IT WAS ABOUT TIME I COVERED UP THAT OLD SOLAR SYSTEM MURAL ANYWAY. I'VE ONLY BEEN LOOKING AT IT SINCE SECOND GRADE.
NOW RAINBOW BITE WOULD BE THE FIRST THING I SAW IN THE MORNING, AND THE LAST THING I SAW AT NIGHT.
Rollers
NEXT, I MADE A LIST USING EVERYTHING I KNEW FROM WATCHING SPORTS MOVIES.
1) Roller skate!!
!!!!!!!!!!!!!!!!!!!!
2) Lift weights
3) Eat raw eggs
4) watch more sports movies

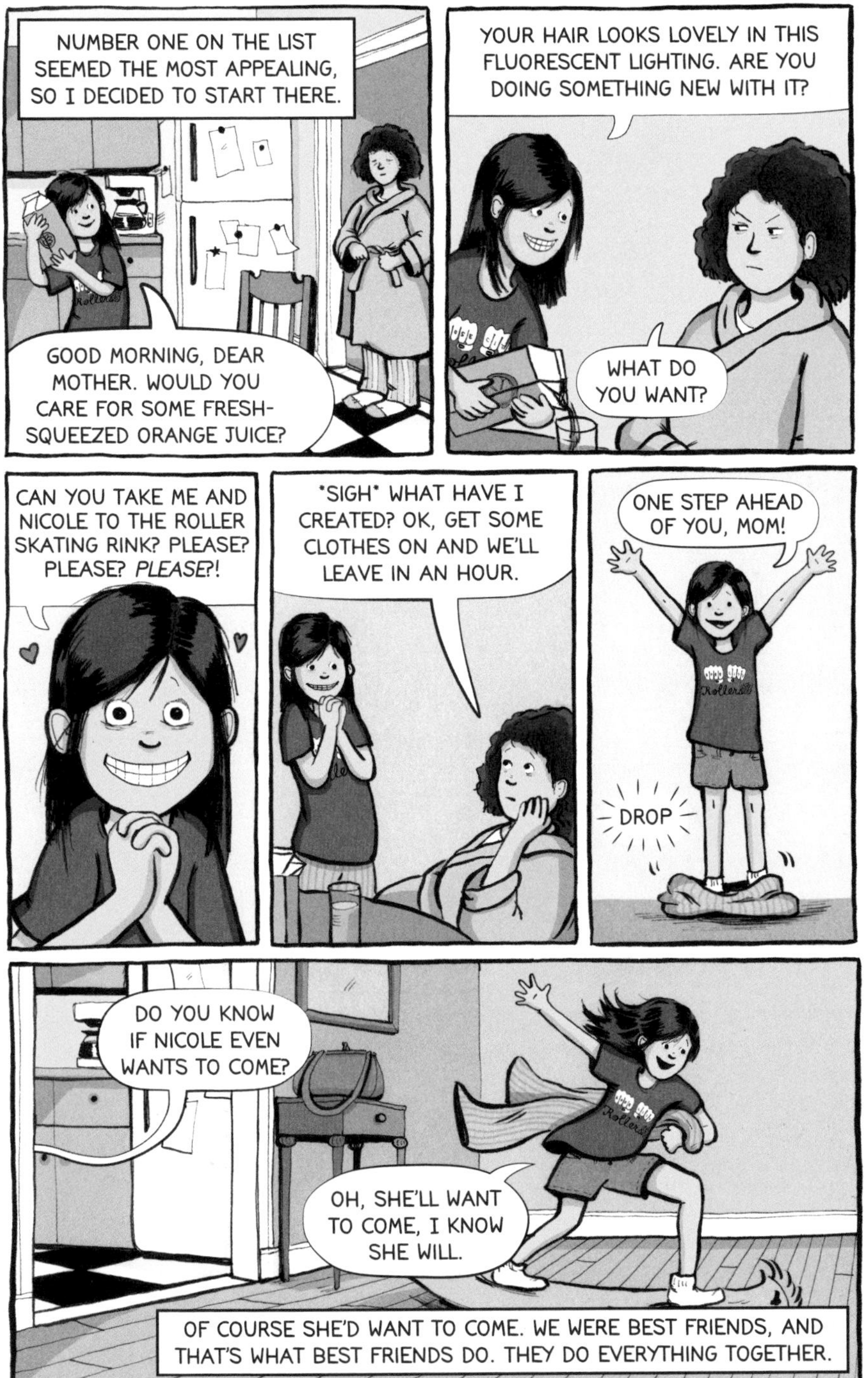
NUMBER ONE ON THE LIST SEEMED THE MOST APPEALING, SO I DECIDED TO START THERE.
GOOD MORNING, DEAR MOTHER. WOULD YOU CARE FOR SOME FRESH-SQUEEZED ORANGE JUICE?
YOUR HAIR LOOKS LOVELY IN THIS FLUORESCENT LIGHTING. ARE YOU DOING SOMETHING NEW WITH IT?
WHAT DO YOU WANT?
CAN YOU TAKE ME AND NICOLE TO THE ROLLER SKATING RINK? PLEASE? PLEASE? *PLEASE*?!
SIGH WHAT HAVE I CREATED? OK, GET SOME CLOTHES ON AND WE'LL LEAVE IN AN HOUR.
ONE STEP AHEAD OF YOU, MOM!
DROP
DO YOU KNOW IF NICOLE EVEN WANTS TO COME?
OH, SHE'LL WANT TO COME, I KNOW SHE WILL.
OF COURSE SHE'D WANT TO COME. WE WERE BEST FRIENDS, AND THAT'S WHAT BEST FRIENDS DO. THEY DO EVERYTHING TOGETHER.

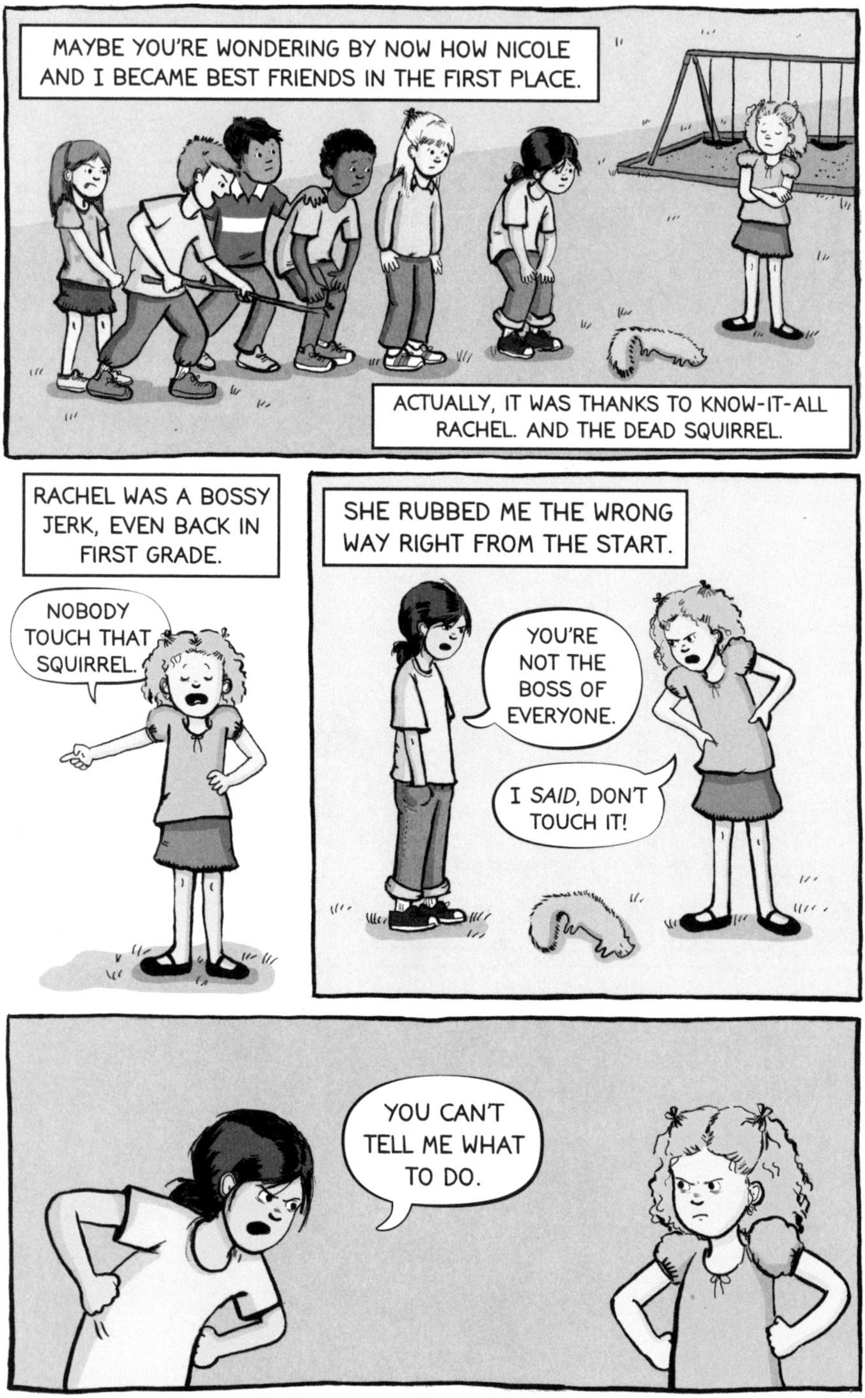
MAYBE YOU'RE WONDERING BY NOW HOW NICOLE AND I BECAME BEST FRIENDS IN THE FIRST PLACE.
ACTUALLY, IT WAS THANKS TO KNOW-IT-ALL RACHEL. AND THE DEAD SQUIRREL.
RACHEL WAS A BOSSY JERK, EVEN BACK IN FIRST GRADE.
NOBODY TOUCH THAT SQUIRREL.
SHE RUBBED ME THE WRONG WAY RIGHT FROM THE START.
YOU'RE NOT THE BOSS OF EVERYONE.
I *SAID*, DON'T TOUCH IT!
YOU CAN'T TELL ME WHAT TO DO.

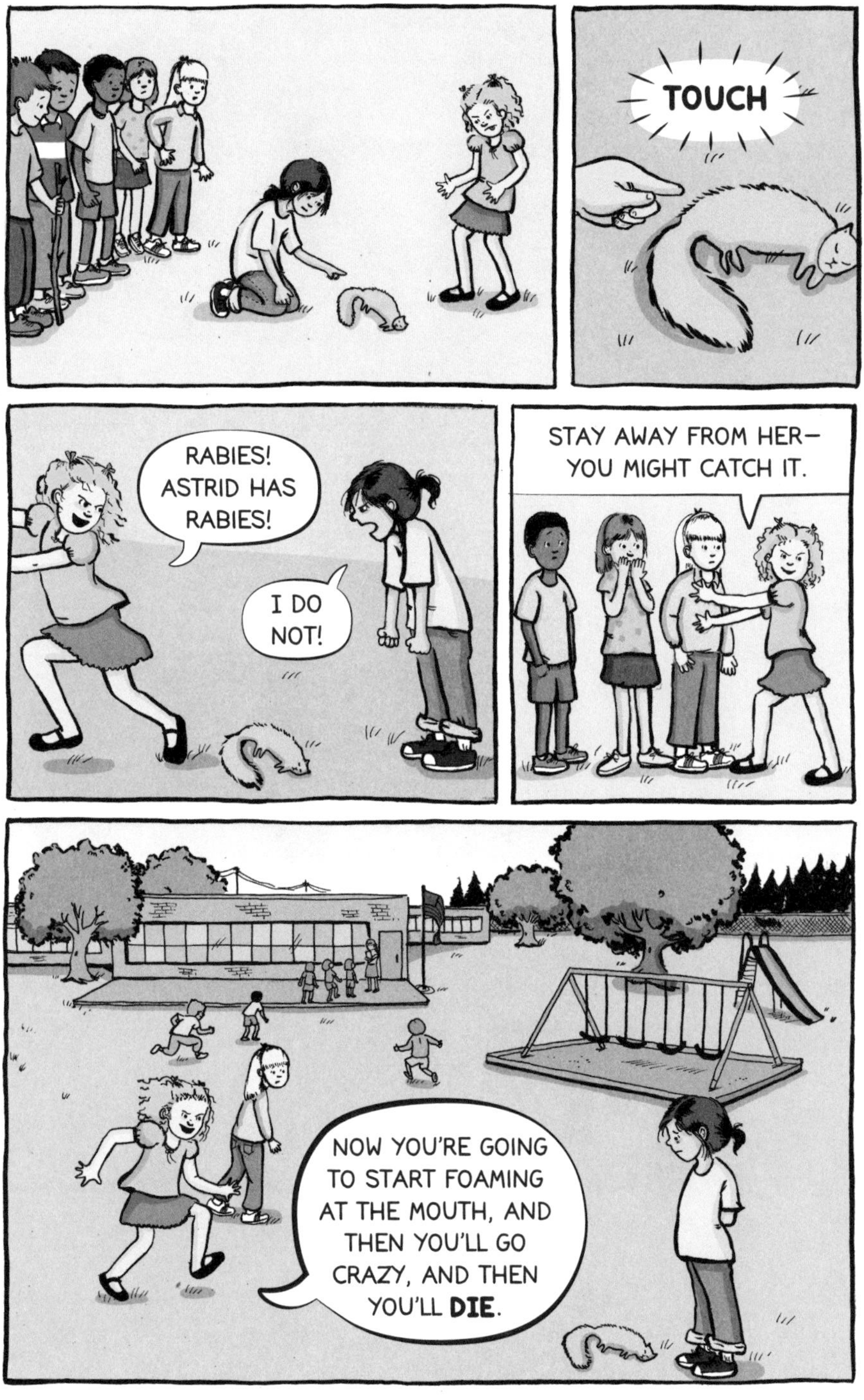
TOUCH
RABIES! ASTRID HAS RABIES!
I DO NOT!
STAY AWAY FROM HER— YOU MIGHT CATCH IT.
NOW YOU'RE GOING TO START FOAMING AT THE MOUTH, AND THEN YOU'LL GO CRAZY, AND THEN YOU'LL **DIE**.

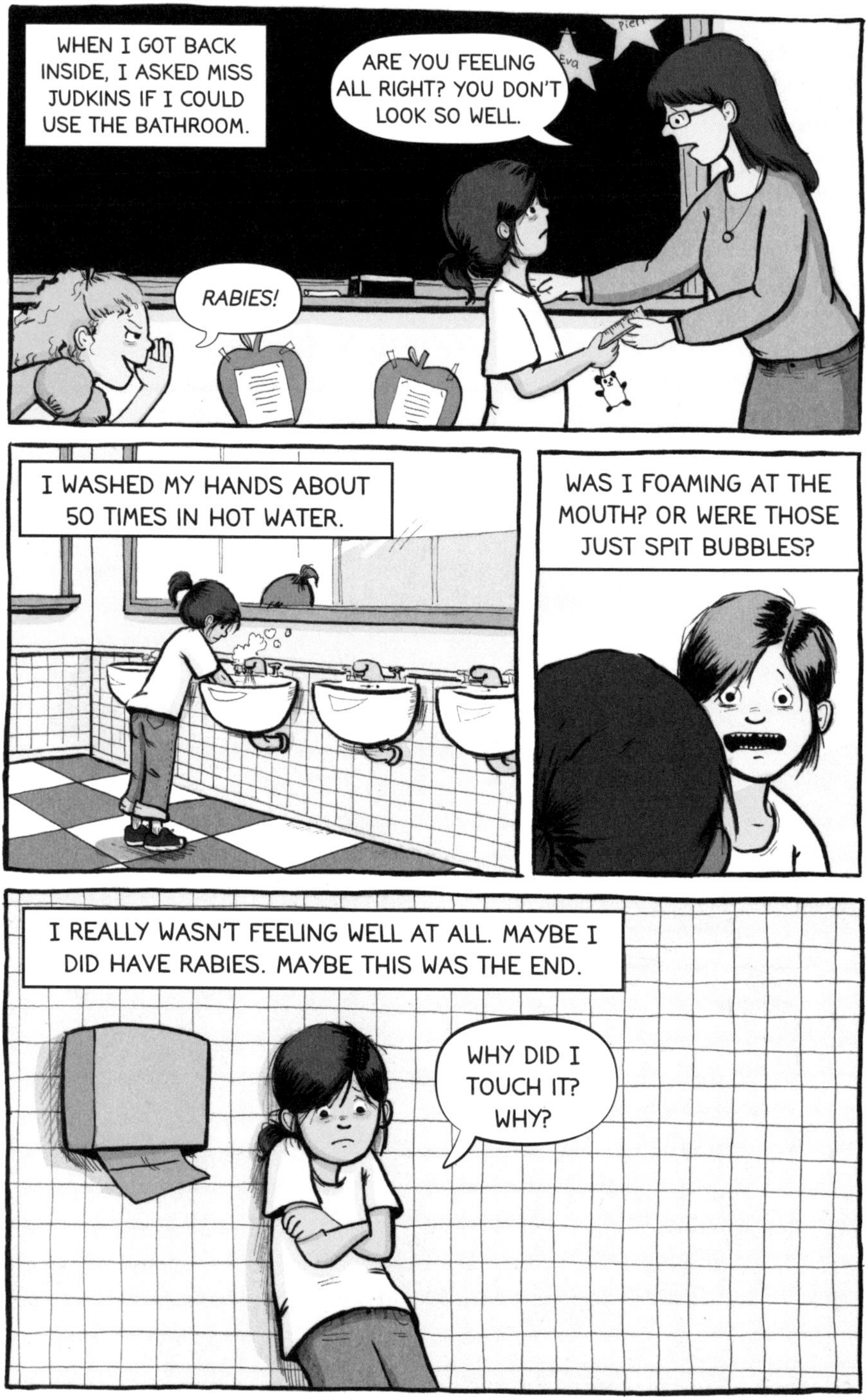
WHEN I GOT BACK INSIDE, I ASKED MISS JUDKINS IF I COULD USE THE BATHROOM.
Eva
ARE YOU FEELING ALL RIGHT? YOU DON'T LOOK SO WELL.
RABIES!
I WASHED MY HANDS ABOUT 50 TIMES IN HOT WATER.
WAS I FOAMING AT THE MOUTH? OR WERE THOSE JUST SPIT BUBBLES?
I REALLY WASN'T FEELING WELL AT ALL. MAYBE I DID HAVE RABIES. MAYBE THIS WAS THE END.
WHY DID I TOUCH IT? WHY?

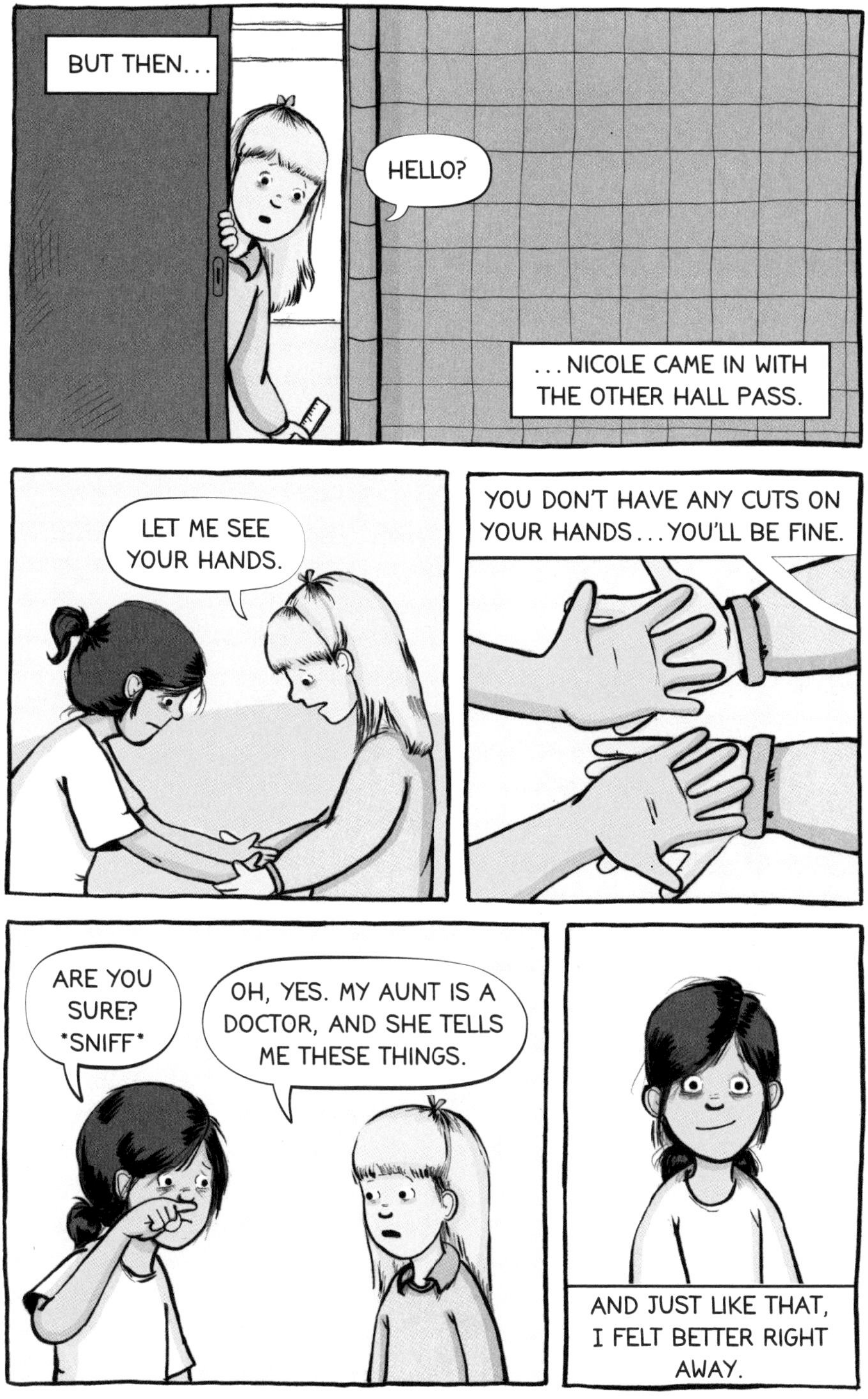
BUT THEN...
HELLO?
...NICOLE CAME IN WITH THE OTHER HALL PASS.
LET ME SEE YOUR HANDS.
YOU DON'T HAVE ANY CUTS ON YOUR HANDS...YOU'LL BE FINE.
ARE YOU SURE? *SNIFF*
OH, YES. MY AUNT IS A DOCTOR, AND SHE TELLS ME THESE THINGS.
AND JUST LIKE THAT, I FELT BETTER RIGHT AWAY.

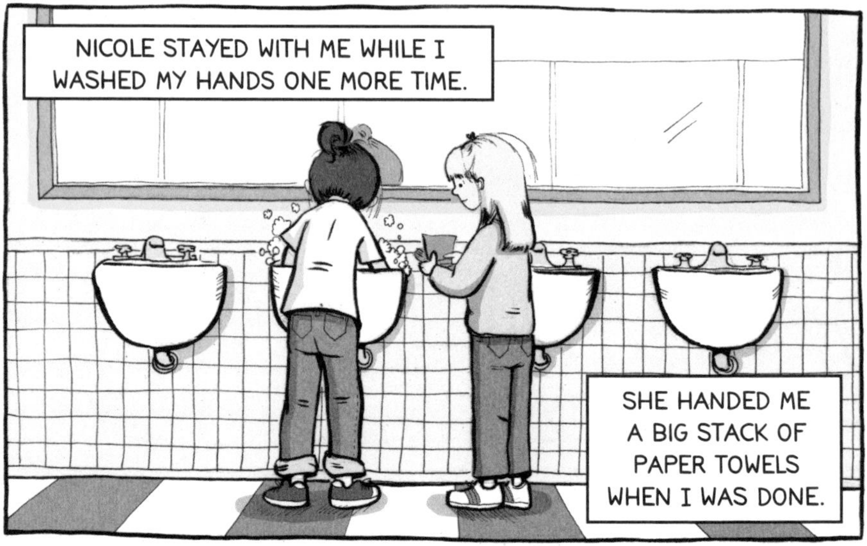
NICOLE STAYED WITH ME WHILE I WASHED MY HANDS ONE MORE TIME.
SHE HANDED ME A BIG STACK OF PAPER TOWELS WHEN I WAS DONE.

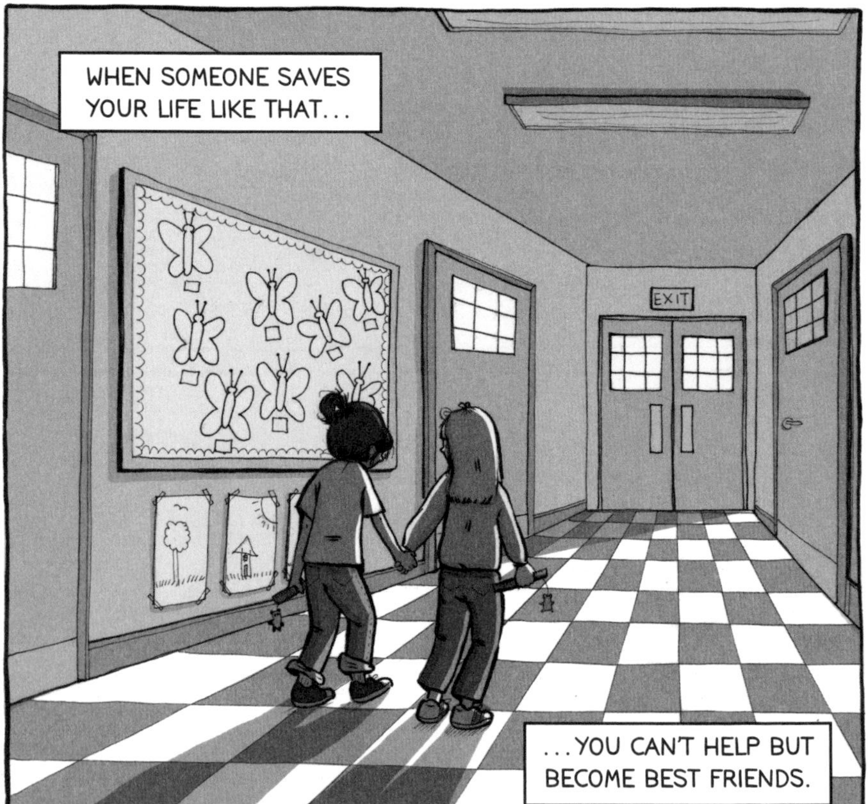
WHEN SOMEONE SAVES YOUR LIFE LIKE THAT...
EXIT
...YOU CAN'T HELP BUT BECOME BEST FRIENDS.

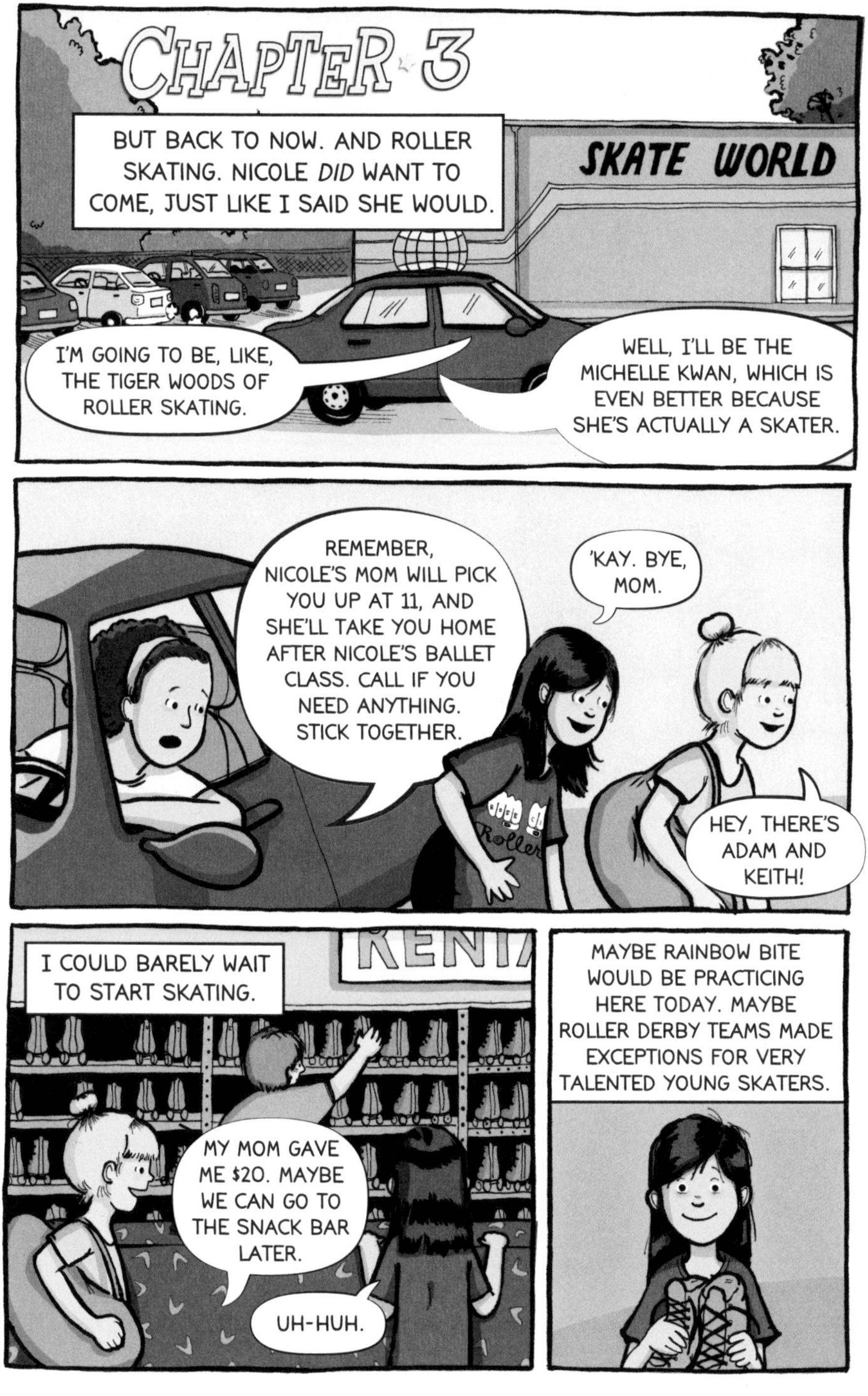
CHAPTER 3
BUT BACK TO NOW. AND ROLLER SKATING. NICOLE *DID* WANT TO COME, JUST LIKE I SAID SHE WOULD.
SKATE WORLD
I'M GOING TO BE, LIKE, THE TIGER WOODS OF ROLLER SKATING.
WELL, I'LL BE THE MICHELLE KWAN, WHICH IS EVEN BETTER BECAUSE SHE'S ACTUALLY A SKATER.
REMEMBER, NICOLE'S MOM WILL PICK YOU UP AT 11, AND SHE'LL TAKE YOU HOME AFTER NICOLE'S BALLET CLASS. CALL IF YOU NEED ANYTHING. STICK TOGETHER.
'KAY. BYE, MOM.
HEY, THERE'S ADAM AND KEITH!
I COULD BARELY WAIT TO START SKATING.
MY MOM GAVE ME $20. MAYBE WE CAN GO TO THE SNACK BAR LATER.
UH-HUH.
MAYBE RAINBOW BITE WOULD BE PRACTICING HERE TODAY. MAYBE ROLLER DERBY TEAMS MADE EXCEPTIONS FOR VERY TALENTED YOUNG SKATERS.

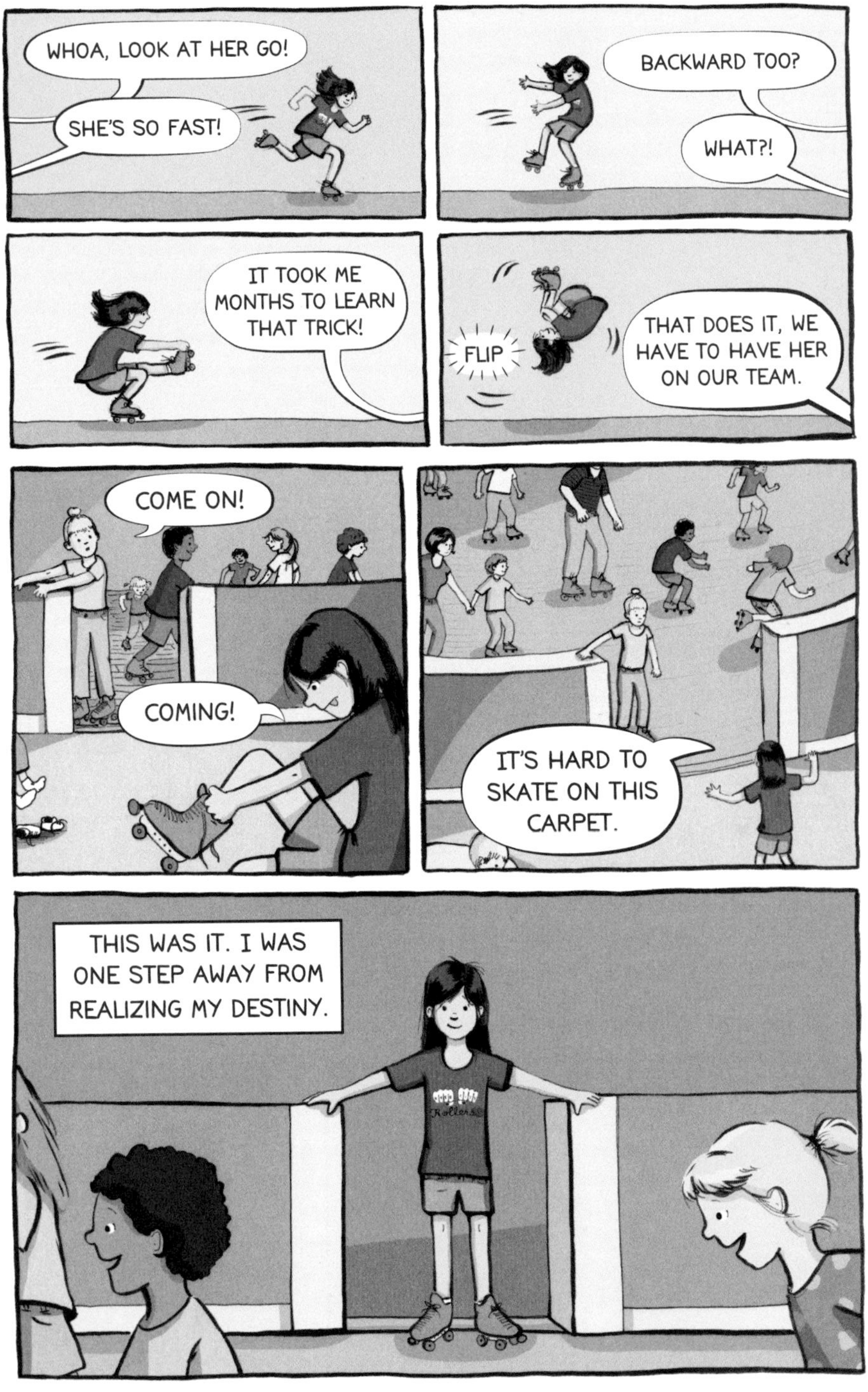
WHOA, LOOK AT HER GO!
SHE'S SO FAST!
BACKWARD TOO?
WHAT?!
IT TOOK ME MONTHS TO LEARN THAT TRICK!
FLIP
THAT DOES IT, WE HAVE TO HAVE HER ON OUR TEAM.
COME ON!
COMING!
IT'S HARD TO SKATE ON THIS CARPET.
THIS WAS IT. I WAS ONE STEP AWAY FROM REALIZING MY DESTINY.

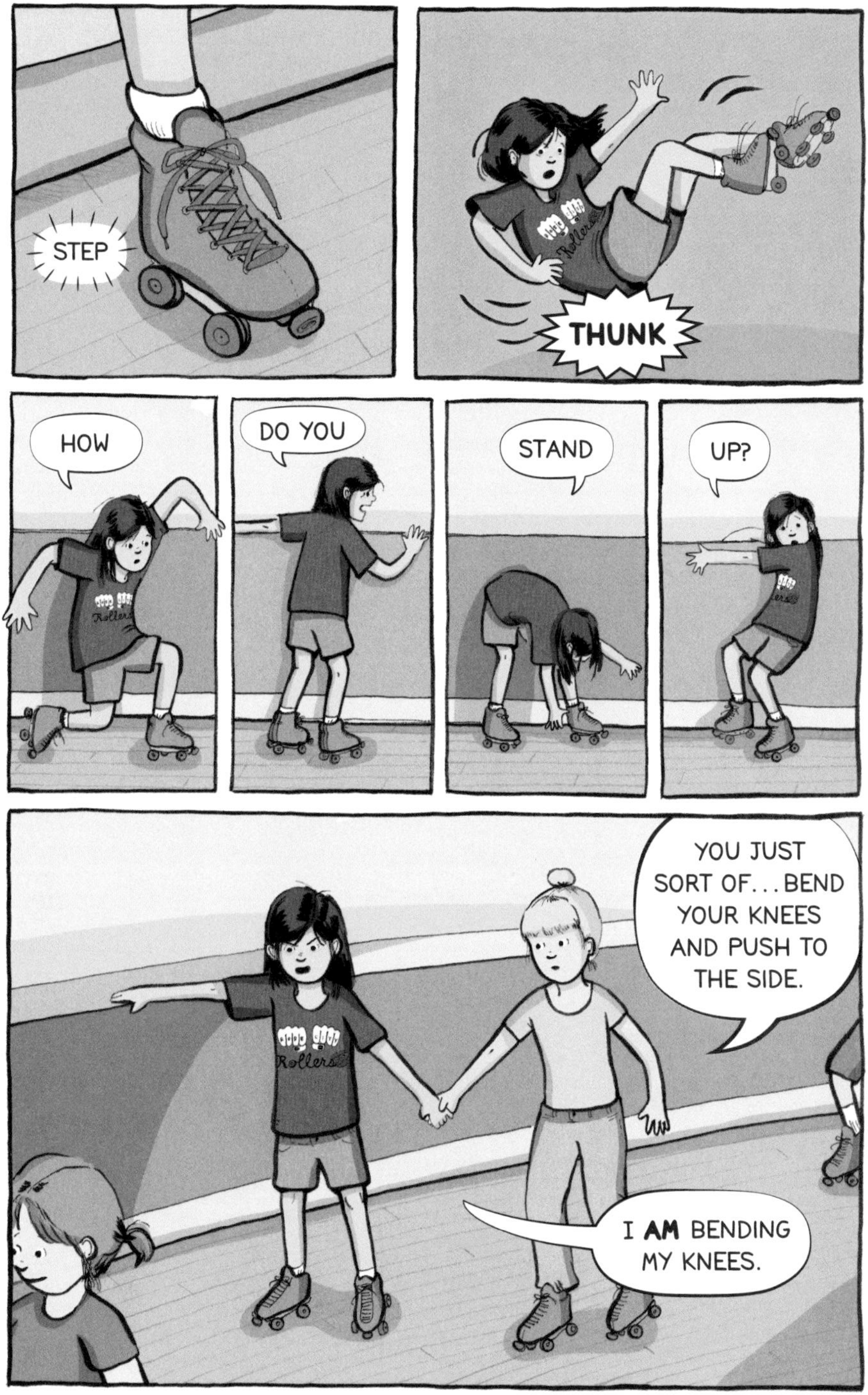
STEP
THUNK
HOW
DO YOU
STAND
UP?
YOU JUST SORT OF... BEND YOUR KNEES AND PUSH TO THE SIDE.
I **AM** BENDING MY KNEES.

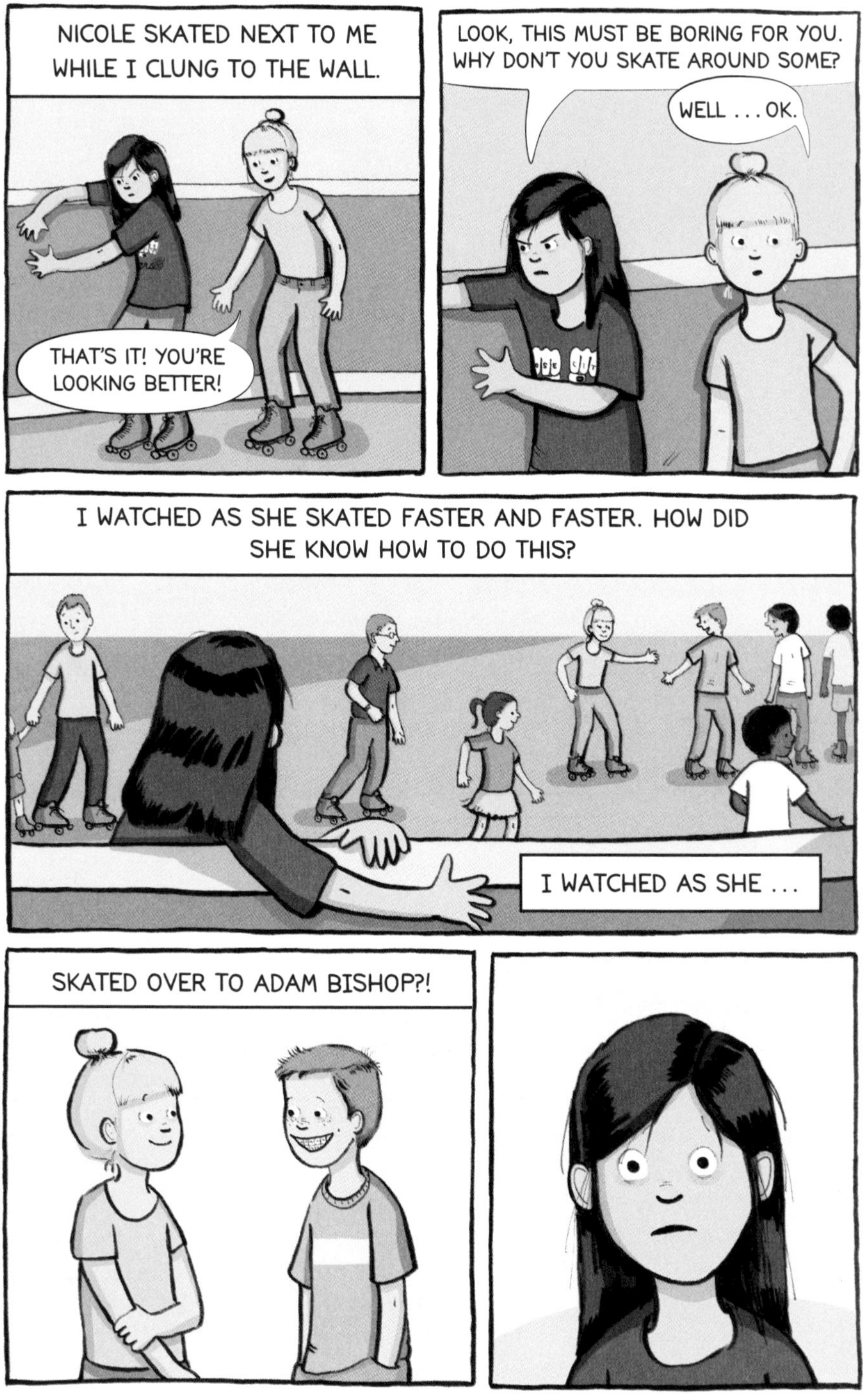
NICOLE SKATED NEXT TO ME WHILE I CLUNG TO THE WALL.
THAT'S IT! YOU'RE LOOKING BETTER!
LOOK, THIS MUST BE BORING FOR YOU. WHY DON'T YOU SKATE AROUND SOME?
WELL . . . OK.
I WATCHED AS SHE SKATED FASTER AND FASTER. HOW DID SHE KNOW HOW TO DO THIS?
I WATCHED AS SHE . . .
SKATED OVER TO ADAM BISHOP?!

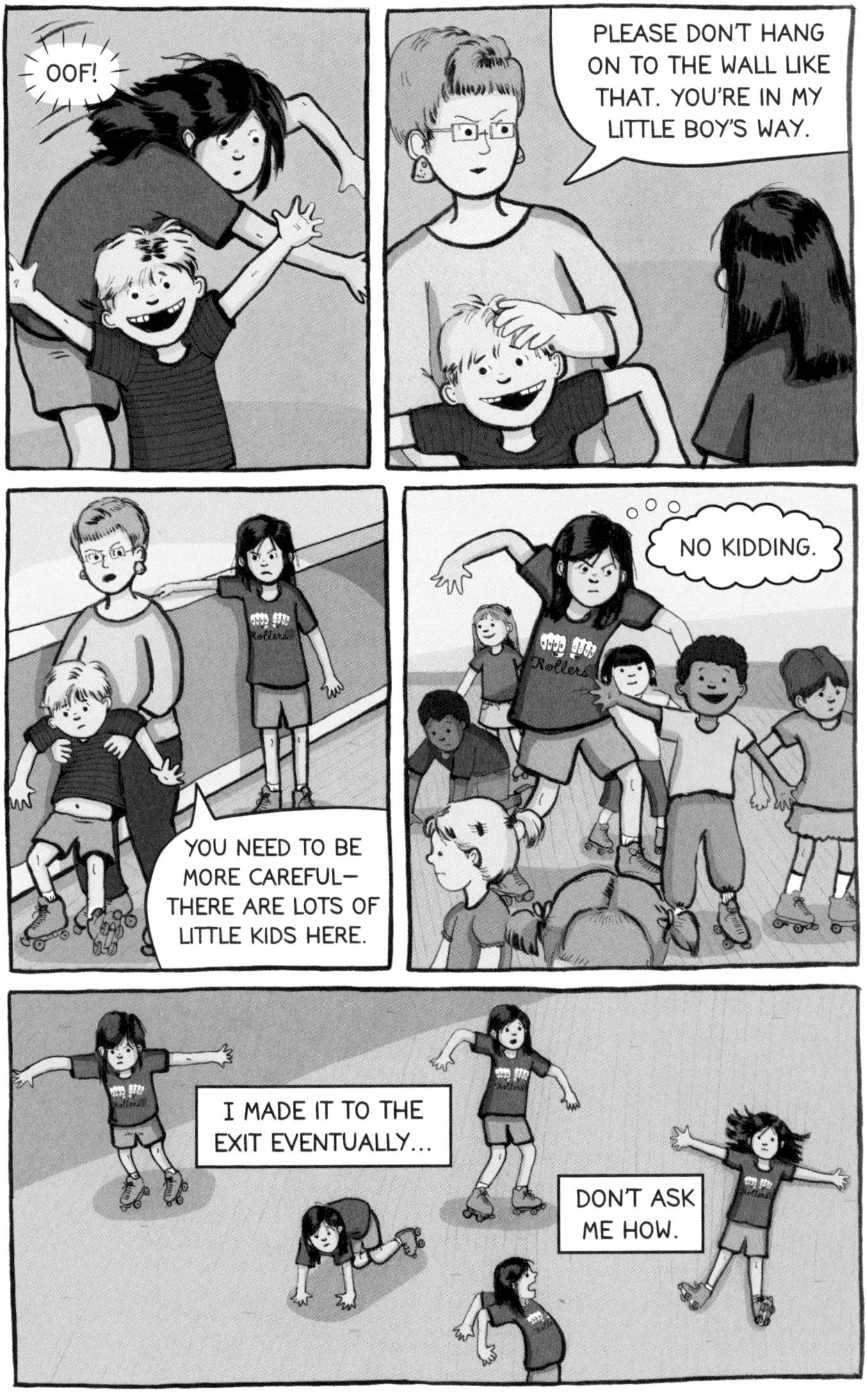
OOF!
PLEASE DON'T HANG ON TO THE WALL LIKE THAT. YOU'RE IN MY LITTLE BOY'S WAY.
YOU NEED TO BE MORE CAREFUL— THERE ARE LOTS OF LITTLE KIDS HERE.
NO KIDDING.
I MADE IT TO THE EXIT EVENTUALLY...
DON'T ASK ME HOW.

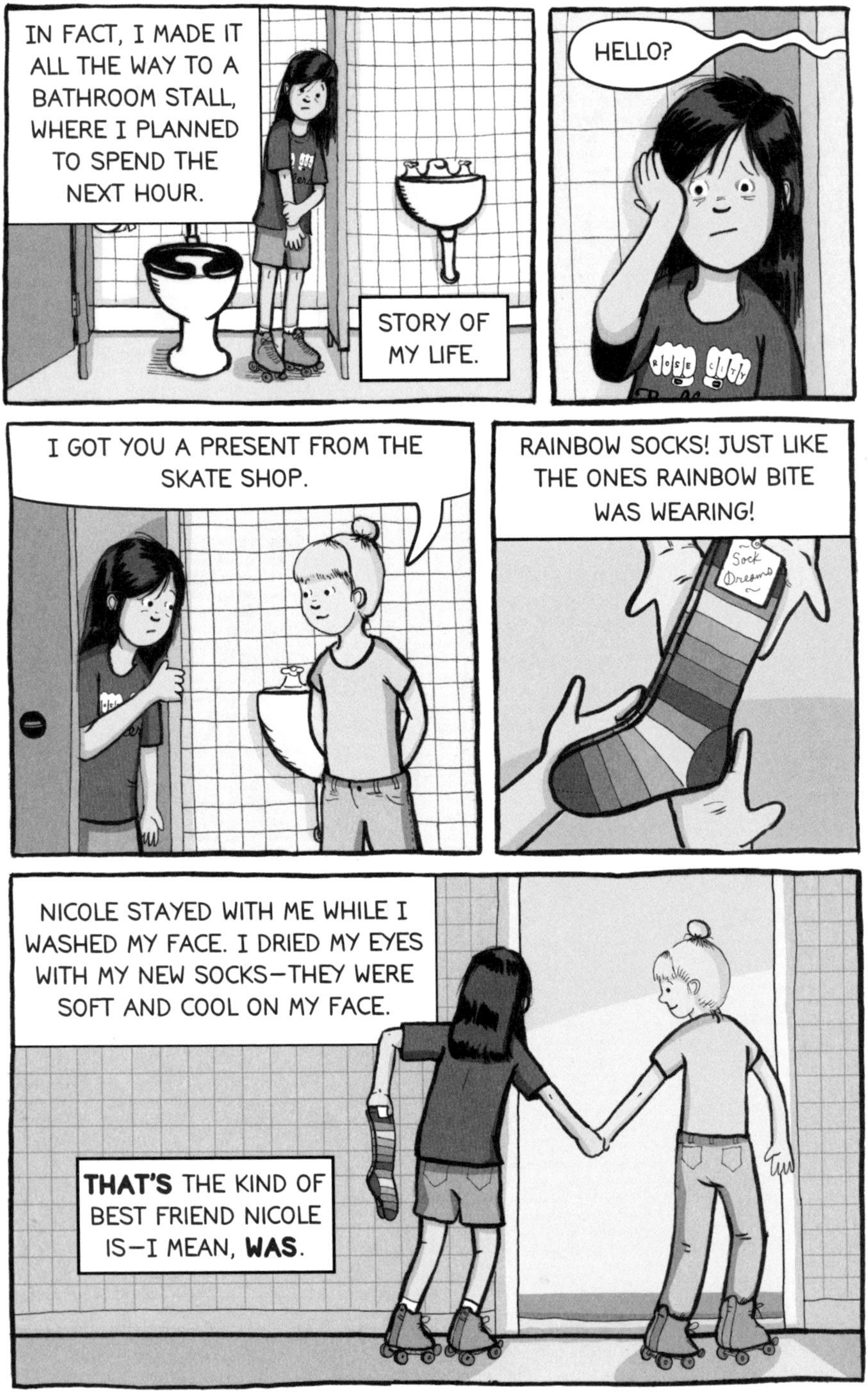
IN FACT, I MADE IT ALL THE WAY TO A BATHROOM STALL, WHERE I PLANNED TO SPEND THE NEXT HOUR.
STORY OF MY LIFE.
HELLO?
ROSE CITY
I GOT YOU A PRESENT FROM THE SKATE SHOP.
RAINBOW SOCKS! JUST LIKE THE ONES RAINBOW BITE WAS WEARING!
Sock Dreams
NICOLE STAYED WITH ME WHILE I WASHED MY FACE. I DRIED MY EYES WITH MY NEW SOCKS—THEY WERE SOFT AND COOL ON MY FACE.
THAT'S THE KIND OF BEST FRIEND NICOLE IS—I MEAN, **WAS**.

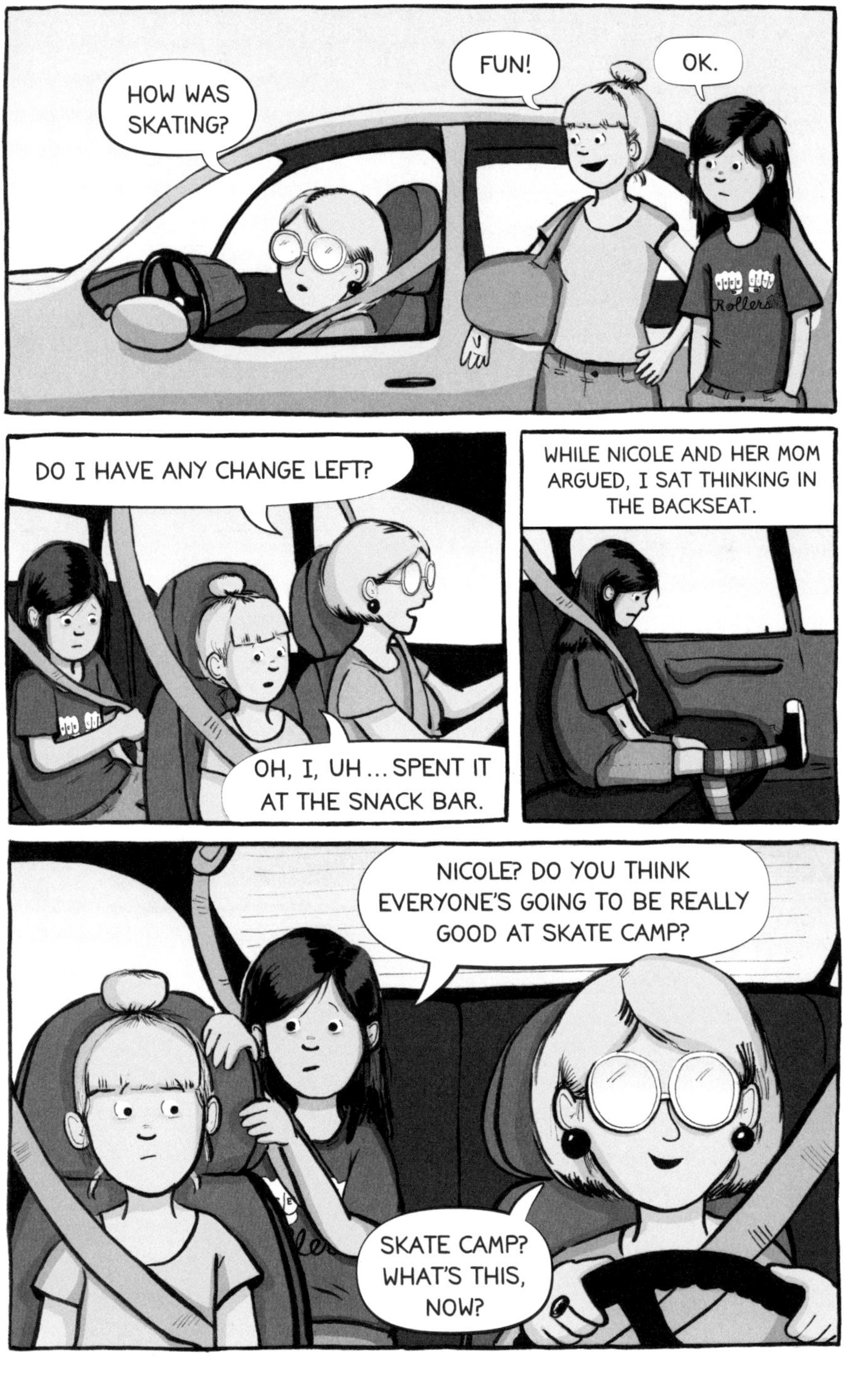
HOW WAS SKATING?
FUN!
OK.
DO I HAVE ANY CHANGE LEFT?
OH, I, UH... SPENT IT AT THE SNACK BAR.
WHILE NICOLE AND HER MOM ARGUED, I SAT THINKING IN THE BACKSEAT.
NICOLE? DO YOU THINK EVERYONE'S GOING TO BE REALLY GOOD AT SKATE CAMP?
SKATE CAMP? WHAT'S THIS, NOW?

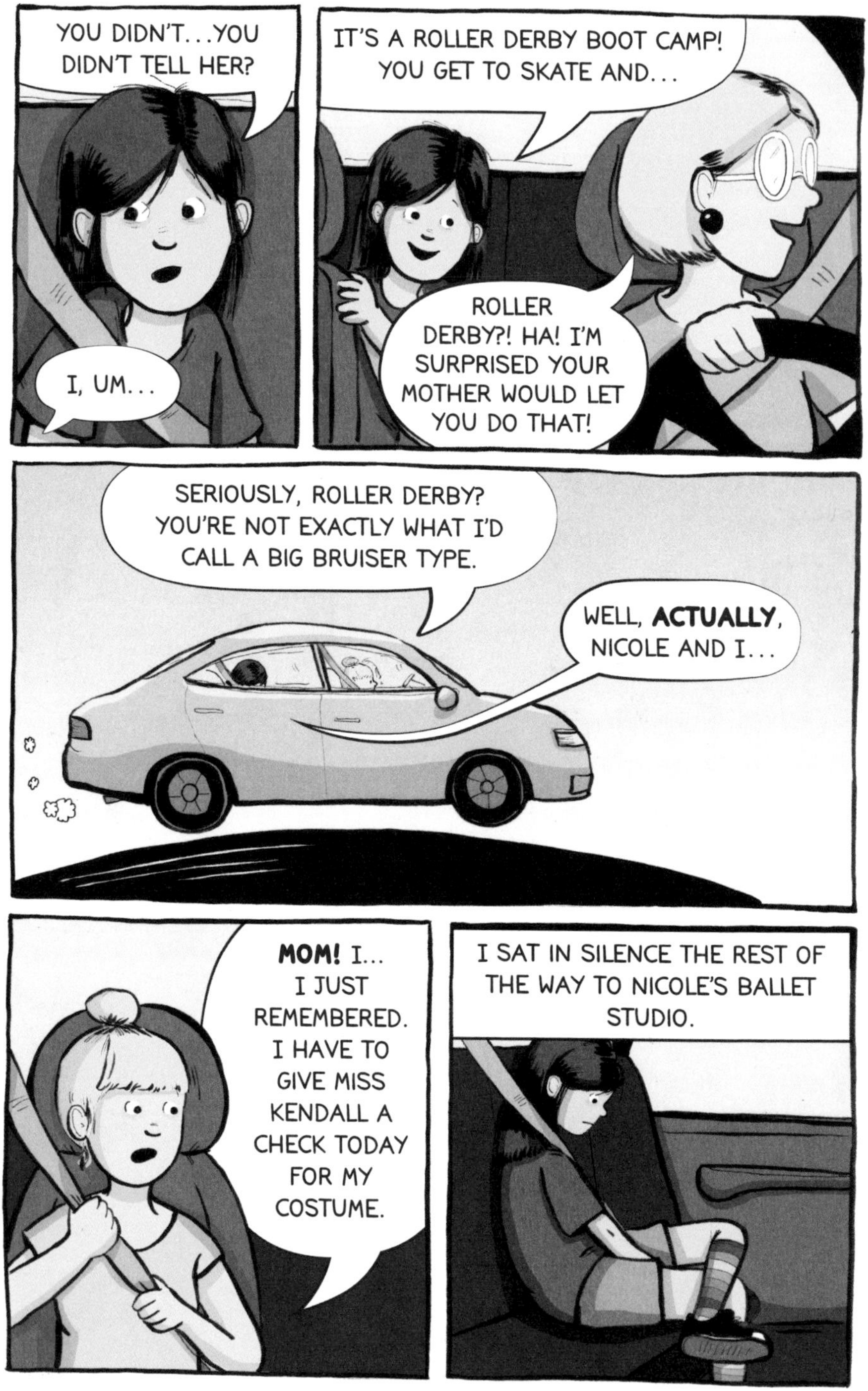
YOU DIDN'T...YOU DIDN'T TELL HER?
I, UM...
IT'S A ROLLER DERBY BOOT CAMP! YOU GET TO SKATE AND...
ROLLER DERBY?! HA! I'M SURPRISED YOUR MOTHER WOULD LET YOU DO THAT!
SERIOUSLY, ROLLER DERBY? YOU'RE NOT EXACTLY WHAT I'D CALL A BIG BRUISER TYPE.
WELL, **ACTUALLY**, NICOLE AND I...
MOM! I... I JUST REMEMBERED. I HAVE TO GIVE MISS KENDALL A CHECK TODAY FOR MY COSTUME.
I SAT IN SILENCE THE REST OF THE WAY TO NICOLE'S BALLET STUDIO.

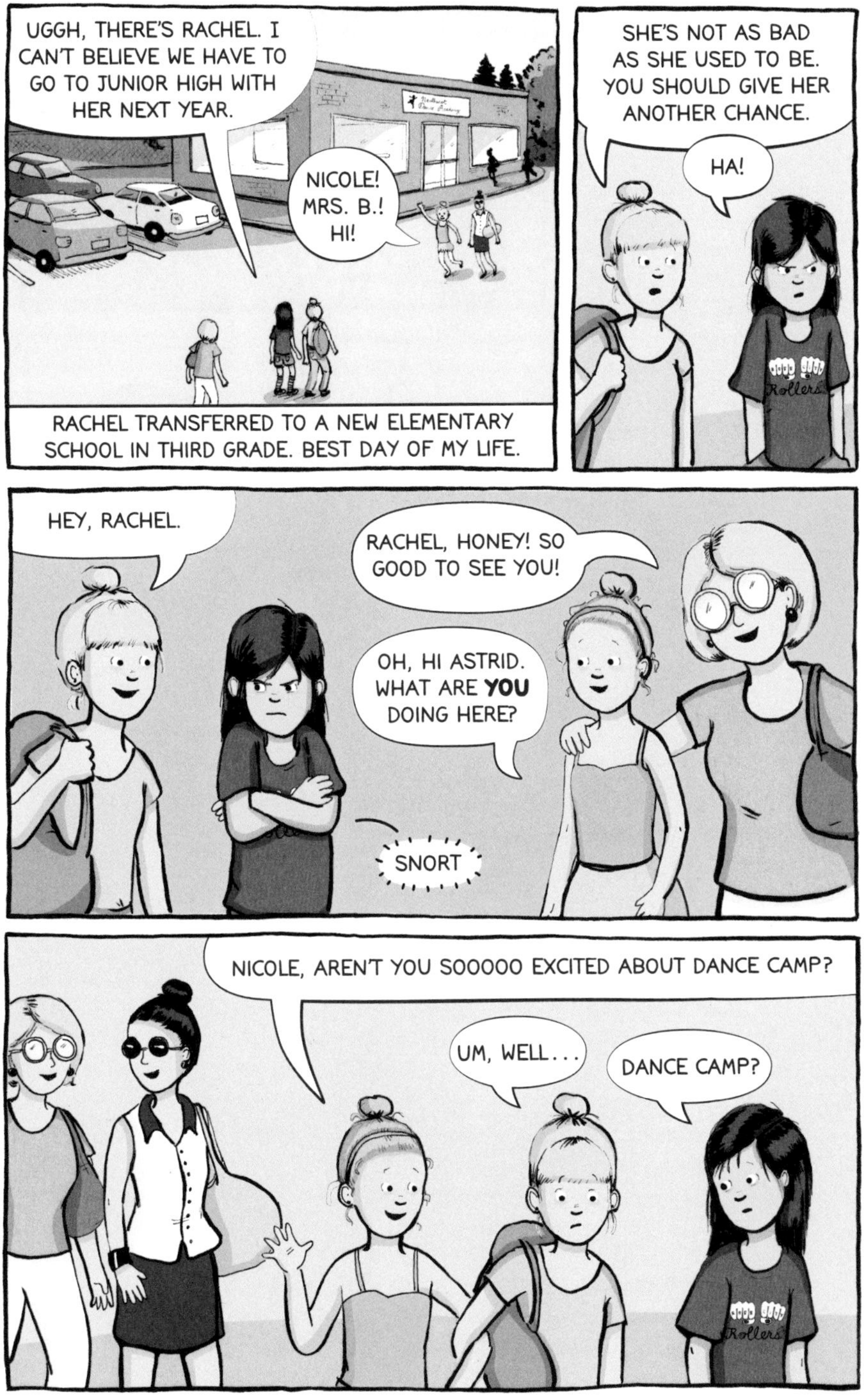
UGGH, THERE'S RACHEL. I CAN'T BELIEVE WE HAVE TO GO TO JUNIOR HIGH WITH HER NEXT YEAR.
NICOLE! MRS. B.! HI!
RACHEL TRANSFERRED TO A NEW ELEMENTARY SCHOOL IN THIRD GRADE. BEST DAY OF MY LIFE.
SHE'S NOT AS BAD AS SHE USED TO BE. YOU SHOULD GIVE HER ANOTHER CHANCE.
HA!
HEY, RACHEL.
RACHEL, HONEY! SO GOOD TO SEE YOU!
OH, HI ASTRID. WHAT ARE **YOU** DOING HERE?
SNORT
NICOLE, AREN'T YOU SOOOOO EXCITED ABOUT DANCE CAMP?
UM, WELL...
DANCE CAMP?

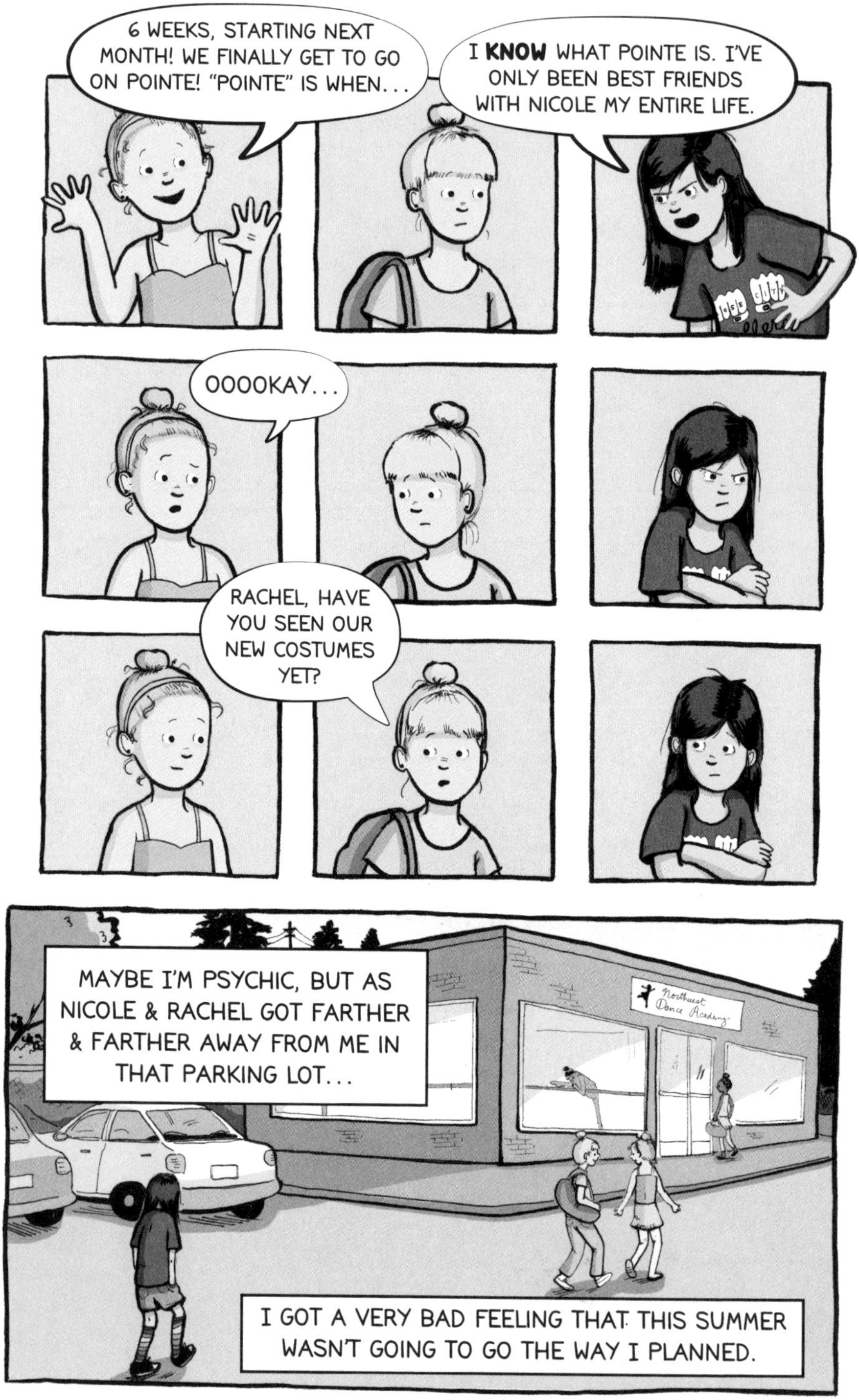
6 WEEKS, STARTING NEXT MONTH! WE FINALLY GET TO GO ON POINTE! "POINTE" IS WHEN...
I **KNOW** WHAT POINTE IS. I'VE ONLY BEEN BEST FRIENDS WITH NICOLE MY ENTIRE LIFE.
OOOOKAY...
RACHEL, HAVE YOU SEEN OUR NEW COSTUMES YET?
MAYBE I'M PSYCHIC, BUT AS NICOLE & RACHEL GOT FARTHER & FARTHER AWAY FROM ME IN THAT PARKING LOT...
Northwest Dance Academy
I GOT A VERY BAD FEELING THAT THIS SUMMER WASN'T GOING TO GO THE WAY I PLANNED.

CHAPTER 4

THE FIRST FEW DAYS OF SUMMER WERE PRETTY UNEVENTFUL. MOM SIGNED ME UP FOR DERBY CAMP.

DO YOU WANT TO INVITE NICOLE OVER SO YOU CAN SIGN UP TOGETHER?

UMMM... NO, THAT'S OK. SHE'S GOING TO SIGN UP ON HER OWN.

REMIND ME, I HAVE TO CALL HER MOM TO TALK ABOUT CARPOOLING.

Rose City Rollers

Junior Roller Derby Camp

I'M CLICKING "YES"... YOU'RE REALLY SURE?

orth in this agreement and will not hold Rose City Rollers liable for any injuries.

Yes, I agree.

WAS I SURE? I PRETTY MUCH STUNK AT SKATING. NICOLE WAS ACTING REALLY WEIRD. BUT...

I'M SURE.

I THINK.

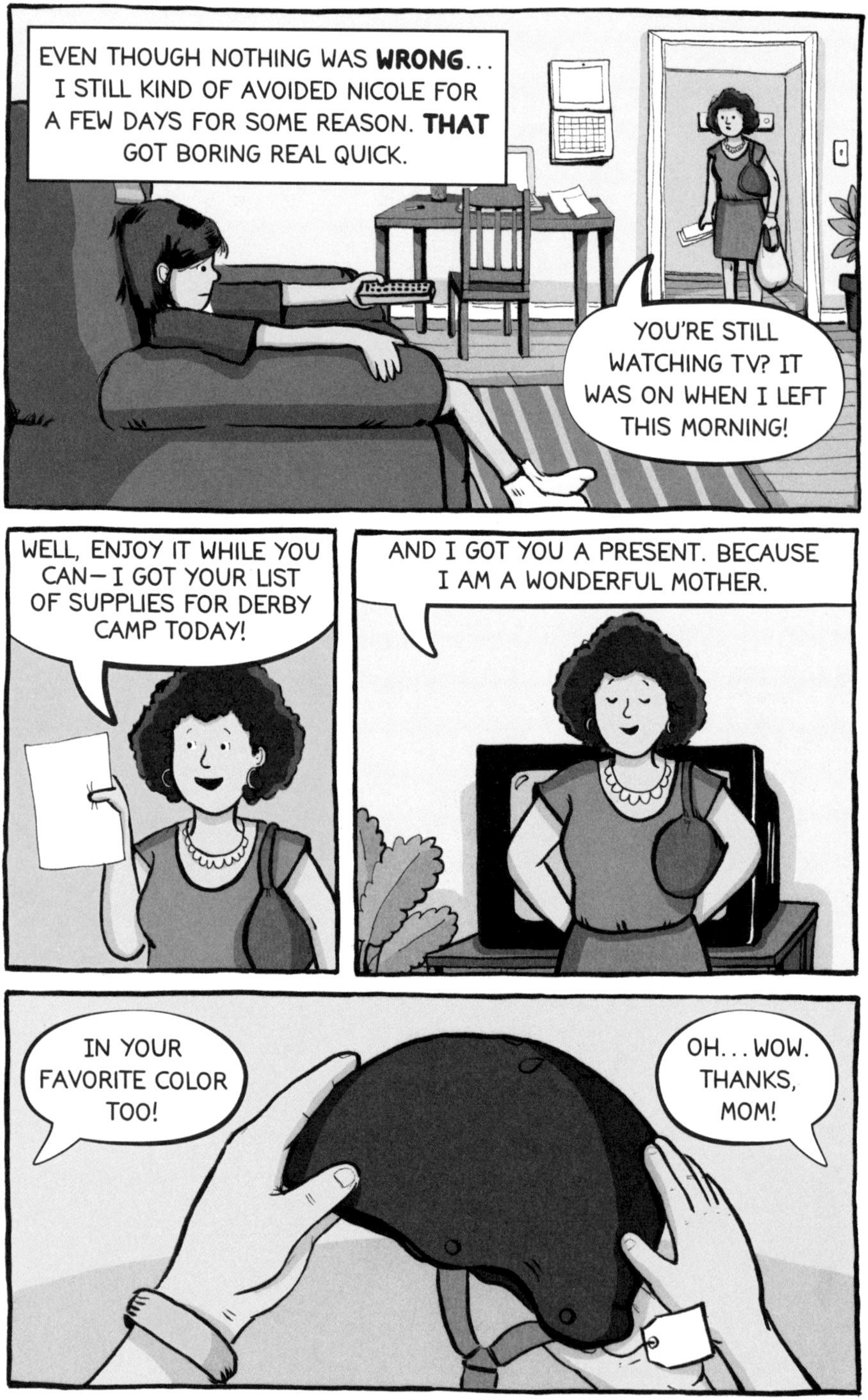
EVEN THOUGH NOTHING WAS **WRONG**... I STILL KIND OF AVOIDED NICOLE FOR A FEW DAYS FOR SOME REASON. **THAT** GOT BORING REAL QUICK.
YOU'RE STILL WATCHING TV? IT WAS ON WHEN I LEFT THIS MORNING!
WELL, ENJOY IT WHILE YOU CAN—I GOT YOUR LIST OF SUPPLIES FOR DERBY CAMP TODAY!
AND I GOT YOU A PRESENT. BECAUSE I AM A WONDERFUL MOTHER.
IN YOUR FAVORITE COLOR TOO!
OH... WOW. THANKS, MOM!

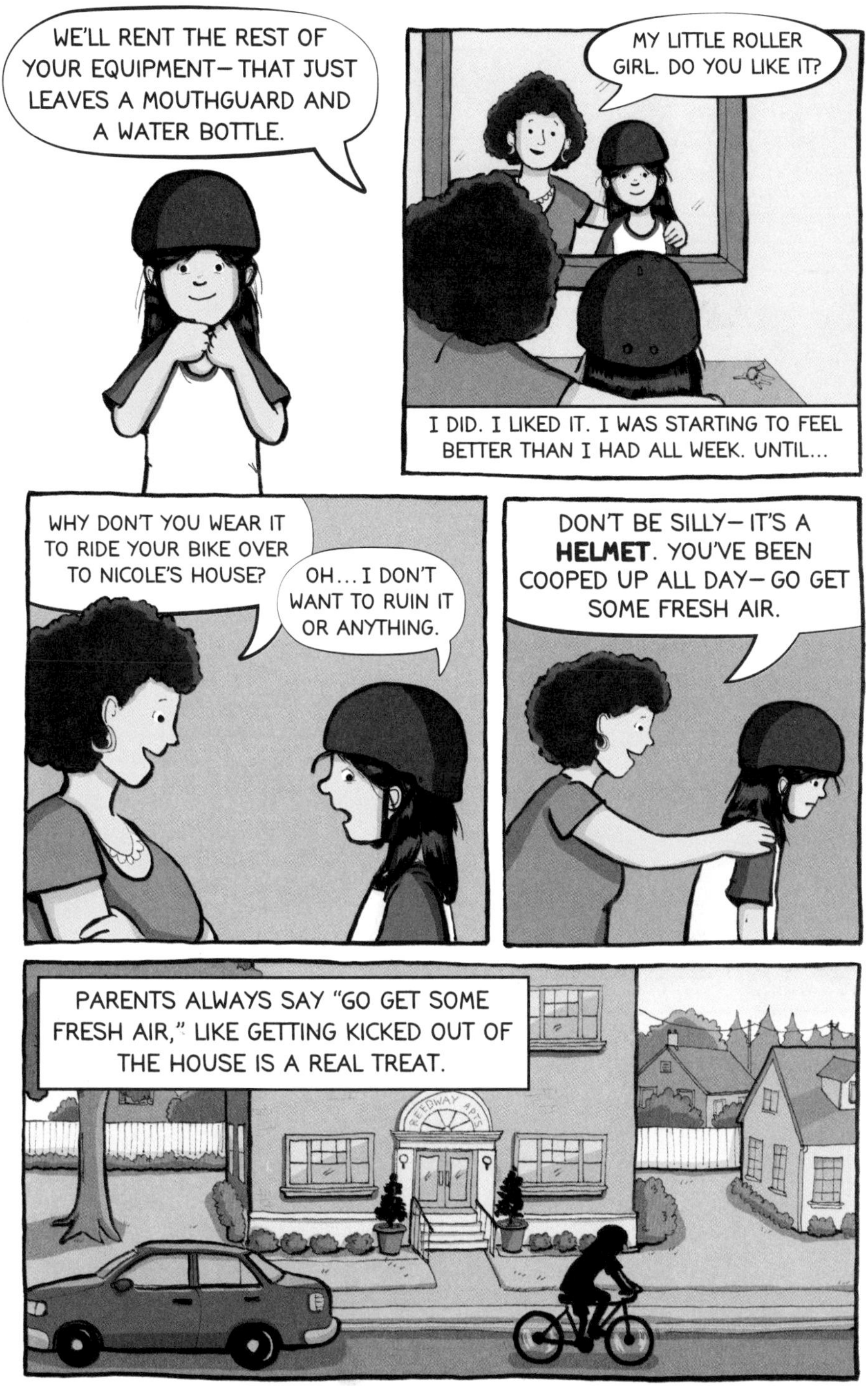
WE'LL RENT THE REST OF YOUR EQUIPMENT— THAT JUST LEAVES A MOUTHGUARD AND A WATER BOTTLE.
MY LITTLE ROLLER GIRL. DO YOU LIKE IT?
I DID. I LIKED IT. I WAS STARTING TO FEEL BETTER THAN I HAD ALL WEEK. UNTIL...
WHY DON'T YOU WEAR IT TO RIDE YOUR BIKE OVER TO NICOLE'S HOUSE?
OH... I DON'T WANT TO RUIN IT OR ANYTHING.
DON'T BE SILLY— IT'S A **HELMET**. YOU'VE BEEN COOPED UP ALL DAY— GO GET SOME FRESH AIR.
PARENTS ALWAYS SAY "GO GET SOME FRESH AIR," LIKE GETTING KICKED OUT OF THE HOUSE IS A REAL TREAT.
REEDWAY APTS

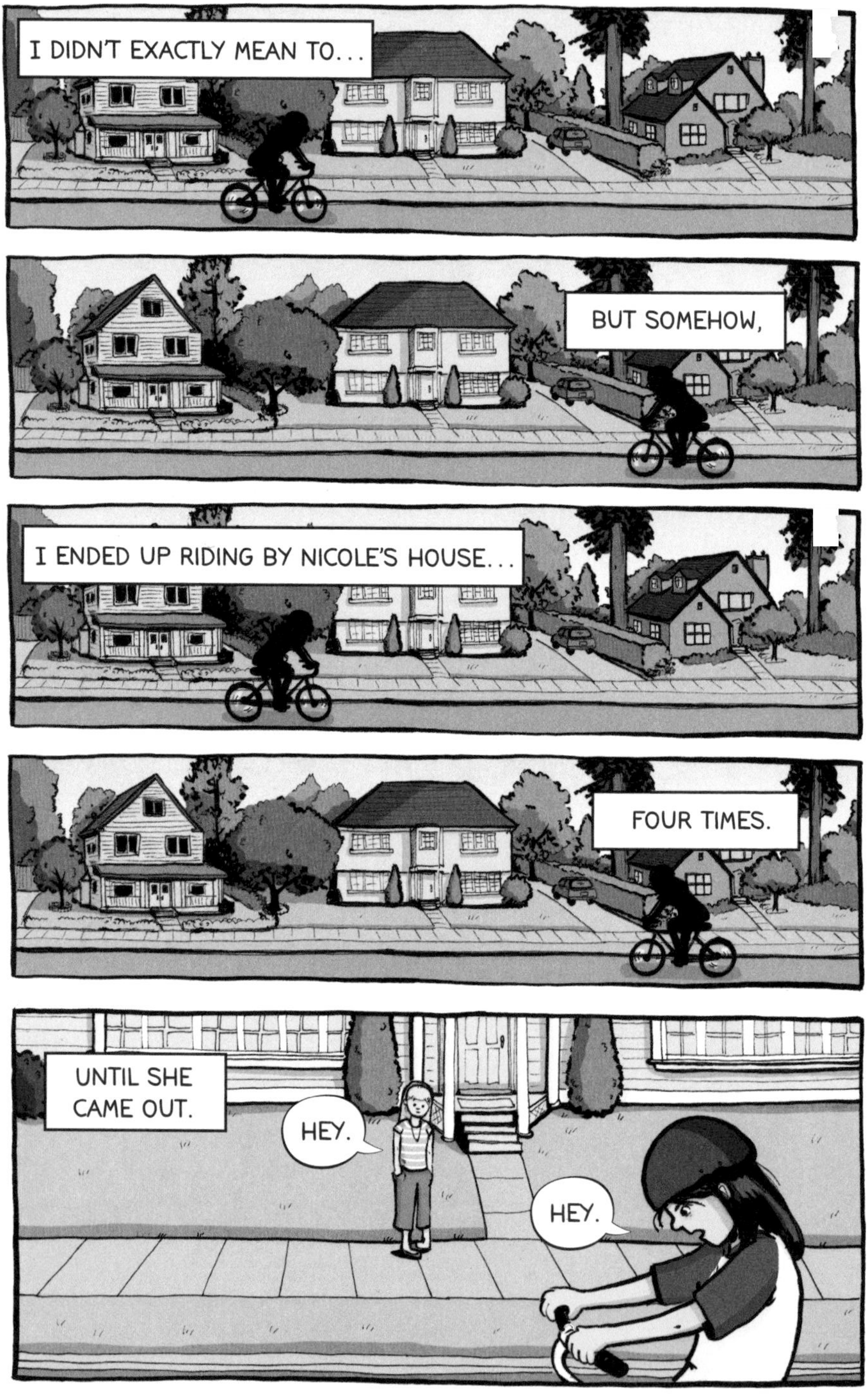
I DIDN'T EXACTLY MEAN TO...
BUT SOMEHOW,
I ENDED UP RIDING BY NICOLE'S HOUSE...
FOUR TIMES.
UNTIL SHE CAME OUT.
HEY.
HEY.

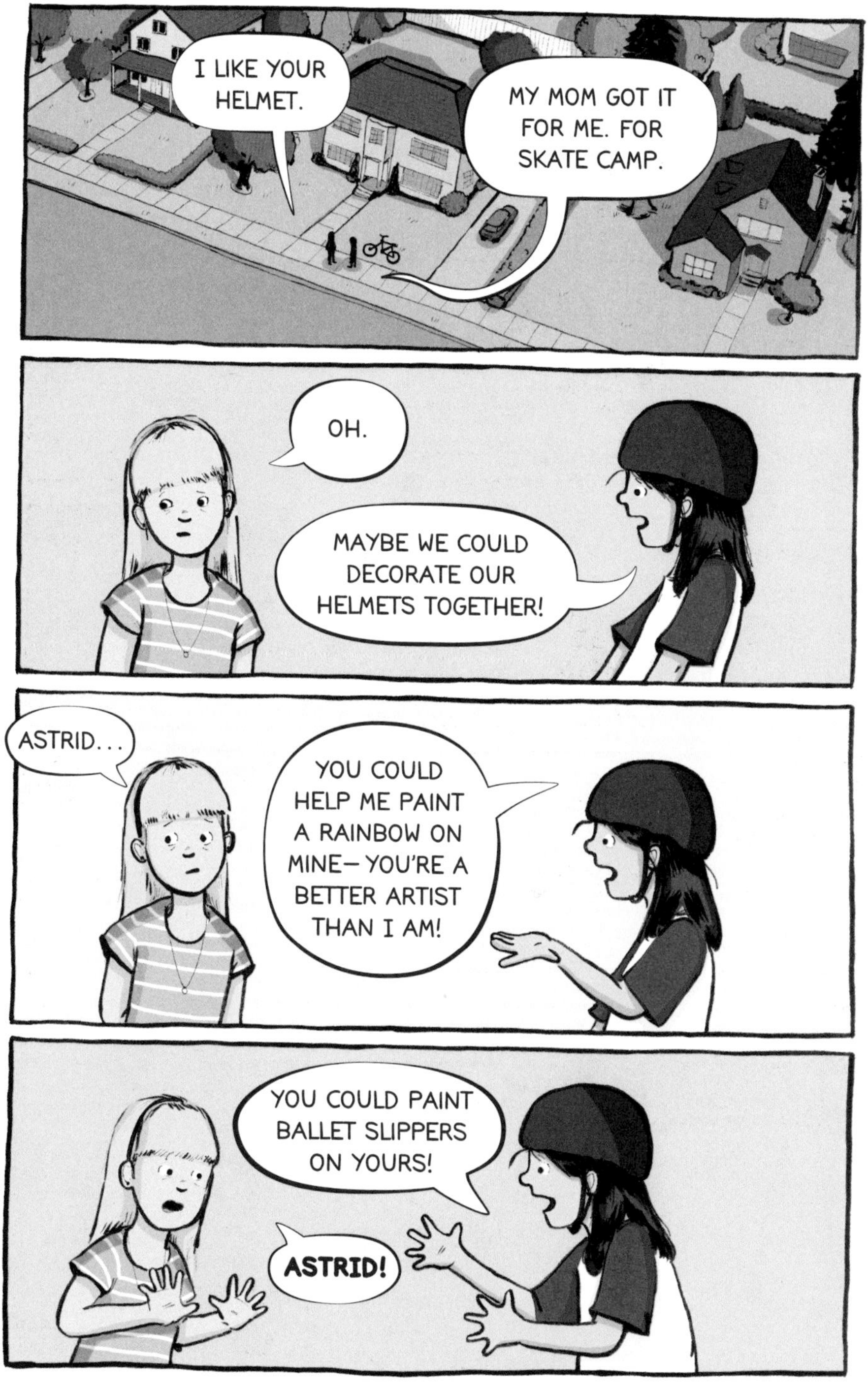
I LIKE YOUR HELMET.
MY MOM GOT IT FOR ME. FOR SKATE CAMP.
OH.
MAYBE WE COULD DECORATE OUR HELMETS TOGETHER!
ASTRID...
YOU COULD HELP ME PAINT A RAINBOW ON MINE—YOU'RE A BETTER ARTIST THAN I AM!
YOU COULD PAINT BALLET SLIPPERS ON YOURS!
ASTRID!

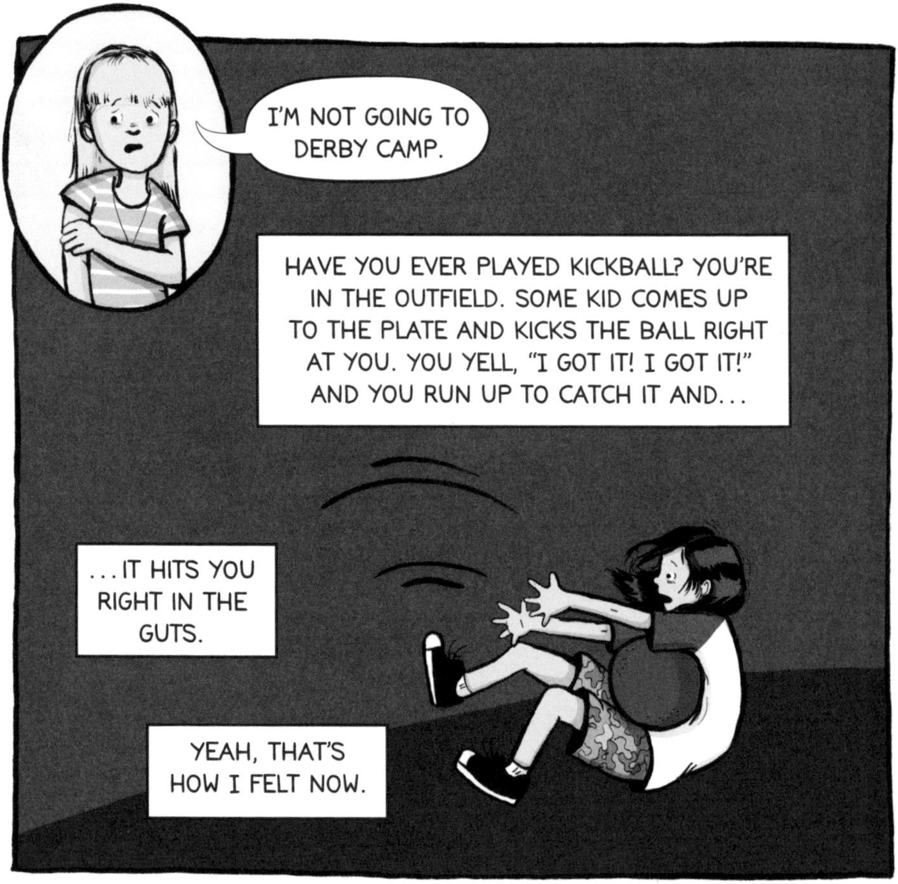
I'M NOT GOING TO DERBY CAMP.
HAVE YOU EVER PLAYED KICKBALL? YOU'RE IN THE OUTFIELD. SOME KID COMES UP TO THE PLATE AND KICKS THE BALL RIGHT AT YOU. YOU YELL, "I GOT IT! I GOT IT!" AND YOU RUN UP TO CATCH IT AND...
...IT HITS YOU RIGHT IN THE GUTS.
YEAH, THAT'S HOW I FELT NOW.

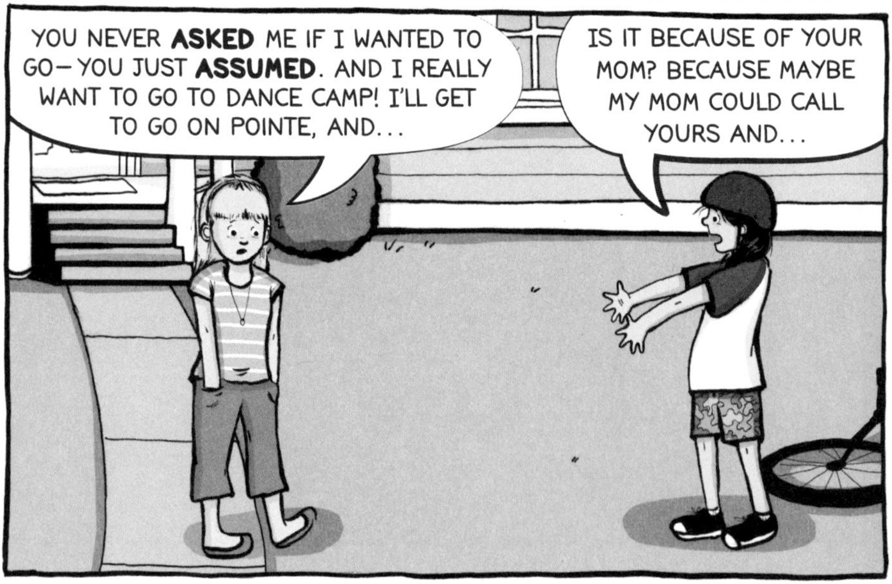
YOU NEVER **ASKED** ME IF I WANTED TO GO— YOU JUST **ASSUMED**. AND I REALLY WANT TO GO TO DANCE CAMP! I'LL GET TO GO ON POINTE, AND...
IS IT BECAUSE OF YOUR MOM? BECAUSE MAYBE MY MOM COULD CALL YOURS AND...

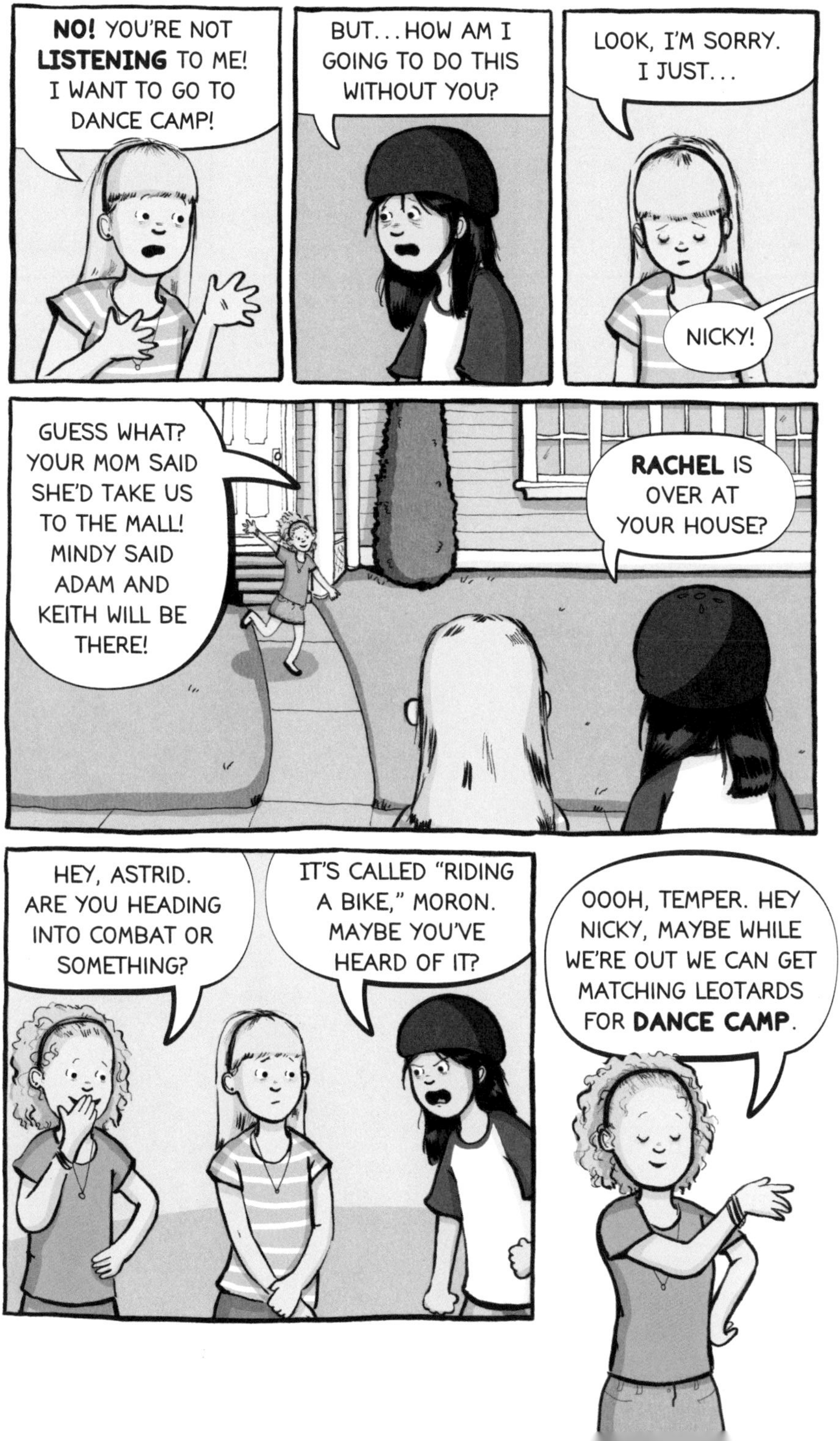

NO! YOU'RE NOT **LISTENING** TO ME! I WANT TO GO TO DANCE CAMP!
BUT... HOW AM I GOING TO DO THIS WITHOUT YOU?
LOOK, I'M SORRY. I JUST...
NICKY!
GUESS WHAT? YOUR MOM SAID SHE'D TAKE US TO THE MALL! MINDY SAID ADAM AND KEITH WILL BE THERE!
RACHEL IS OVER AT YOUR HOUSE?
HEY, ASTRID. ARE YOU HEADING INTO COMBAT OR SOMETHING?
IT'S CALLED "RIDING A BIKE," MORON. MAYBE YOU'VE HEARD OF IT?
OOOH, TEMPER. HEY NICKY, MAYBE WHILE WE'RE OUT WE CAN GET MATCHING LEOTARDS FOR **DANCE CAMP**.

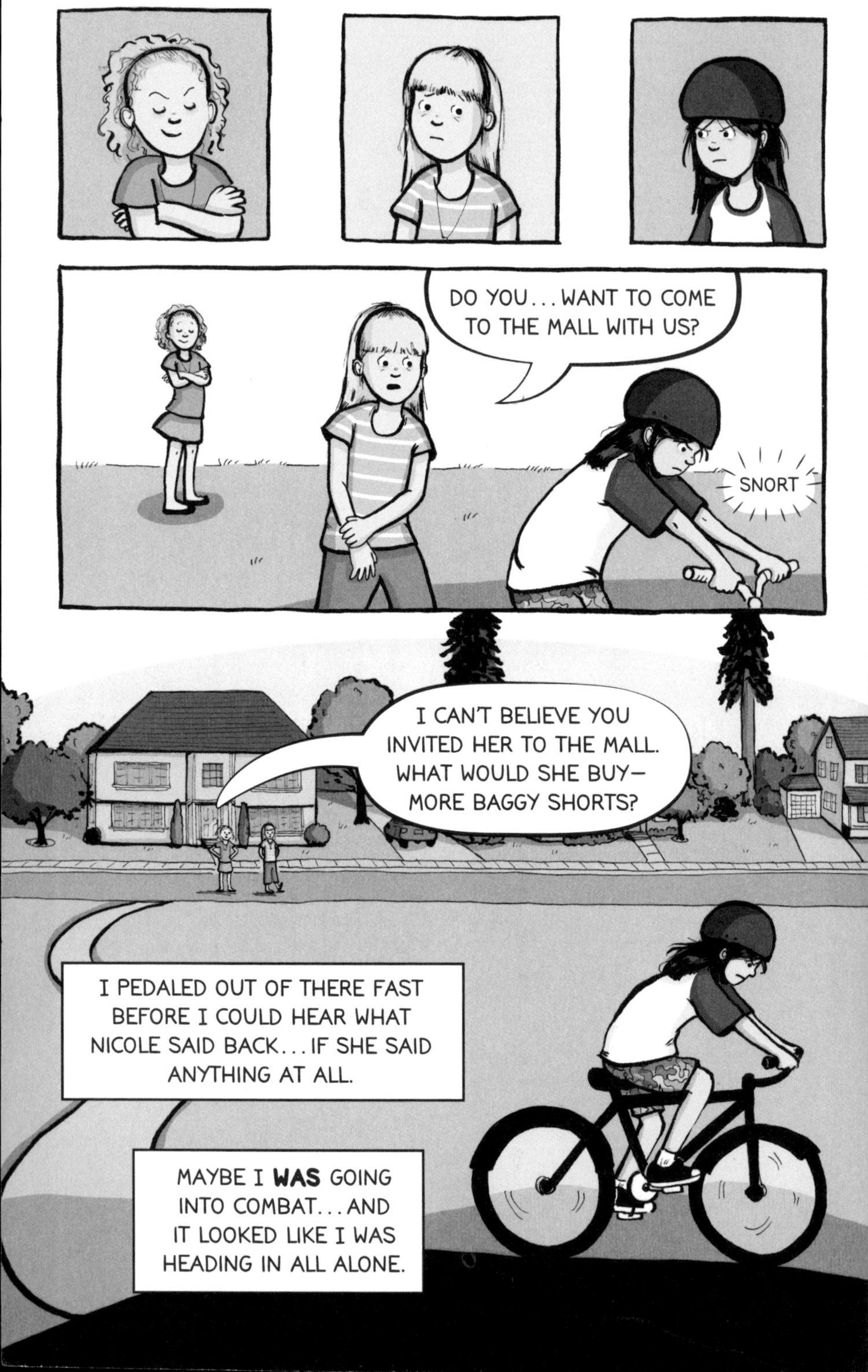
DO YOU...WANT TO COME TO THE MALL WITH US?
SNORT
I CAN'T BELIEVE YOU INVITED HER TO THE MALL. WHAT WOULD SHE BUY—MORE BAGGY SHORTS?
I PEDALED OUT OF THERE FAST BEFORE I COULD HEAR WHAT NICOLE SAID BACK...IF SHE SAID ANYTHING AT ALL.
MAYBE I **WAS** GOING INTO COMBAT...AND IT LOOKED LIKE I WAS HEADING IN ALL ALONE.

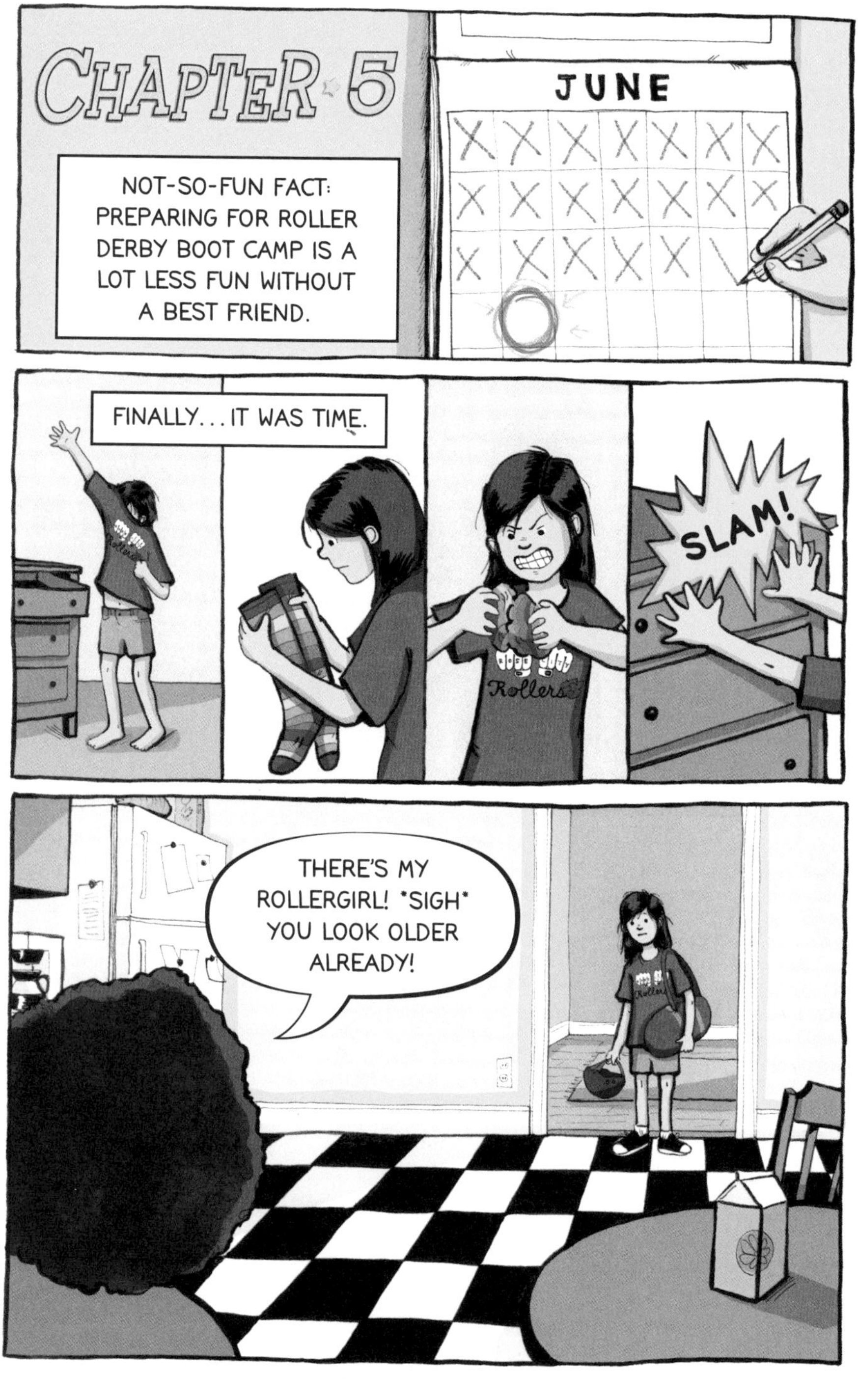
CHAPTER 5
NOT-SO-FUN FACT: PREPARING FOR ROLLER DERBY BOOT CAMP IS A LOT LESS FUN WITHOUT A BEST FRIEND.
JUNE
FINALLY... IT WAS TIME.
Rollers
SLAM!
THERE'S MY ROLLERGIRL! *SIGH* YOU LOOK OLDER ALREADY!

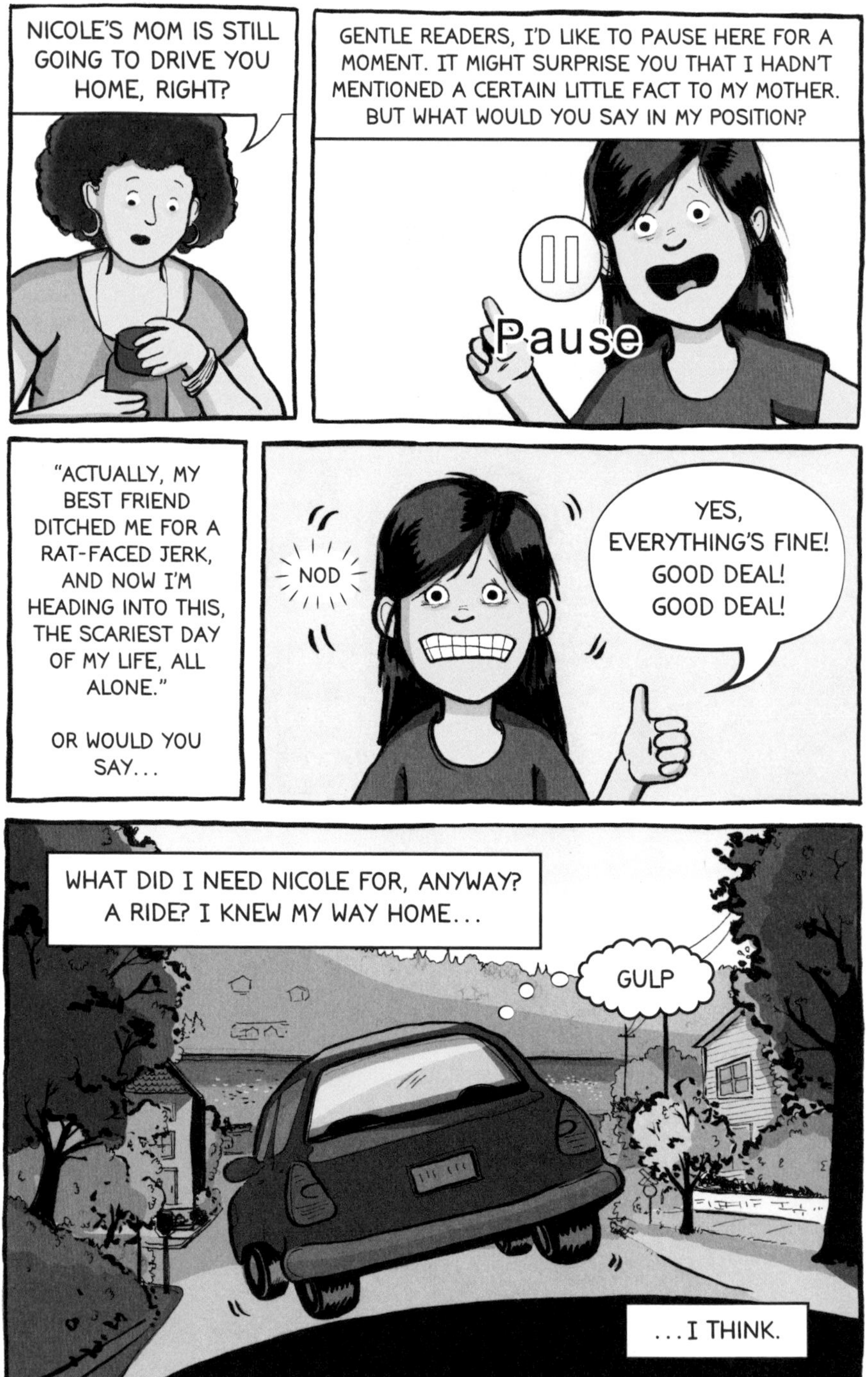
NICOLE'S MOM IS STILL GOING TO DRIVE YOU HOME, RIGHT?
GENTLE READERS, I'D LIKE TO PAUSE HERE FOR A MOMENT. IT MIGHT SURPRISE YOU THAT I HADN'T MENTIONED A CERTAIN LITTLE FACT TO MY MOTHER. BUT WHAT WOULD YOU SAY IN MY POSITION?
Pause
"ACTUALLY, MY BEST FRIEND DITCHED ME FOR A RAT-FACED JERK, AND NOW I'M HEADING INTO THIS, THE SCARIEST DAY OF MY LIFE, ALL ALONE."
OR WOULD YOU SAY...
NOD
YES, EVERYTHING'S FINE! GOOD DEAL! GOOD DEAL!
WHAT DID I NEED NICOLE FOR, ANYWAY? A RIDE? I KNEW MY WAY HOME...
GULP
...I THINK.

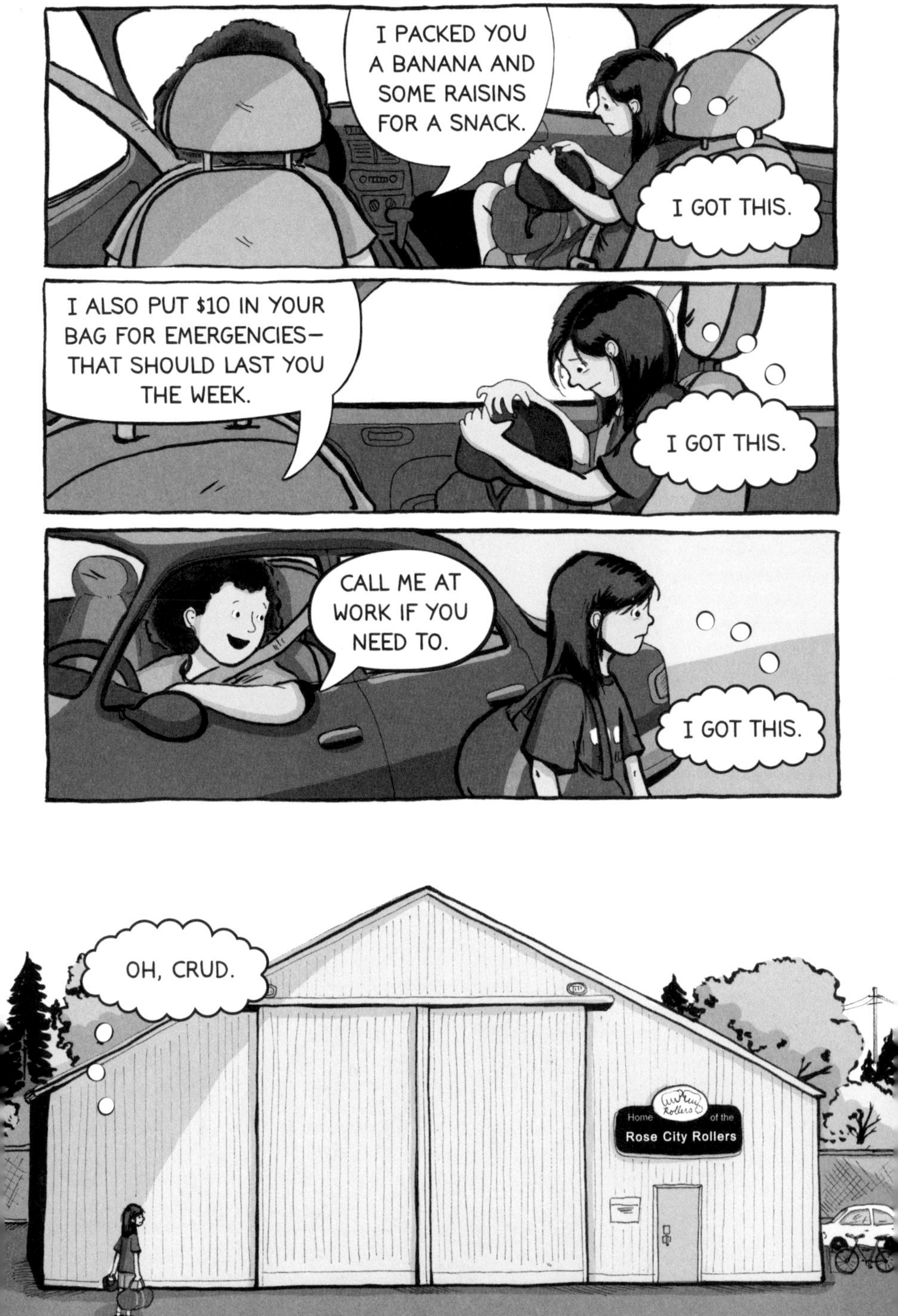
I PACKED YOU A BANANA AND SOME RAISINS FOR A SNACK.
I GOT THIS.
I ALSO PUT $10 IN YOUR BAG FOR EMERGENCIES—THAT SHOULD LAST YOU THE WEEK.
I GOT THIS.
CALL ME AT WORK IF YOU NEED TO.
I GOT THIS.
OH, CRUD.
Home of the Rose City Rollers

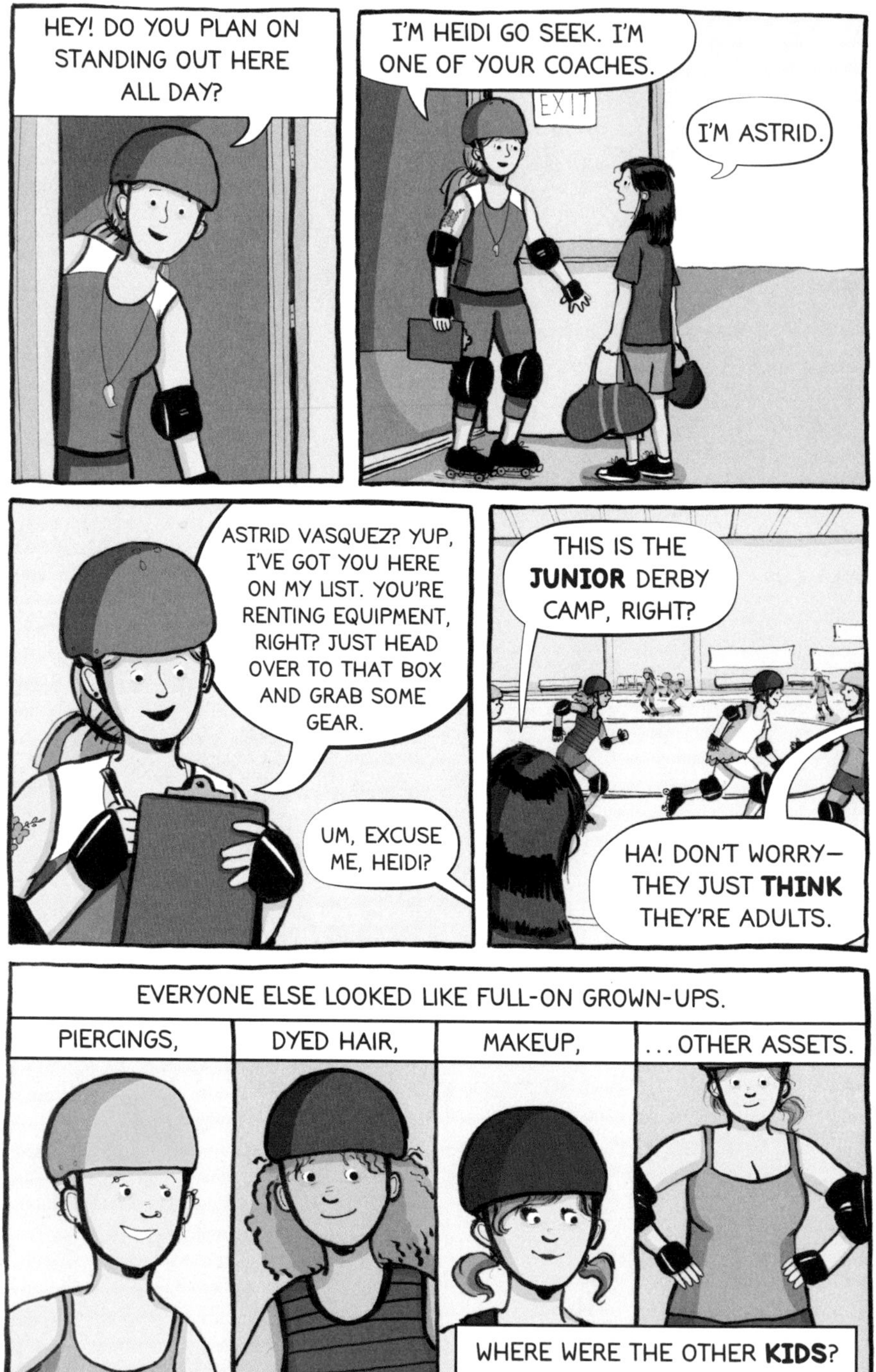
HEY! DO YOU PLAN ON STANDING OUT HERE ALL DAY?
I'M HEIDI GO SEEK. I'M ONE OF YOUR COACHES.
EXIT
I'M ASTRID.
ASTRID VASQUEZ? YUP, I'VE GOT YOU HERE ON MY LIST. YOU'RE RENTING EQUIPMENT, RIGHT? JUST HEAD OVER TO THAT BOX AND GRAB SOME GEAR.
UM, EXCUSE ME, HEIDI?
THIS IS THE **JUNIOR** DERBY CAMP, RIGHT?
HA! DON'T WORRY— THEY JUST **THINK** THEY'RE ADULTS.
EVERYONE ELSE LOOKED LIKE FULL-ON GROWN-UPS.
PIERCINGS,
DYED HAIR,
MAKEUP,
. . . OTHER ASSETS.
WHERE WERE THE OTHER **KIDS**?

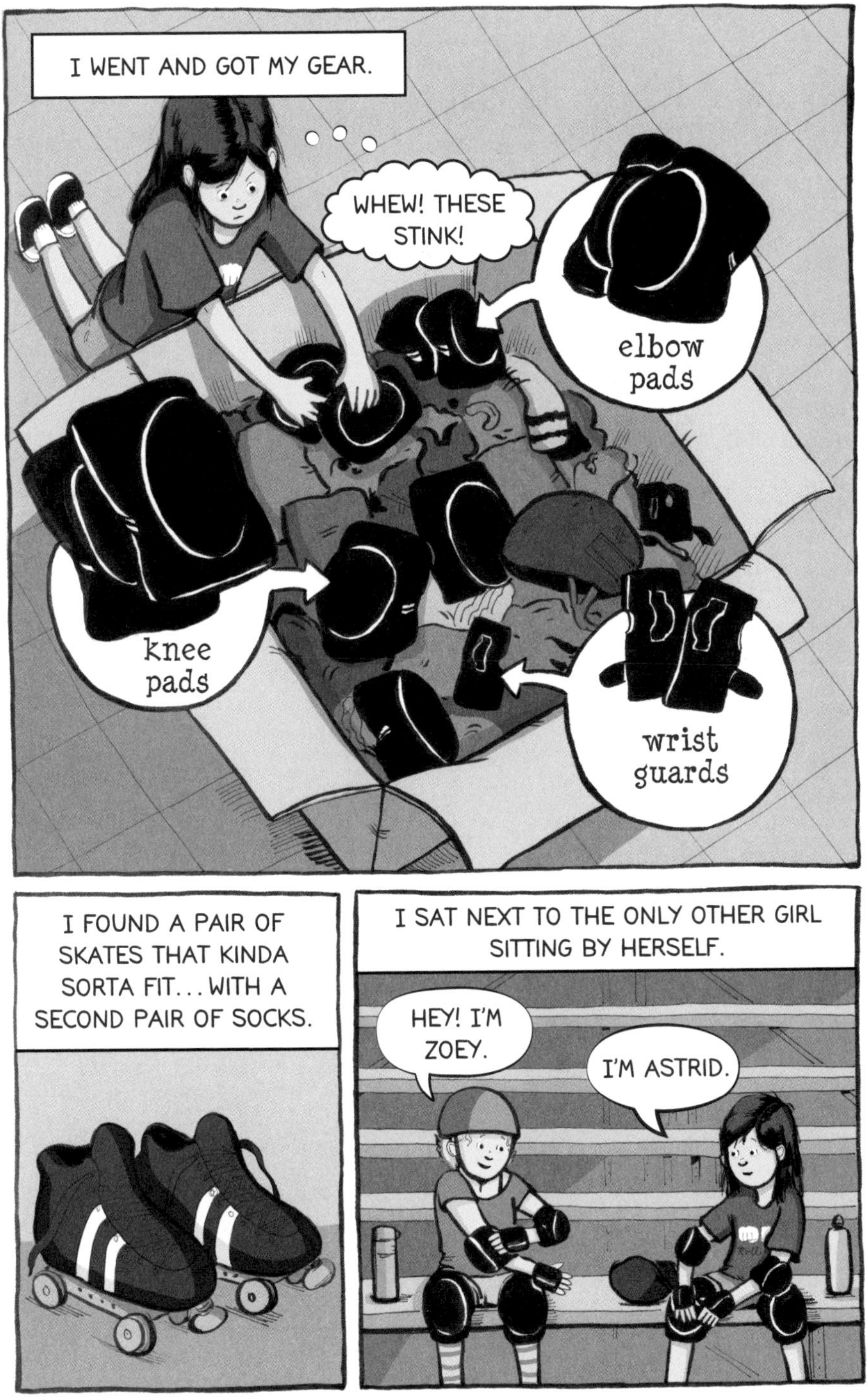
I WENT AND GOT MY GEAR.
WHEW! THESE STINK!
elbow pads
knee pads
wrist guards
I FOUND A PAIR OF SKATES THAT KINDA SORTA FIT. . . WITH A SECOND PAIR OF SOCKS.
I SAT NEXT TO THE ONLY OTHER GIRL SITTING BY HERSELF.
HEY! I'M ZOEY.
I'M ASTRID.

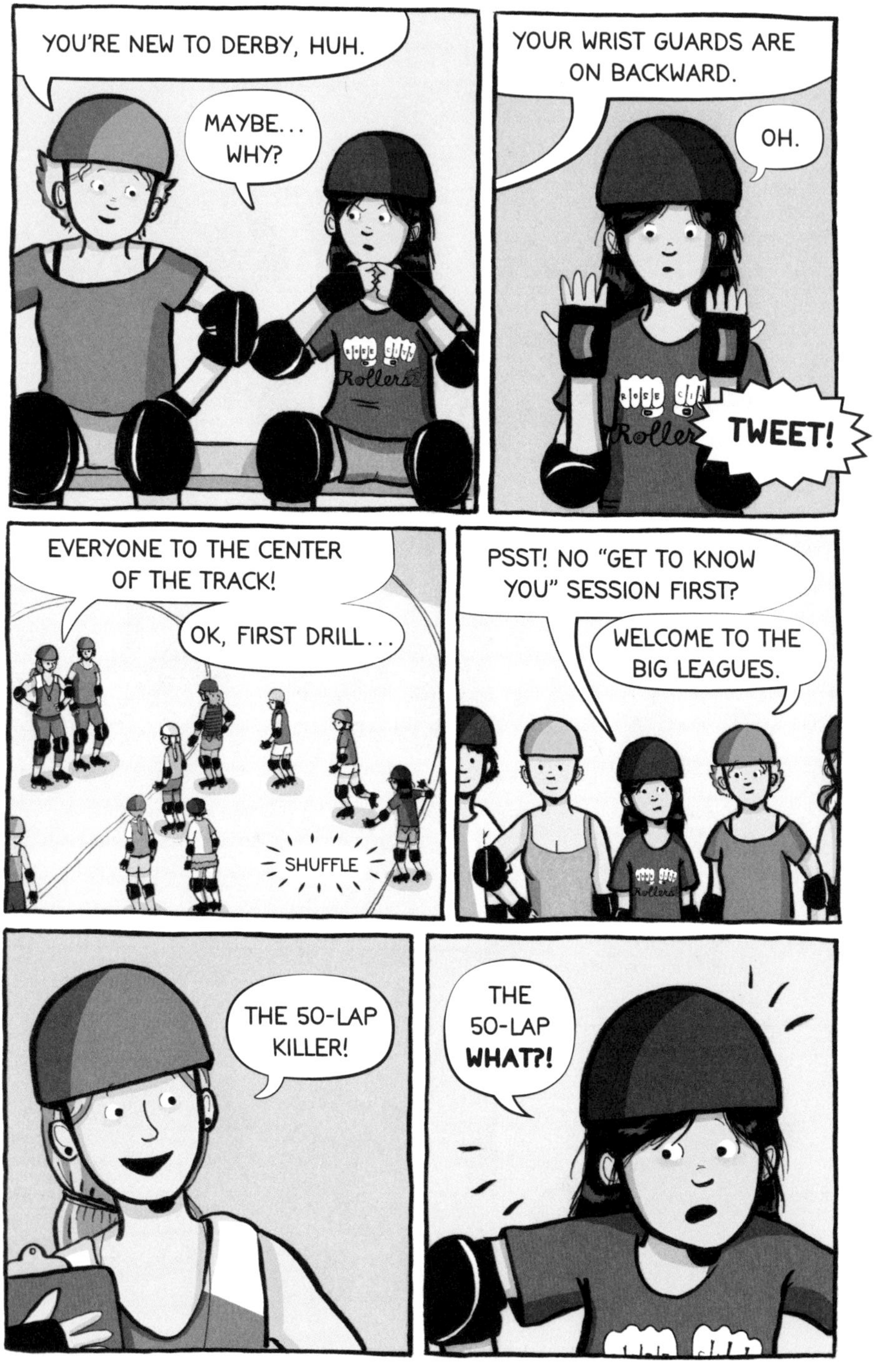
YOU'RE NEW TO DERBY, HUH.
MAYBE... WHY?
YOUR WRIST GUARDS ARE ON BACKWARD.
OH.
ROSE CITY Rollers
TWEET!
EVERYONE TO THE CENTER OF THE TRACK!
OK, FIRST DRILL...
SHUFFLE
PSST! NO "GET TO KNOW YOU" SESSION FIRST?
WELCOME TO THE BIG LEAGUES.
THE 50-LAP KILLER!
THE 50-LAP **WHAT?!**

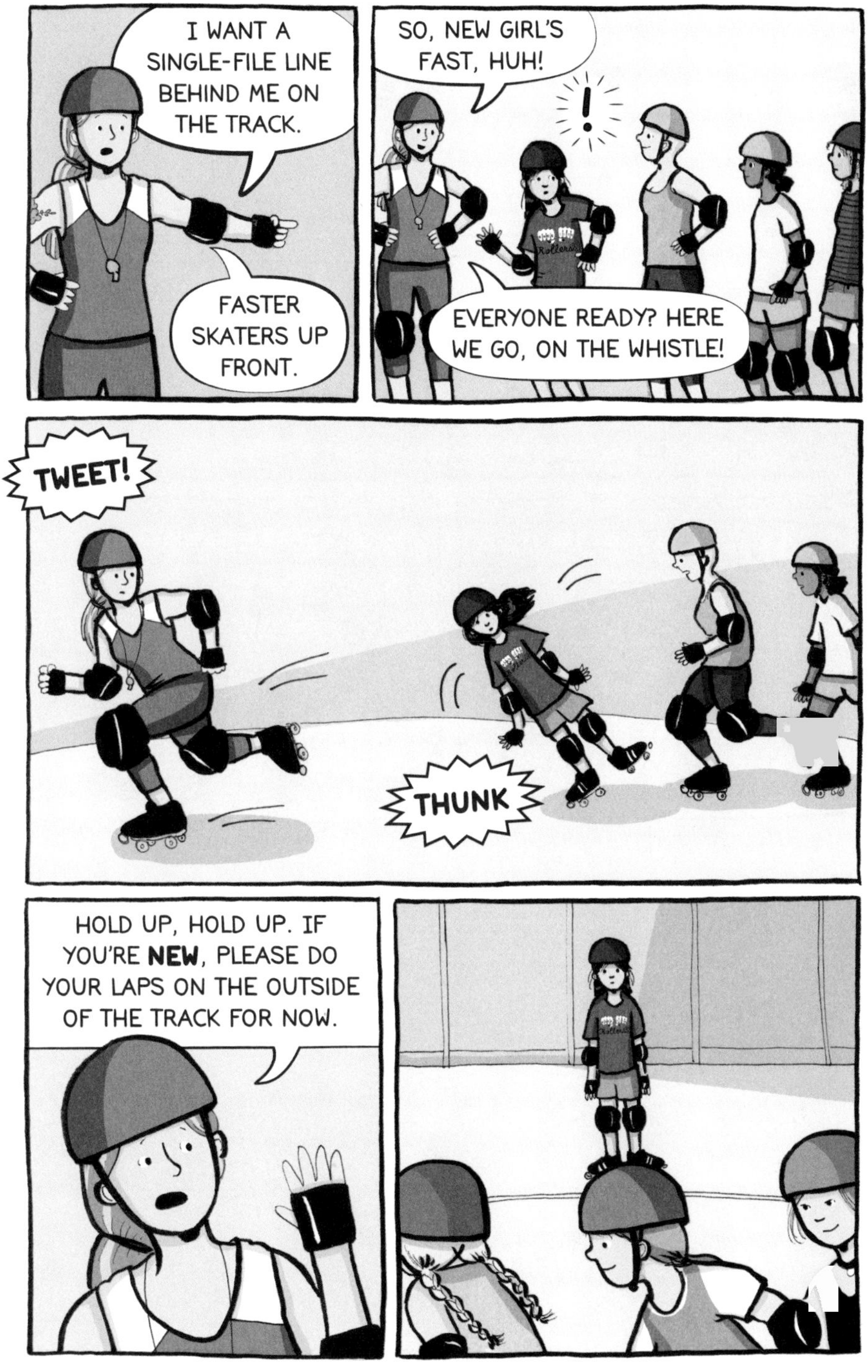

I WANT A SINGLE-FILE LINE BEHIND ME ON THE TRACK.
FASTER SKATERS UP FRONT.
SO, NEW GIRL'S FAST, HUH!
!
EVERYONE READY? HERE WE GO, ON THE WHISTLE!
TWEET!
THUNK
HOLD UP, HOLD UP. IF YOU'RE **NEW**, PLEASE DO YOUR LAPS ON THE OUTSIDE OF THE TRACK FOR NOW.

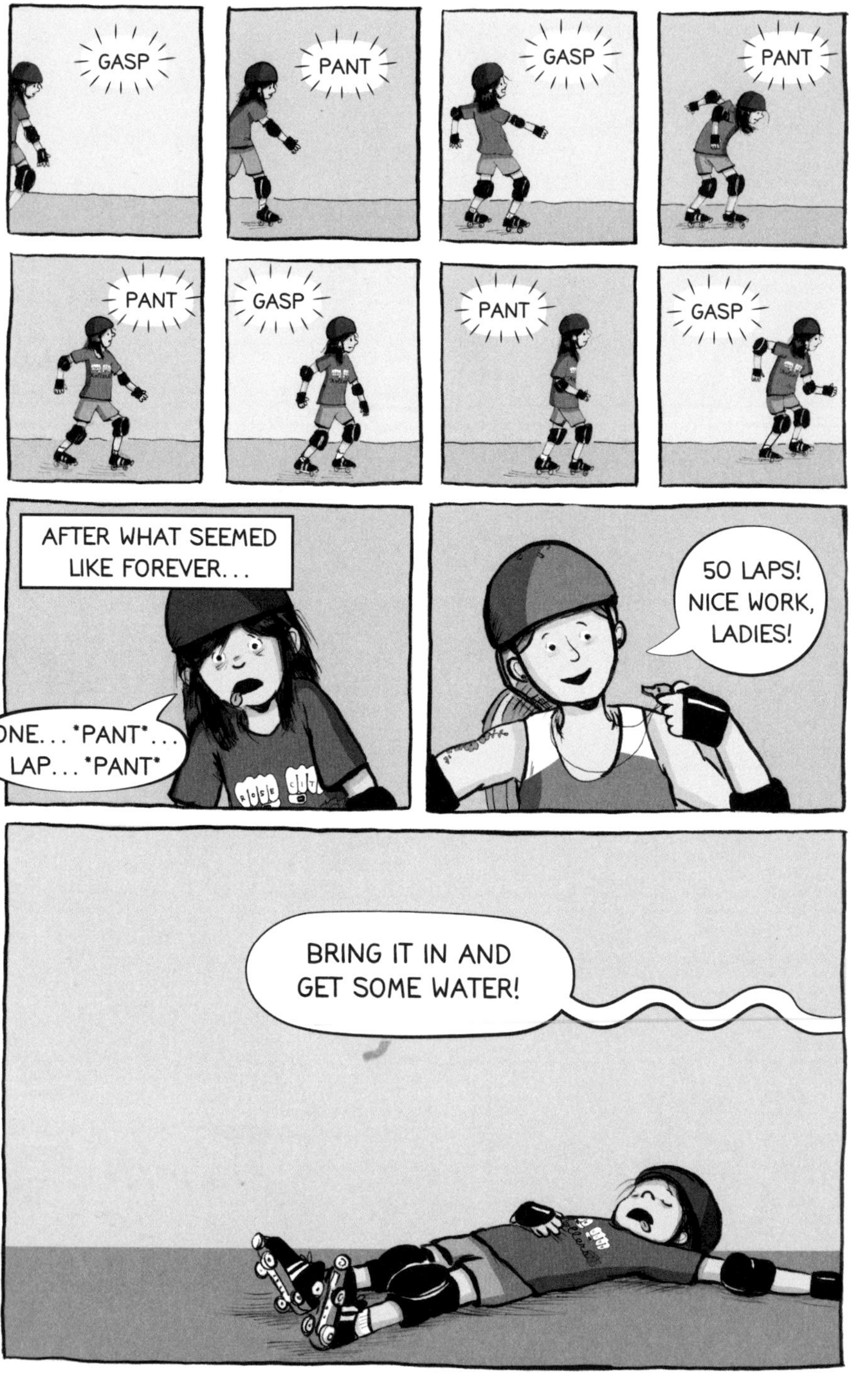
GASP
PANT
GASP
PANT
PANT
GASP
PANT
GASP
AFTER WHAT SEEMED LIKE FOREVER...
ONE... *PANT*... LAP... *PANT*
50 LAPS! NICE WORK, LADIES!
BRING IT IN AND GET SOME WATER!

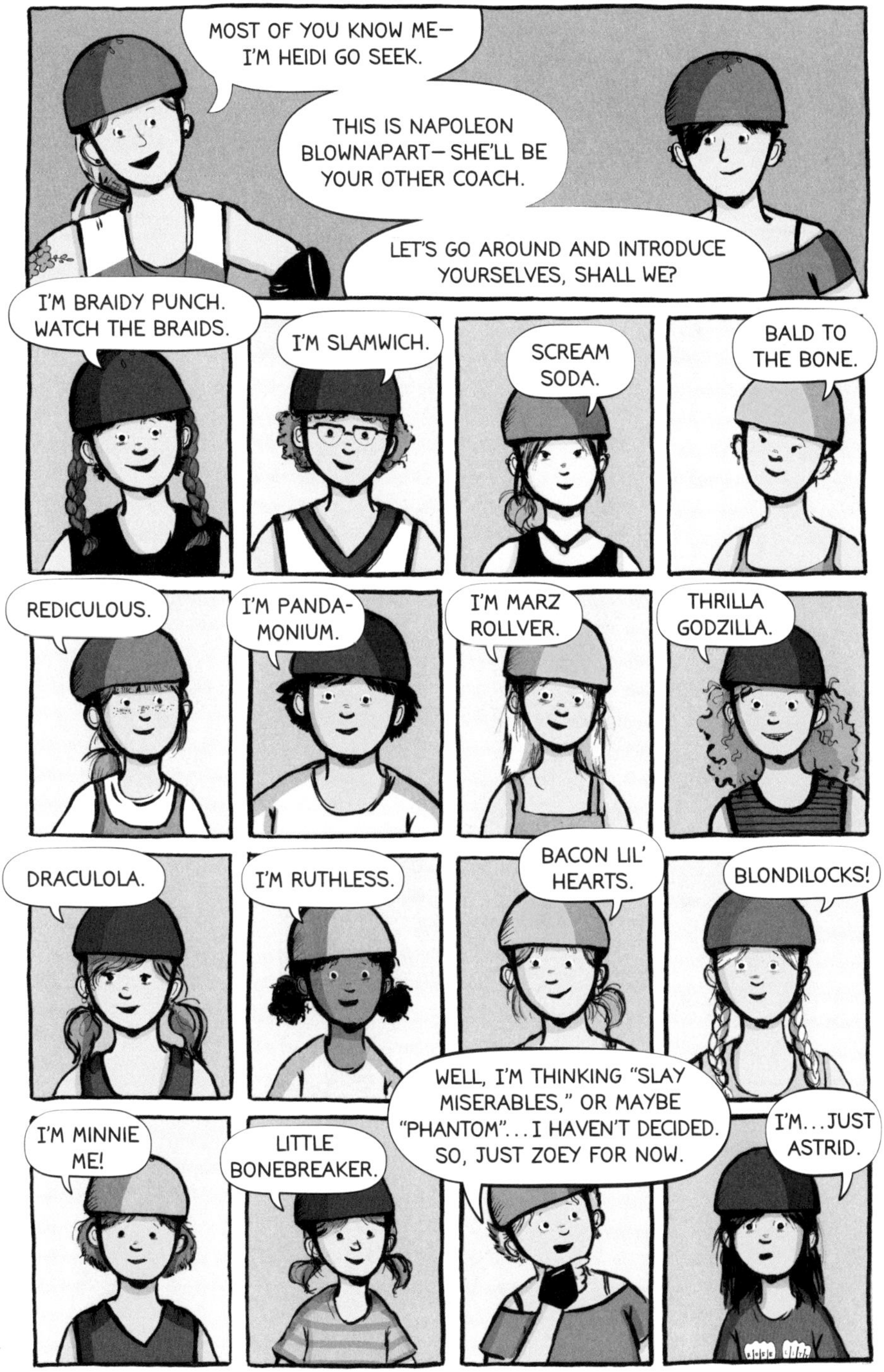
MOST OF YOU KNOW ME—
I'M HEIDI GO SEEK.
THIS IS NAPOLEON BLOWNAPART—SHE'LL BE YOUR OTHER COACH.
LET'S GO AROUND AND INTRODUCE YOURSELVES, SHALL WE?
I'M BRAIDY PUNCH. WATCH THE BRAIDS.
I'M SLAMWICH.
SCREAM SODA.
BALD TO THE BONE.
REDICULOUS.
I'M PANDA-MONIUM.
I'M MARZ ROLLVER.
THRILLA GODZILLA.
DRACULOLA.
I'M RUTHLESS.
BACON LIL' HEARTS.
BLONDILOCKS!
I'M MINNIE ME!
LITTLE BONEBREAKER.
WELL, I'M THINKING "SLAY MISERABLES," OR MAYBE "PHANTOM"... I HAVEN'T DECIDED. SO, JUST ZOEY FOR NOW.
I'M...JUST ASTRID.

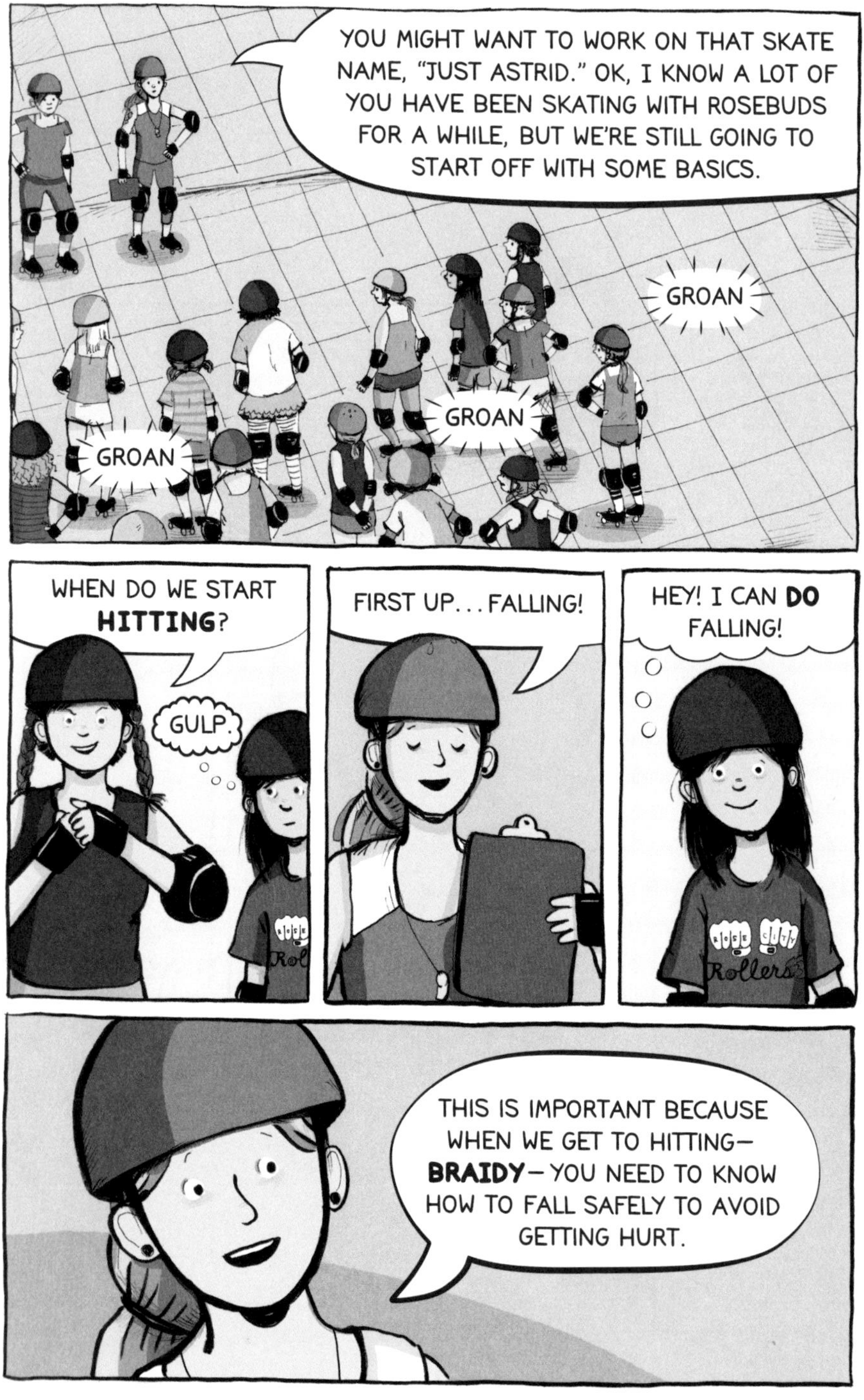
YOU MIGHT WANT TO WORK ON THAT SKATE NAME, "JUST ASTRID." OK, I KNOW A LOT OF YOU HAVE BEEN SKATING WITH ROSEBUDS FOR A WHILE, BUT WE'RE STILL GOING TO START OFF WITH SOME BASICS.
GROAN
GROAN
GROAN
WHEN DO WE START **HITTING**?
GULP.
FIRST UP... FALLING!
HEY! I CAN **DO** FALLING!
THIS IS IMPORTANT BECAUSE WHEN WE GET TO HITTING— **BRAIDY**— YOU NEED TO KNOW HOW TO FALL SAFELY TO AVOID GETTING HURT.

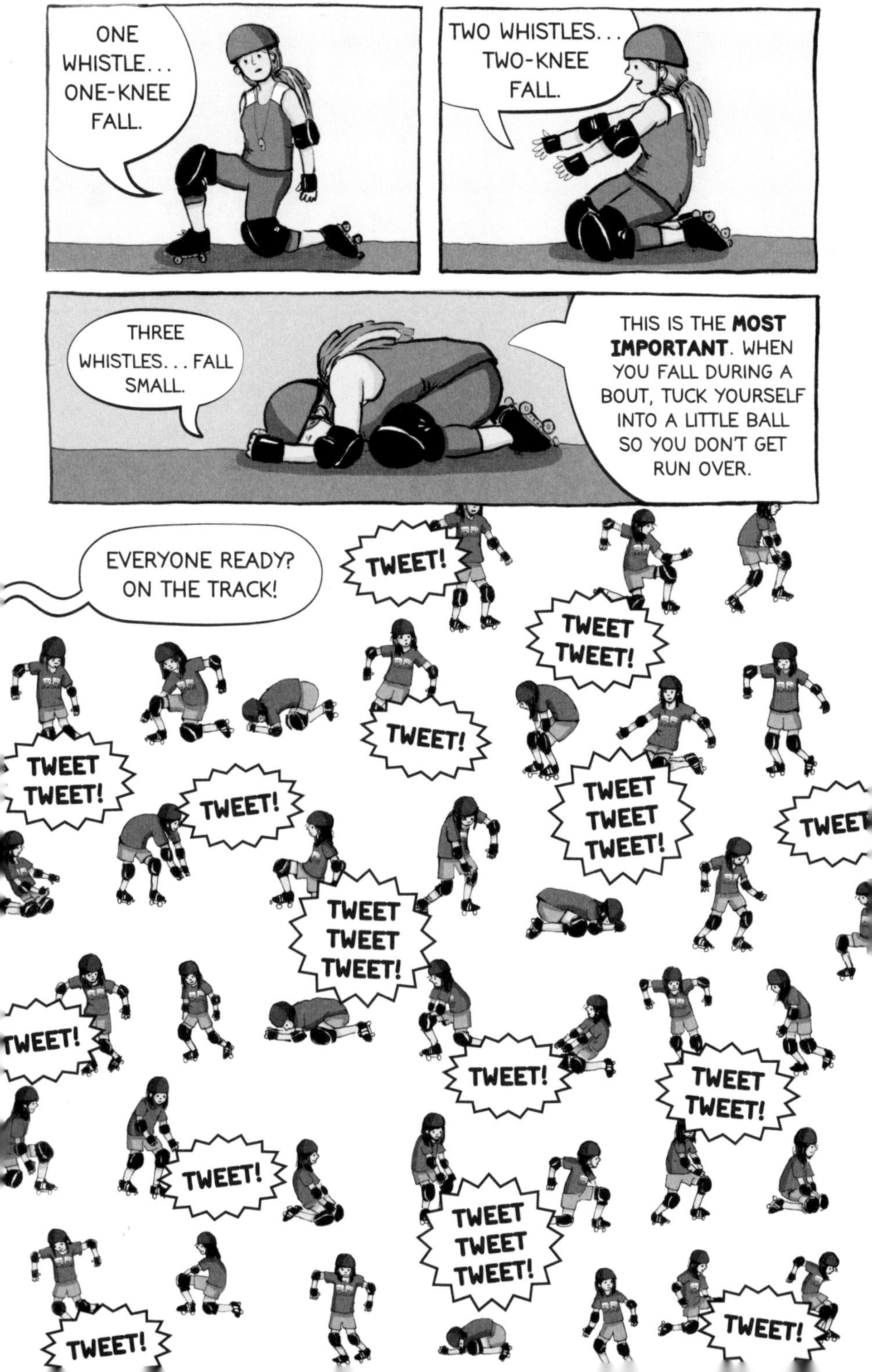

ONE WHISTLE... ONE-KNEE FALL.
TWO WHISTLES... TWO-KNEE FALL.
THREE WHISTLES... FALL SMALL.
THIS IS THE **MOST IMPORTANT**. WHEN YOU FALL DURING A BOUT, TUCK YOURSELF INTO A LITTLE BALL SO YOU DON'T GET RUN OVER.
EVERYONE READY? ON THE TRACK!
TWEET!
TWEET TWEET!
TWEET!
TWEET TWEET!
TWEET!
TWEET TWEET TWEET!
TWEET TWEET TWEET!
TWEET!
TWEET!
TWEET TWEET!
TWEET!
TWEET TWEET TWEET!
TWEET!
TWEET!

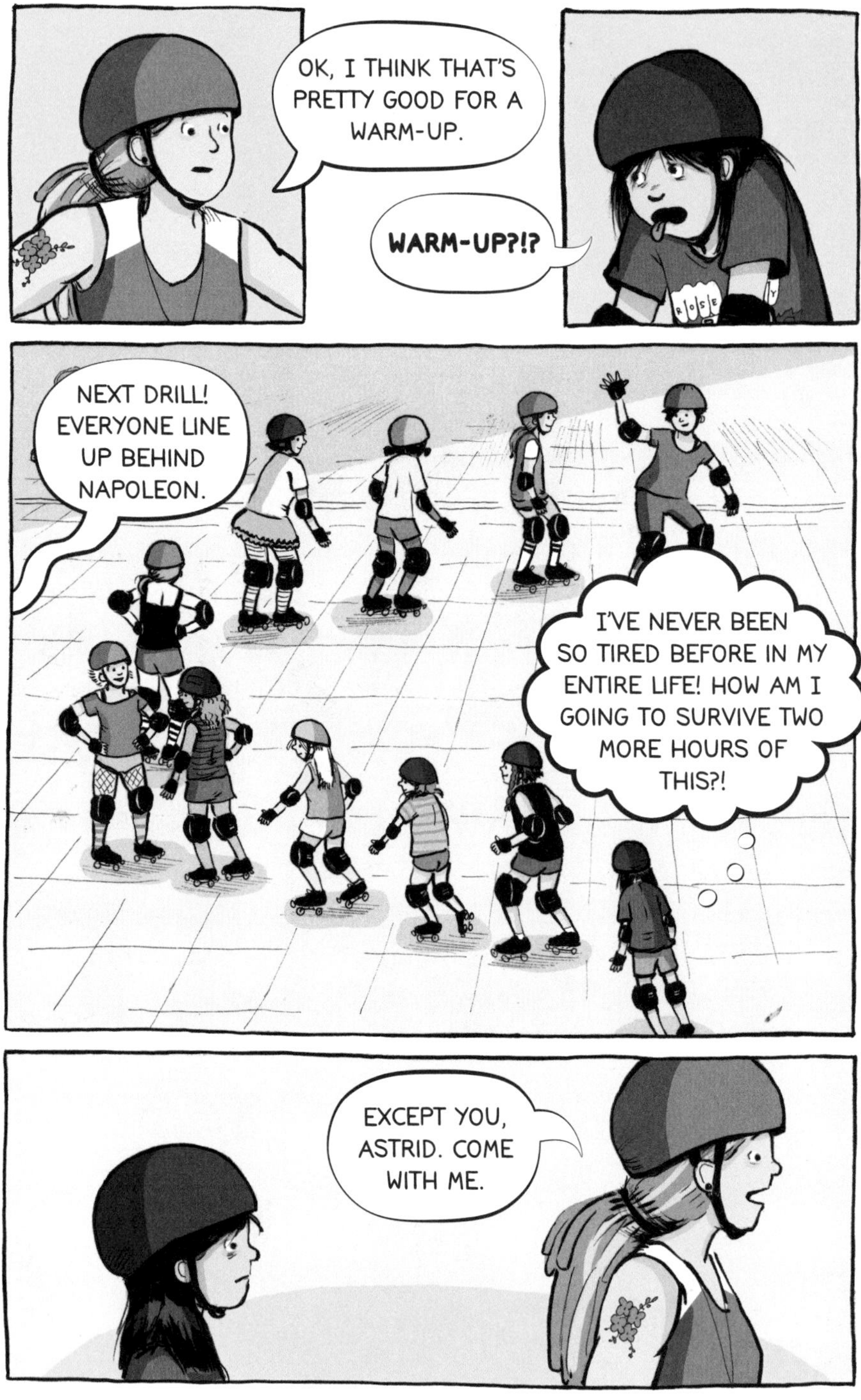
OK, I THINK THAT'S PRETTY GOOD FOR A WARM-UP.
WARM-UP?!?
ROSE
NEXT DRILL! EVERYONE LINE UP BEHIND NAPOLEON.
I'VE NEVER BEEN SO TIRED BEFORE IN MY ENTIRE LIFE! HOW AM I GOING TO SURVIVE TWO MORE HOURS OF THIS?!
EXCEPT YOU, ASTRID. COME WITH ME.

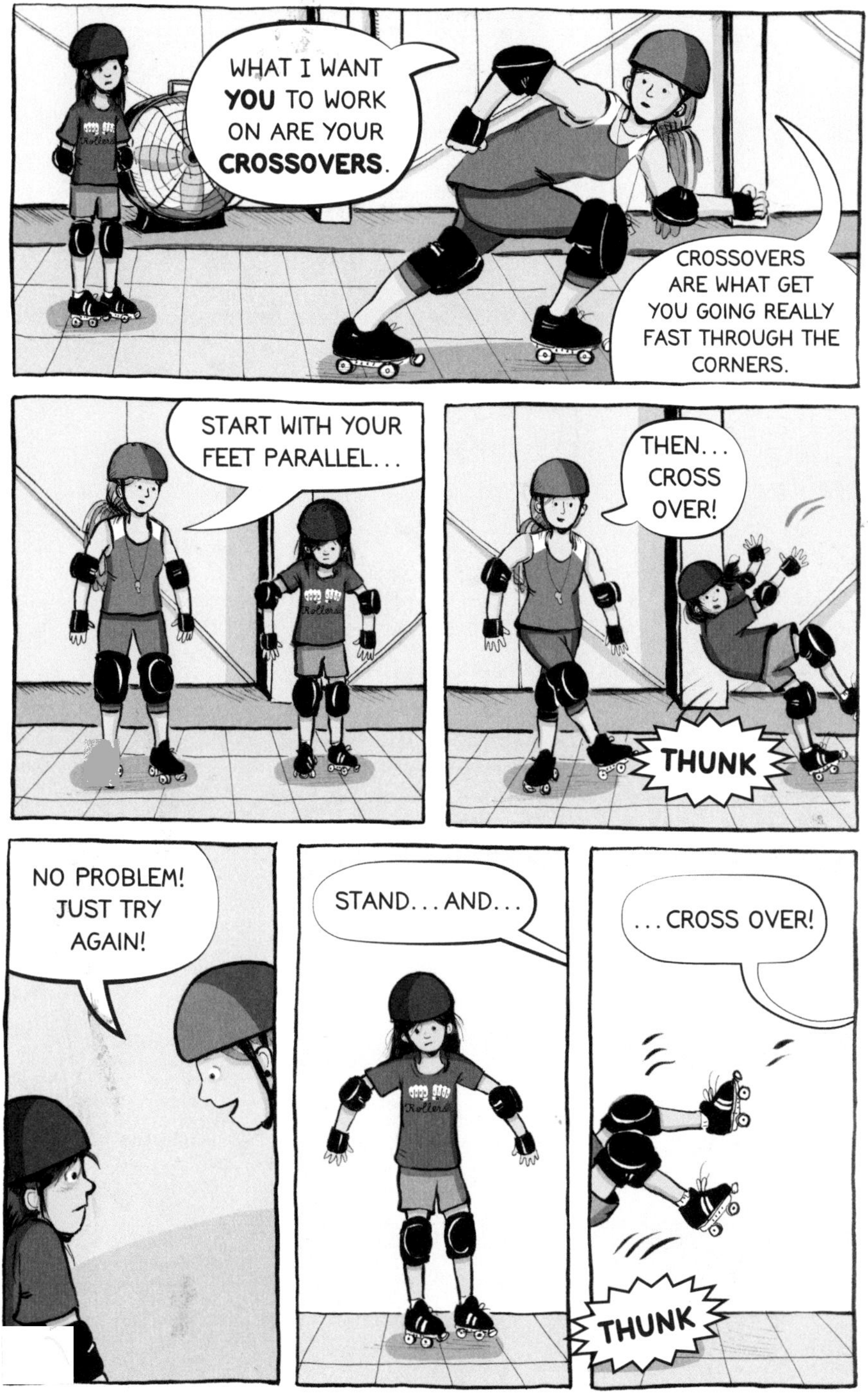
WHAT I WANT **YOU** TO WORK ON ARE YOUR **CROSSOVERS**.
CROSSOVERS ARE WHAT GET YOU GOING REALLY FAST THROUGH THE CORNERS.
START WITH YOUR FEET PARALLEL...
THEN... CROSS OVER!
THUNK
NO PROBLEM! JUST TRY AGAIN!
STAND...AND...
...CROSS OVER!
THUNK

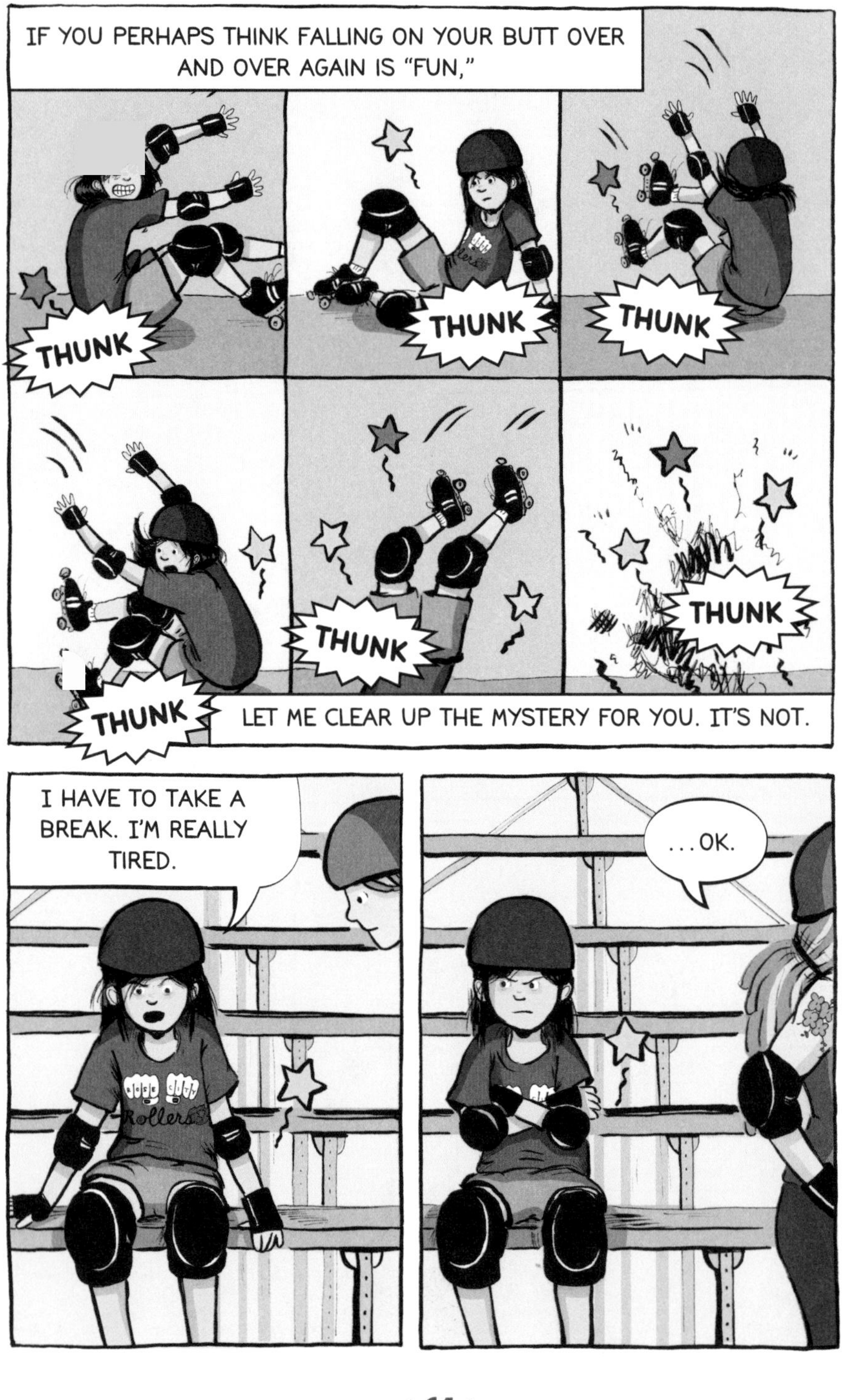
IF YOU PERHAPS THINK FALLING ON YOUR BUTT OVER AND OVER AGAIN IS "FUN,"
THUNK
THUNK
THUNK
THUNK
THUNK
THUNK
LET ME CLEAR UP THE MYSTERY FOR YOU. IT'S NOT.
I HAVE TO TAKE A BREAK. I'M REALLY TIRED.
...OK.

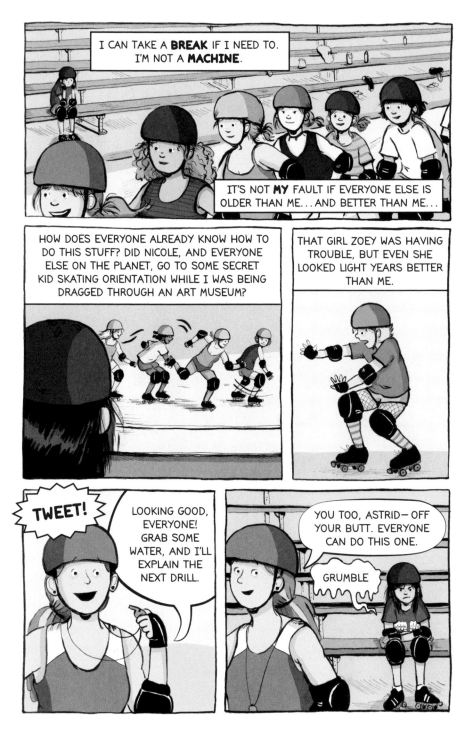

I CAN TAKE A **BREAK** IF I NEED TO. I'M NOT A **MACHINE**.

IT'S NOT **MY** FAULT IF EVERYONE ELSE IS OLDER THAN ME... AND BETTER THAN ME...

HOW DOES EVERYONE ALREADY KNOW HOW TO DO THIS STUFF? DID NICOLE, AND EVERYONE ELSE ON THE PLANET, GO TO SOME SECRET KID SKATING ORIENTATION WHILE I WAS BEING DRAGGED THROUGH AN ART MUSEUM?

THAT GIRL ZOEY WAS HAVING TROUBLE, BUT EVEN SHE LOOKED LIGHT YEARS BETTER THAN ME.

TWEET!

LOOKING GOOD, EVERYONE! GRAB SOME WATER, AND I'LL EXPLAIN THE NEXT DRILL.

YOU TOO, ASTRID— OFF YOUR BUTT. EVERYONE CAN DO THIS ONE.

GRUMBLE

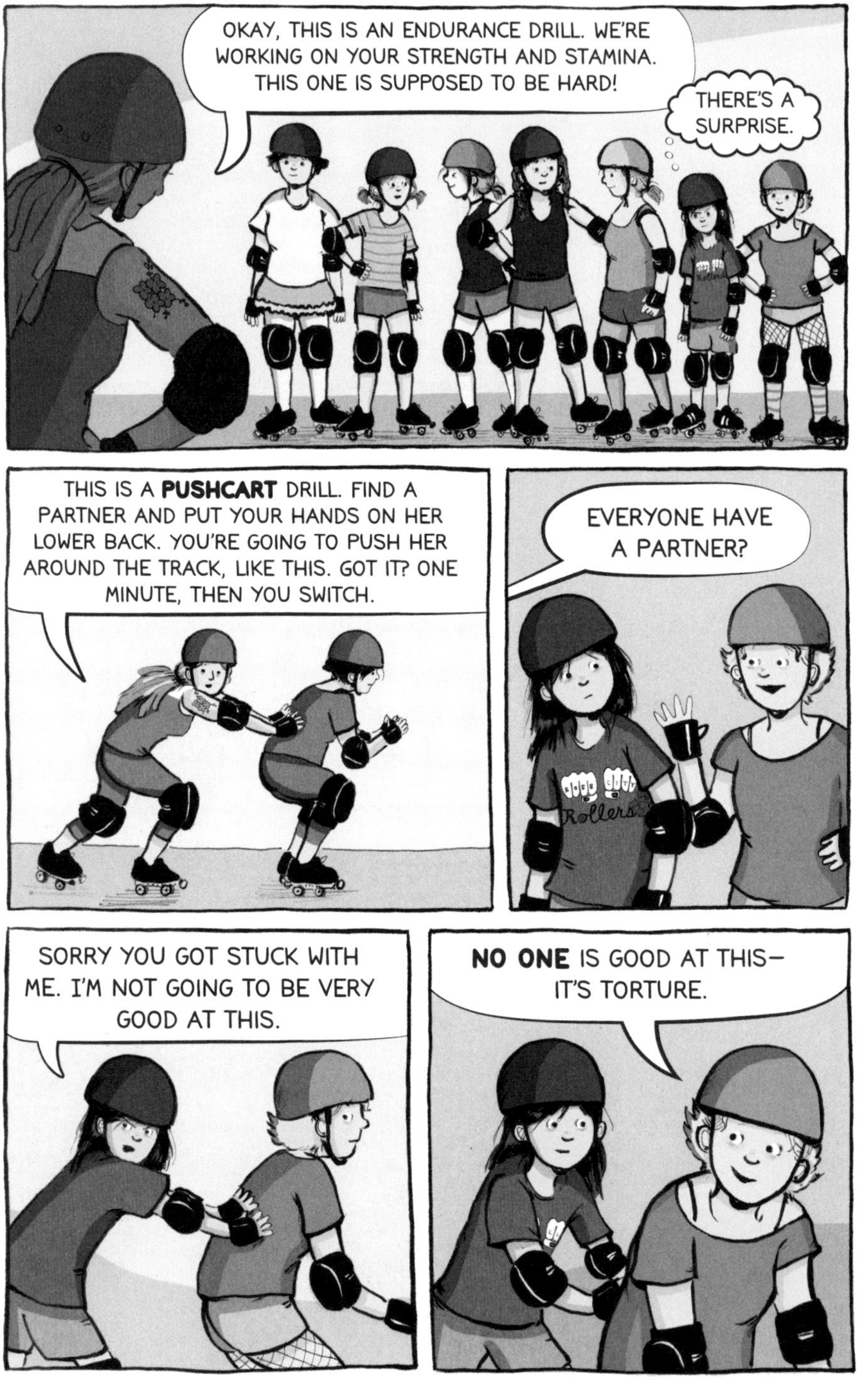
OKAY, THIS IS AN ENDURANCE DRILL. WE'RE WORKING ON YOUR STRENGTH AND STAMINA. THIS ONE IS SUPPOSED TO BE HARD!
THERE'S A SURPRISE.
THIS IS A **PUSHCART** DRILL. FIND A PARTNER AND PUT YOUR HANDS ON HER LOWER BACK. YOU'RE GOING TO PUSH HER AROUND THE TRACK, LIKE THIS. GOT IT? ONE MINUTE, THEN YOU SWITCH.
EVERYONE HAVE A PARTNER?
SORRY YOU GOT STUCK WITH ME. I'M NOT GOING TO BE VERY GOOD AT THIS.
NO ONE IS GOOD AT THIS—IT'S TORTURE.

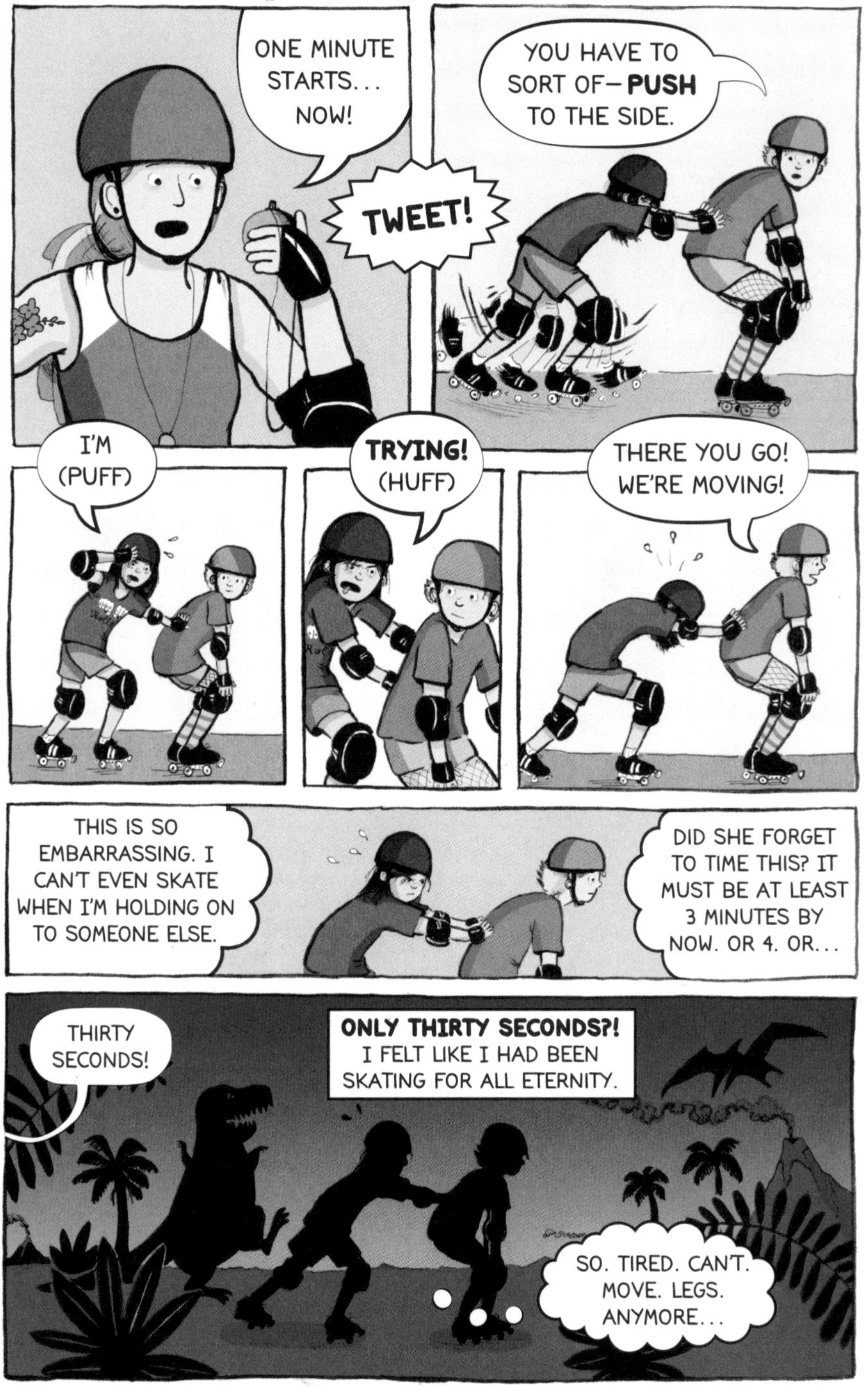
ONE MINUTE STARTS... NOW!
TWEET!
YOU HAVE TO SORT OF—**PUSH** TO THE SIDE.
I'M (PUFF)
TRYING! (HUFF)
THERE YOU GO! WE'RE MOVING!
THIS IS SO EMBARRASSING. I CAN'T EVEN SKATE WHEN I'M HOLDING ON TO SOMEONE ELSE.
DID SHE FORGET TO TIME THIS? IT MUST BE AT LEAST 3 MINUTES BY NOW. OR 4. OR...
THIRTY SECONDS!
ONLY THIRTY SECONDS?! I FELT LIKE I HAD BEEN SKATING FOR ALL ETERNITY.
SO. TIRED. CAN'T. MOVE. LEGS. ANYMORE...

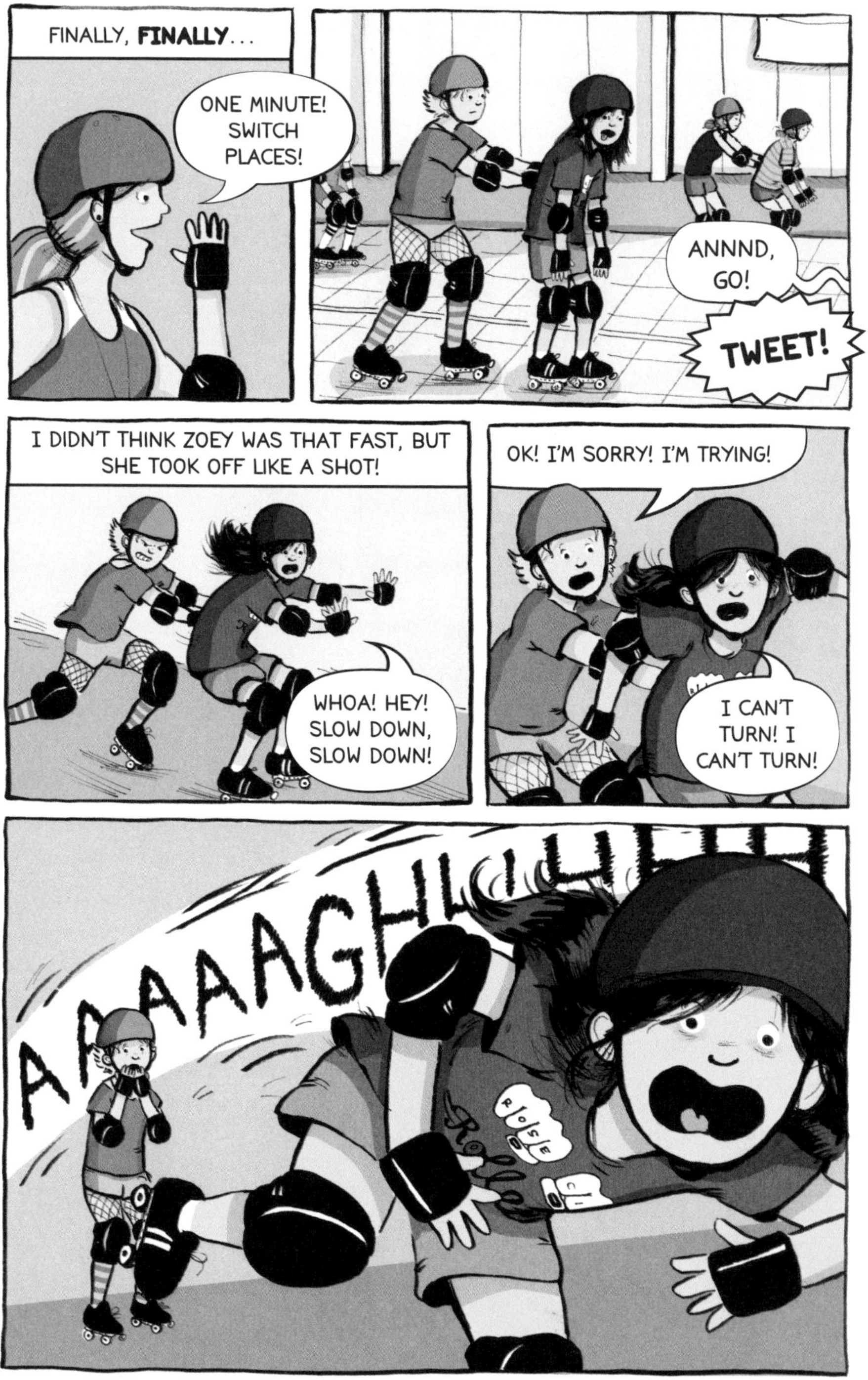
FINALLY, **FINALLY**...
ONE MINUTE! SWITCH PLACES!
ANNND, GO!
TWEET!
I DIDN'T THINK ZOEY WAS THAT FAST, BUT SHE TOOK OFF LIKE A SHOT!
WHOA! HEY! SLOW DOWN, SLOW DOWN!
OK! I'M SORRY! I'M TRYING!
I CAN'T TURN! I CAN'T TURN!
AAAAAGHHHHHH

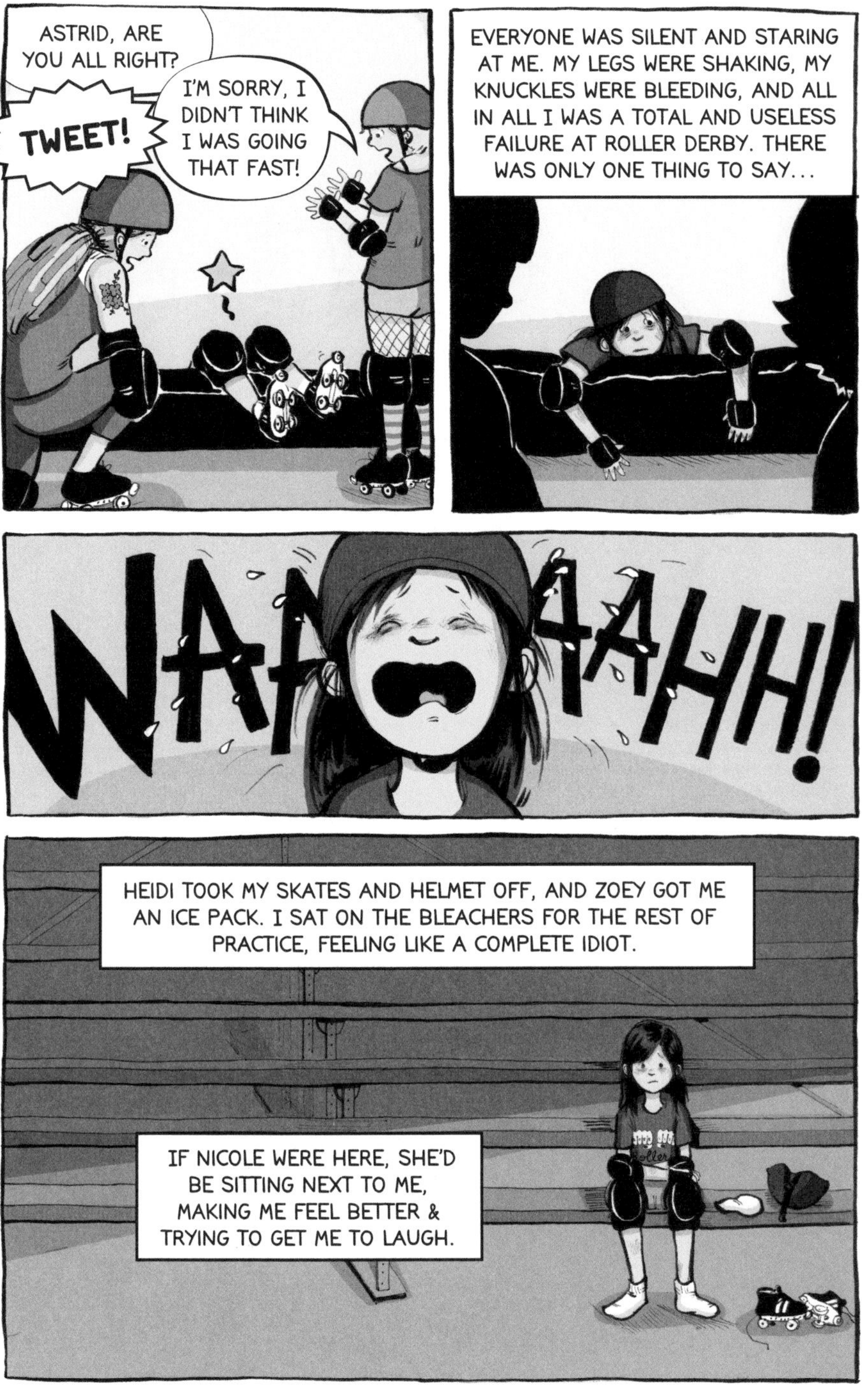
ASTRID, ARE YOU ALL RIGHT?
TWEET!
I'M SORRY, I DIDN'T THINK I WAS GOING THAT FAST!
EVERYONE WAS SILENT AND STARING AT ME. MY LEGS WERE SHAKING, MY KNUCKLES WERE BLEEDING, AND ALL IN ALL I WAS A TOTAL AND USELESS FAILURE AT ROLLER DERBY. THERE WAS ONLY ONE THING TO SAY...
WAAAAHH!
HEIDI TOOK MY SKATES AND HELMET OFF, AND ZOEY GOT ME AN ICE PACK. I SAT ON THE BLEACHERS FOR THE REST OF PRACTICE, FEELING LIKE A COMPLETE IDIOT.
IF NICOLE WERE HERE, SHE'D BE SITTING NEXT TO ME, MAKING ME FEEL BETTER & TRYING TO GET ME TO LAUGH.

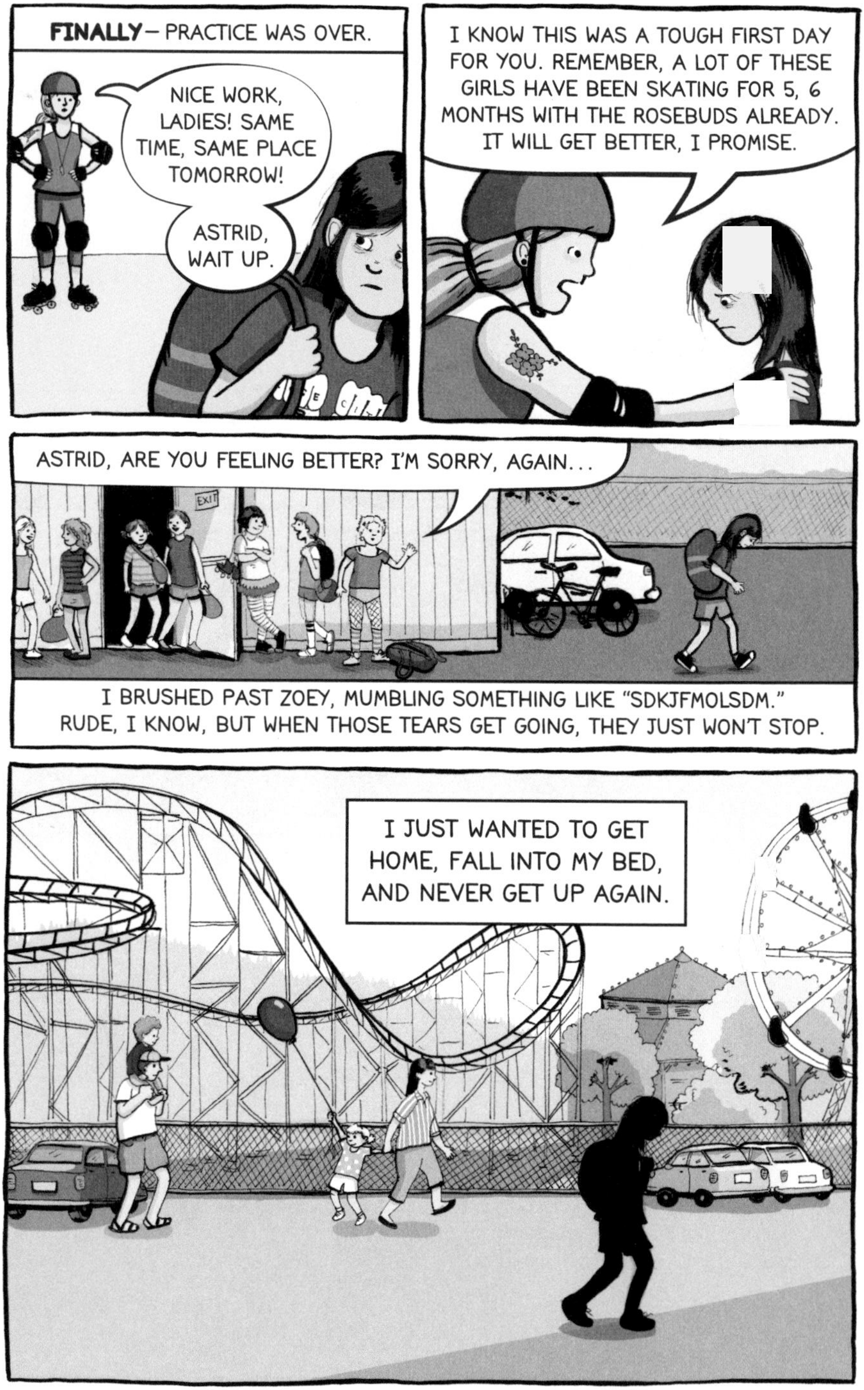
FINALLY— PRACTICE WAS OVER.
NICE WORK, LADIES! SAME TIME, SAME PLACE TOMORROW!
ASTRID, WAIT UP.
I KNOW THIS WAS A TOUGH FIRST DAY FOR YOU. REMEMBER, A LOT OF THESE GIRLS HAVE BEEN SKATING FOR 5, 6 MONTHS WITH THE ROSEBUDS ALREADY. IT WILL GET BETTER, I PROMISE.
ASTRID, ARE YOU FEELING BETTER? I'M SORRY, AGAIN...
EXIT
I BRUSHED PAST ZOEY, MUMBLING SOMETHING LIKE "SDKJFMOLSDM." RUDE, I KNOW, BUT WHEN THOSE TEARS GET GOING, THEY JUST WON'T STOP.
I JUST WANTED TO GET HOME, FALL INTO MY BED, AND NEVER GET UP AGAIN.

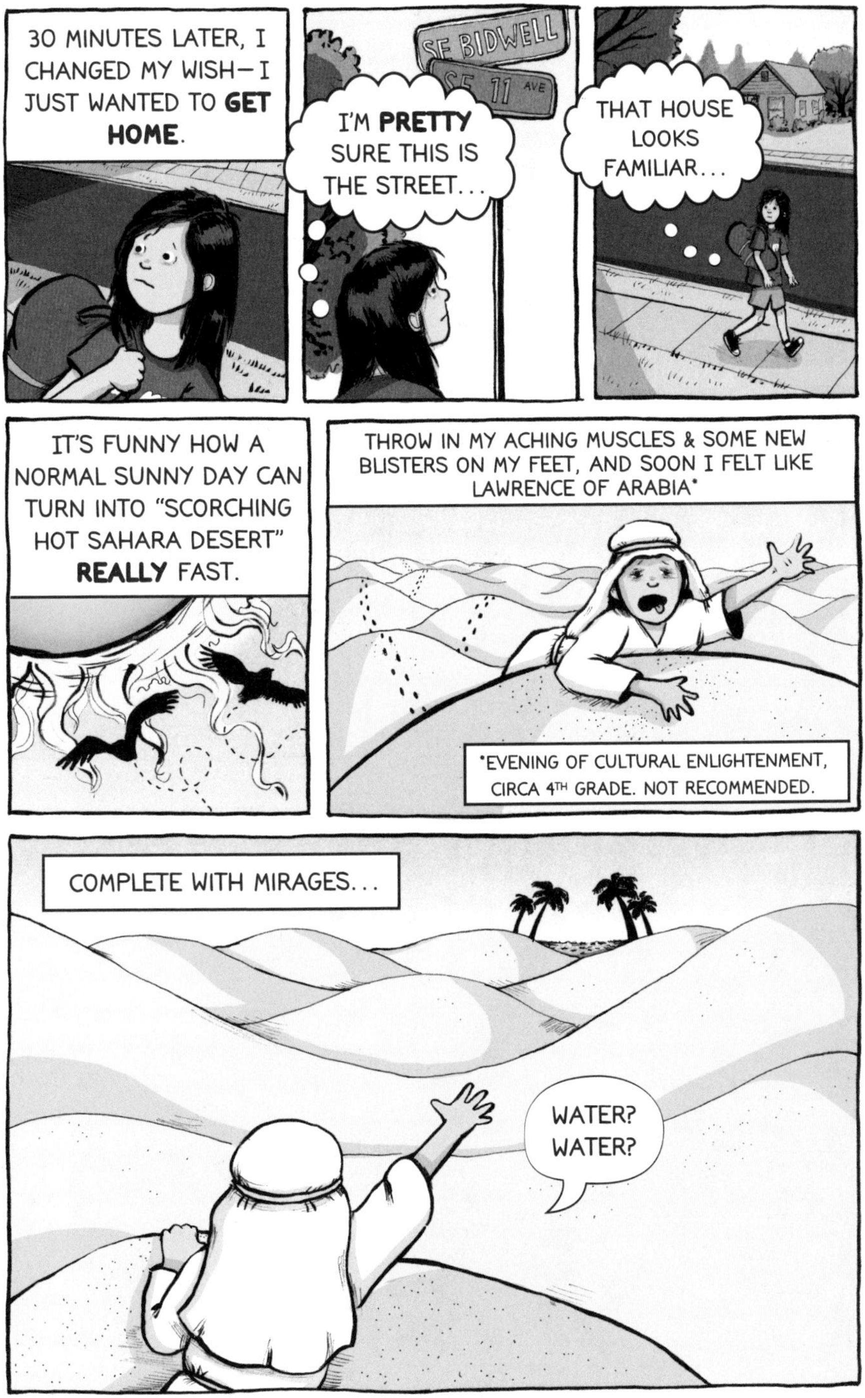
30 MINUTES LATER, I CHANGED MY WISH—I JUST WANTED TO **GET HOME**.
SE BIDWELL
SE 11 AVE
I'M **PRETTY** SURE THIS IS THE STREET...
THAT HOUSE LOOKS FAMILIAR...
IT'S FUNNY HOW A NORMAL SUNNY DAY CAN TURN INTO "SCORCHING HOT SAHARA DESERT" **REALLY** FAST.
THROW IN MY ACHING MUSCLES & SOME NEW BLISTERS ON MY FEET, AND SOON I FELT LIKE LAWRENCE OF ARABIA*
*EVENING OF CULTURAL ENLIGHTENMENT, CIRCA 4TH GRADE. NOT RECOMMENDED.
COMPLETE WITH MIRAGES...
WATER? WATER?

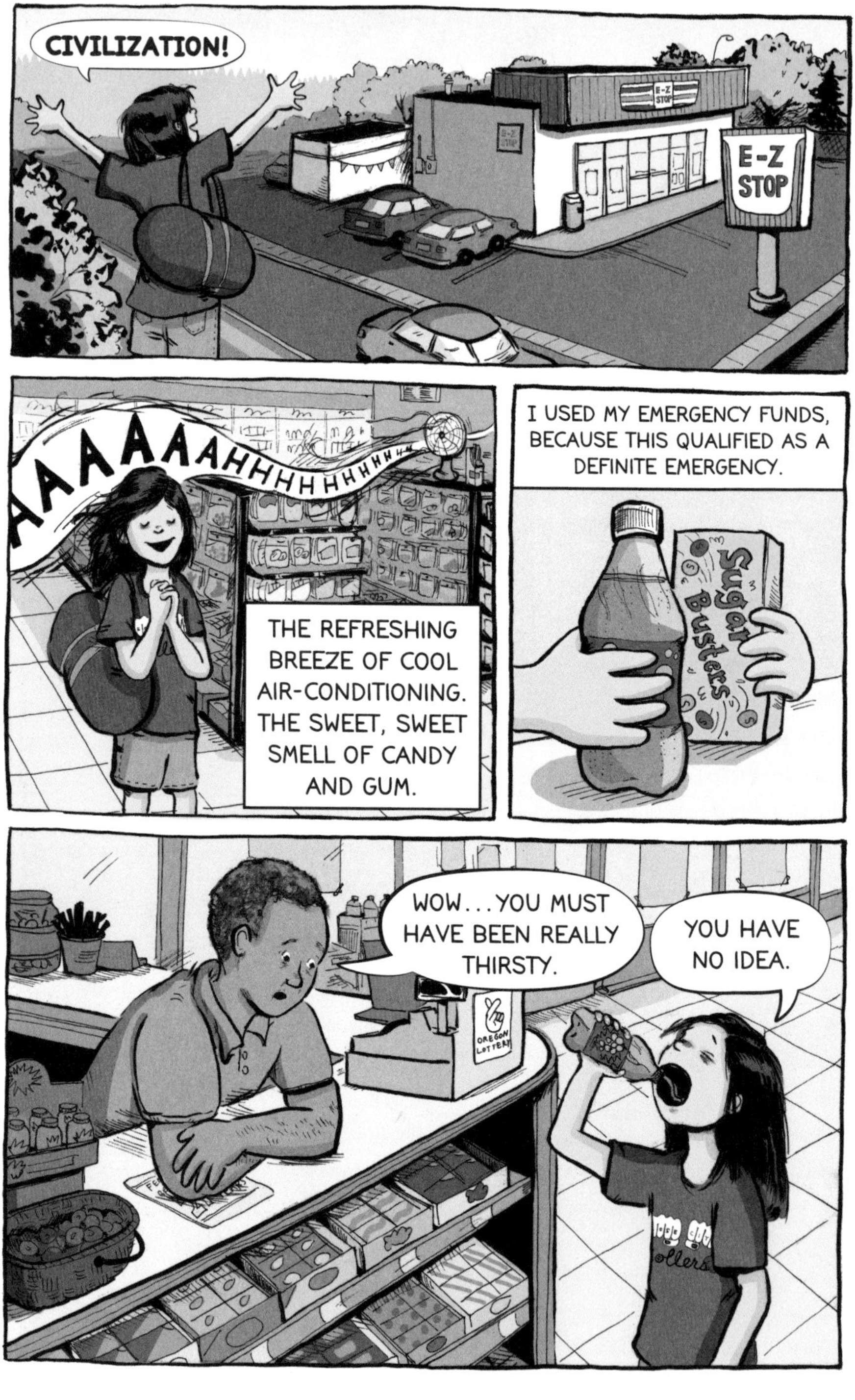
CIVILIZATION!
E-Z STOP
E-Z STOP
AAAAAAHHHHHHHHHHHH
THE REFRESHING BREEZE OF COOL AIR-CONDITIONING. THE SWEET, SWEET SMELL OF CANDY AND GUM.
I USED MY EMERGENCY FUNDS, BECAUSE THIS QUALIFIED AS A DEFINITE EMERGENCY.
Sugar Busters
WOW...YOU MUST HAVE BEEN REALLY THIRSTY.
YOU HAVE NO IDEA.
OREGON LOTTERY

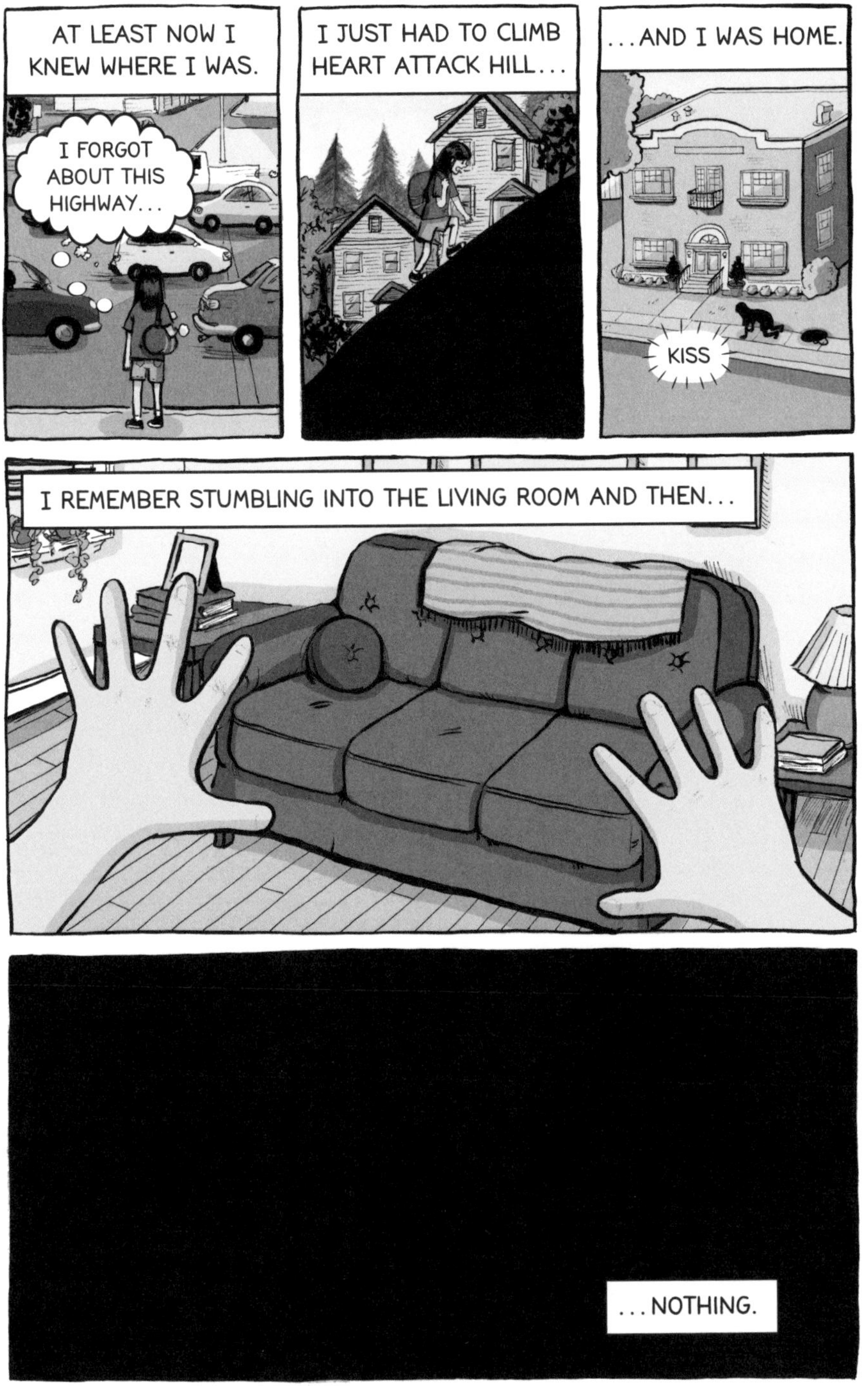
AT LEAST NOW I KNEW WHERE I WAS.
I FORGOT ABOUT THIS HIGHWAY...
I JUST HAD TO CLIMB HEART ATTACK HILL...
...AND I WAS HOME.
KISS
I REMEMBER STUMBLING INTO THE LIVING ROOM AND THEN...
...NOTHING.

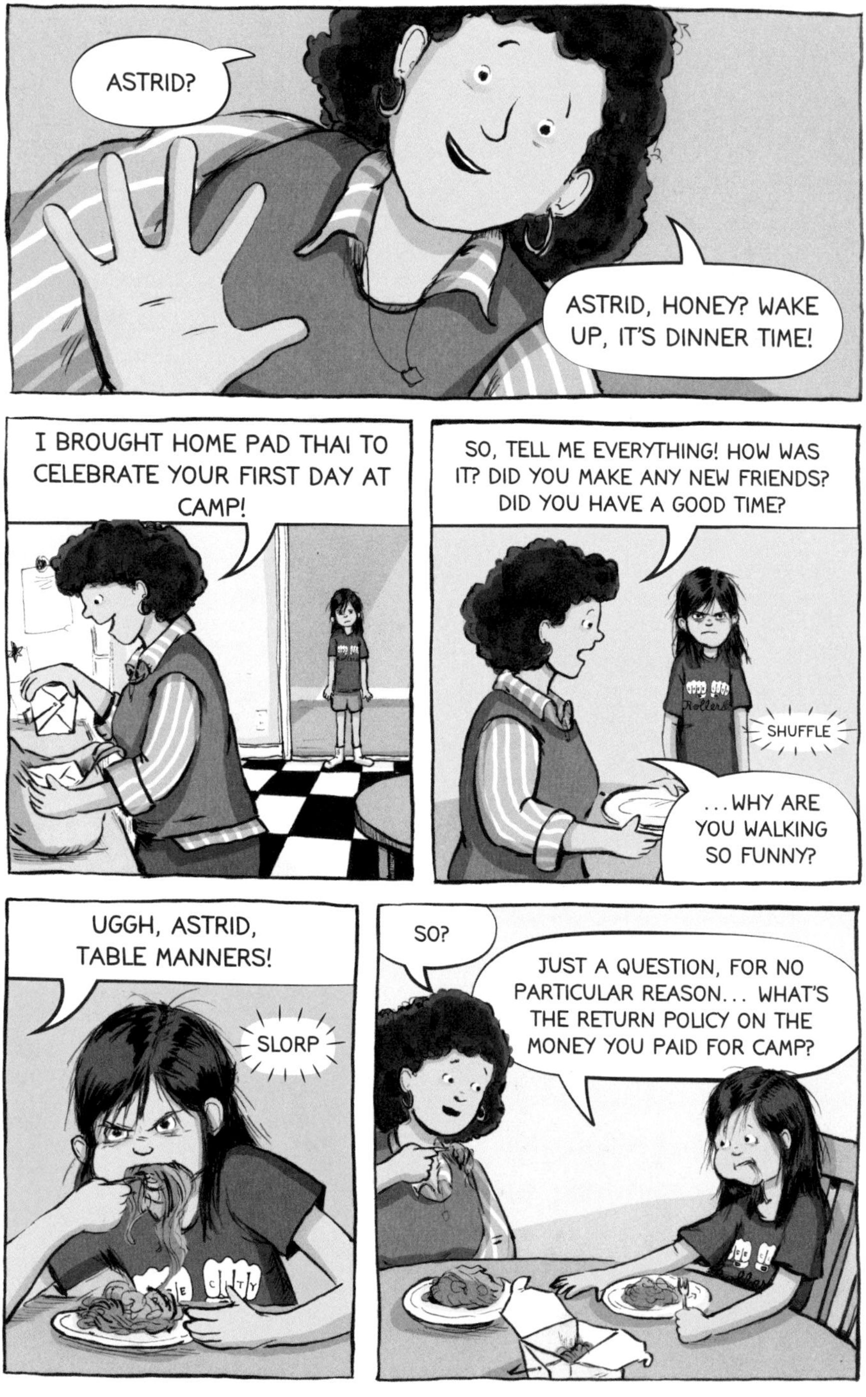
ASTRID?
ASTRID, HONEY? WAKE UP, IT'S DINNER TIME!
I BROUGHT HOME PAD THAI TO CELEBRATE YOUR FIRST DAY AT CAMP!
SO, TELL ME EVERYTHING! HOW WAS IT? DID YOU MAKE ANY NEW FRIENDS? DID YOU HAVE A GOOD TIME?
SHUFFLE
...WHY ARE YOU WALKING SO FUNNY?
UGGH, ASTRID, TABLE MANNERS!
SLORP
SO?
JUST A QUESTION, FOR NO PARTICULAR REASON... WHAT'S THE RETURN POLICY ON THE MONEY YOU PAID FOR CAMP?

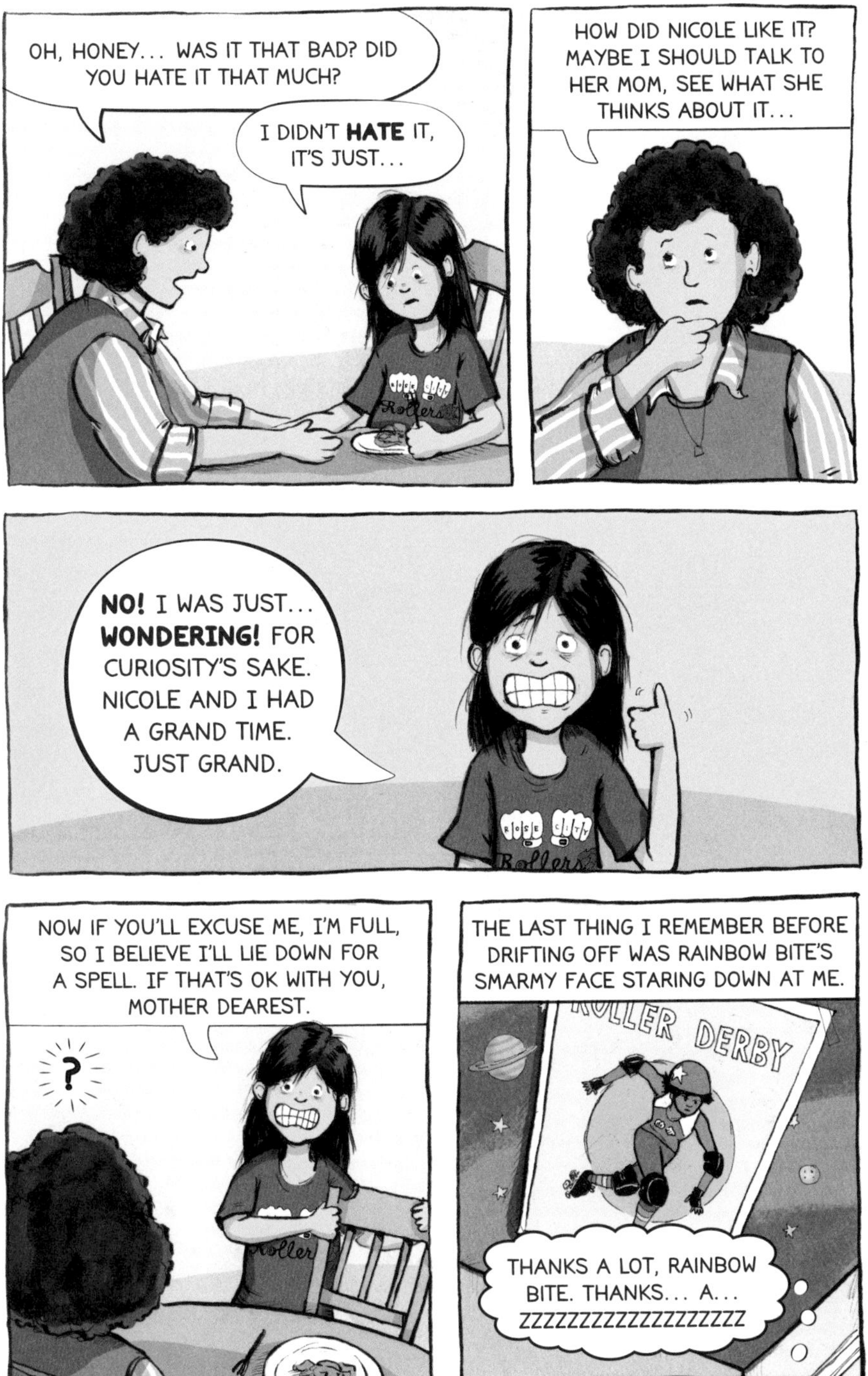
OH, HONEY... WAS IT THAT BAD? DID YOU HATE IT THAT MUCH?
I DIDN'T **HATE** IT, IT'S JUST...
HOW DID NICOLE LIKE IT? MAYBE I SHOULD TALK TO HER MOM, SEE WHAT SHE THINKS ABOUT IT...
NO! I WAS JUST... **WONDERING!** FOR CURIOSITY'S SAKE. NICOLE AND I HAD A GRAND TIME. JUST GRAND.
NOW IF YOU'LL EXCUSE ME, I'M FULL, SO I BELIEVE I'LL LIE DOWN FOR A SPELL. IF THAT'S OK WITH YOU, MOTHER DEAREST.
?
THE LAST THING I REMEMBER BEFORE DRIFTING OFF WAS RAINBOW BITE'S SMARMY FACE STARING DOWN AT ME.
DERBY
THANKS A LOT, RAINBOW BITE. THANKS... A... ZZZZZZZZZZZZZZZZZZZZ

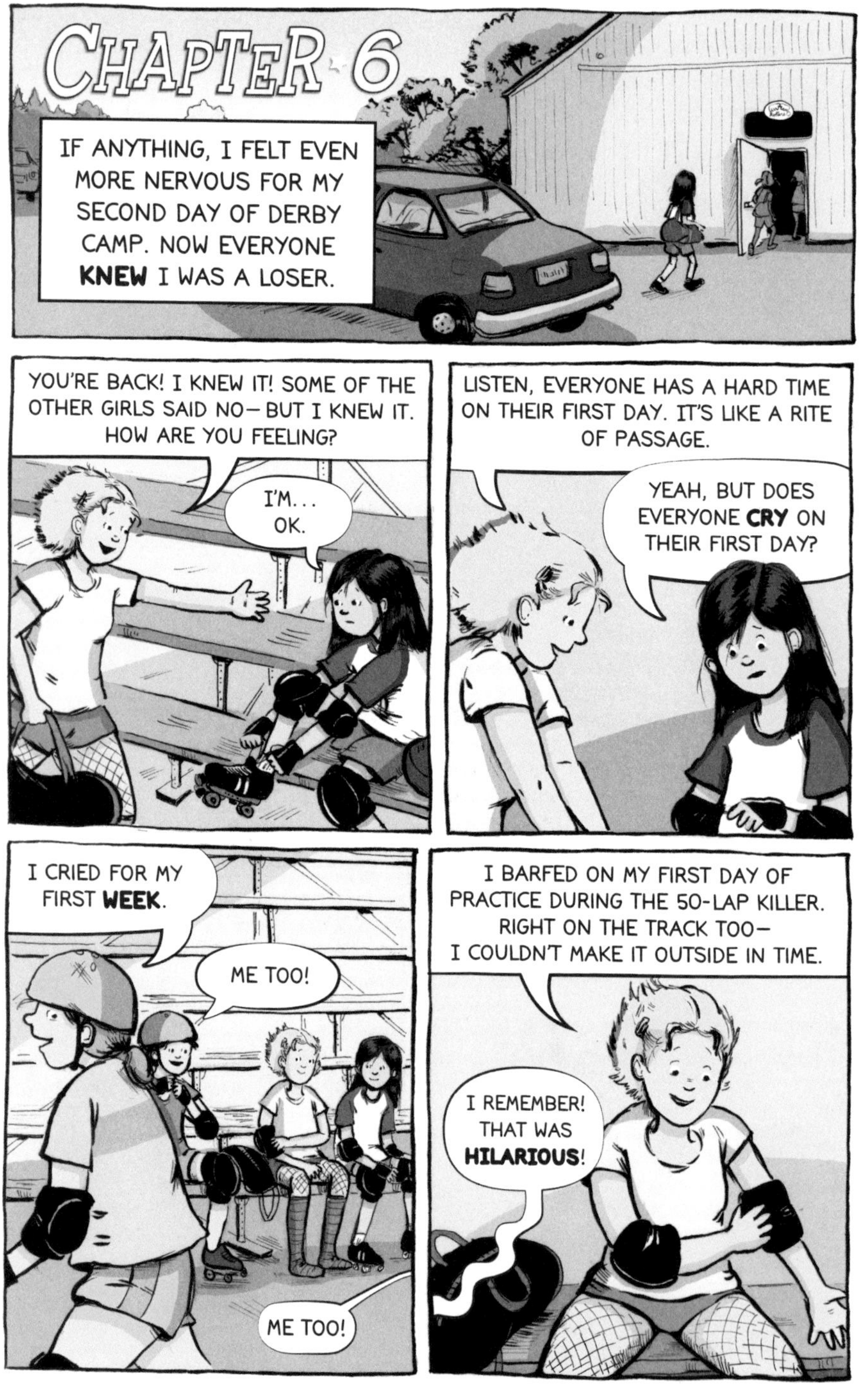
CHAPTER 6
IF ANYTHING, I FELT EVEN MORE NERVOUS FOR MY SECOND DAY OF DERBY CAMP. NOW EVERYONE **KNEW** I WAS A LOSER.
YOU'RE BACK! I KNEW IT! SOME OF THE OTHER GIRLS SAID NO— BUT I KNEW IT. HOW ARE YOU FEELING?
I'M... OK.
LISTEN, EVERYONE HAS A HARD TIME ON THEIR FIRST DAY. IT'S LIKE A RITE OF PASSAGE.
YEAH, BUT DOES EVERYONE **CRY** ON THEIR FIRST DAY?
I CRIED FOR MY FIRST **WEEK**.
ME TOO!
ME TOO!
I BARFED ON MY FIRST DAY OF PRACTICE DURING THE 50-LAP KILLER. RIGHT ON THE TRACK TOO— I COULDN'T MAKE IT OUTSIDE IN TIME.
I REMEMBER! THAT WAS **HILARIOUS**!

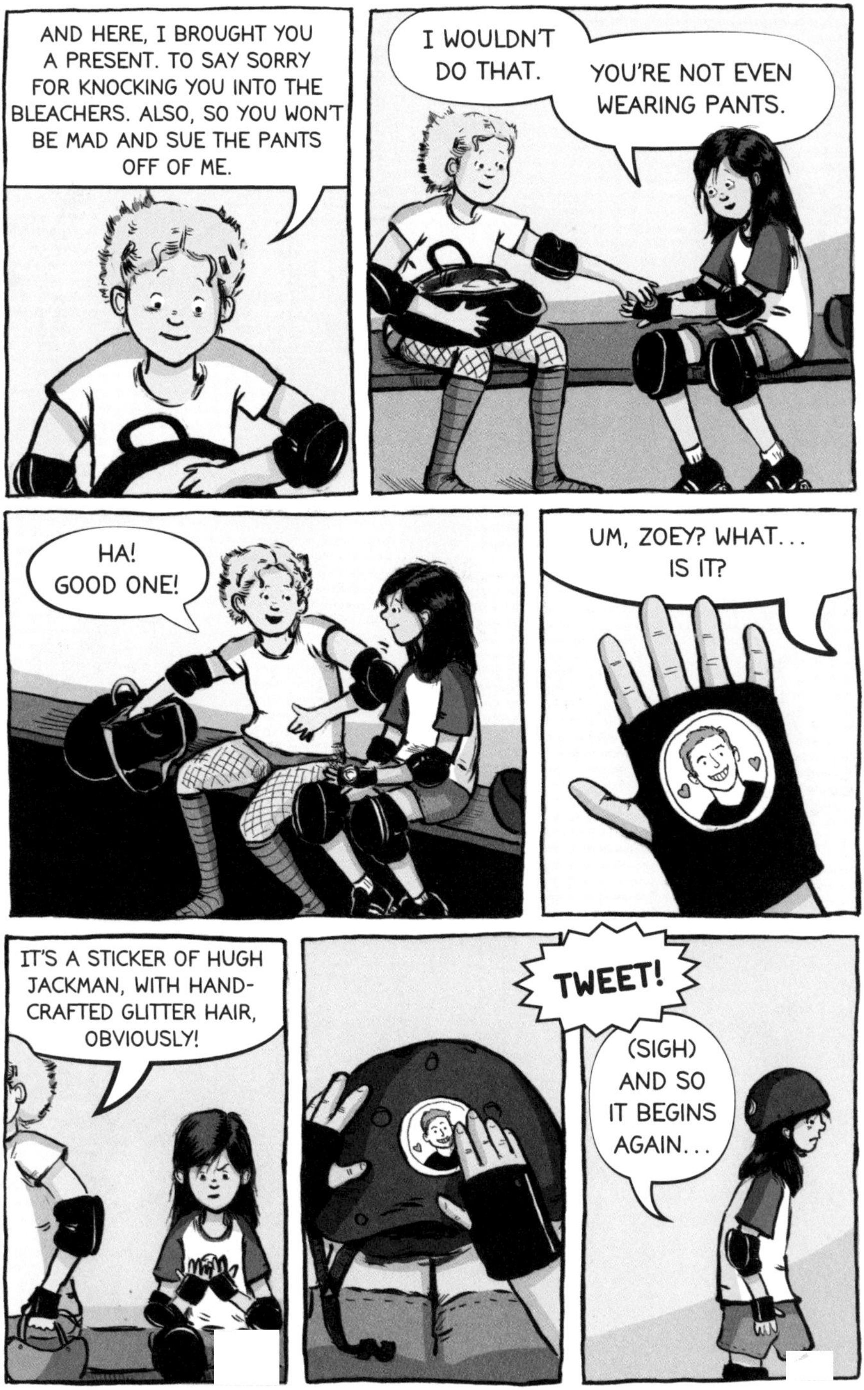
AND HERE, I BROUGHT YOU A PRESENT. TO SAY SORRY FOR KNOCKING YOU INTO THE BLEACHERS. ALSO, SO YOU WON'T BE MAD AND SUE THE PANTS OFF OF ME.
I WOULDN'T DO THAT.
YOU'RE NOT EVEN WEARING PANTS.
HA! GOOD ONE!
UM, ZOEY? WHAT... IS IT?
IT'S A STICKER OF HUGH JACKMAN, WITH HAND-CRAFTED GLITTER HAIR, OBVIOUSLY!
TWEET!
(SIGH) AND SO IT BEGINS AGAIN...

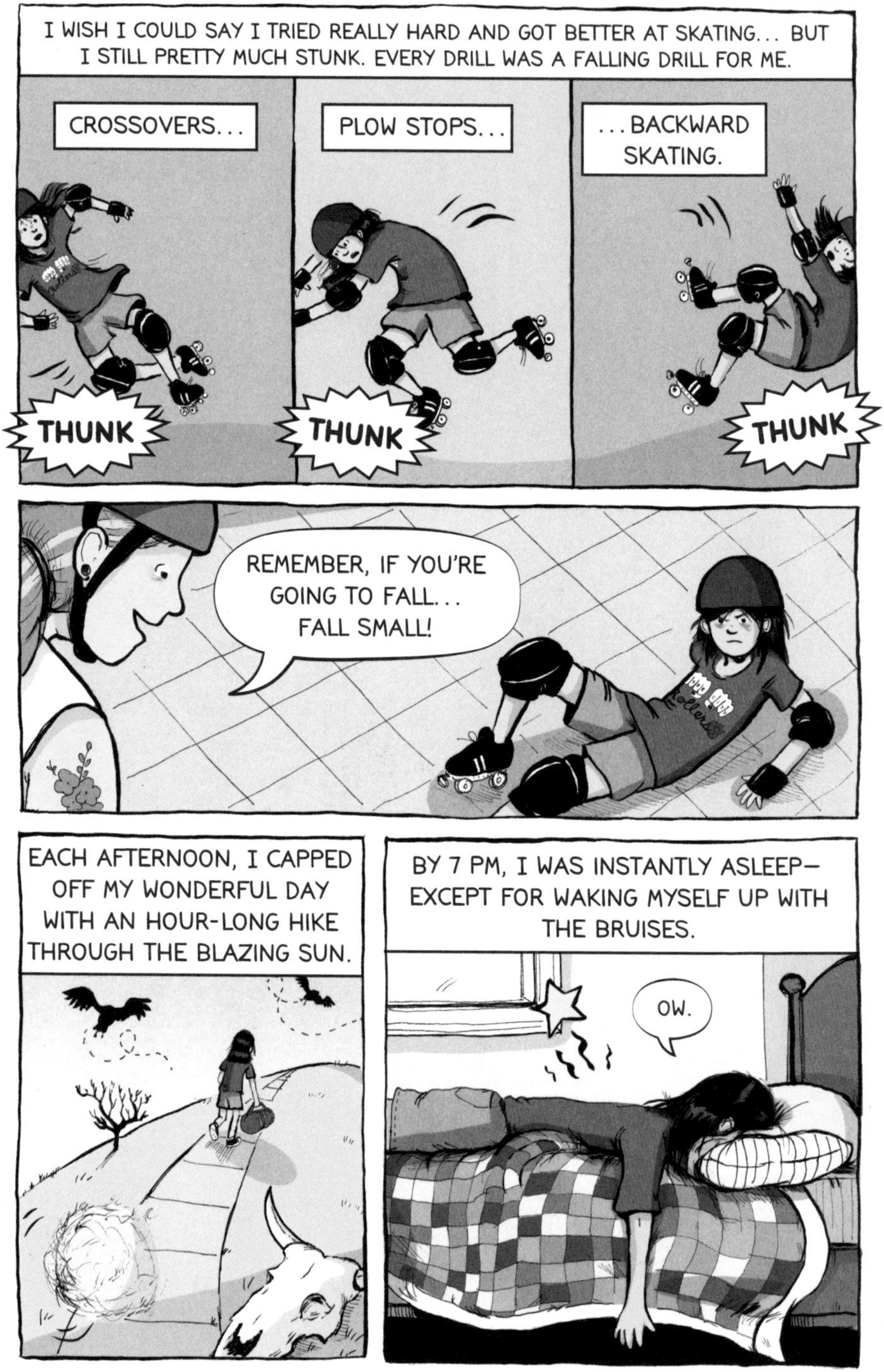
I WISH I COULD SAY I TRIED REALLY HARD AND GOT BETTER AT SKATING... BUT I STILL PRETTY MUCH STUNK. EVERY DRILL WAS A FALLING DRILL FOR ME.
CROSSOVERS...
THUNK
PLOW STOPS...
THUNK
...BACKWARD SKATING.
THUNK
REMEMBER, IF YOU'RE GOING TO FALL... FALL SMALL!
EACH AFTERNOON, I CAPPED OFF MY WONDERFUL DAY WITH AN HOUR-LONG HIKE THROUGH THE BLAZING SUN.
BY 7 PM, I WAS INSTANTLY ASLEEP— EXCEPT FOR WAKING MYSELF UP WITH THE BRUISES.
OW.

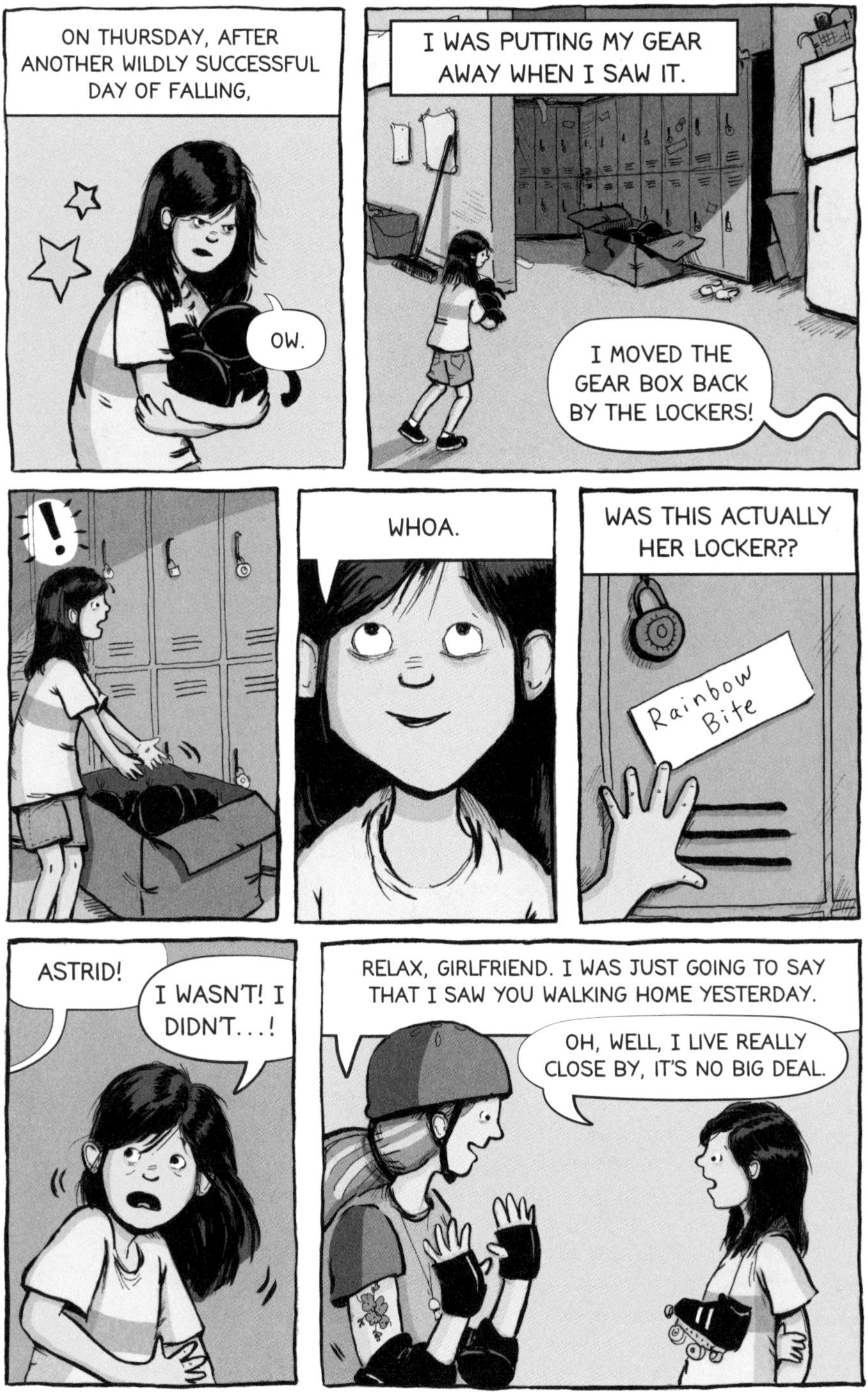
ON THURSDAY, AFTER ANOTHER WILDLY SUCCESSFUL DAY OF FALLING,
OW.
I WAS PUTTING MY GEAR AWAY WHEN I SAW IT.
I MOVED THE GEAR BOX BACK BY THE LOCKERS!
!
WHOA.
WAS THIS ACTUALLY HER LOCKER??
Rainbow Bite
ASTRID!
I WASN'T! I DIDN'T...!
RELAX, GIRLFRIEND. I WAS JUST GOING TO SAY THAT I SAW YOU WALKING HOME YESTERDAY.
OH, WELL, I LIVE REALLY CLOSE BY, IT'S NO BIG DEAL.

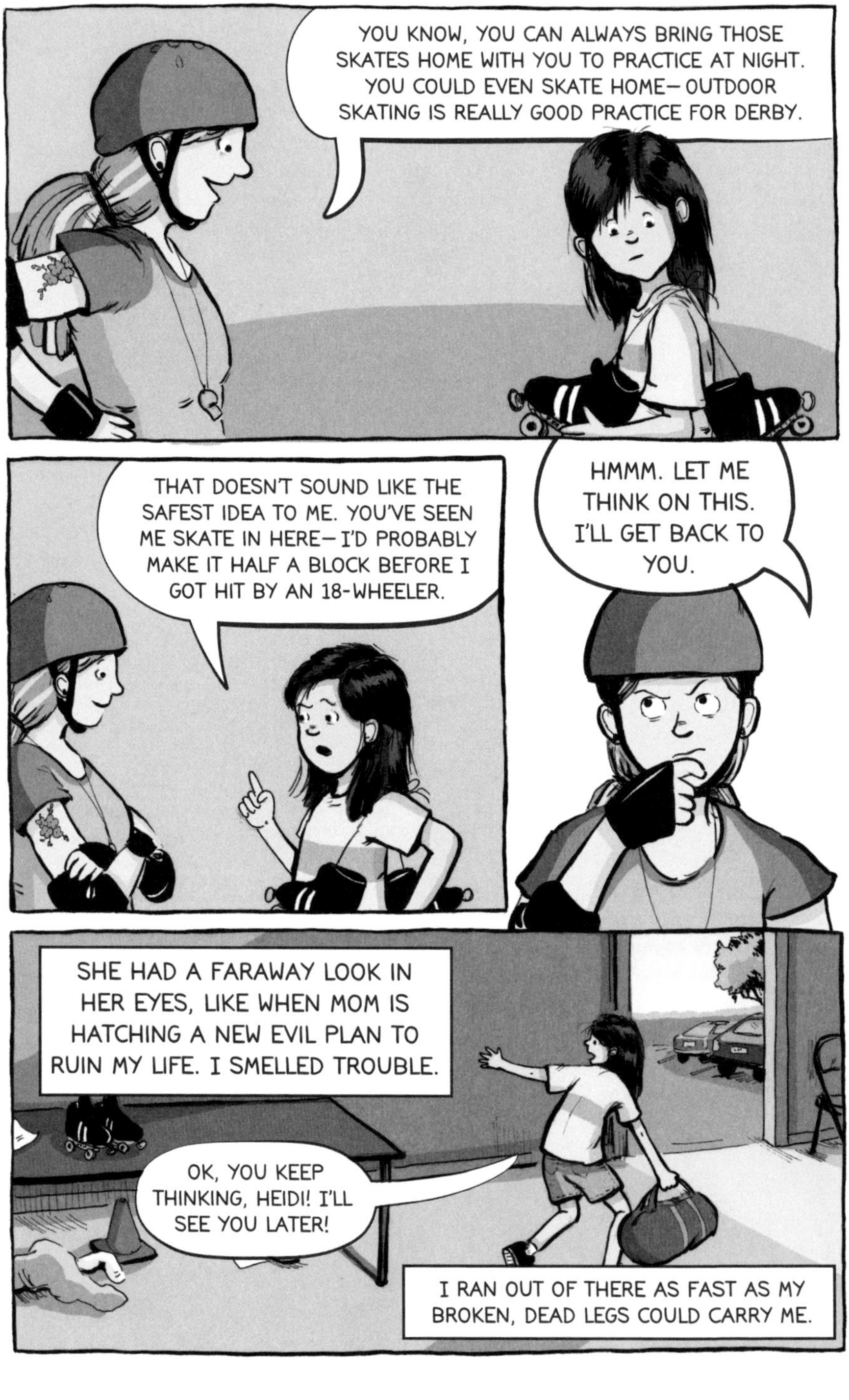
YOU KNOW, YOU CAN ALWAYS BRING THOSE SKATES HOME WITH YOU TO PRACTICE AT NIGHT. YOU COULD EVEN SKATE HOME— OUTDOOR SKATING IS REALLY GOOD PRACTICE FOR DERBY.
THAT DOESN'T SOUND LIKE THE SAFEST IDEA TO ME. YOU'VE SEEN ME SKATE IN HERE— I'D PROBABLY MAKE IT HALF A BLOCK BEFORE I GOT HIT BY AN 18-WHEELER.
HMMM. LET ME THINK ON THIS. I'LL GET BACK TO YOU.
SHE HAD A FARAWAY LOOK IN HER EYES, LIKE WHEN MOM IS HATCHING A NEW EVIL PLAN TO RUIN MY LIFE. I SMELLED TROUBLE.
OK, YOU KEEP THINKING, HEIDI! I'LL SEE YOU LATER!
I RAN OUT OF THERE AS FAST AS MY BROKEN, DEAD LEGS COULD CARRY ME.

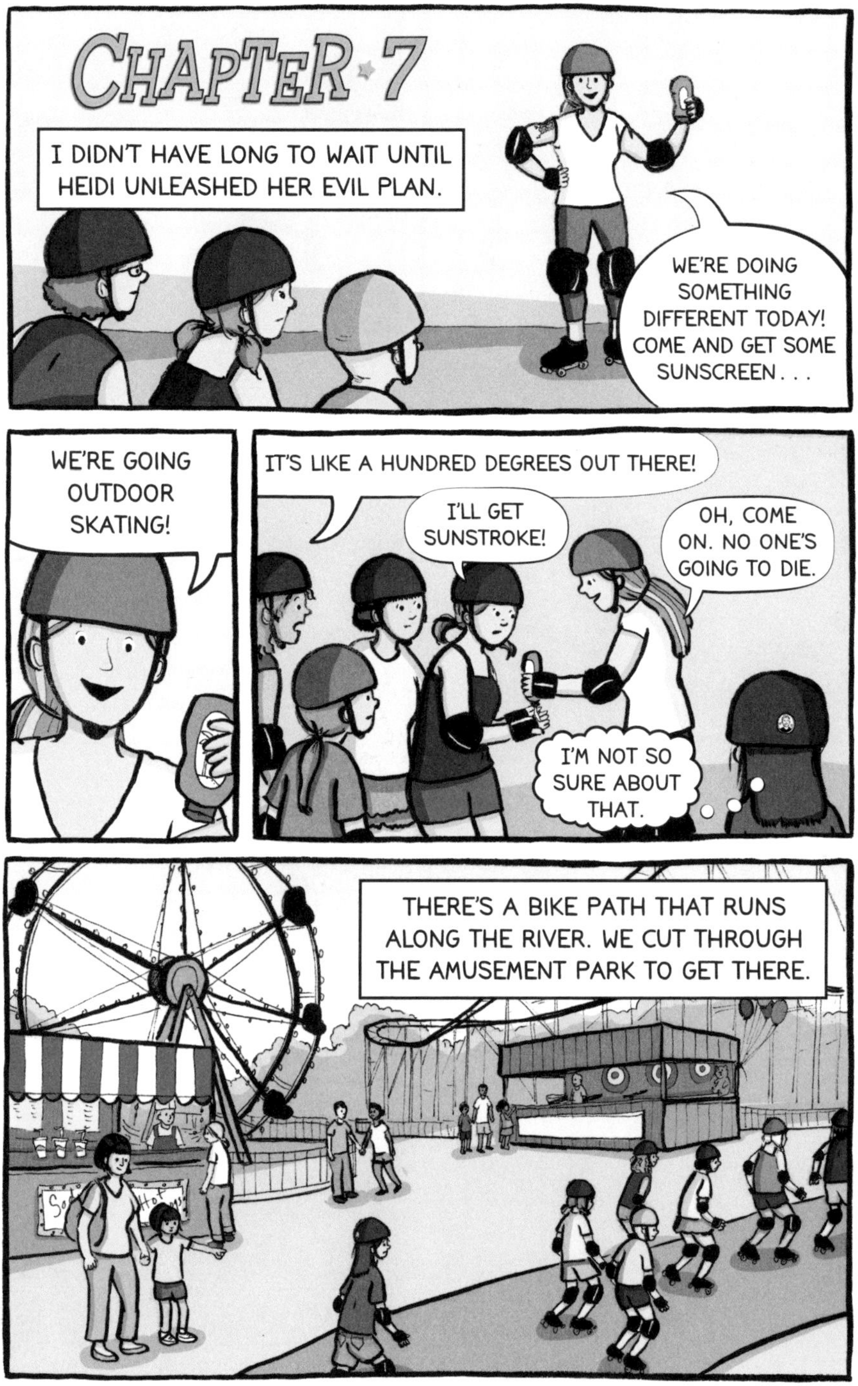
CHAPTER 7
I DIDN'T HAVE LONG TO WAIT UNTIL HEIDI UNLEASHED HER EVIL PLAN.
WE'RE DOING SOMETHING DIFFERENT TODAY! COME AND GET SOME SUNSCREEN . . .
WE'RE GOING OUTDOOR SKATING!
IT'S LIKE A HUNDRED DEGREES OUT THERE!
I'LL GET SUNSTROKE!
OH, COME ON. NO ONE'S GOING TO DIE.
I'M NOT SO SURE ABOUT THAT.
THERE'S A BIKE PATH THAT RUNS ALONG THE RIVER. WE CUT THROUGH THE AMUSEMENT PARK TO GET THERE.

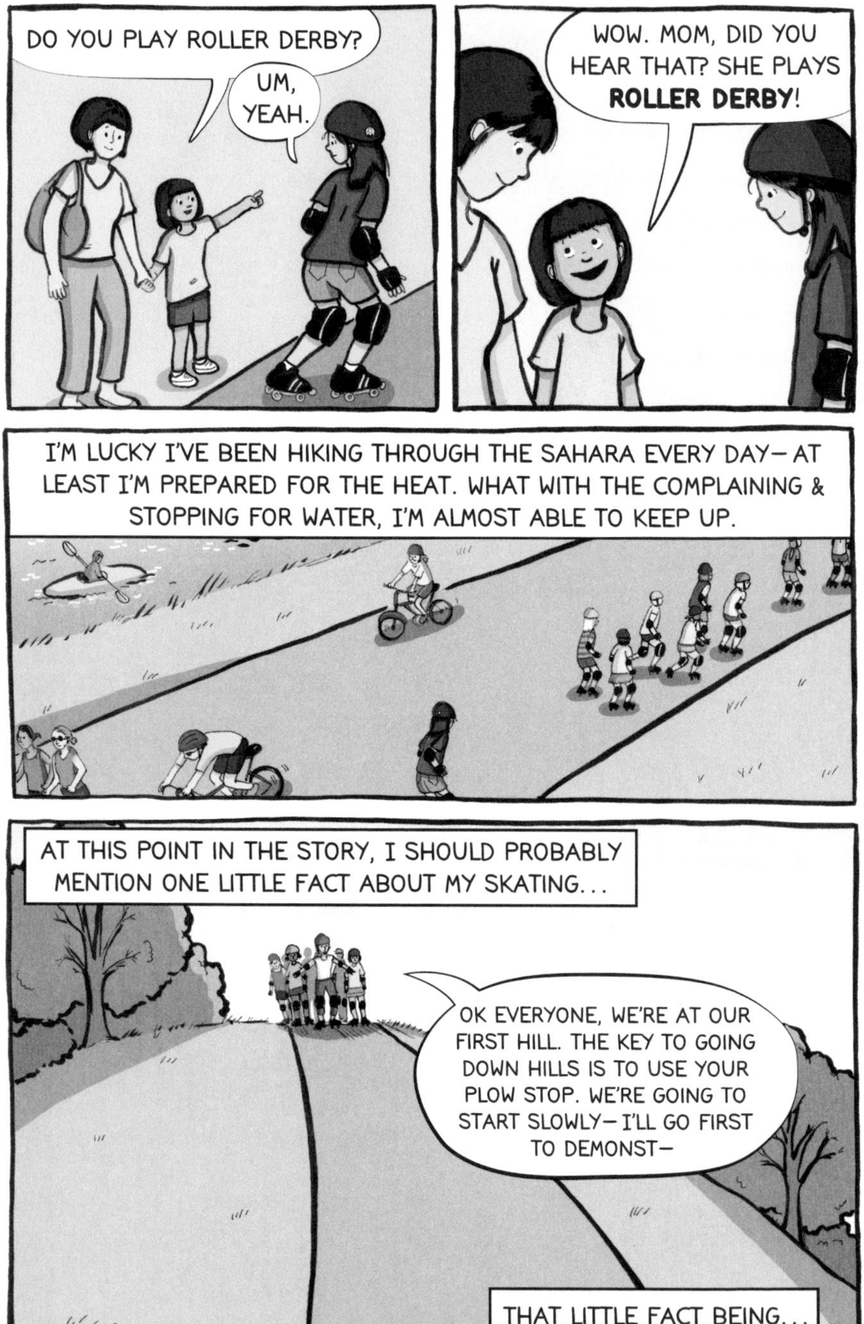
DO YOU PLAY ROLLER DERBY?
UM, YEAH.
WOW. MOM, DID YOU HEAR THAT? SHE PLAYS **ROLLER DERBY**!
I'M LUCKY I'VE BEEN HIKING THROUGH THE SAHARA EVERY DAY— AT LEAST I'M PREPARED FOR THE HEAT. WHAT WITH THE COMPLAINING & STOPPING FOR WATER, I'M ALMOST ABLE TO KEEP UP.
AT THIS POINT IN THE STORY, I SHOULD PROBABLY MENTION ONE LITTLE FACT ABOUT MY SKATING...
OK EVERYONE, WE'RE AT OUR FIRST HILL. THE KEY TO GOING DOWN HILLS IS TO USE YOUR PLOW STOP. WE'RE GOING TO START SLOWLY— I'LL GO FIRST TO DEMONST—
THAT LITTLE FACT BEING...

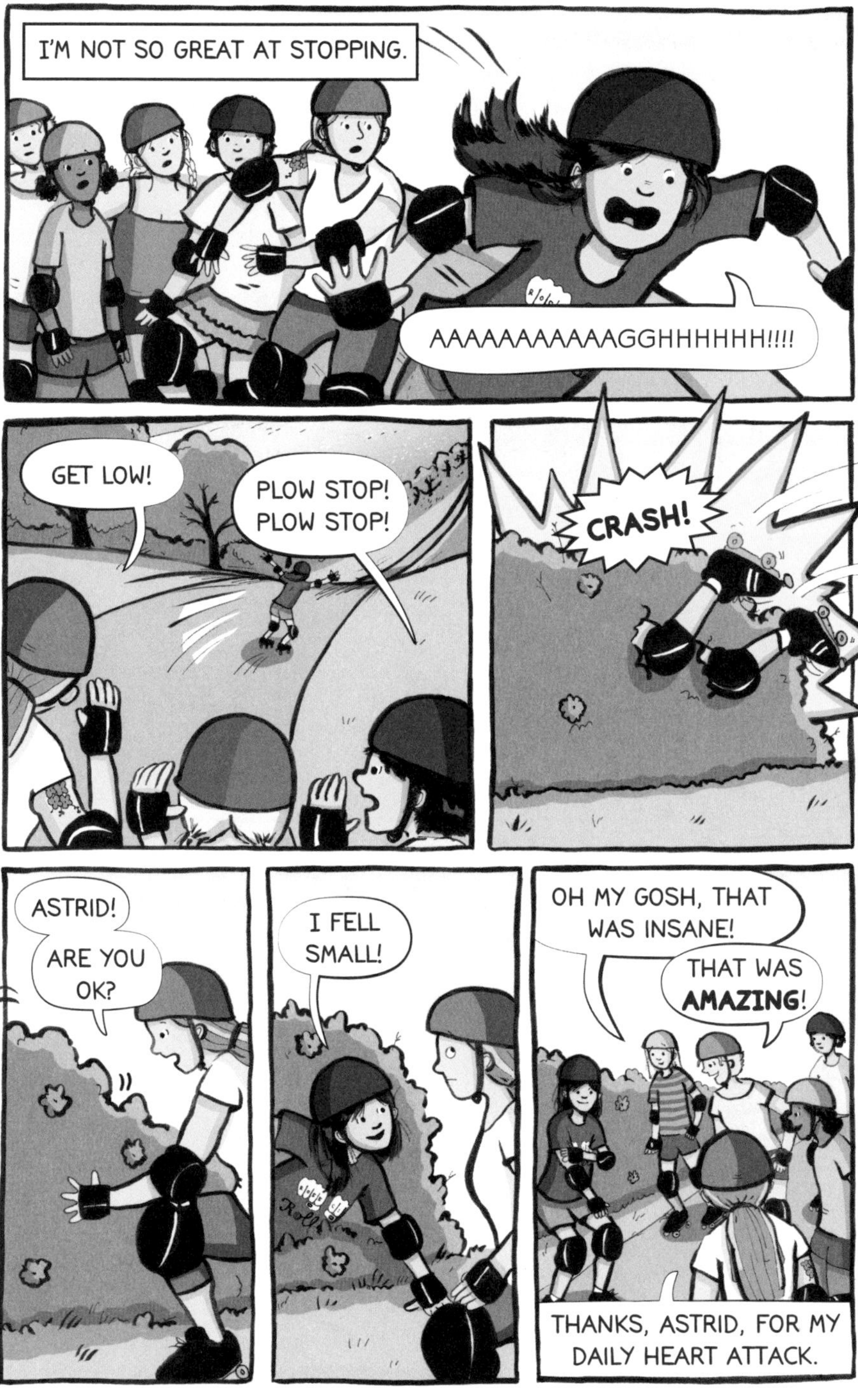
I'M NOT SO GREAT AT STOPPING.
AAAAAAAAAAAAGGHHHHHH!!!!
GET LOW!
PLOW STOP! PLOW STOP!
CRASH!
ASTRID!
ARE YOU OK?
I FELL SMALL!
OH MY GOSH, THAT WAS INSANE!
THAT WAS **AMAZING**!
THANKS, ASTRID, FOR MY DAILY HEART ATTACK.

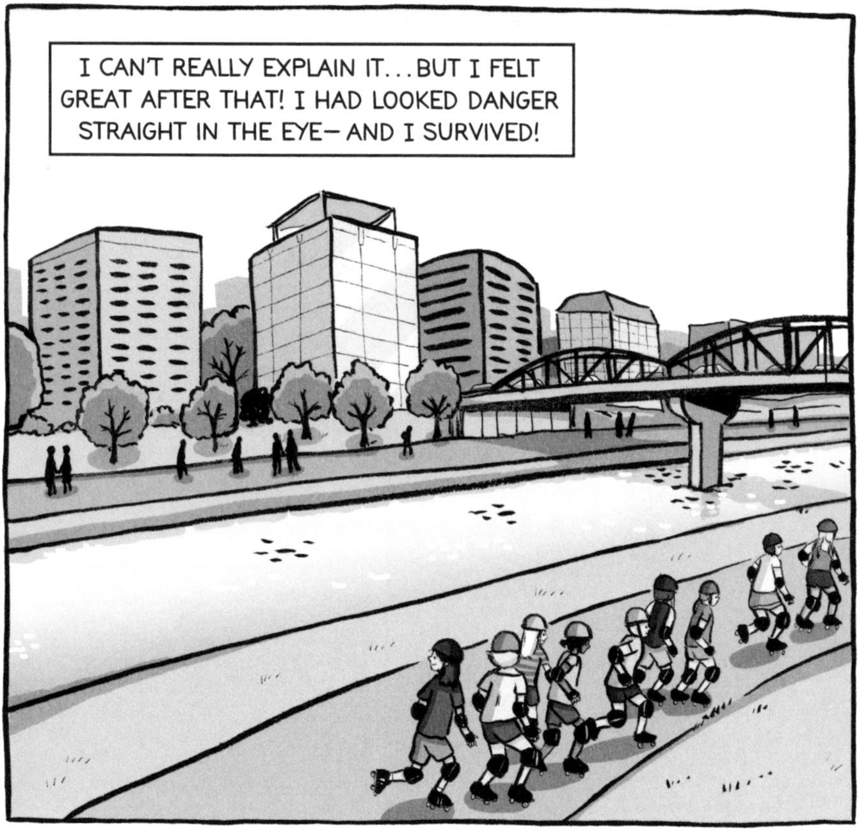
I CAN'T REALLY EXPLAIN IT... BUT I FELT GREAT AFTER THAT! I HAD LOOKED DANGER STRAIGHT IN THE EYE— AND I SURVIVED!

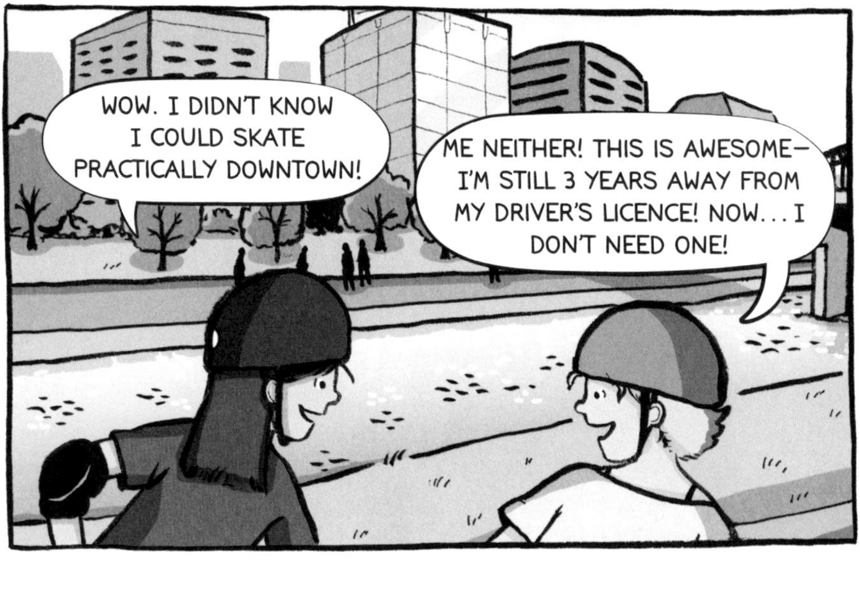
WOW. I DIDN'T KNOW I COULD SKATE PRACTICALLY DOWNTOWN!
ME NEITHER! THIS IS AWESOME— I'M STILL 3 YEARS AWAY FROM MY DRIVER'S LICENCE! NOW... I DON'T NEED ONE!

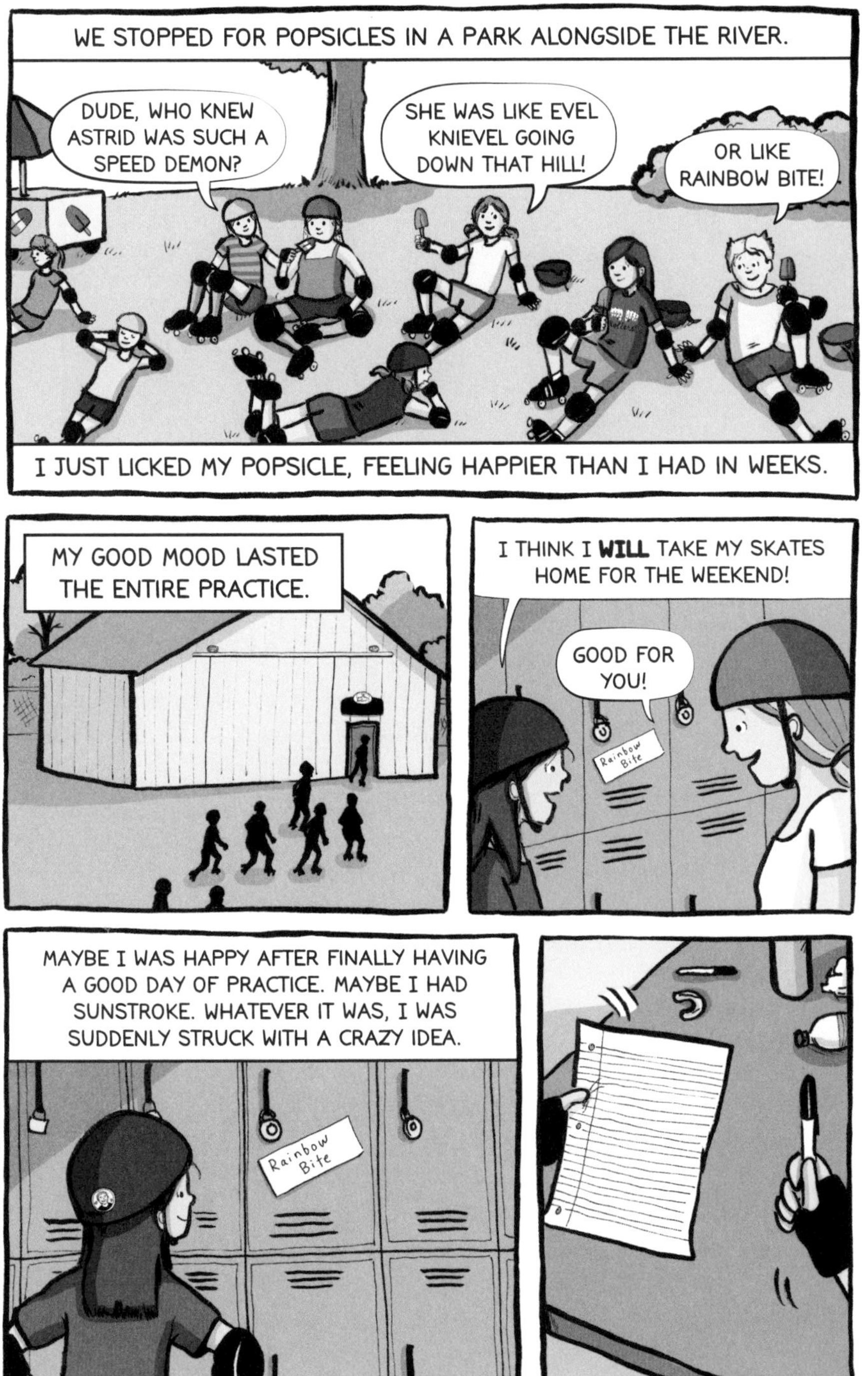
WE STOPPED FOR POPSICLES IN A PARK ALONGSIDE THE RIVER.
DUDE, WHO KNEW ASTRID WAS SUCH A SPEED DEMON?
SHE WAS LIKE EVEL KNIEVEL GOING DOWN THAT HILL!
OR LIKE RAINBOW BITE!
I JUST LICKED MY POPSICLE, FEELING HAPPIER THAN I HAD IN WEEKS.
MY GOOD MOOD LASTED THE ENTIRE PRACTICE.
I THINK I **WILL** TAKE MY SKATES HOME FOR THE WEEKEND!
GOOD FOR YOU!
Rainbow Bite
MAYBE I WAS HAPPY AFTER FINALLY HAVING A GOOD DAY OF PRACTICE. MAYBE I HAD SUNSTROKE. WHATEVER IT WAS, I WAS SUDDENLY STRUCK WITH A CRAZY IDEA.
Rainbow Bite

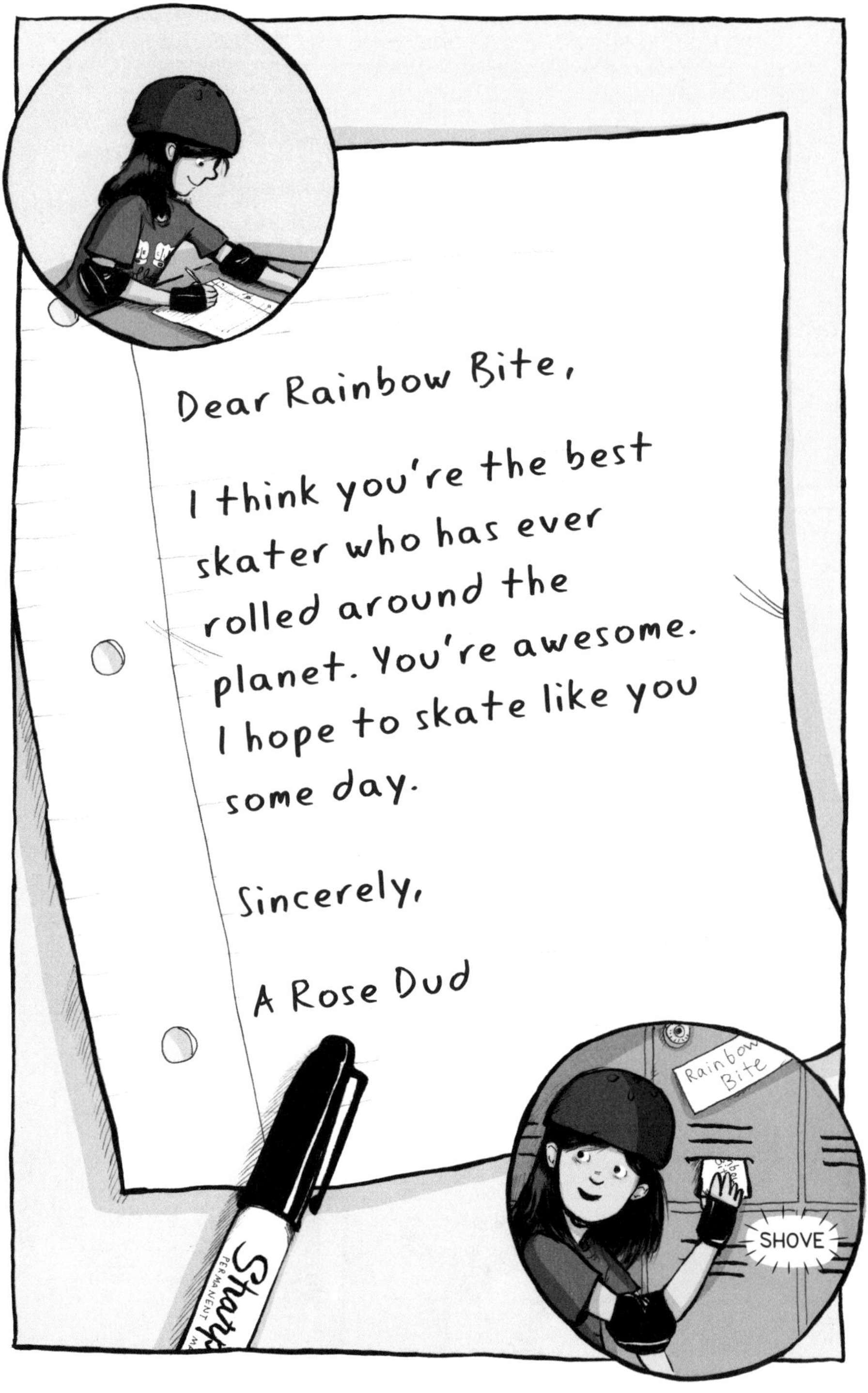
Dear Rainbow Bite,
I think you're the best skater who has ever rolled around the planet. You're awesome. I hope to skate like you some day.
Sincerely,
A Rose Dud
Rainbow Bite
SHOVE
Sharpie
PERMANENT MA

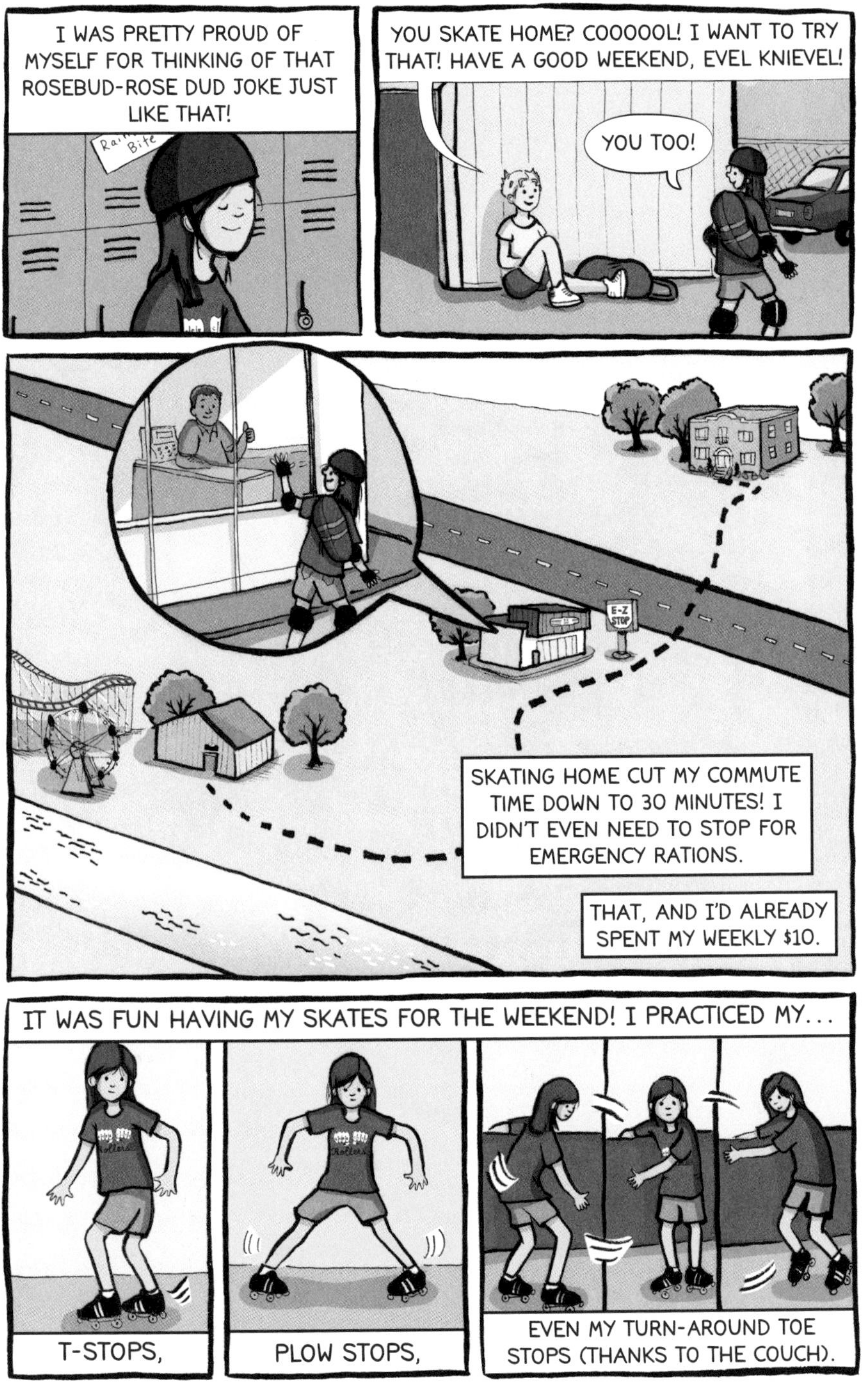

I WAS PRETTY PROUD OF MYSELF FOR THINKING OF THAT ROSEBUD-ROSE DUD JOKE JUST LIKE THAT!
YOU SKATE HOME? COOOOOL! I WANT TO TRY THAT! HAVE A GOOD WEEKEND, EVEL KNIEVEL!
YOU TOO!
E-Z STOP
SKATING HOME CUT MY COMMUTE TIME DOWN TO 30 MINUTES! I DIDN'T EVEN NEED TO STOP FOR EMERGENCY RATIONS.
THAT, AND I'D ALREADY SPENT MY WEEKLY $10.
IT WAS FUN HAVING MY SKATES FOR THE WEEKEND! I PRACTICED MY...
T-STOPS,
PLOW STOPS,
EVEN MY TURN-AROUND TOE STOPS (THANKS TO THE COUCH).

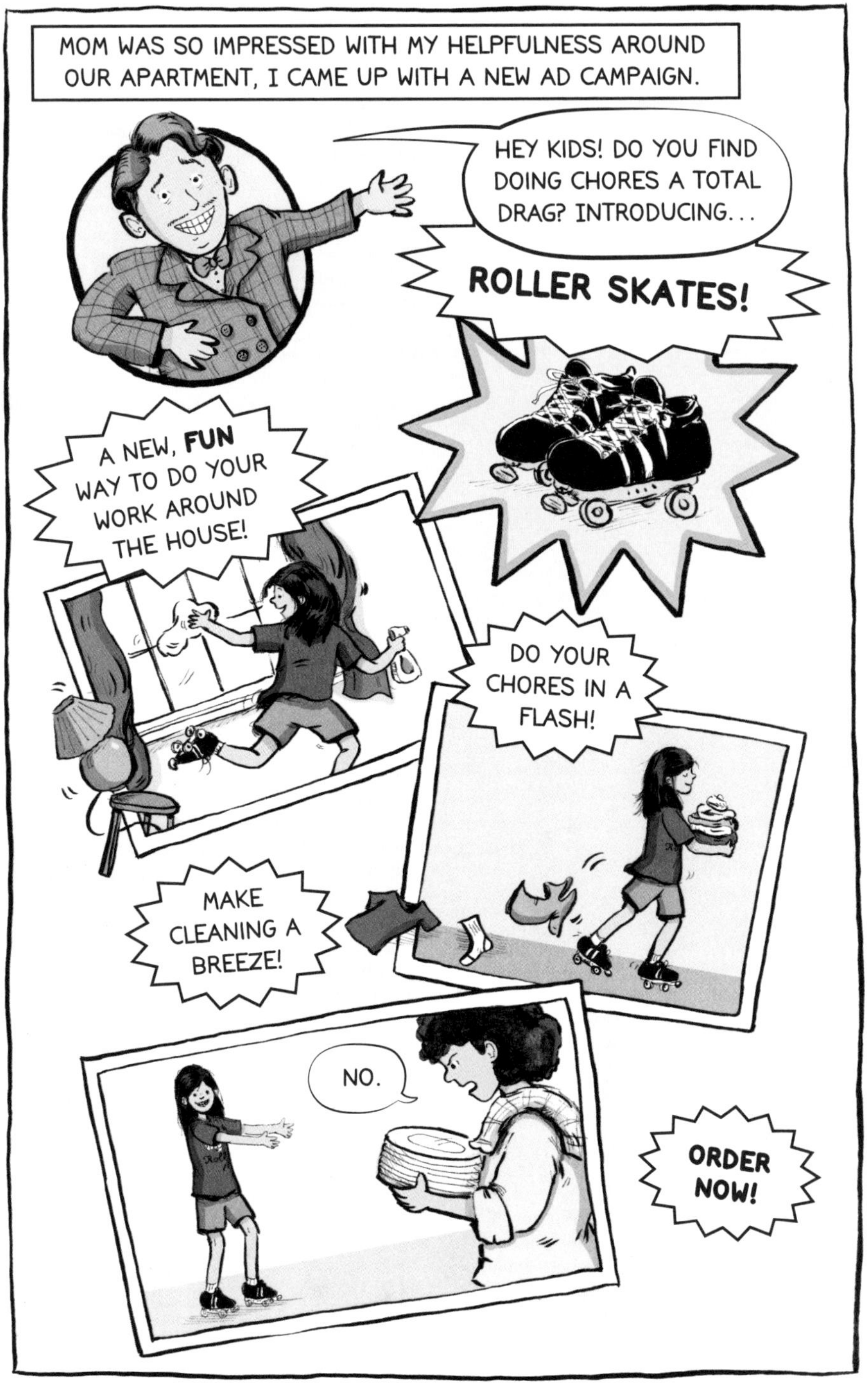
MOM WAS SO IMPRESSED WITH MY HELPFULNESS AROUND OUR APARTMENT, I CAME UP WITH A NEW AD CAMPAIGN.
HEY KIDS! DO YOU FIND DOING CHORES A TOTAL DRAG? INTRODUCING. . .
ROLLER SKATES!
A NEW, FUN WAY TO DO YOUR WORK AROUND THE HOUSE!
DO YOUR CHORES IN A FLASH!
MAKE CLEANING A BREEZE!
NO.
ORDER NOW!

YOU'LL THANK ME, TRUST ME. NOW GO PUT ON A CLEAN SHIRT.

I DON'T **HAVE** ANY CLEAN SHIRTS!

THAT'S NOT MY FAULT. IF IT'S NOT IN THE HAMPER, IT DOESN'T GET WASHED. BESIDES, YOU HAVE THAT WHOLE BAG OF CLOTHES MRS. KEMP GAVE YOU LAST WEEK—I HAVEN'T SEEN YOU WEARING ANY OF **THOSE**.

YEAH, BECAUSE I'M NOT A COLOR-BLIND 3-YEAR-OLD.

I'LL BE IN THE CAR. YOU'VE GOT FIVE MINUTES.

MRS. KEMP WAS MY MOM'S CO-WORKER. SHE THOUGHT SHE WAS BEING NICE BY SENDING OVER HER DAUGHTER BRITTNEY'S HAND-ME-DOWNS.

GRUMBLE

BY ALL ACCOUNTS, BRITTNEY WAS 13 YEARS OLD. I DO NOT BELIEVE THIS.

SERIOUSLY, WHAT 13-YEAR-OLD WEARS THIS STUFF?

Princess

Purr-fect!!

I REFUSE TO WEAR ANYTHING PINK, SO THAT RULED OUT 98% OF HER COLLECTION.

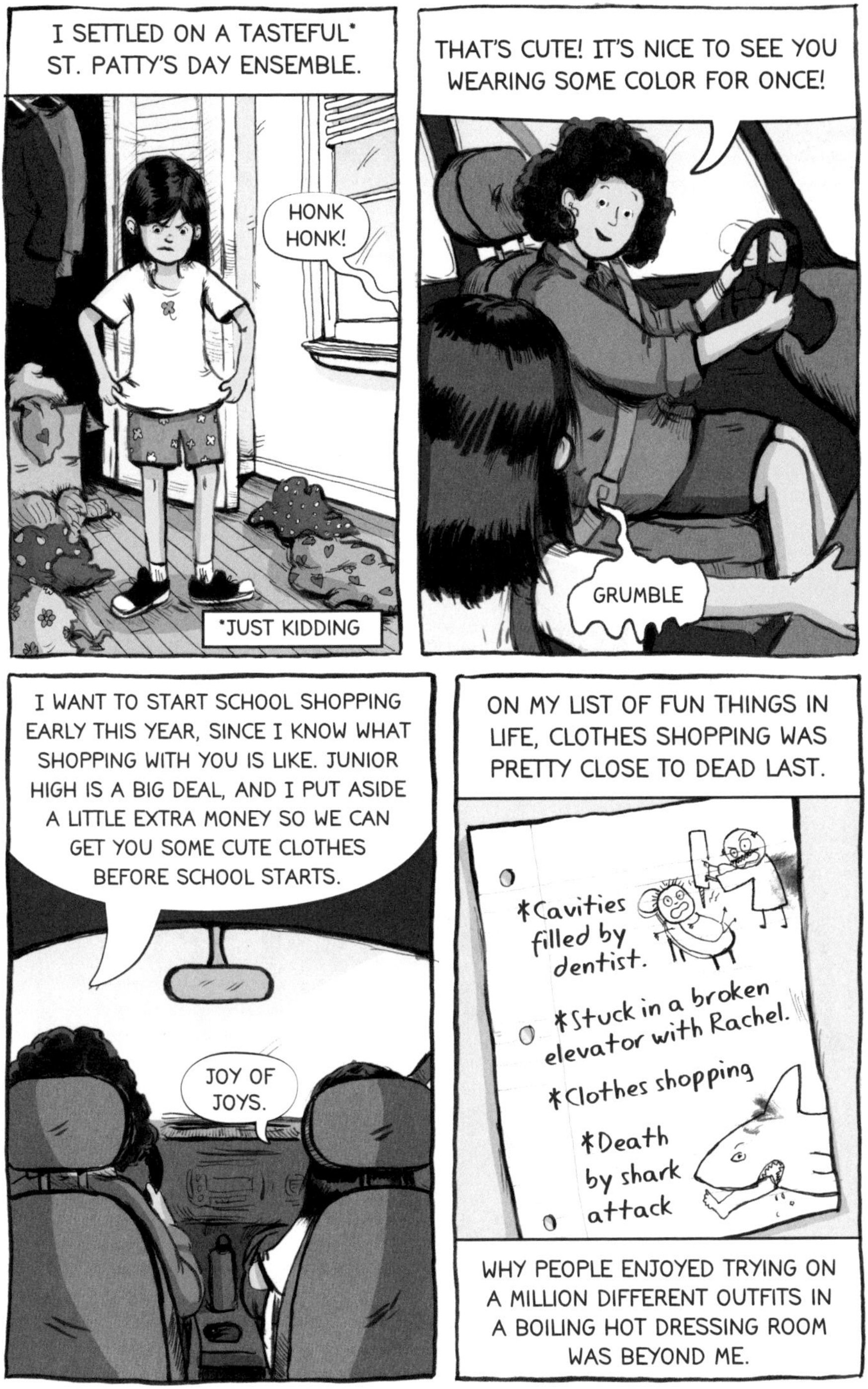

I SETTLED ON A TASTEFUL* ST. PATTY'S DAY ENSEMBLE.
HONK HONK!
*JUST KIDDING
THAT'S CUTE! IT'S NICE TO SEE YOU WEARING SOME COLOR FOR ONCE!
GRUMBLE
I WANT TO START SCHOOL SHOPPING EARLY THIS YEAR, SINCE I KNOW WHAT SHOPPING WITH YOU IS LIKE. JUNIOR HIGH IS A BIG DEAL, AND I PUT ASIDE A LITTLE EXTRA MONEY SO WE CAN GET YOU SOME CUTE CLOTHES BEFORE SCHOOL STARTS.
JOY OF JOYS.
ON MY LIST OF FUN THINGS IN LIFE, CLOTHES SHOPPING WAS PRETTY CLOSE TO DEAD LAST.
*Cavities filled by dentist.
*Stuck in a broken elevator with Rachel.
*Clothes shopping
*Death by shark attack
WHY PEOPLE ENJOYED TRYING ON A MILLION DIFFERENT OUTFITS IN A BOILING HOT DRESSING ROOM WAS BEYOND ME.

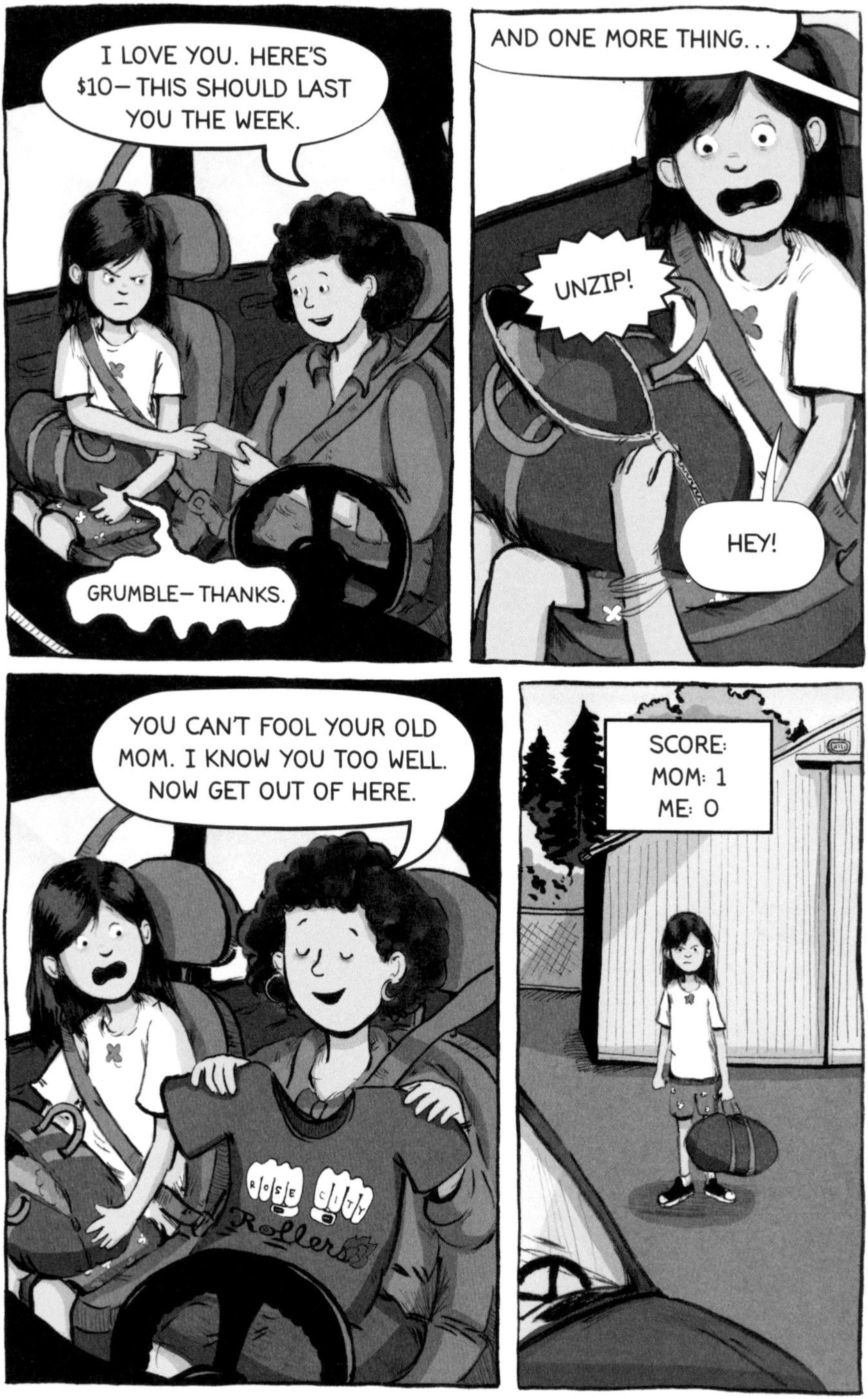
I LOVE YOU. HERE'S $10—THIS SHOULD LAST YOU THE WEEK.
GRUMBLE—THANKS.
AND ONE MORE THING...
UNZIP!
HEY!
YOU CAN'T FOOL YOUR OLD MOM. I KNOW YOU TOO WELL. NOW GET OUT OF HERE.
ROSE CITY
Rollers
SCORE:
MOM: 1
ME: 0

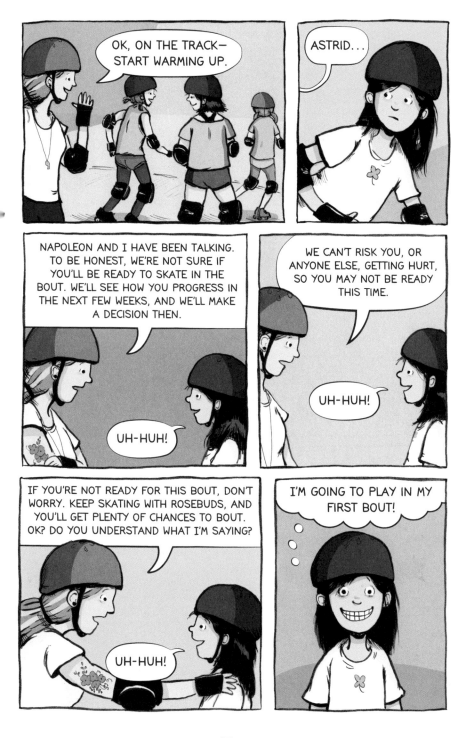

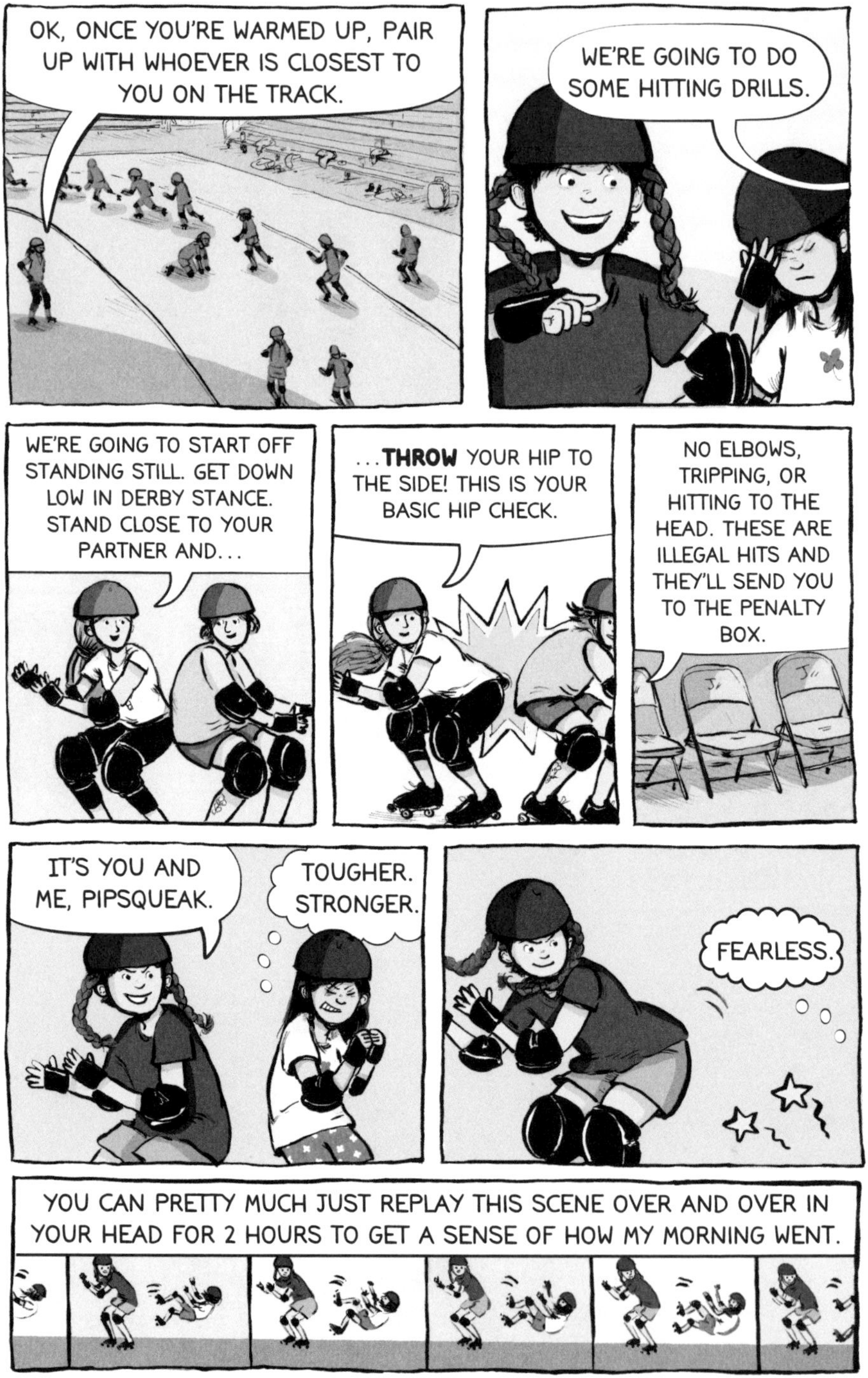

OK, ONCE YOU'RE WARMED UP, PAIR UP WITH WHOEVER IS CLOSEST TO YOU ON THE TRACK.
WE'RE GOING TO DO SOME HITTING DRILLS.
WE'RE GOING TO START OFF STANDING STILL. GET DOWN LOW IN DERBY STANCE. STAND CLOSE TO YOUR PARTNER AND...
...**THROW** YOUR HIP TO THE SIDE! THIS IS YOUR BASIC HIP CHECK.
NO ELBOWS, TRIPPING, OR HITTING TO THE HEAD. THESE ARE ILLEGAL HITS AND THEY'LL SEND YOU TO THE PENALTY BOX.
IT'S YOU AND ME, PIPSQUEAK.
TOUGHER. STRONGER.
FEARLESS.
YOU CAN PRETTY MUCH JUST REPLAY THIS SCENE OVER AND OVER IN YOUR HEAD FOR 2 HOURS TO GET A SENSE OF HOW MY MORNING WENT.

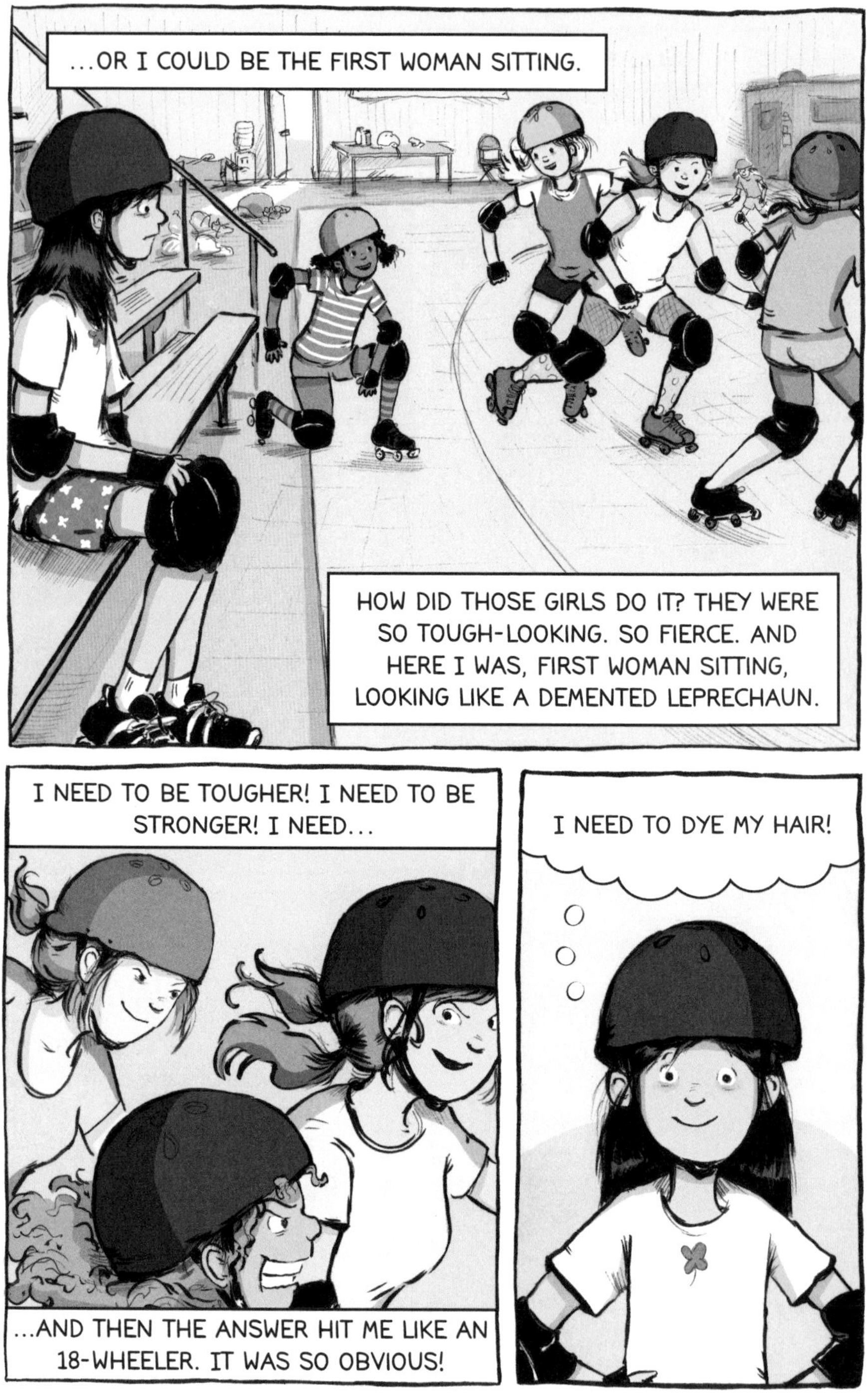
...OR I COULD BE THE FIRST WOMAN SITTING.
HOW DID THOSE GIRLS DO IT? THEY WERE SO TOUGH-LOOKING. SO FIERCE. AND HERE I WAS, FIRST WOMAN SITTING, LOOKING LIKE A DEMENTED LEPRECHAUN.
I NEED TO BE TOUGHER! I NEED TO BE STRONGER! I NEED...
...AND THEN THE ANSWER HIT ME LIKE AN 18-WHEELER. IT WAS SO OBVIOUS!
I NEED TO DYE MY HAIR!

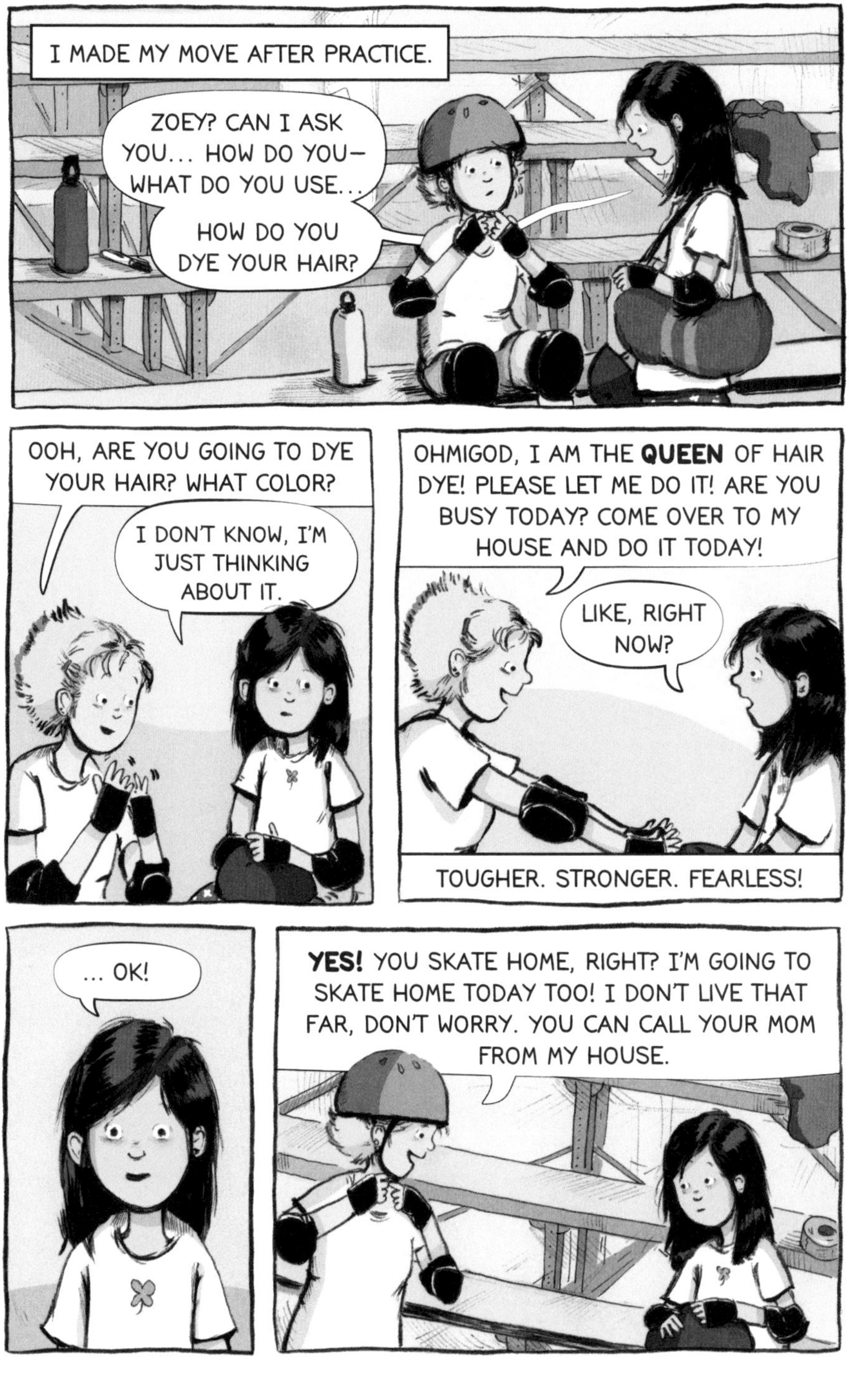
I MADE MY MOVE AFTER PRACTICE.
ZOEY? CAN I ASK YOU... HOW DO YOU— WHAT DO YOU USE...
HOW DO YOU DYE YOUR HAIR?
OOH, ARE YOU GOING TO DYE YOUR HAIR? WHAT COLOR?
I DON'T KNOW, I'M JUST THINKING ABOUT IT.
OHMIGOD, I AM THE **QUEEN** OF HAIR DYE! PLEASE LET ME DO IT! ARE YOU BUSY TODAY? COME OVER TO MY HOUSE AND DO IT TODAY!
LIKE, RIGHT NOW?
TOUGHER. STRONGER. FEARLESS!
... OK!
YES! YOU SKATE HOME, RIGHT? I'M GOING TO SKATE HOME TODAY TOO! I DON'T LIVE THAT FAR, DON'T WORRY. YOU CAN CALL YOUR MOM FROM MY HOUSE.

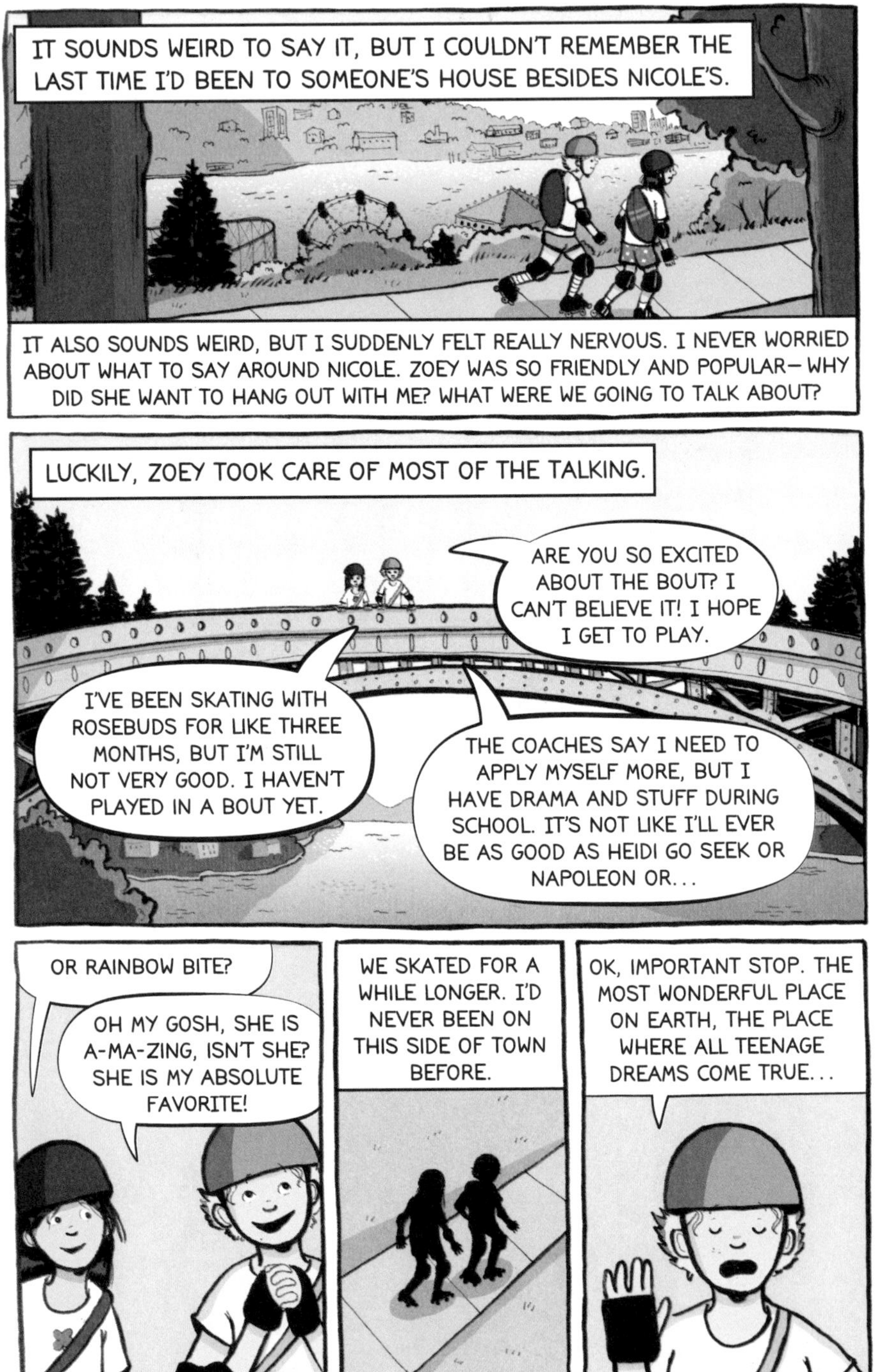
IT SOUNDS WEIRD TO SAY IT, BUT I COULDN'T REMEMBER THE LAST TIME I'D BEEN TO SOMEONE'S HOUSE BESIDES NICOLE'S.
IT ALSO SOUNDS WEIRD, BUT I SUDDENLY FELT REALLY NERVOUS. I NEVER WORRIED ABOUT WHAT TO SAY AROUND NICOLE. ZOEY WAS SO FRIENDLY AND POPULAR— WHY DID SHE WANT TO HANG OUT WITH ME? WHAT WERE WE GOING TO TALK ABOUT?
LUCKILY, ZOEY TOOK CARE OF MOST OF THE TALKING.
ARE YOU SO EXCITED ABOUT THE BOUT? I CAN'T BELIEVE IT! I HOPE I GET TO PLAY.
I'VE BEEN SKATING WITH ROSEBUDS FOR LIKE THREE MONTHS, BUT I'M STILL NOT VERY GOOD. I HAVEN'T PLAYED IN A BOUT YET.
THE COACHES SAY I NEED TO APPLY MYSELF MORE, BUT I HAVE DRAMA AND STUFF DURING SCHOOL. IT'S NOT LIKE I'LL EVER BE AS GOOD AS HEIDI GO SEEK OR NAPOLEON OR...
OR RAINBOW BITE?
OH MY GOSH, SHE IS A-MA-ZING, ISN'T SHE? SHE IS MY ABSOLUTE FAVORITE!
WE SKATED FOR A WHILE LONGER. I'D NEVER BEEN ON THIS SIDE OF TOWN BEFORE.
OK, IMPORTANT STOP. THE MOST WONDERFUL PLACE ON EARTH, THE PLACE WHERE ALL TEENAGE DREAMS COME TRUE...

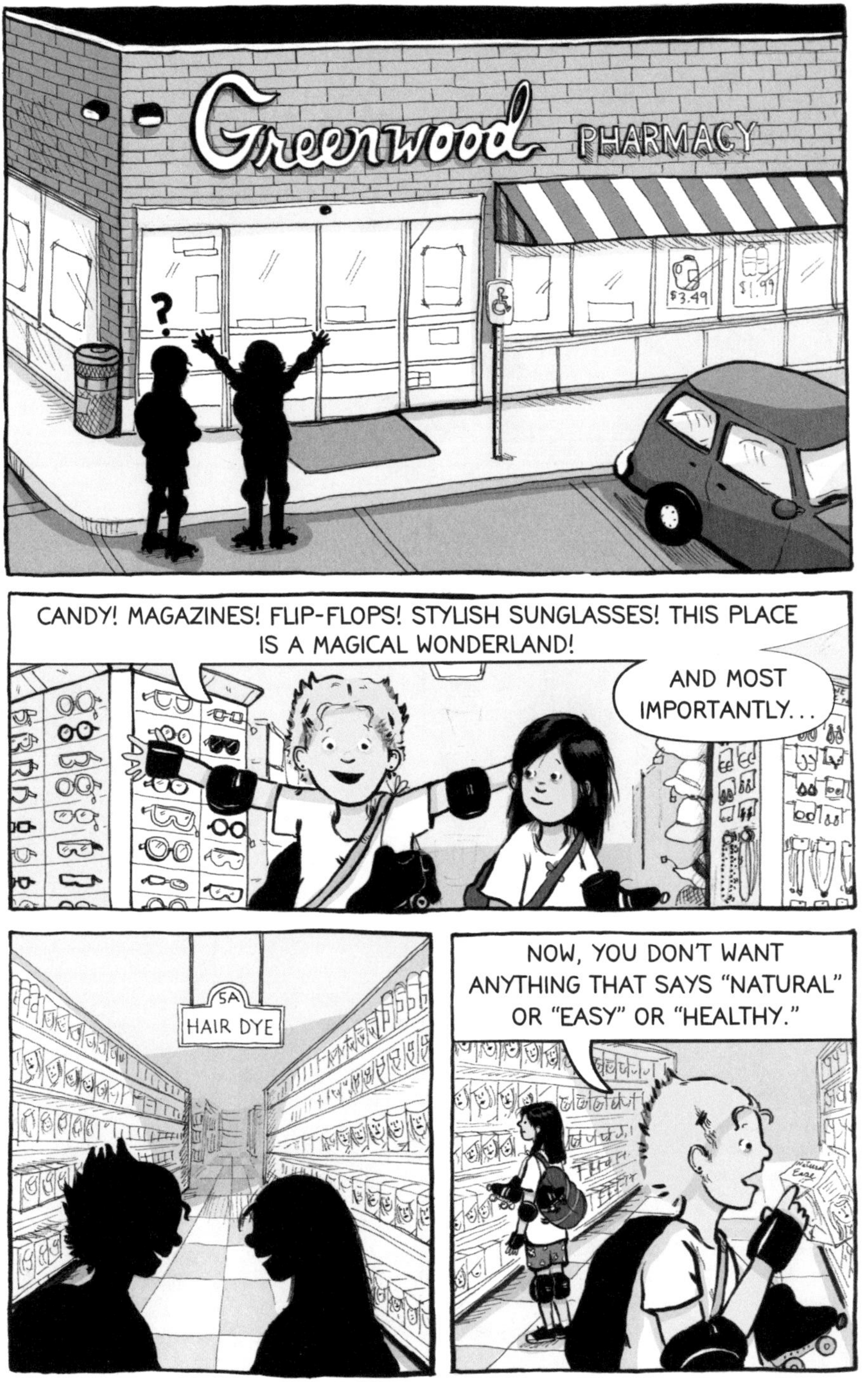
Greenwood PHARMACY
$3.49
$1.99
?
CANDY! MAGAZINES! FLIP-FLOPS! STYLISH SUNGLASSES! THIS PLACE IS A MAGICAL WONDERLAND!
AND MOST IMPORTANTLY...
5A
HAIR DYE
NOW, YOU DON'T WANT ANYTHING THAT SAYS "NATURAL" OR "EASY" OR "HEALTHY."

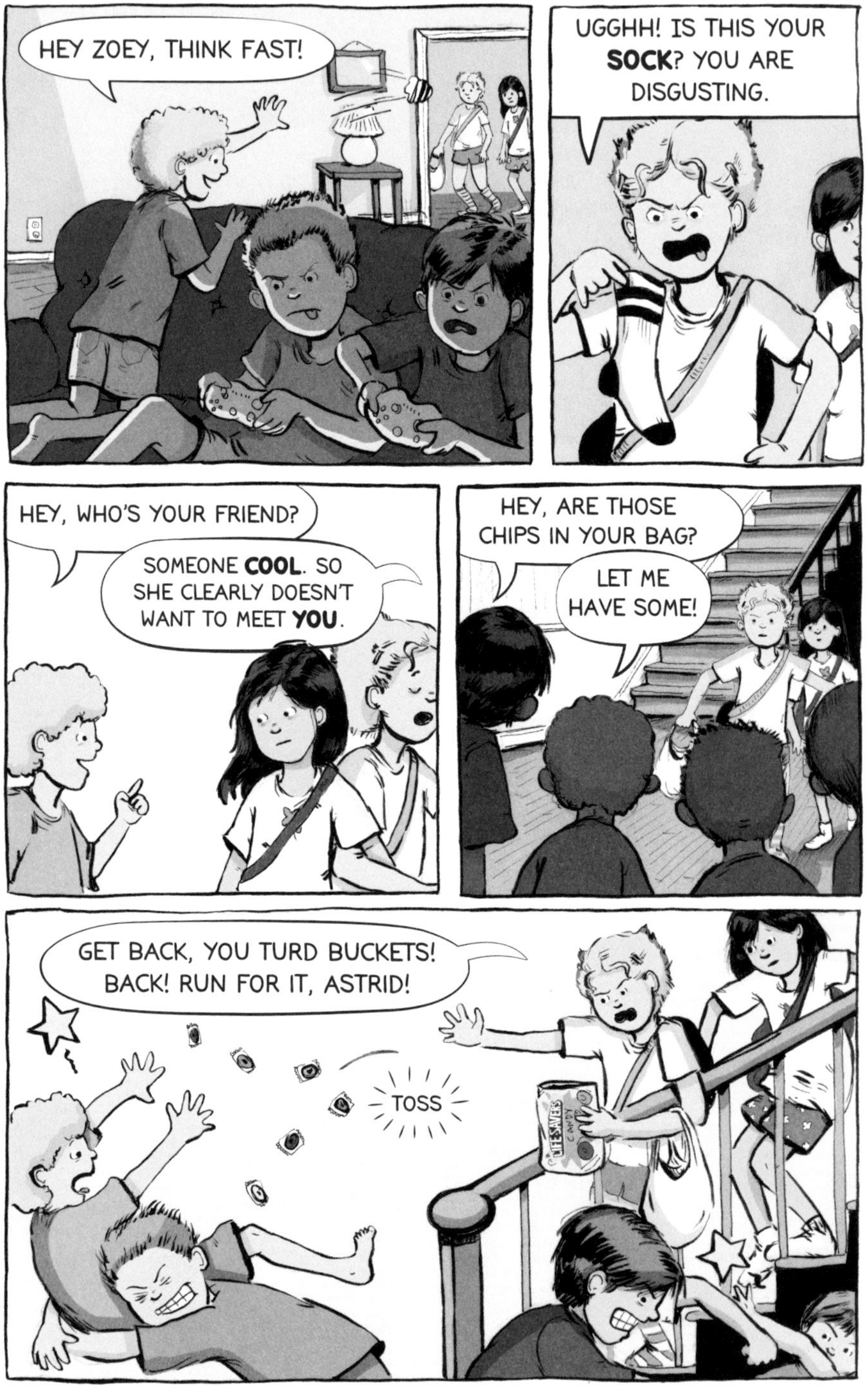
HEY ZOEY, THINK FAST!
UGGHH! IS THIS YOUR **SOCK**? YOU ARE DISGUSTING.
HEY, WHO'S YOUR FRIEND?
SOMEONE **COOL**. SO SHE CLEARLY DOESN'T WANT TO MEET **YOU**.
HEY, ARE THOSE CHIPS IN YOUR BAG?
LET ME HAVE SOME!
GET BACK, YOU TURD BUCKETS! BACK! RUN FOR IT, ASTRID!
TOSS
LIFESAVERS CANDY

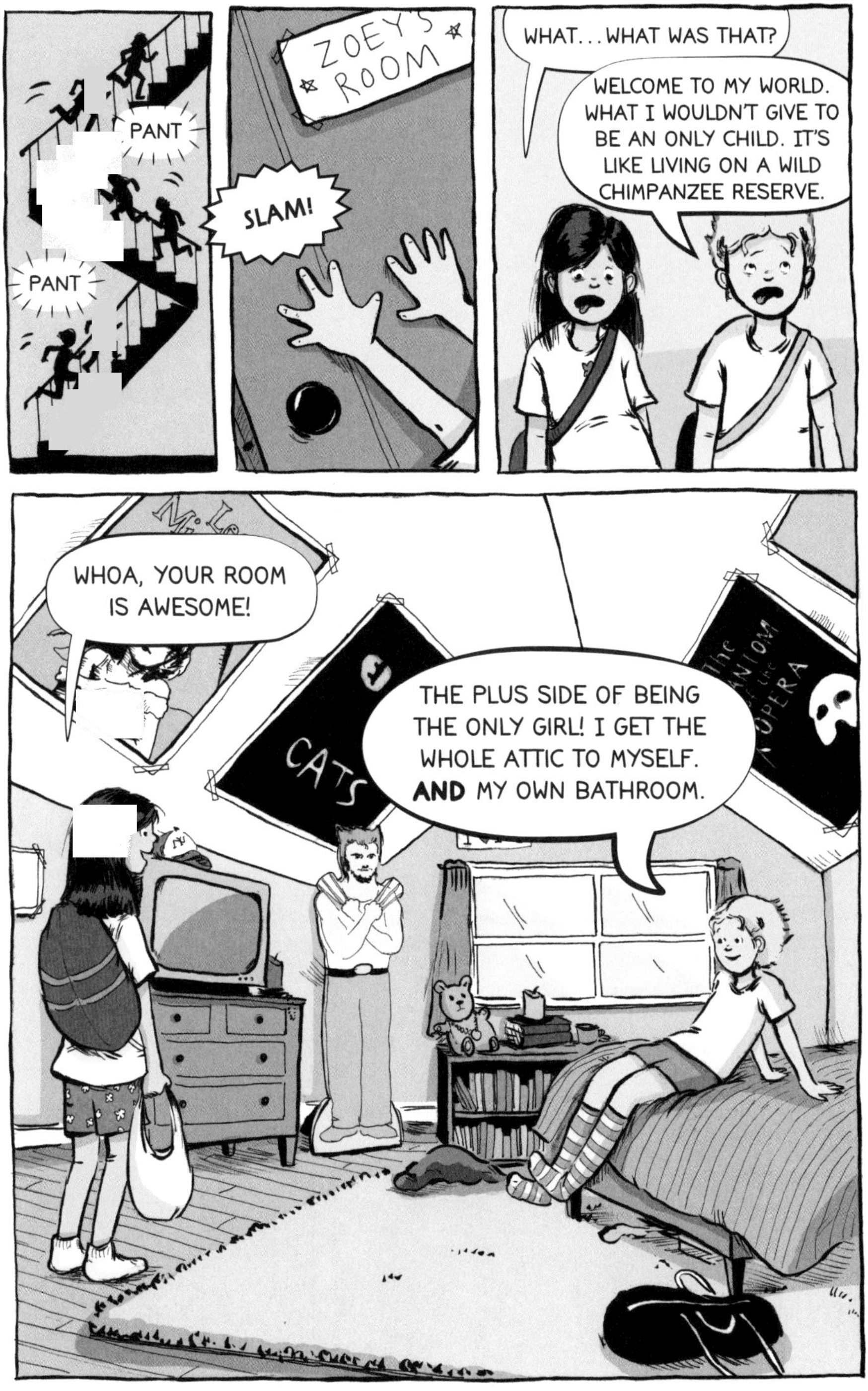
PANT
PANT
SLAM!
ZOEY'S ROOM
WHAT... WHAT WAS THAT?
WELCOME TO MY WORLD. WHAT I WOULDN'T GIVE TO BE AN ONLY CHILD. IT'S LIKE LIVING ON A WILD CHIMPANZEE RESERVE.
WHOA, YOUR ROOM IS AWESOME!
CATS
The PHANTOM of the OPERA
THE PLUS SIDE OF BEING THE ONLY GIRL! I GET THE WHOLE ATTIC TO MYSELF. **AND** MY OWN BATHROOM.

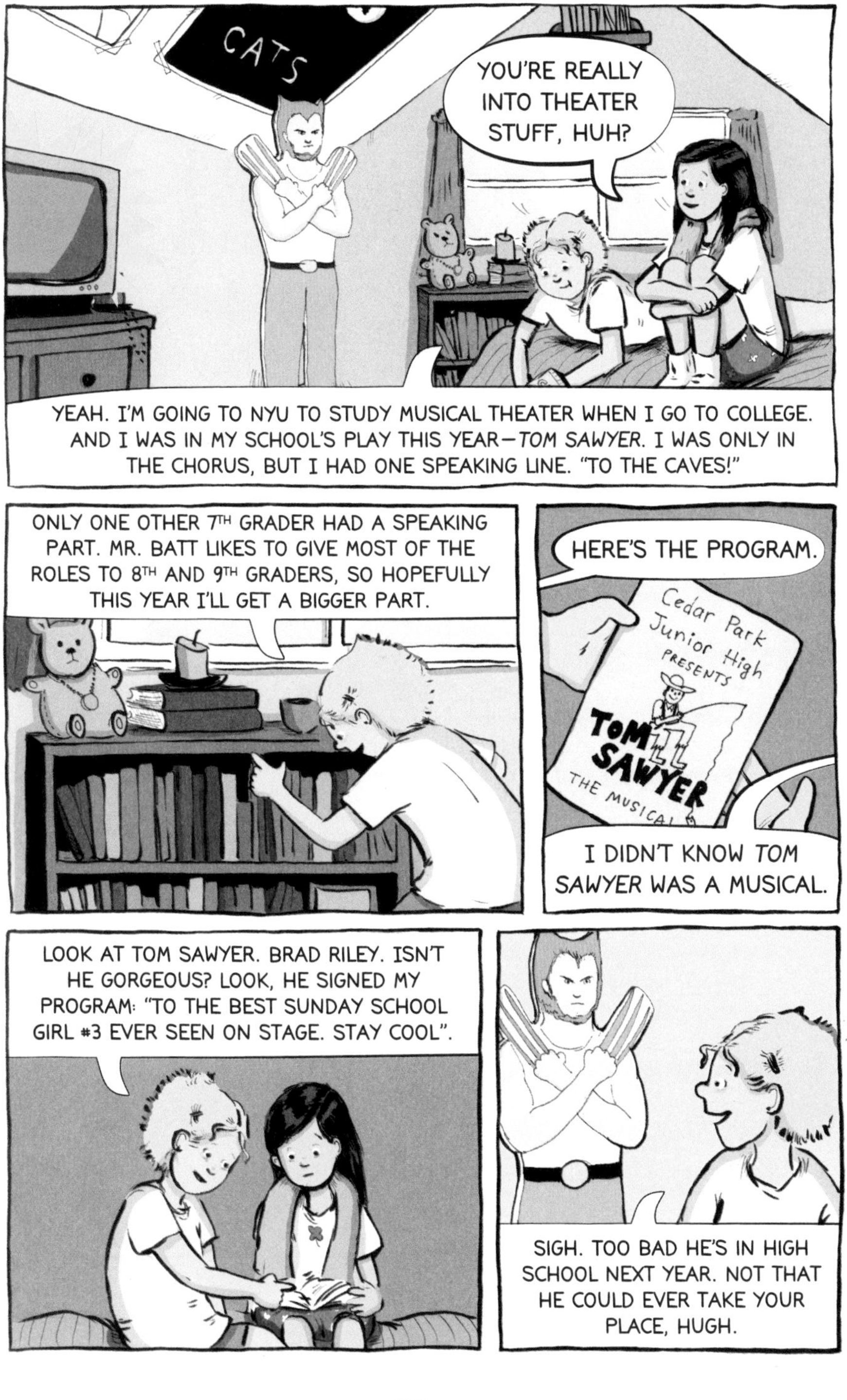
CATS
YOU'RE REALLY INTO THEATER STUFF, HUH?
YEAH. I'M GOING TO NYU TO STUDY MUSICAL THEATER WHEN I GO TO COLLEGE. AND I WAS IN MY SCHOOL'S PLAY THIS YEAR—*TOM SAWYER*. I WAS ONLY IN THE CHORUS, BUT I HAD ONE SPEAKING LINE. "TO THE CAVES!"
ONLY ONE OTHER 7TH GRADER HAD A SPEAKING PART. MR. BATT LIKES TO GIVE MOST OF THE ROLES TO 8TH AND 9TH GRADERS, SO HOPEFULLY THIS YEAR I'LL GET A BIGGER PART.
HERE'S THE PROGRAM.
Cedar Park Junior High PRESENTS
TOM SAWYER
THE MUSICAL
I DIDN'T KNOW *TOM SAWYER* WAS A MUSICAL.
LOOK AT TOM SAWYER. BRAD RILEY. ISN'T HE GORGEOUS? LOOK, HE SIGNED MY PROGRAM: "TO THE BEST SUNDAY SCHOOL GIRL #3 EVER SEEN ON STAGE. STAY COOL".
SIGH. TOO BAD HE'S IN HIGH SCHOOL NEXT YEAR. NOT THAT HE COULD EVER TAKE YOUR PLACE, HUGH.

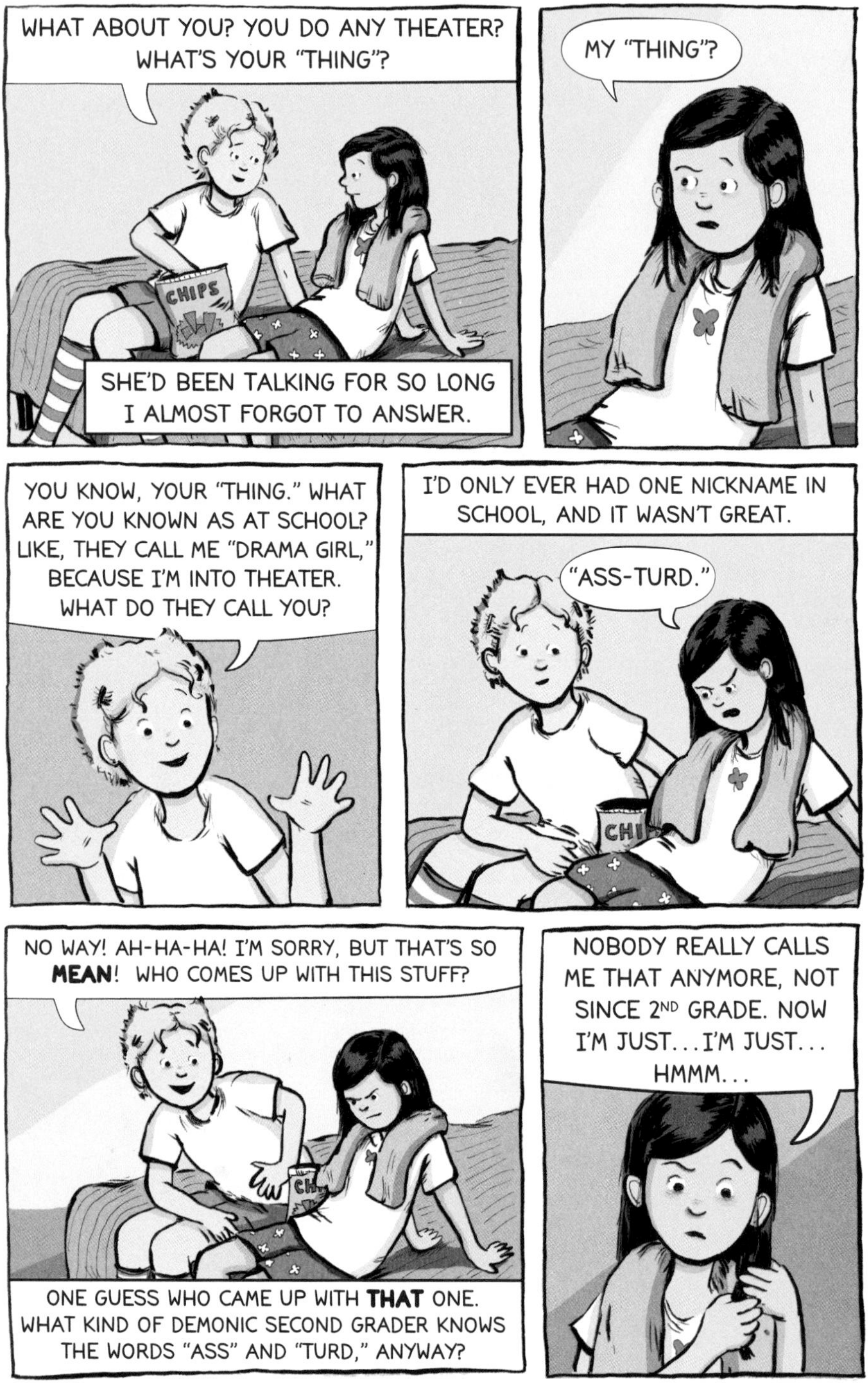
WHAT ABOUT YOU? YOU DO ANY THEATER? WHAT'S YOUR "THING"?
CHIPS
SHE'D BEEN TALKING FOR SO LONG I ALMOST FORGOT TO ANSWER.
MY "THING"?
YOU KNOW, YOUR "THING." WHAT ARE YOU KNOWN AS AT SCHOOL? LIKE, THEY CALL ME "DRAMA GIRL," BECAUSE I'M INTO THEATER. WHAT DO THEY CALL YOU?
I'D ONLY EVER HAD ONE NICKNAME IN SCHOOL, AND IT WASN'T GREAT.
"ASS-TURD."
NO WAY! AH-HA-HA! I'M SORRY, BUT THAT'S SO **MEAN**! WHO COMES UP WITH THIS STUFF?
ONE GUESS WHO CAME UP WITH **THAT** ONE. WHAT KIND OF DEMONIC SECOND GRADER KNOWS THE WORDS "ASS" AND "TURD," ANYWAY?
NOBODY REALLY CALLS ME THAT ANYMORE, NOT SINCE 2ND GRADE. NOW I'M JUST... I'M JUST... HMMM...

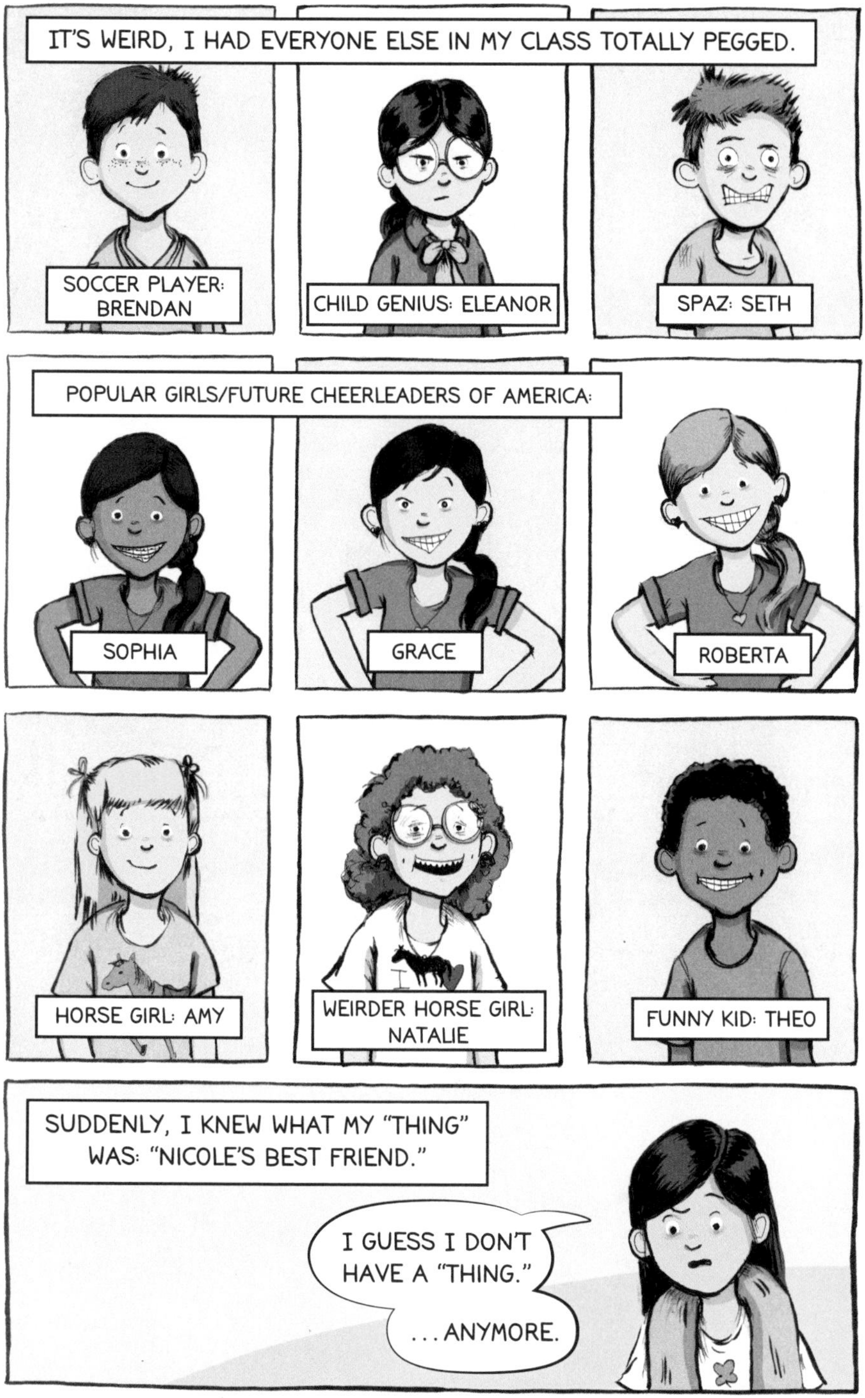
IT'S WEIRD, I HAD EVERYONE ELSE IN MY CLASS TOTALLY PEGGED.
SOCCER PLAYER: BRENDAN
CHILD GENIUS: ELEANOR
SPAZ: SETH
POPULAR GIRLS/FUTURE CHEERLEADERS OF AMERICA:
SOPHIA
GRACE
ROBERTA
HORSE GIRL: AMY
WEIRDER HORSE GIRL: NATALIE
FUNNY KID: THEO
SUDDENLY, I KNEW WHAT MY "THING" WAS: "NICOLE'S BEST FRIEND."
I GUESS I DON'T HAVE A "THING."
. . . ANYMORE.

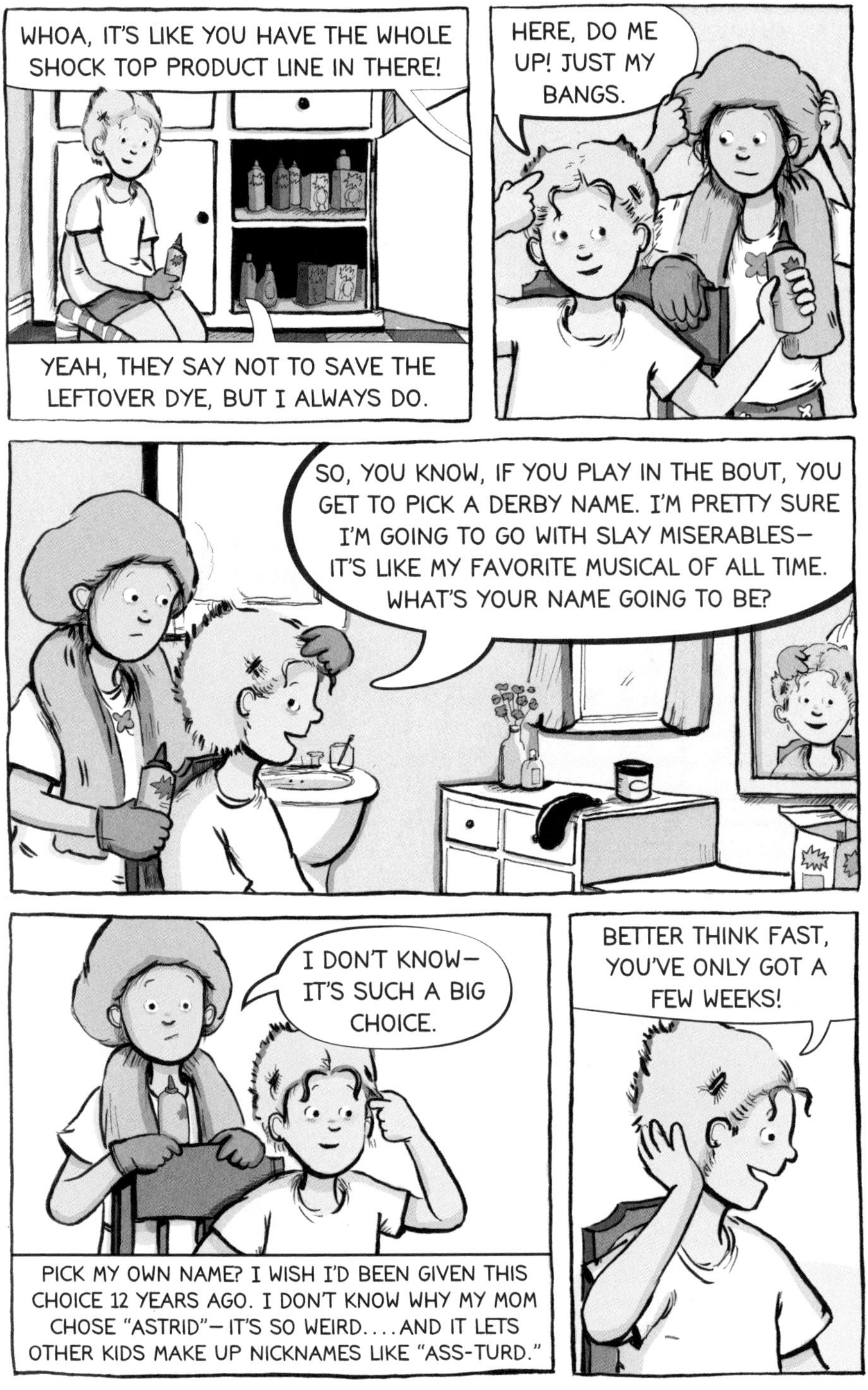
WHOA, IT'S LIKE YOU HAVE THE WHOLE SHOCK TOP PRODUCT LINE IN THERE!
YEAH, THEY SAY NOT TO SAVE THE LEFTOVER DYE, BUT I ALWAYS DO.
HERE, DO ME UP! JUST MY BANGS.
SO, YOU KNOW, IF YOU PLAY IN THE BOUT, YOU GET TO PICK A DERBY NAME. I'M PRETTY SURE I'M GOING TO GO WITH SLAY MISERABLES— IT'S LIKE MY FAVORITE MUSICAL OF ALL TIME. WHAT'S YOUR NAME GOING TO BE?
I DON'T KNOW— IT'S SUCH A BIG CHOICE.
PICK MY OWN NAME? I WISH I'D BEEN GIVEN THIS CHOICE 12 YEARS AGO. I DON'T KNOW WHY MY MOM CHOSE "ASTRID"— IT'S SO WEIRD. . . . AND IT LETS OTHER KIDS MAKE UP NICKNAMES LIKE "ASS-TURD."
BETTER THINK FAST, YOU'VE ONLY GOT A FEW WEEKS!

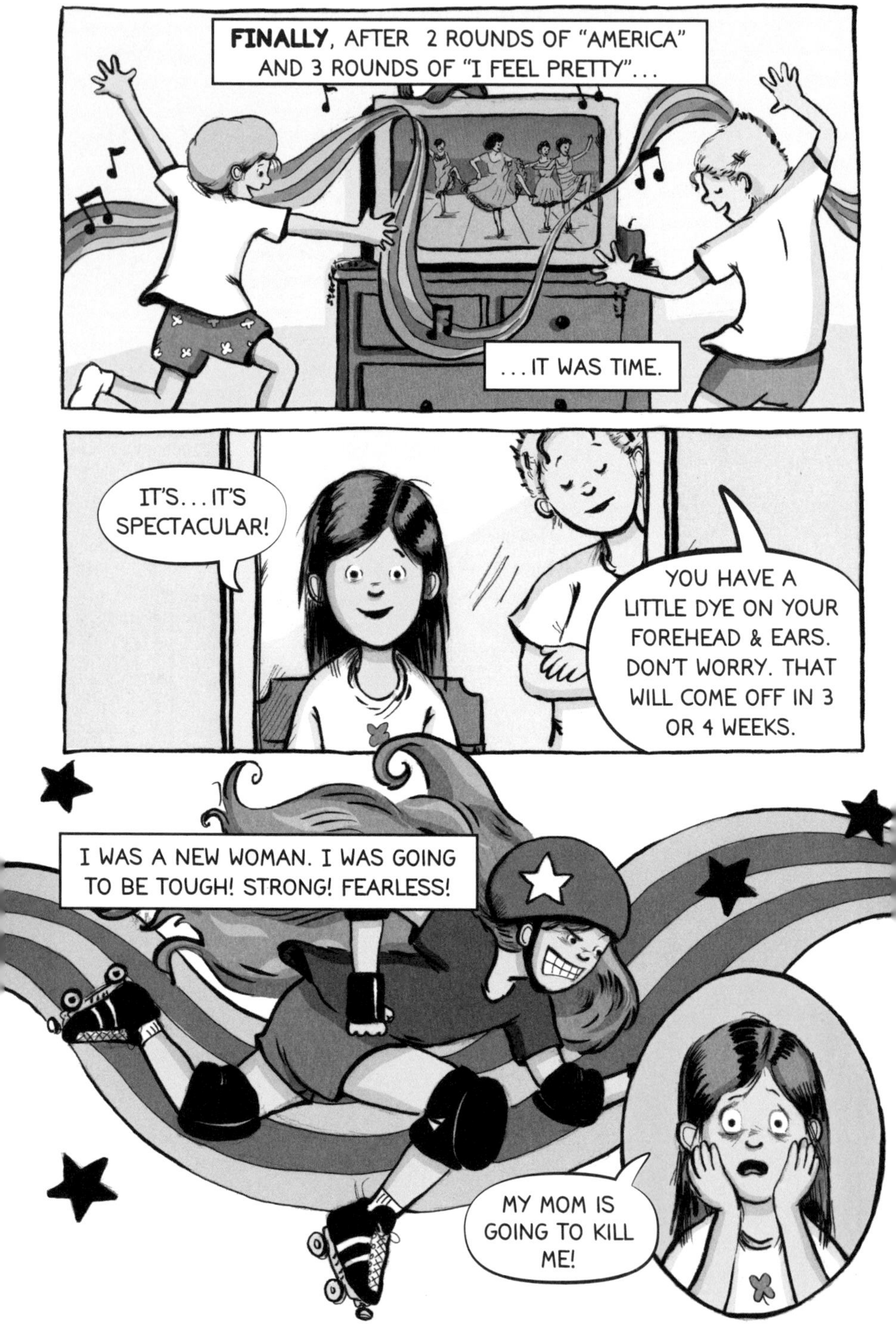
FINALLY, AFTER 2 ROUNDS OF "AMERICA" AND 3 ROUNDS OF "I FEEL PRETTY"...
...IT WAS TIME.
IT'S...IT'S SPECTACULAR!
YOU HAVE A LITTLE DYE ON YOUR FOREHEAD & EARS. DON'T WORRY. THAT WILL COME OFF IN 3 OR 4 WEEKS.
I WAS A NEW WOMAN. I WAS GOING TO BE TOUGH! STRONG! FEARLESS!
MY MOM IS GOING TO KILL ME!

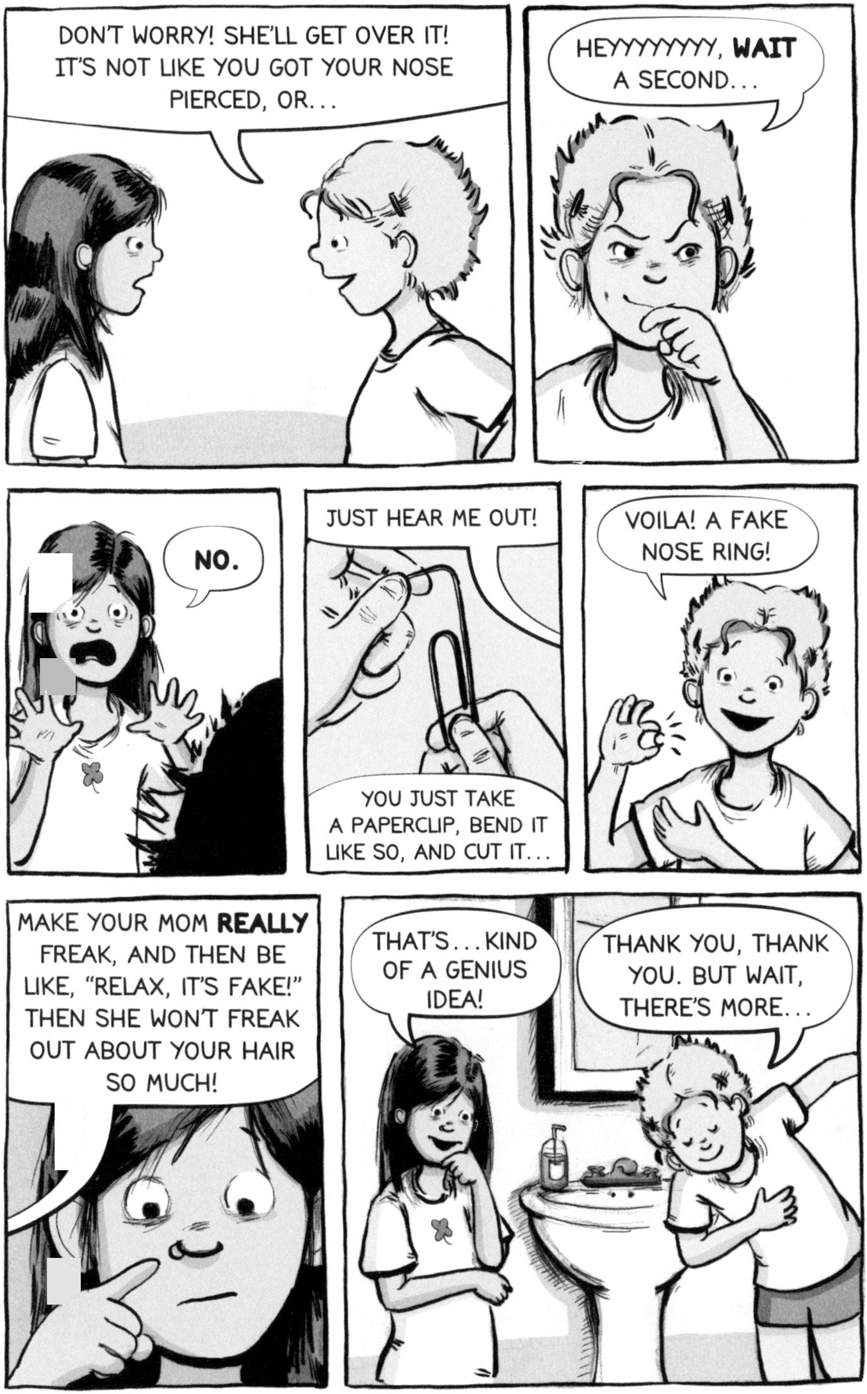

DON'T WORRY! SHE'LL GET OVER IT! IT'S NOT LIKE YOU GOT YOUR NOSE PIERCED, OR...
HEYYYYYYYY, **WAIT** A SECOND...
NO.
JUST HEAR ME OUT!
YOU JUST TAKE A PAPERCLIP, BEND IT LIKE SO, AND CUT IT...
VOILA! A FAKE NOSE RING!
MAKE YOUR MOM **REALLY** FREAK, AND THEN BE LIKE, "RELAX, IT'S FAKE!" THEN SHE WON'T FREAK OUT ABOUT YOUR HAIR SO MUCH!
THAT'S...KIND OF A GENIUS IDEA!
THANK YOU, THANK YOU. BUT WAIT, THERE'S MORE...

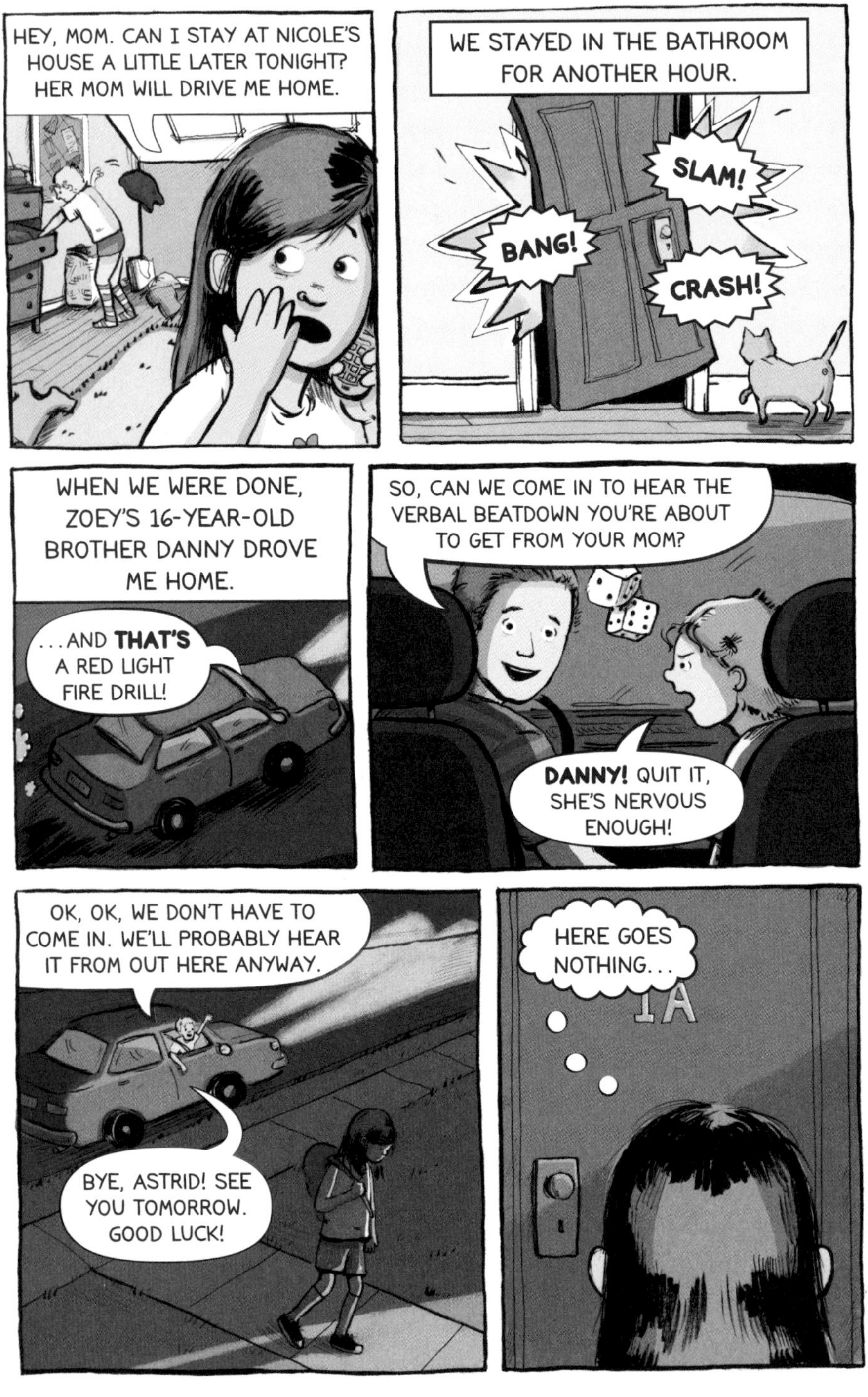
HEY, MOM. CAN I STAY AT NICOLE'S HOUSE A LITTLE LATER TONIGHT? HER MOM WILL DRIVE ME HOME.
WE STAYED IN THE BATHROOM FOR ANOTHER HOUR.
SLAM!
BANG!
CRASH!
WHEN WE WERE DONE, ZOEY'S 16-YEAR-OLD BROTHER DANNY DROVE ME HOME.
...AND **THAT'S** A RED LIGHT FIRE DRILL!
SO, CAN WE COME IN TO HEAR THE VERBAL BEATDOWN YOU'RE ABOUT TO GET FROM YOUR MOM?
DANNY! QUIT IT, SHE'S NERVOUS ENOUGH!
OK, OK, WE DON'T HAVE TO COME IN. WE'LL PROBABLY HEAR IT FROM OUT HERE ANYWAY.
BYE, ASTRID! SEE YOU TOMORROW. GOOD LUCK!
HERE GOES NOTHING...
1A

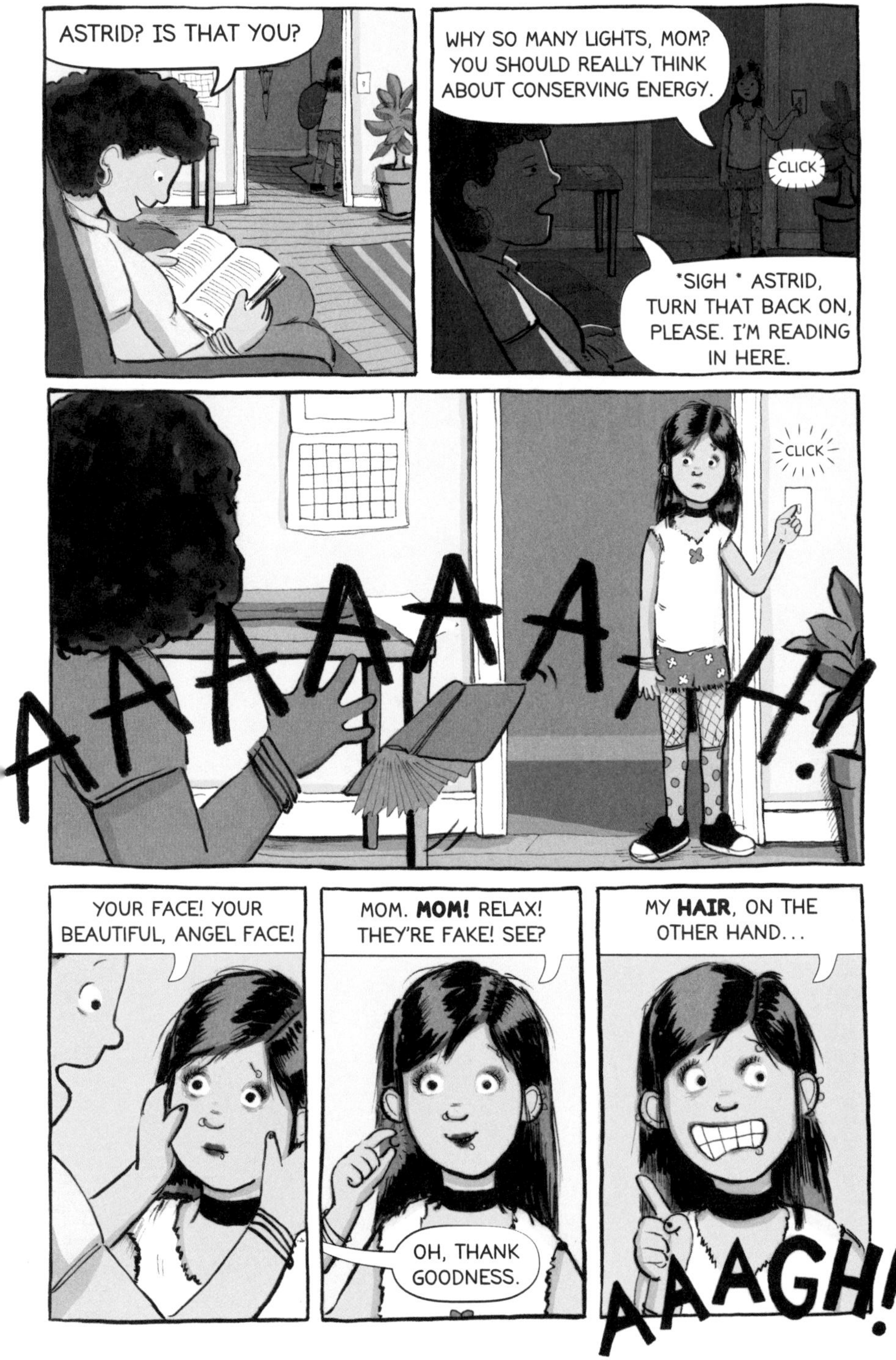
ASTRID? IS THAT YOU?
WHY SO MANY LIGHTS, MOM? YOU SHOULD REALLY THINK ABOUT CONSERVING ENERGY.
CLICK
*SIGH * ASTRID, TURN THAT BACK ON, PLEASE. I'M READING IN HERE.
CLICK
AAAAAAH!
YOUR FACE! YOUR BEAUTIFUL, ANGEL FACE!
MOM. **MOM!** RELAX! THEY'RE FAKE! SEE?
OH, THANK GOODNESS.
MY **HAIR**, ON THE OTHER HAND...
AAAGH!

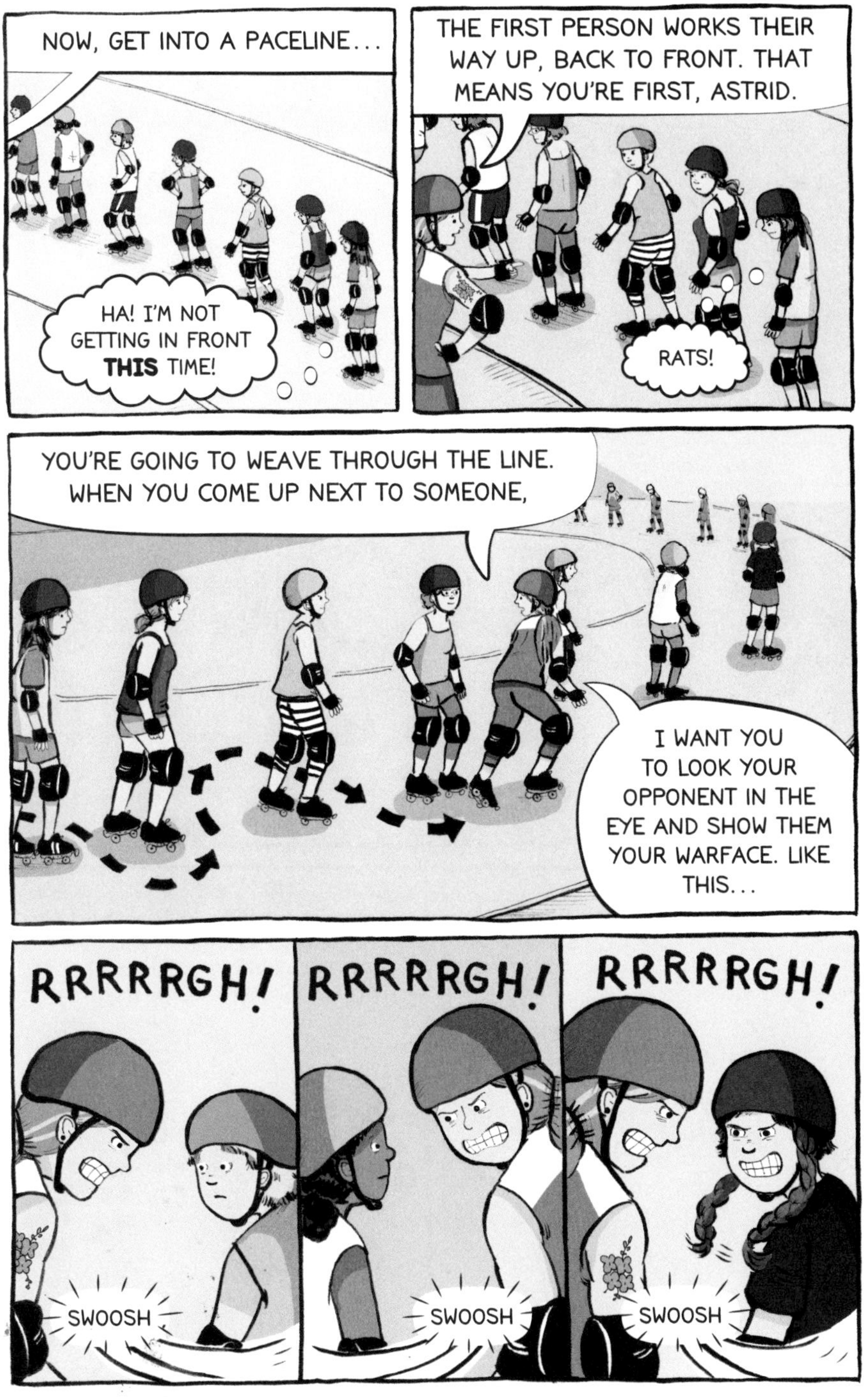
NOW, GET INTO A PACELINE...
HA! I'M NOT GETTING IN FRONT **THIS** TIME!
THE FIRST PERSON WORKS THEIR WAY UP, BACK TO FRONT. THAT MEANS YOU'RE FIRST, ASTRID.
RATS!
YOU'RE GOING TO WEAVE THROUGH THE LINE. WHEN YOU COME UP NEXT TO SOMEONE,
I WANT YOU TO LOOK YOUR OPPONENT IN THE EYE AND SHOW THEM YOUR WARFACE. LIKE THIS...
RRRRRGH!
SWOOSH
RRRRRGH!
SWOOSH
RRRRRGH!
SWOOSH

* 124 *

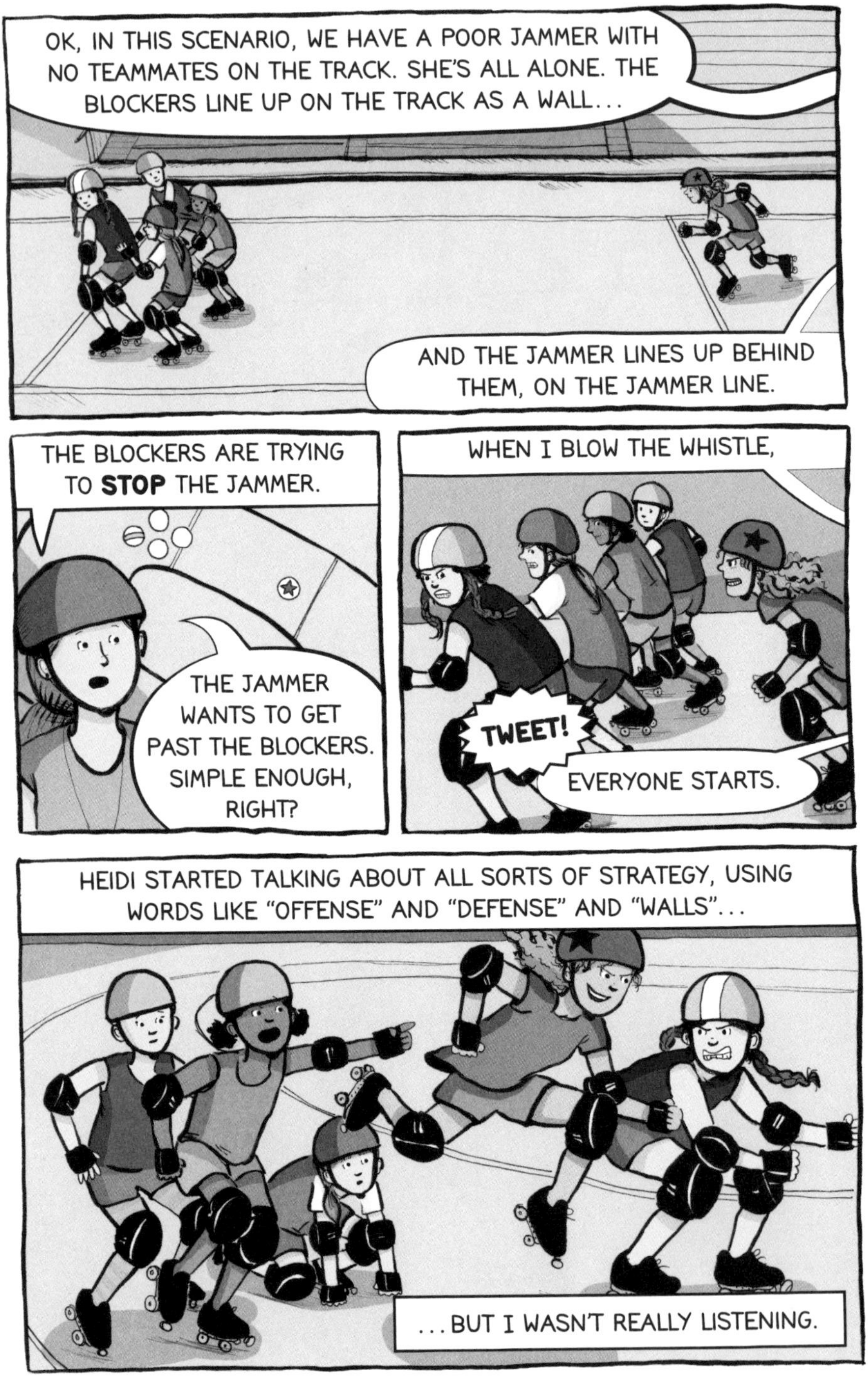
OK, IN THIS SCENARIO, WE HAVE A POOR JAMMER WITH NO TEAMMATES ON THE TRACK. SHE'S ALL ALONE. THE BLOCKERS LINE UP ON THE TRACK AS A WALL...
AND THE JAMMER LINES UP BEHIND THEM, ON THE JAMMER LINE.
THE BLOCKERS ARE TRYING TO **STOP** THE JAMMER.
THE JAMMER WANTS TO GET PAST THE BLOCKERS. SIMPLE ENOUGH, RIGHT?
WHEN I BLOW THE WHISTLE,
TWEET!
EVERYONE STARTS.
HEIDI STARTED TALKING ABOUT ALL SORTS OF STRATEGY, USING WORDS LIKE "OFFENSE" AND "DEFENSE" AND "WALLS"...
...BUT I WASN'T REALLY LISTENING.

IT DIDN'T STOP ME FROM TRYING— LIKE ON FRIDAY, WHEN SHE ASKED FOR VOLUNTEERS TO HAND OUT FLYERS FOR THE UPCOMING BOUT.

I NEED A FEW OF YOU TO COME TO OAKS PARK TONIGHT FROM 5 TO 7. IT'S FAMILY FUN NIGHT, AND IT WOULD BE A GREAT PLACE TO HAND OUT FLYERS AND TALK TO PEOPLE ABOUT ROLLER DERBY.

I'LL DO IT, HEIDI!

FRIENDLY, HELPFUL, TEAM-PLAYER SMILE.

OOOKAYYYY... THANKS, ASTRID!

I CAN COME WITH YOU!

COOL! YOU CAN COME OVER TO MY HOUSE FOR DINNER IF YOU WANT!

SO, ZOEY SKATED HOME WITH ME AFTER CAMP. I MADE MY USUAL STOP.

E-Z STOP

MY BEST CUSTOMER! SURE, YOU CAN PUT A FLYER IN THE WINDOW!

SOMETHING CAUGHT MY EYE AS I WAS HANGING UP MY FLYER...

FANCY THAT— NICOLE'S DANCE CAMP WAS HAVING A RECITAL THE WEEK AFTER OUR BOUT.

Northwest Dance Academy

Summer Recital
July 30th, 7 pm

ROLLER DERBY

TECHNICALLY, I'M NOT ALLOWED TO HAVE FRIENDS OVER WHEN MOM'S NOT HOME... SO WE HAD TO DO A LITTLE WORK-AROUND.

MOM! I'M HOME!

CAN ZOEY STAY FOR DINNER?

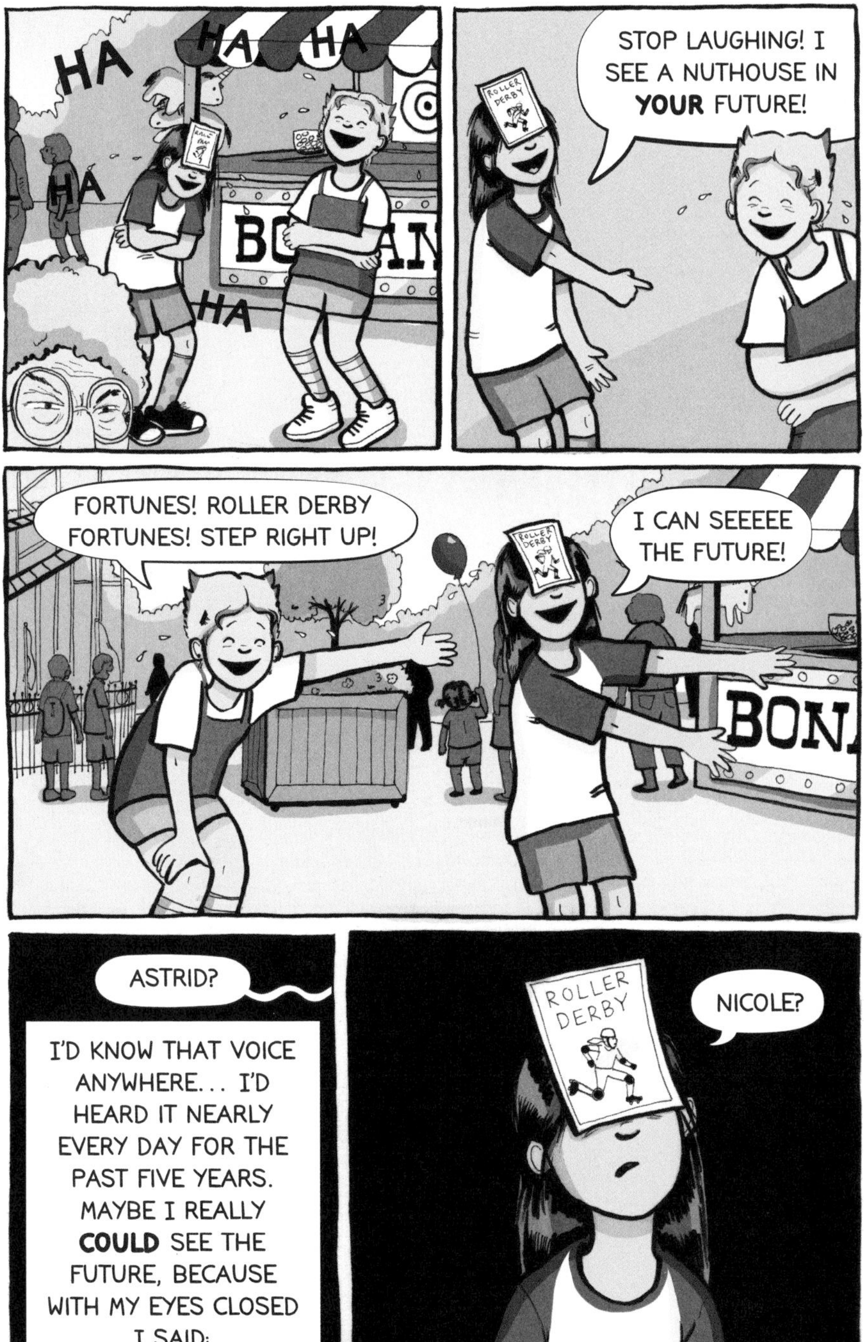
HA HA HA
HA
HA
STOP LAUGHING! I SEE A NUTHOUSE IN **YOUR** FUTURE!
FORTUNES! ROLLER DERBY FORTUNES! STEP RIGHT UP!
I CAN SEEEEE THE FUTURE!
ASTRID?
I'D KNOW THAT VOICE ANYWHERE... I'D HEARD IT NEARLY EVERY DAY FOR THE PAST FIVE YEARS. MAYBE I REALLY **COULD** SEE THE FUTURE, BECAUSE WITH MY EYES CLOSED I SAID:
ROLLER DERBY
NICOLE?

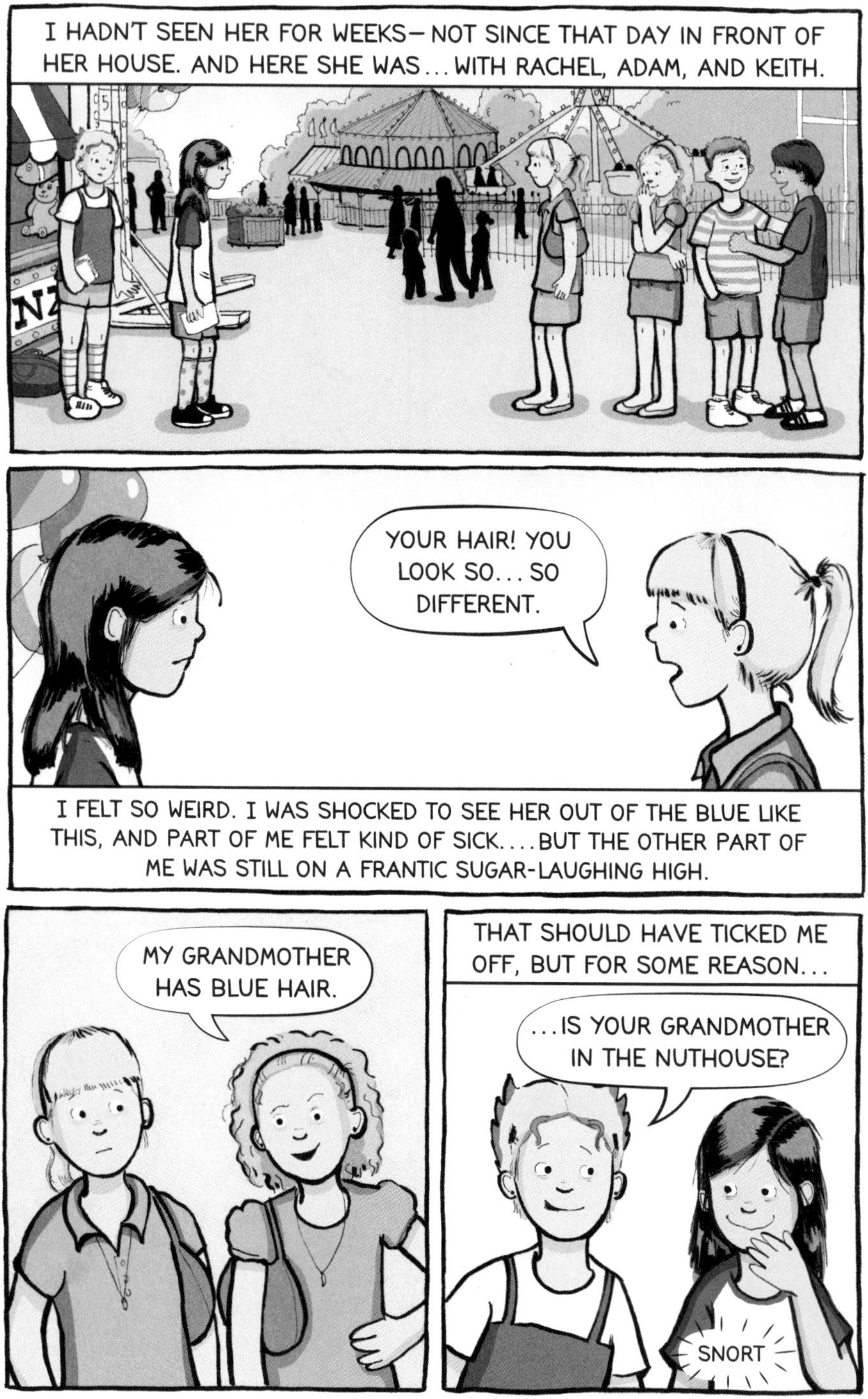
I HADN'T SEEN HER FOR WEEKS— NOT SINCE THAT DAY IN FRONT OF HER HOUSE. AND HERE SHE WAS... WITH RACHEL, ADAM, AND KEITH.
YOUR HAIR! YOU LOOK SO... SO DIFFERENT.
I FELT SO WEIRD. I WAS SHOCKED TO SEE HER OUT OF THE BLUE LIKE THIS, AND PART OF ME FELT KIND OF SICK.... BUT THE OTHER PART OF ME WAS STILL ON A FRANTIC SUGAR-LAUGHING HIGH.
MY GRANDMOTHER HAS BLUE HAIR.
THAT SHOULD HAVE TICKED ME OFF, BUT FOR SOME REASON...
...IS YOUR GRANDMOTHER IN THE NUTHOUSE?
SNORT

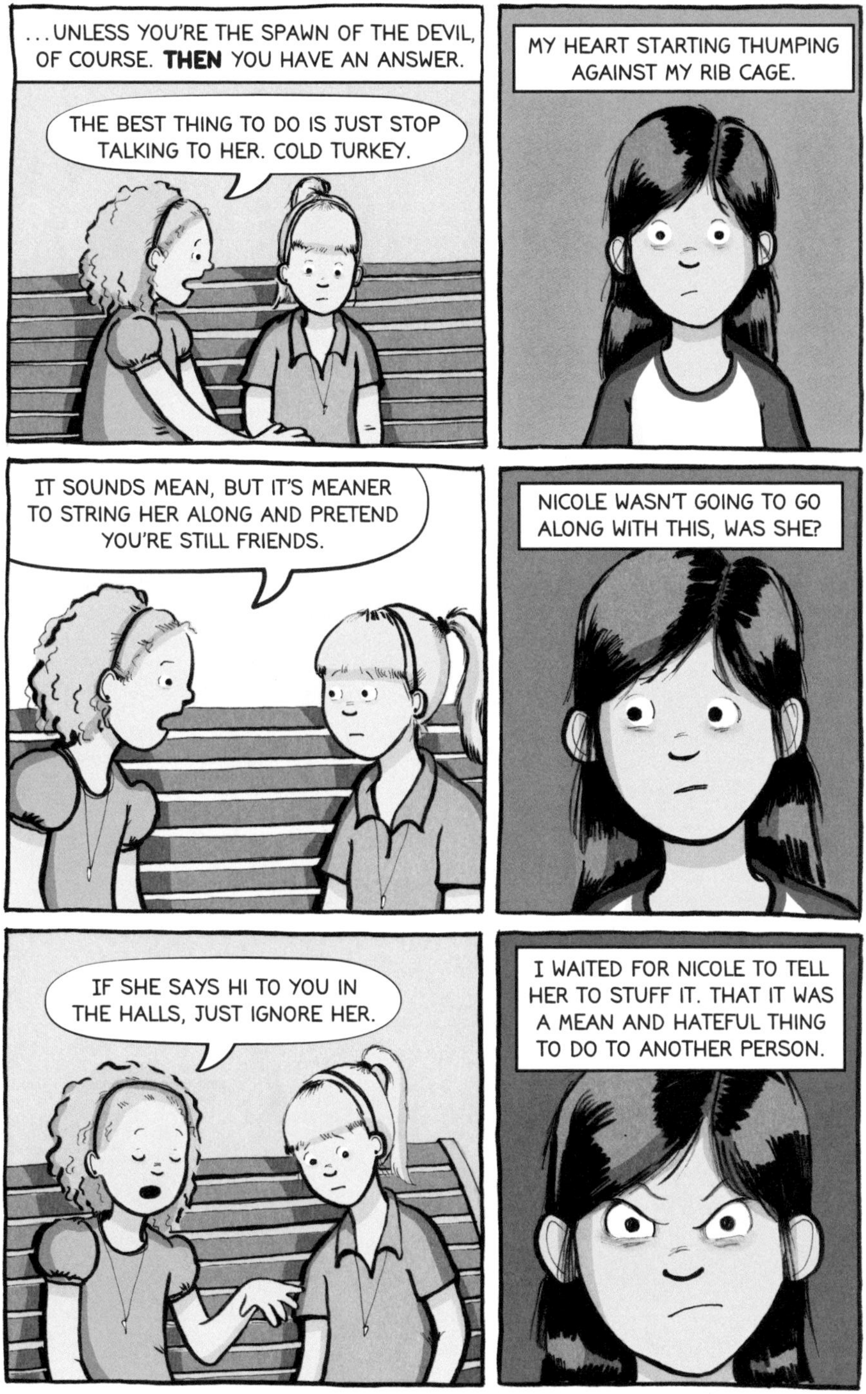
...UNLESS YOU'RE THE SPAWN OF THE DEVIL, OF COURSE. **THEN** YOU HAVE AN ANSWER.
THE BEST THING TO DO IS JUST STOP TALKING TO HER. COLD TURKEY.
MY HEART STARTING THUMPING AGAINST MY RIB CAGE.
IT SOUNDS MEAN, BUT IT'S MEANER TO STRING HER ALONG AND PRETEND YOU'RE STILL FRIENDS.
NICOLE WASN'T GOING TO GO ALONG WITH THIS, WAS SHE?
IF SHE SAYS HI TO YOU IN THE HALLS, JUST IGNORE HER.
I WAITED FOR NICOLE TO TELL HER TO STUFF IT. THAT IT WAS A MEAN AND HATEFUL THING TO DO TO ANOTHER PERSON.

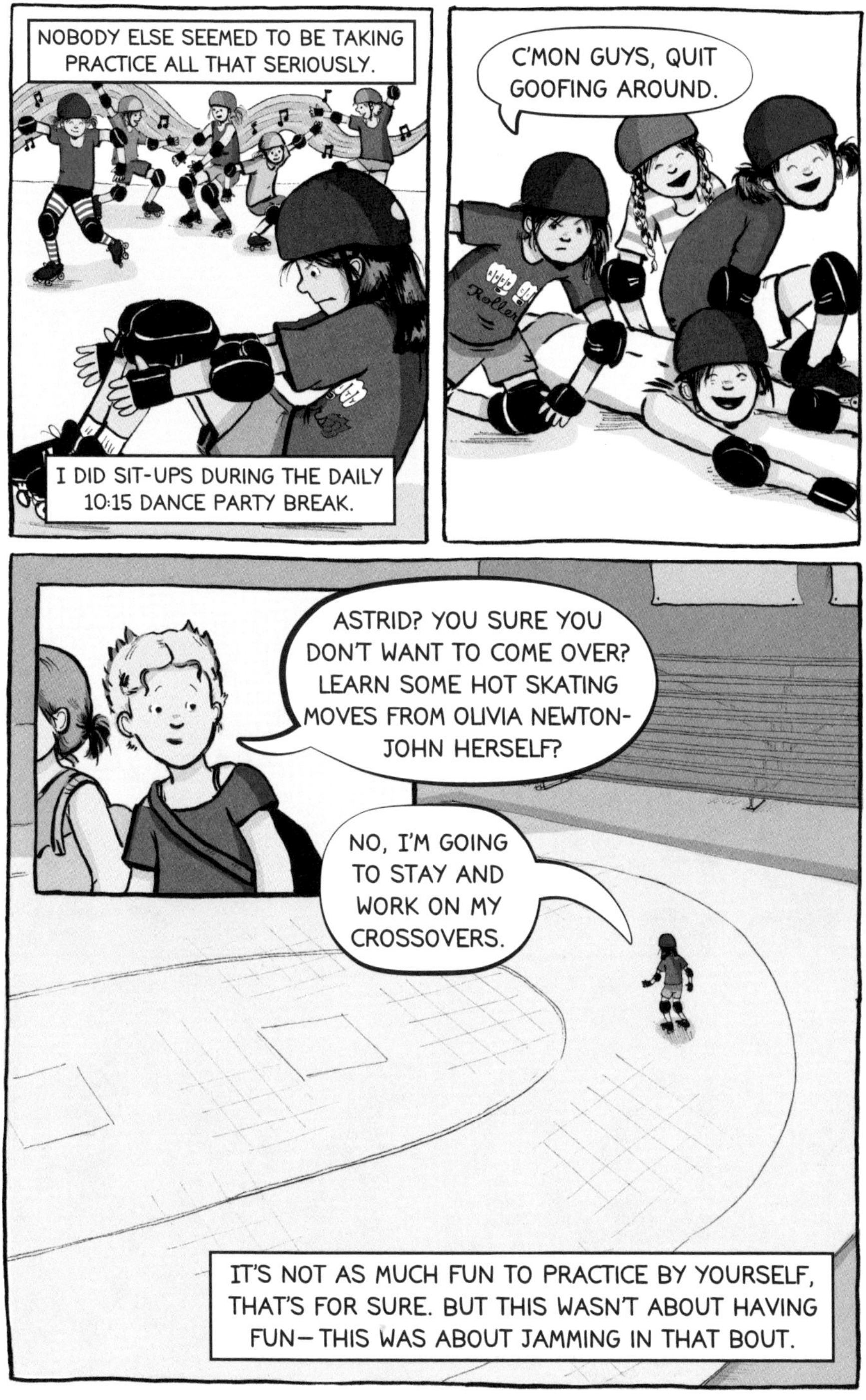
NOBODY ELSE SEEMED TO BE TAKING PRACTICE ALL THAT SERIOUSLY.
I DID SIT-UPS DURING THE DAILY 10:15 DANCE PARTY BREAK.
C'MON GUYS, QUIT GOOFING AROUND.
ASTRID? YOU SURE YOU DON'T WANT TO COME OVER? LEARN SOME HOT SKATING MOVES FROM OLIVIA NEWTON-JOHN HERSELF?
NO, I'M GOING TO STAY AND WORK ON MY CROSSOVERS.
IT'S NOT AS MUCH FUN TO PRACTICE BY YOURSELF, THAT'S FOR SURE. BUT THIS WASN'T ABOUT HAVING FUN—THIS WAS ABOUT JAMMING IN THAT BOUT.

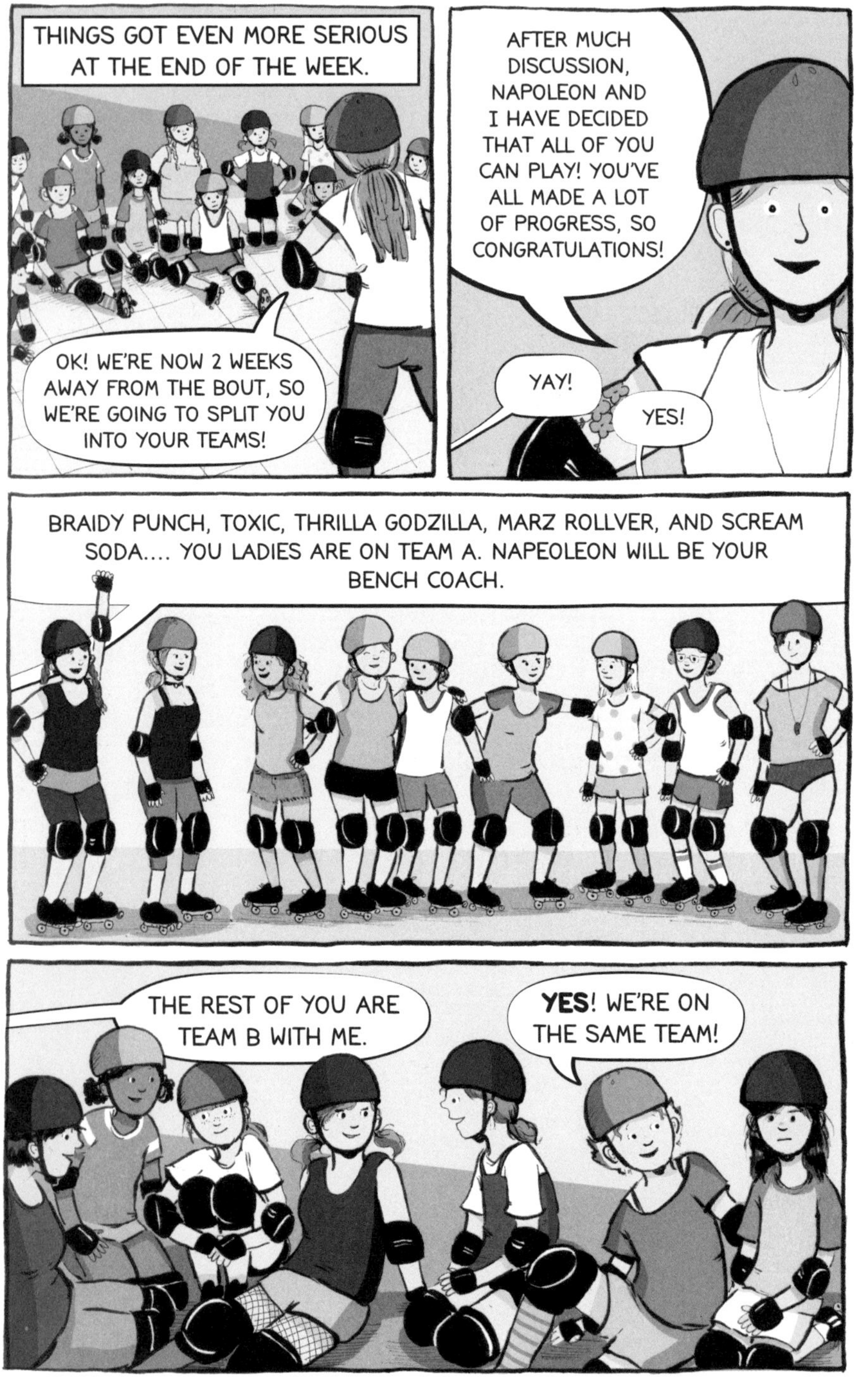
THINGS GOT EVEN MORE SERIOUS AT THE END OF THE WEEK.
OK! WE'RE NOW 2 WEEKS AWAY FROM THE BOUT, SO WE'RE GOING TO SPLIT YOU INTO YOUR TEAMS!
AFTER MUCH DISCUSSION, NAPOLEON AND I HAVE DECIDED THAT ALL OF YOU CAN PLAY! YOU'VE ALL MADE A LOT OF PROGRESS, SO CONGRATULATIONS!
YAY!
YES!
BRAIDY PUNCH, TOXIC, THRILLA GODZILLA, MARZ ROLLVER, AND SCREAM SODA.... YOU LADIES ARE ON TEAM A. NAPEOLEON WILL BE YOUR BENCH COACH.
THE REST OF YOU ARE TEAM B WITH ME.
YES! WE'RE ON THE SAME TEAM!

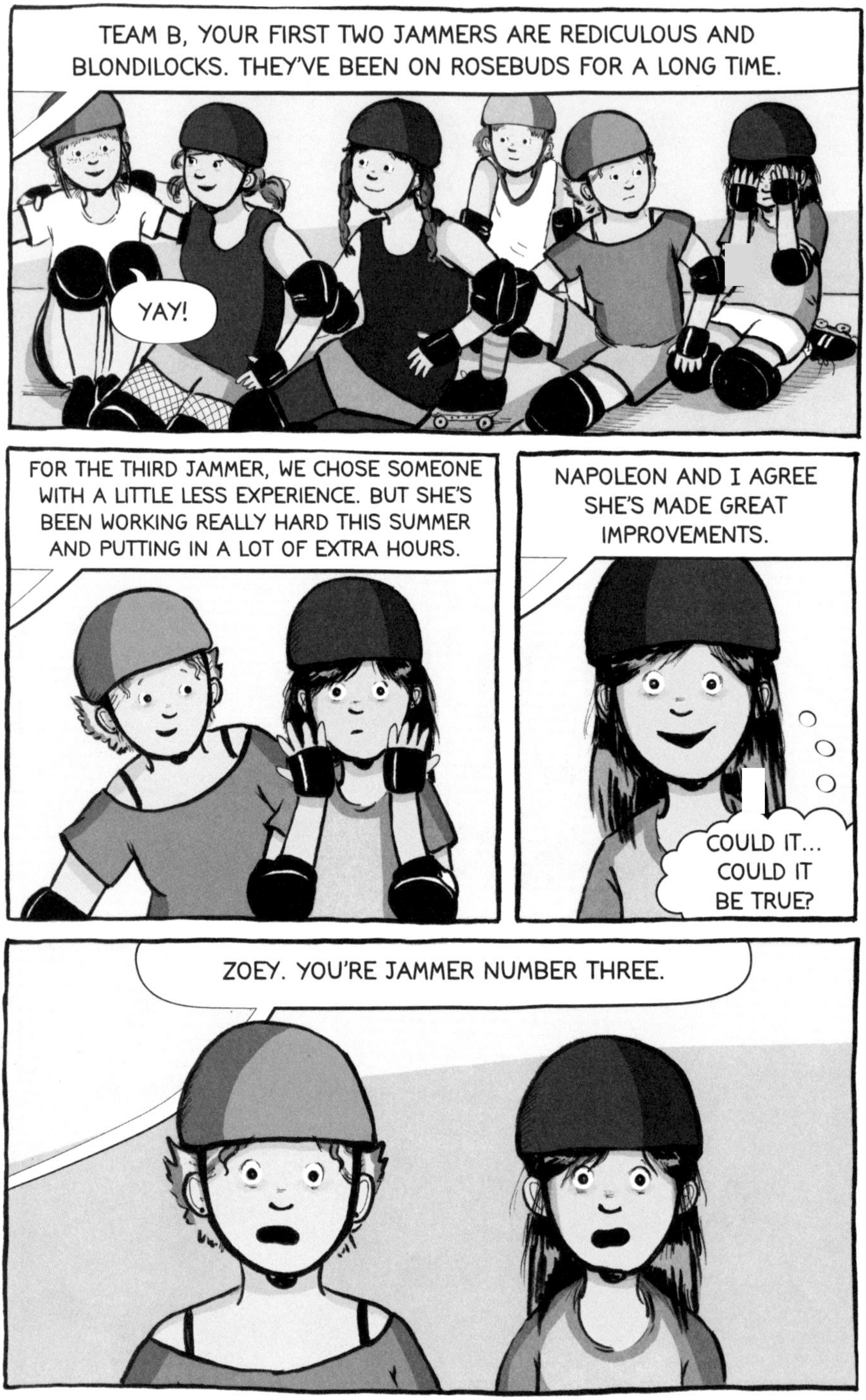
TEAM B, YOUR FIRST TWO JAMMERS ARE REDICULOUS AND BLONDILOCKS. THEY'VE BEEN ON ROSEBUDS FOR A LONG TIME.
YAY!
FOR THE THIRD JAMMER, WE CHOSE SOMEONE WITH A LITTLE LESS EXPERIENCE. BUT SHE'S BEEN WORKING REALLY HARD THIS SUMMER AND PUTTING IN A LOT OF EXTRA HOURS.
NAPOLEON AND I AGREE SHE'S MADE GREAT IMPROVEMENTS.
COULD IT... COULD IT BE TRUE?
ZOEY. YOU'RE JAMMER NUMBER THREE.

OKAY...BYE, SWEETIE. IT WAS NICE TO SEE YOU.

IS SOMETHING WRONG? YOU'RE BOTH ACTING VERY STRANGE.

NOTHING'S **WRONG**, EXCEPT THAT I HAVE BEEN SEEN IN PUBLIC IN THIS HUMILIATING DRESS. CAN WE **PLEASE** GET OUT OF HERE NOW?

SLAM!

MY KNEES WERE SHAKING WITH RELIEF AND BOTTLED-UP STRESS. IS IT POSSIBLE TO GIVE YOURSELF AN ULCER IN 5 MINUTES? AT THE RIPE AGE OF 12?

YOU KNOW, SOME WOMEN FIND SHOPPING TO BE A RELAXING AND ENJOYABLE EXPERIENCE. IMAGINE THAT.

I DIDN'T BOTHER TO ANSWER. I WAS SO CONFUSED. WHY DID NICOLE SAVE MY HIDE BACK THERE IN YOUNG MISSES?

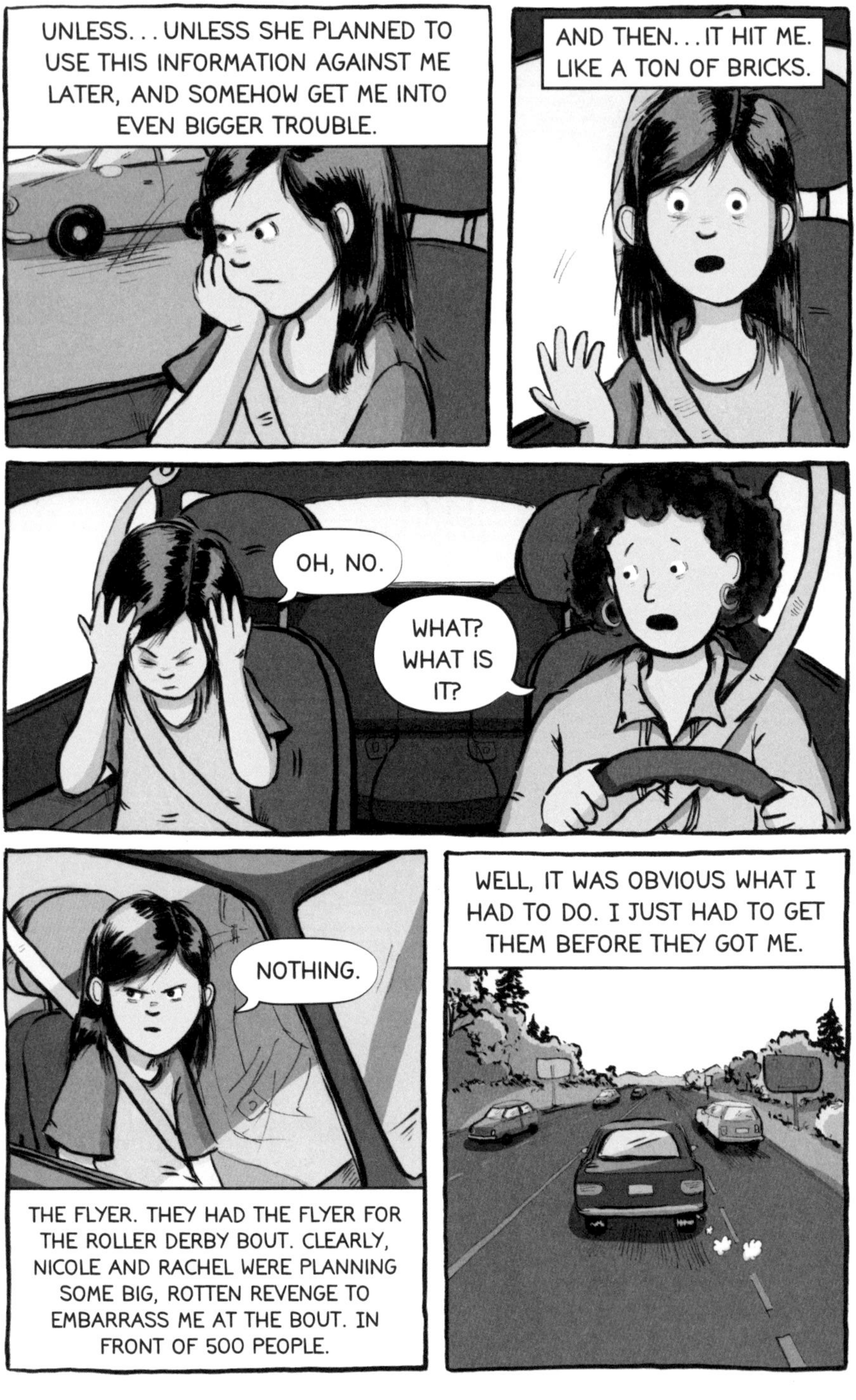
UNLESS. . . UNLESS SHE PLANNED TO USE THIS INFORMATION AGAINST ME LATER, AND SOMEHOW GET ME INTO EVEN BIGGER TROUBLE.
AND THEN. . . IT HIT ME. LIKE A TON OF BRICKS.
OH, NO.
WHAT? WHAT IS IT?
NOTHING.
THE FLYER. THEY HAD THE FLYER FOR THE ROLLER DERBY BOUT. CLEARLY, NICOLE AND RACHEL WERE PLANNING SOME BIG, ROTTEN REVENGE TO EMBARRASS ME AT THE BOUT. IN FRONT OF 500 PEOPLE.
WELL, IT WAS OBVIOUS WHAT I HAD TO DO. I JUST HAD TO GET THEM BEFORE THEY GOT ME.

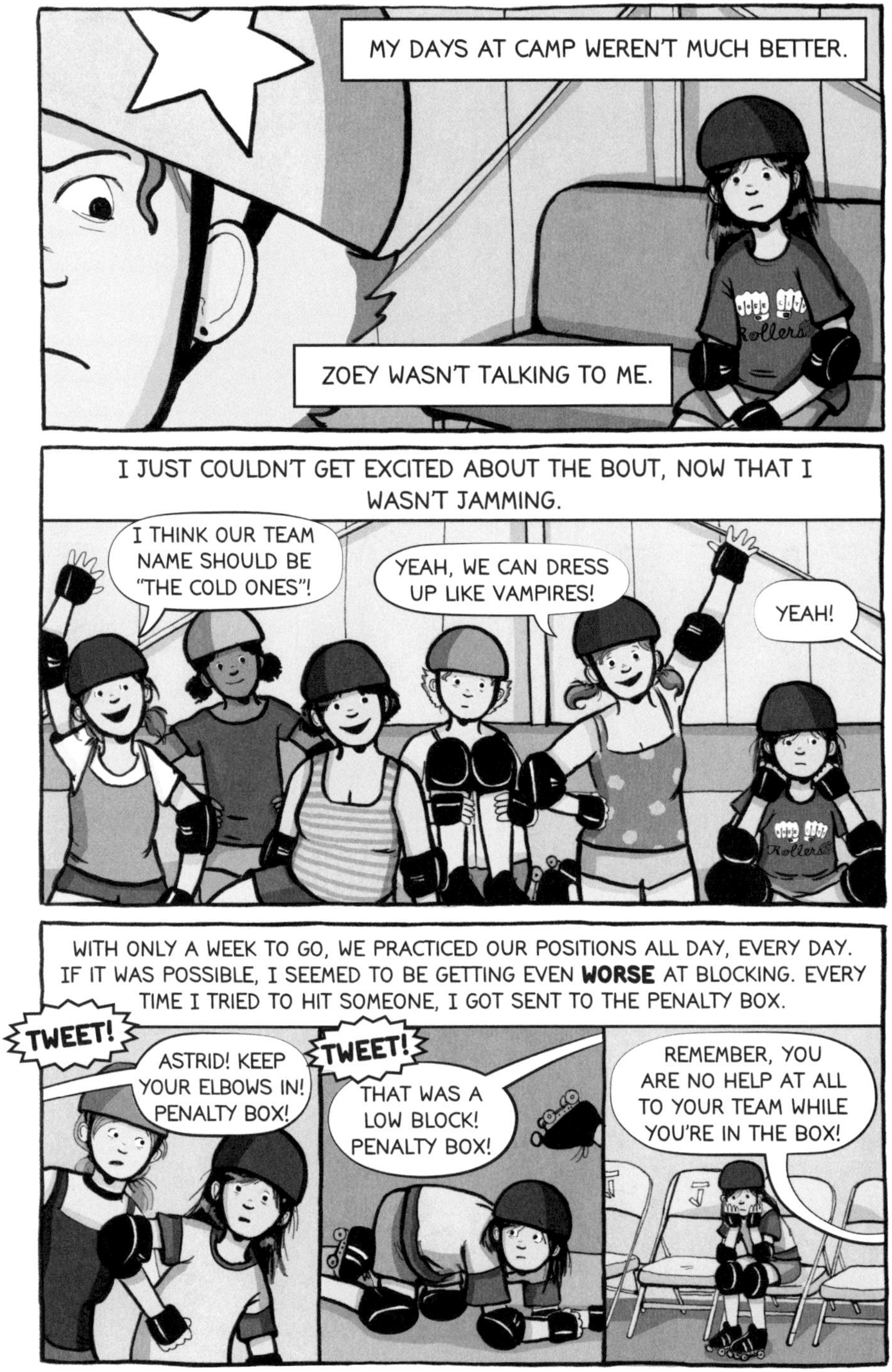
MY DAYS AT CAMP WEREN'T MUCH BETTER.
ZOEY WASN'T TALKING TO ME.
I JUST COULDN'T GET EXCITED ABOUT THE BOUT, NOW THAT I WASN'T JAMMING.
I THINK OUR TEAM NAME SHOULD BE "THE COLD ONES"!
YEAH, WE CAN DRESS UP LIKE VAMPIRES!
YEAH!
WITH ONLY A WEEK TO GO, WE PRACTICED OUR POSITIONS ALL DAY, EVERY DAY. IF IT WAS POSSIBLE, I SEEMED TO BE GETTING EVEN **WORSE** AT BLOCKING. EVERY TIME I TRIED TO HIT SOMEONE, I GOT SENT TO THE PENALTY BOX.
TWEET!
ASTRID! KEEP YOUR ELBOWS IN! PENALTY BOX!
TWEET!
THAT WAS A LOW BLOCK! PENALTY BOX!
REMEMBER, YOU ARE NO HELP AT ALL TO YOUR TEAM WHILE YOU'RE IN THE BOX!

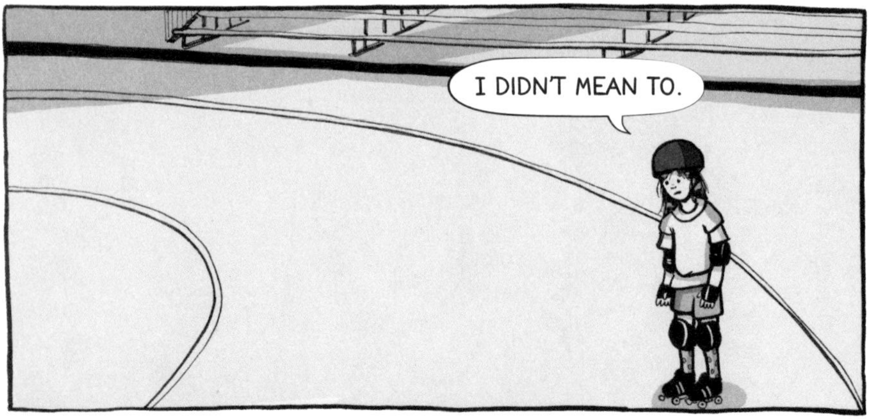
I DIDN'T MEAN TO.

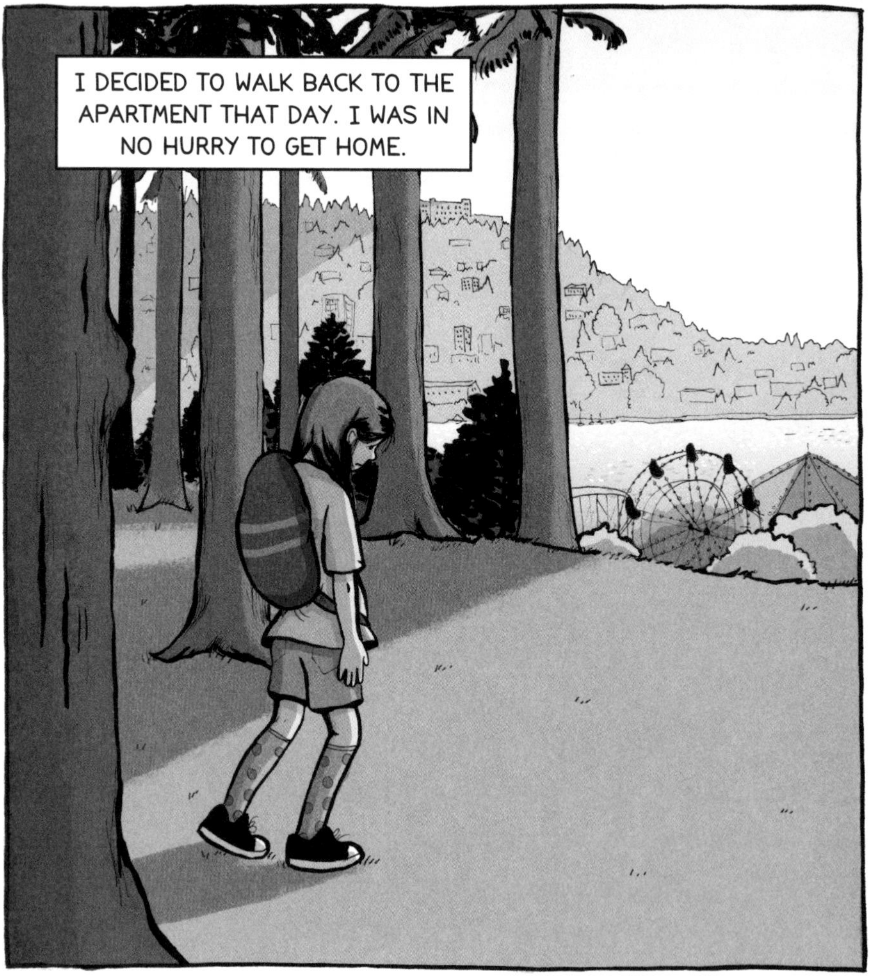
I DECIDED TO WALK BACK TO THE APARTMENT THAT DAY. I WAS IN NO HURRY TO GET HOME.

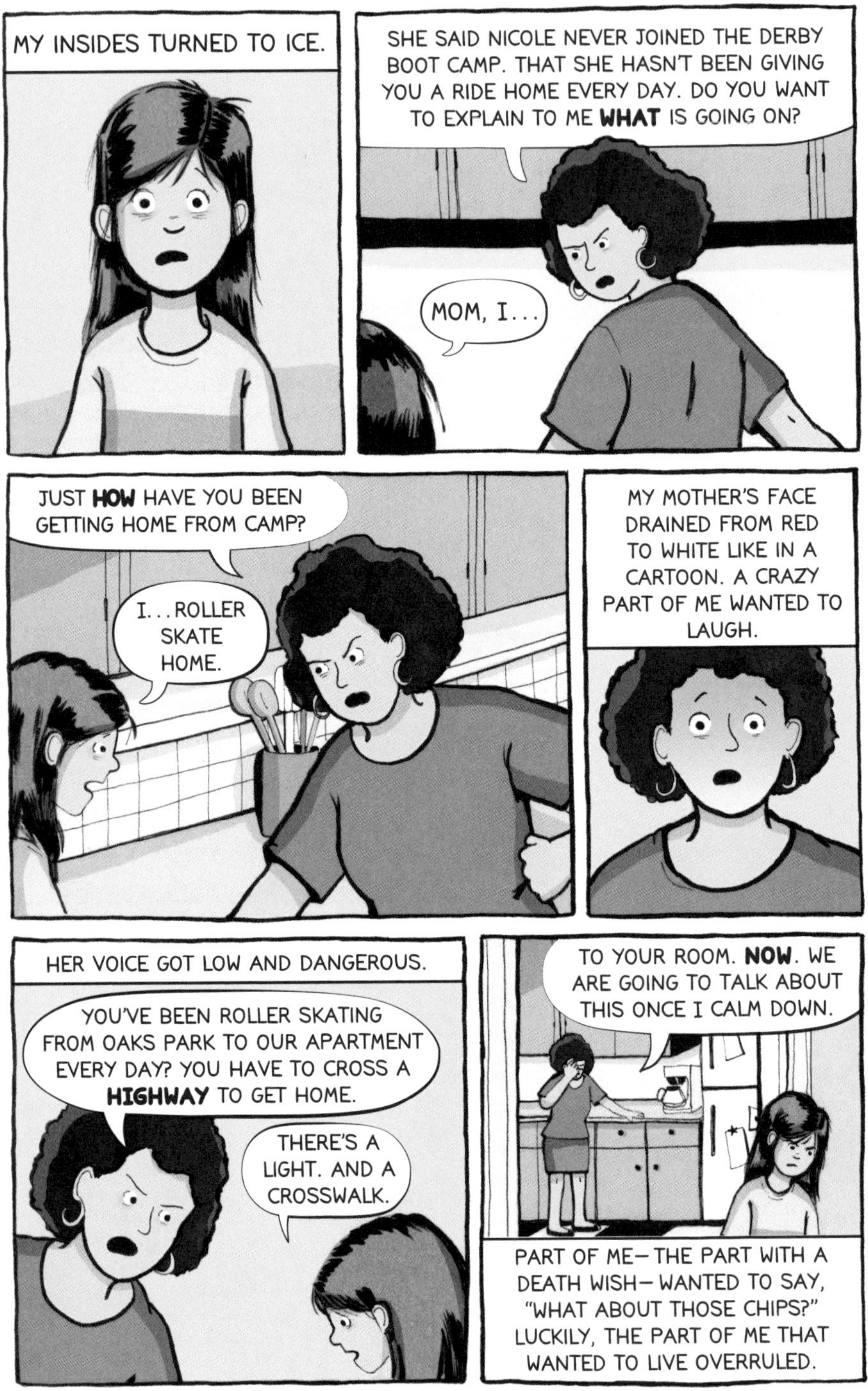
MY INSIDES TURNED TO ICE.
SHE SAID NICOLE NEVER JOINED THE DERBY BOOT CAMP. THAT SHE HASN'T BEEN GIVING YOU A RIDE HOME EVERY DAY. DO YOU WANT TO EXPLAIN TO ME **WHAT** IS GOING ON?
MOM, I...
JUST **HOW** HAVE YOU BEEN GETTING HOME FROM CAMP?
I...ROLLER SKATE HOME.
MY MOTHER'S FACE DRAINED FROM RED TO WHITE LIKE IN A CARTOON. A CRAZY PART OF ME WANTED TO LAUGH.
HER VOICE GOT LOW AND DANGEROUS.
YOU'VE BEEN ROLLER SKATING FROM OAKS PARK TO OUR APARTMENT EVERY DAY? YOU HAVE TO CROSS A **HIGHWAY** TO GET HOME.
THERE'S A LIGHT. AND A CROSSWALK.
TO YOUR ROOM. **NOW**. WE ARE GOING TO TALK ABOUT THIS ONCE I CALM DOWN.
PART OF ME—THE PART WITH A DEATH WISH—WANTED TO SAY, "WHAT ABOUT THOSE CHIPS?" LUCKILY, THE PART OF ME THAT WANTED TO LIVE OVERRULED.

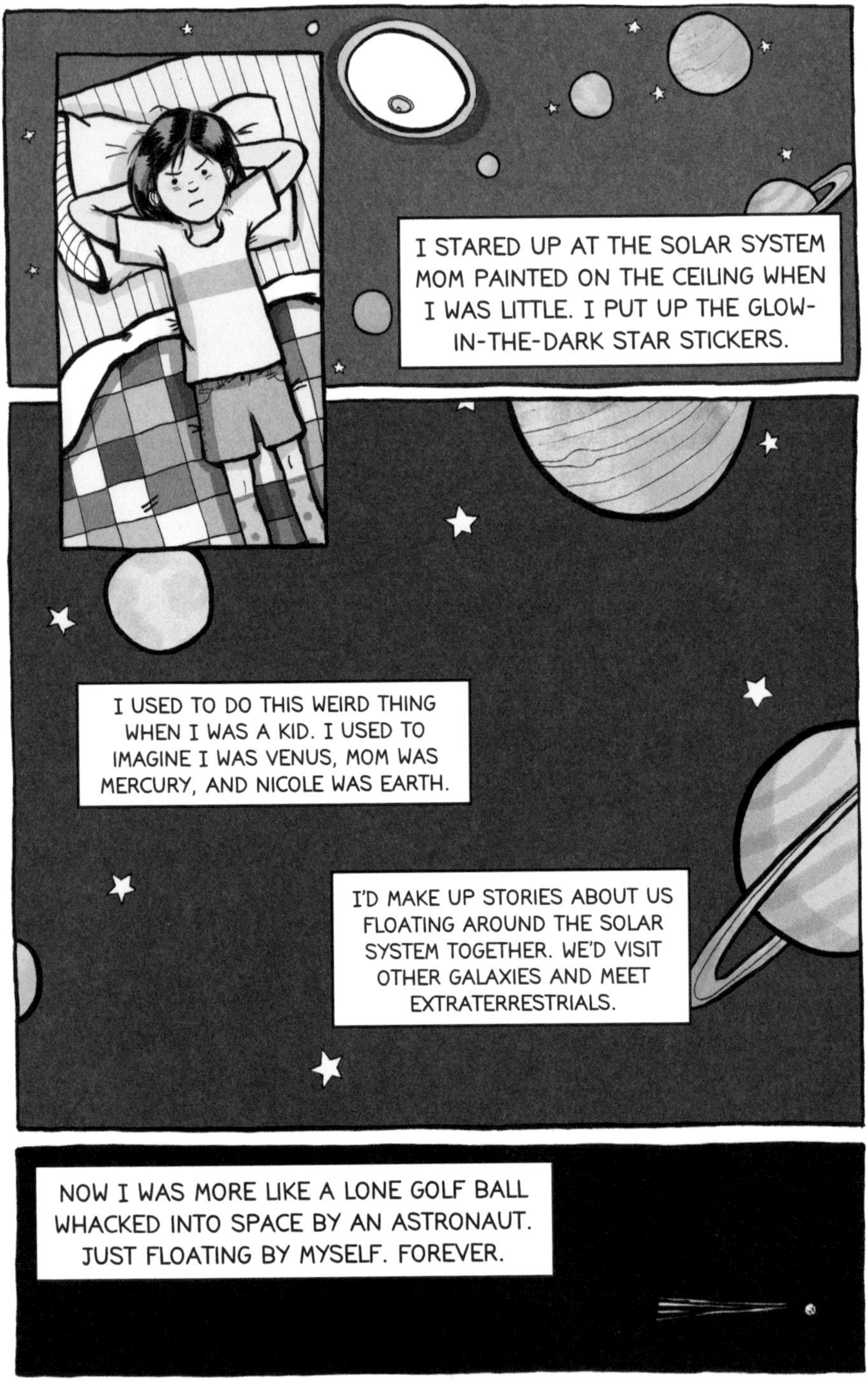
I STARED UP AT THE SOLAR SYSTEM MOM PAINTED ON THE CEILING WHEN I WAS LITTLE. I PUT UP THE GLOW-IN-THE-DARK STAR STICKERS.
I USED TO DO THIS WEIRD THING WHEN I WAS A KID. I USED TO IMAGINE I WAS VENUS, MOM WAS MERCURY, AND NICOLE WAS EARTH.
I'D MAKE UP STORIES ABOUT US FLOATING AROUND THE SOLAR SYSTEM TOGETHER. WE'D VISIT OTHER GALAXIES AND MEET EXTRATERRESTRIALS.
NOW I WAS MORE LIKE A LONE GOLF BALL WHACKED INTO SPACE BY AN ASTRONAUT. JUST FLOATING BY MYSELF. FOREVER.

SOME OF THE LONGEST MOMENTS OF MY LIFE HAVE BEEN SPENT IN MY ROOM, WAITING FOR MOM TO COME IN AND YELL AT ME.

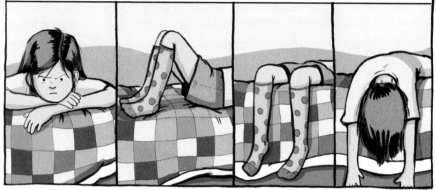

IT WAS WEIRD, THOUGH. SHE JUST SAT THERE. SHE DIDN'T SHOUT. SHE DIDN'T SCREAM. SHE JUST SAT.

OF COURSE, EVENTUALLY, SHE CAME.

FINALLY I FELT LIKE THE SILENCE WAS GOING TO SUFFOCATE ME.

MOM?

I JUST DON'T KNOW WHAT TO DO, ASTRID. FIRST YOU'RE DYEING YOUR HAIR, NOW YOU'RE LYING TO ME...BEING A PARENT WAS SO MUCH EASIER WHEN YOU WERE A LITTLE GIRL.

I'M **NOT** A LITTLE GIRL ANYMORE.

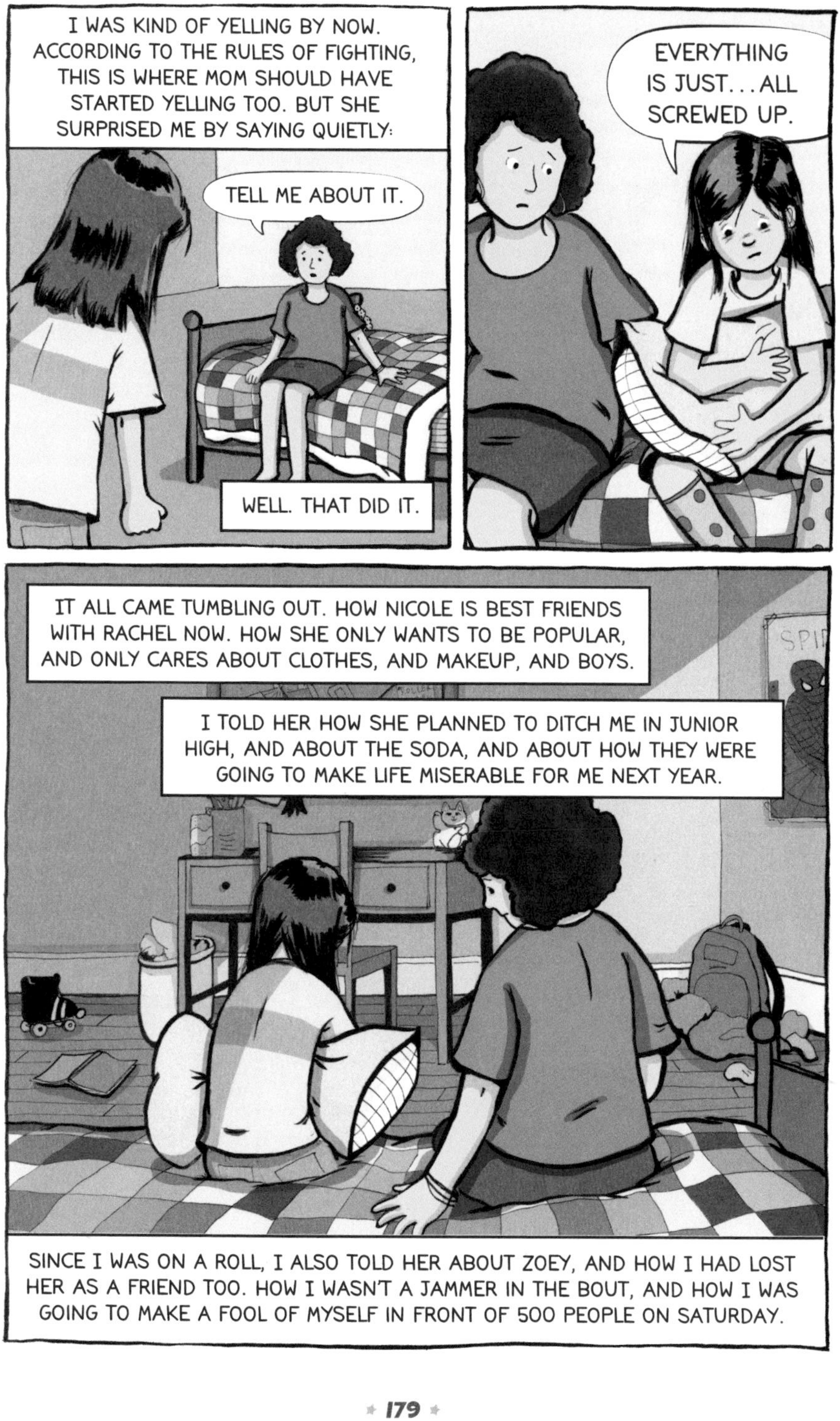

I WAS KIND OF YELLING BY NOW. ACCORDING TO THE RULES OF FIGHTING, THIS IS WHERE MOM SHOULD HAVE STARTED YELLING TOO. BUT SHE SURPRISED ME BY SAYING QUIETLY:
TELL ME ABOUT IT.
WELL. THAT DID IT.
EVERYTHING IS JUST...ALL SCREWED UP.
IT ALL CAME TUMBLING OUT. HOW NICOLE IS BEST FRIENDS WITH RACHEL NOW. HOW SHE ONLY WANTS TO BE POPULAR, AND ONLY CARES ABOUT CLOTHES, AND MAKEUP, AND BOYS.
I TOLD HER HOW SHE PLANNED TO DITCH ME IN JUNIOR HIGH, AND ABOUT THE SODA, AND ABOUT HOW THEY WERE GOING TO MAKE LIFE MISERABLE FOR ME NEXT YEAR.
SINCE I WAS ON A ROLL, I ALSO TOLD HER ABOUT ZOEY, AND HOW I HAD LOST HER AS A FRIEND TOO. HOW I WASN'T A JAMMER IN THE BOUT, AND HOW I WAS GOING TO MAKE A FOOL OF MYSELF IN FRONT OF 500 PEOPLE ON SATURDAY.

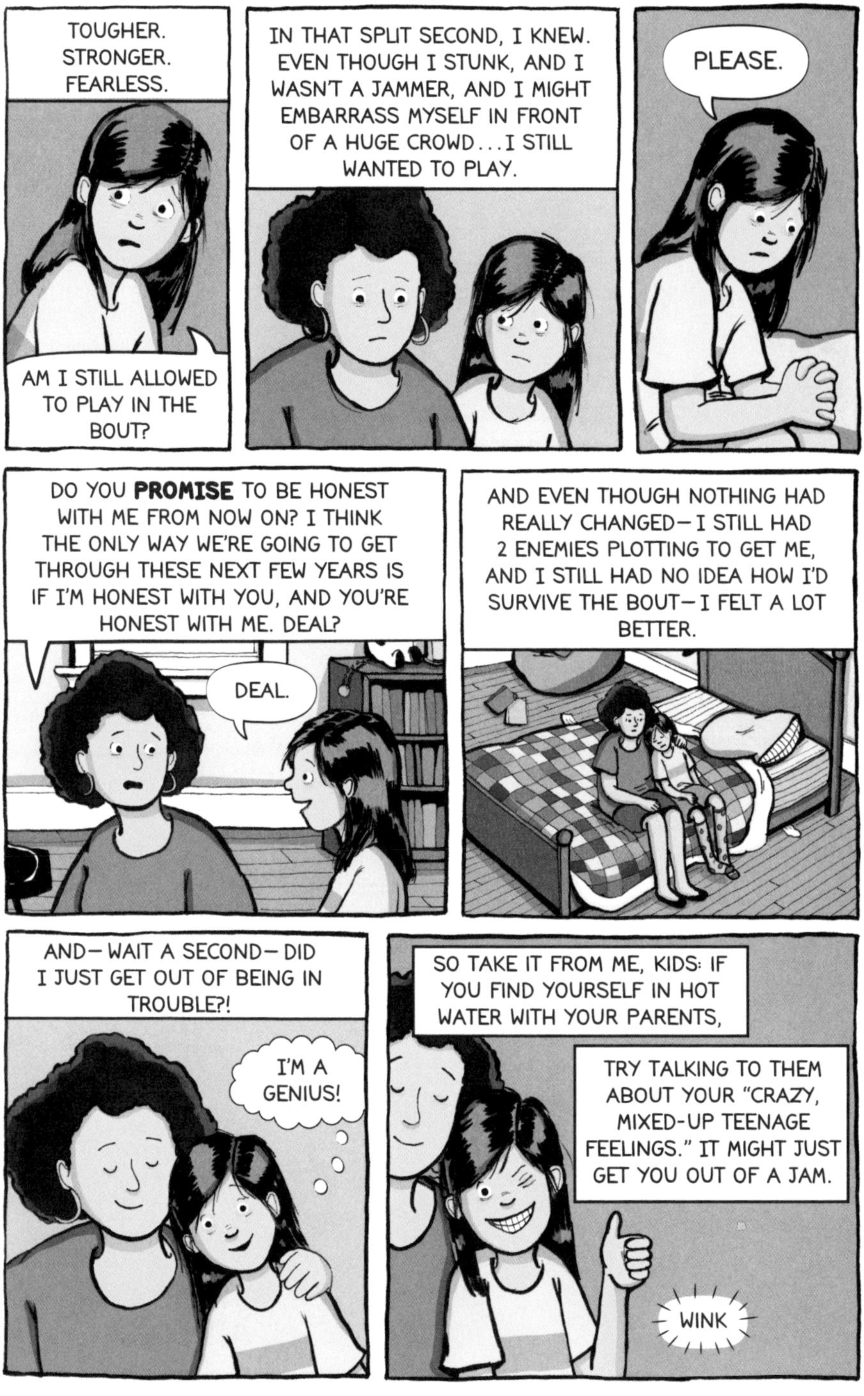
TOUGHER. STRONGER. FEARLESS.
AM I STILL ALLOWED TO PLAY IN THE BOUT?
IN THAT SPLIT SECOND, I KNEW. EVEN THOUGH I STUNK, AND I WASN'T A JAMMER, AND I MIGHT EMBARRASS MYSELF IN FRONT OF A HUGE CROWD...I STILL WANTED TO PLAY.
PLEASE.
DO YOU **PROMISE** TO BE HONEST WITH ME FROM NOW ON? I THINK THE ONLY WAY WE'RE GOING TO GET THROUGH THESE NEXT FEW YEARS IS IF I'M HONEST WITH YOU, AND YOU'RE HONEST WITH ME. DEAL?
DEAL.
AND EVEN THOUGH NOTHING HAD REALLY CHANGED— I STILL HAD 2 ENEMIES PLOTTING TO GET ME, AND I STILL HAD NO IDEA HOW I'D SURVIVE THE BOUT— I FELT A LOT BETTER.
AND— WAIT A SECOND— DID I JUST GET OUT OF BEING IN TROUBLE?!
I'M A GENIUS!
SO TAKE IT FROM ME, KIDS: IF YOU FIND YOURSELF IN HOT WATER WITH YOUR PARENTS,
TRY TALKING TO THEM ABOUT YOUR "CRAZY, MIXED-UP TEENAGE FEELINGS." IT MIGHT JUST GET YOU OUT OF A JAM.
WINK

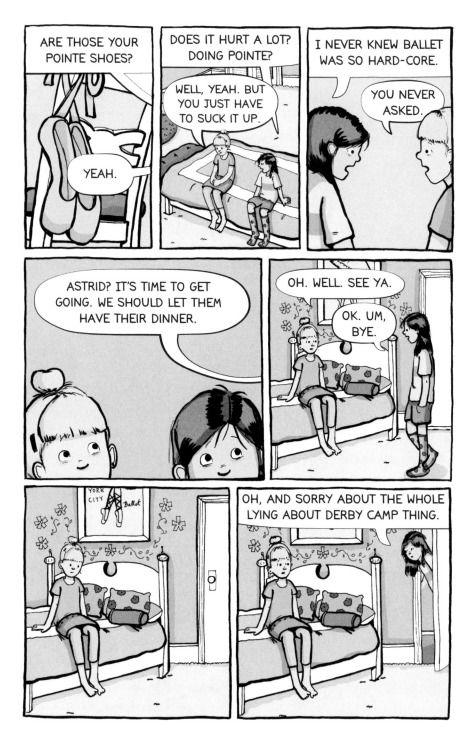

WHEN I WAS IN KINDERGARTEN, MY TEACHER HAD A POSTER THAT WAS SUPPOSED TO TEACH YOU ABOUT FEELINGS.

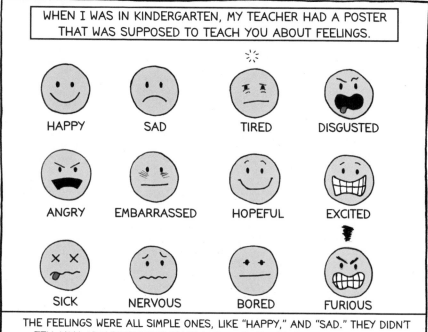

HAPPY	SAD	TIRED	DISGUSTED
ANGRY	EMBARRASSED	HOPEFUL	EXCITED
SICK	NERVOUS	BORED	FURIOUS

THE FEELINGS WERE ALL SIMPLE ONES, LIKE "HAPPY," AND "SAD." THEY DIDN'T TELL YOU ABOUT FEELINGS THAT GOT MIXED TOGETHER LIKE A SMOOTHIE.

I FELT BETTER...BUT NOT COMPLETELY. I WAS STILL A LITTLE MAD AT NICOLE... BUT I FELT LIKE I DID SOMETHING WRONG TOO. I WAS HAPPY THAT I TALKED TO HER...BUT SAD THAT EVERYTHING STILL FELT SO DIFFERENT.

I WAS SHAD.

HAPPY + SAD = SHAD ?

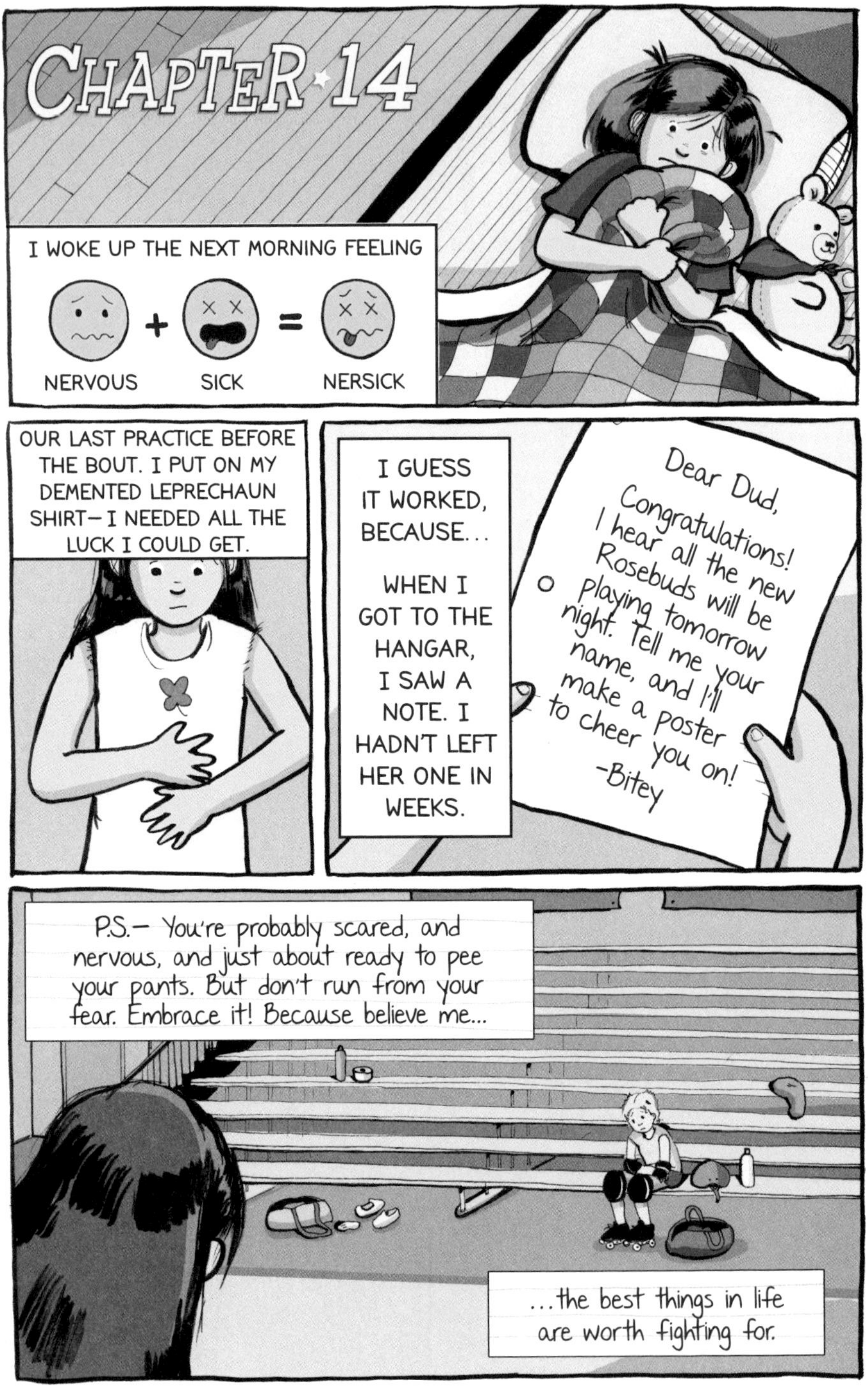
CHAPTER 14
I WOKE UP THE NEXT MORNING FEELING
NERVOUS
+
SICK
=
NERSICK
OUR LAST PRACTICE BEFORE THE BOUT. I PUT ON MY DEMENTED LEPRECHAUN SHIRT— I NEEDED ALL THE LUCK I COULD GET.
I GUESS IT WORKED, BECAUSE...
WHEN I GOT TO THE HANGAR, I SAW A NOTE. I HADN'T LEFT HER ONE IN WEEKS.
Dear Dud,
Congratulations! I hear all the new Rosebuds will be playing tomorrow night. Tell me your name, and I'll make a poster to cheer you on!
-Bitey
P.S.— You're probably scared, and nervous, and just about ready to pee your pants. But don't run from your fear. Embrace it! Because believe me...
...the best things in life are worth fighting for.

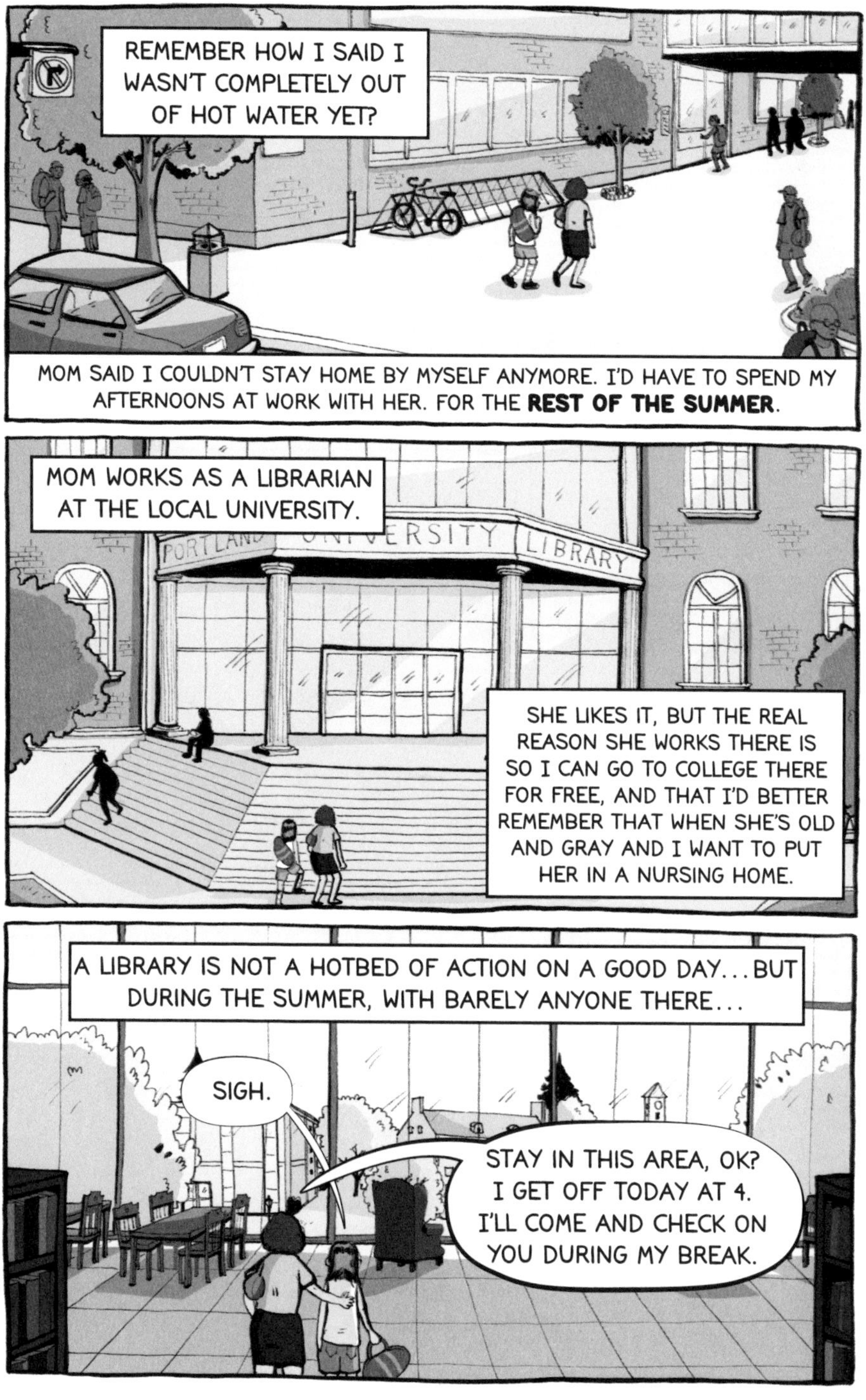
REMEMBER HOW I SAID I WASN'T COMPLETELY OUT OF HOT WATER YET?
MOM SAID I COULDN'T STAY HOME BY MYSELF ANYMORE. I'D HAVE TO SPEND MY AFTERNOONS AT WORK WITH HER. FOR THE **REST OF THE SUMMER**.
MOM WORKS AS A LIBRARIAN AT THE LOCAL UNIVERSITY.
PORTLAND UNIVERSITY LIBRARY
SHE LIKES IT, BUT THE REAL REASON SHE WORKS THERE IS SO I CAN GO TO COLLEGE THERE FOR FREE, AND THAT I'D BETTER REMEMBER THAT WHEN SHE'S OLD AND GRAY AND I WANT TO PUT HER IN A NURSING HOME.
A LIBRARY IS NOT A HOTBED OF ACTION ON A GOOD DAY... BUT DURING THE SUMMER, WITH BARELY ANYONE THERE...
SIGH.
STAY IN THIS AREA, OK? I GET OFF TODAY AT 4. I'LL COME AND CHECK ON YOU DURING MY BREAK.

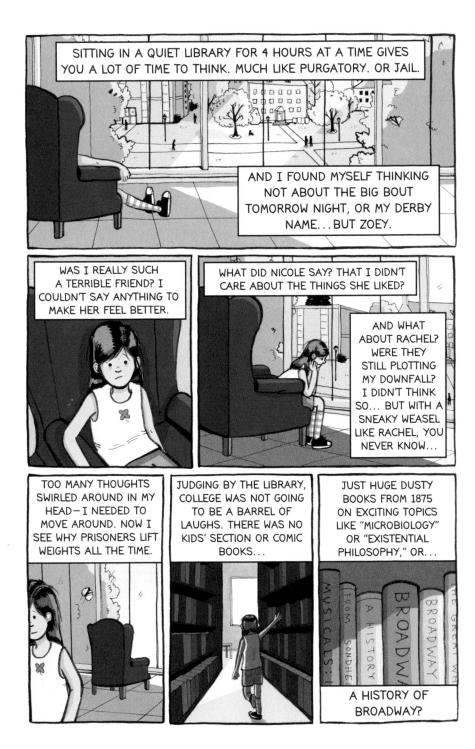

SITTING IN A QUIET LIBRARY FOR 4 HOURS AT A TIME GIVES YOU A LOT OF TIME TO THINK. MUCH LIKE PURGATORY. OR JAIL.

AND I FOUND MYSELF THINKING NOT ABOUT THE BIG BOUT TOMORROW NIGHT, OR MY DERBY NAME... BUT ZOEY.

WAS I REALLY SUCH A TERRIBLE FRIEND? I COULDN'T SAY ANYTHING TO MAKE HER FEEL BETTER.

WHAT DID NICOLE SAY? THAT I DIDN'T CARE ABOUT THE THINGS SHE LIKED?

AND WHAT ABOUT RACHEL? WERE THEY STILL PLOTTING MY DOWNFALL? I DIDN'T THINK SO... BUT WITH A SNEAKY WEASEL LIKE RACHEL, YOU NEVER KNOW...

TOO MANY THOUGHTS SWIRLED AROUND IN MY HEAD—I NEEDED TO MOVE AROUND. NOW I SEE WHY PRISONERS LIFT WEIGHTS ALL THE TIME.

JUDGING BY THE LIBRARY, COLLEGE WAS NOT GOING TO BE A BARREL OF LAUGHS. THERE WAS NO KIDS' SECTION OR COMIC BOOKS...

JUST HUGE DUSTY BOOKS FROM 1875 ON EXCITING TOPICS LIKE "MICROBIOLOGY" OR "EXISTENTIAL PHILOSOPHY," OR...

MUSICALS: FROM SONDHE

A HISTORY

BROADWAY

BROADWAY

THE GREAT WH

A HISTORY OF BROADWAY?

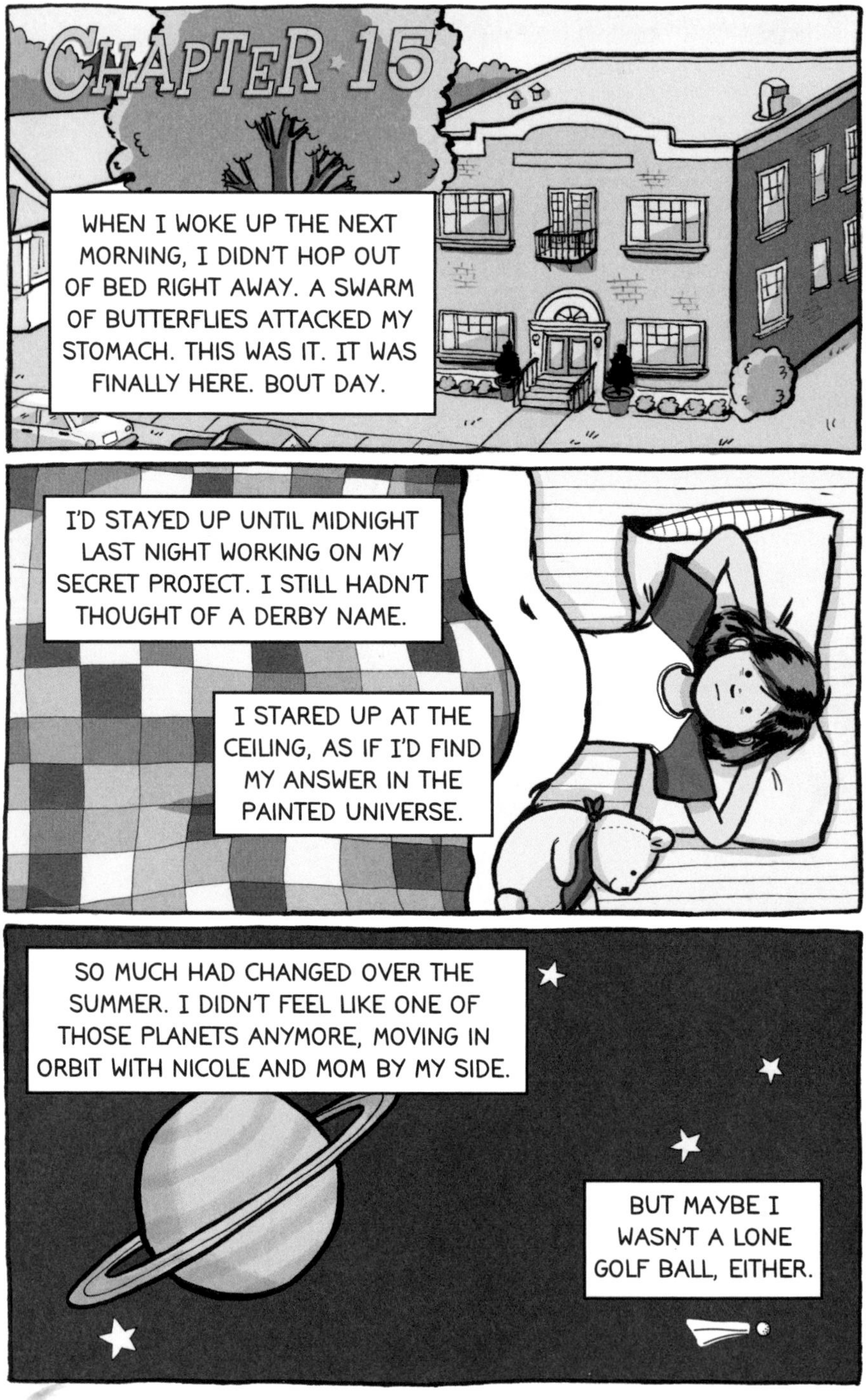
CHAPTER 15
WHEN I WOKE UP THE NEXT MORNING, I DIDN'T HOP OUT OF BED RIGHT AWAY. A SWARM OF BUTTERFLIES ATTACKED MY STOMACH. THIS WAS IT. IT WAS FINALLY HERE. BOUT DAY.
I'D STAYED UP UNTIL MIDNIGHT LAST NIGHT WORKING ON MY SECRET PROJECT. I STILL HADN'T THOUGHT OF A DERBY NAME.
I STARED UP AT THE CEILING, AS IF I'D FIND MY ANSWER IN THE PAINTED UNIVERSE.
SO MUCH HAD CHANGED OVER THE SUMMER. I DIDN'T FEEL LIKE ONE OF THOSE PLANETS ANYMORE, MOVING IN ORBIT WITH NICOLE AND MOM BY MY SIDE.
BUT MAYBE I WASN'T A LONE GOLF BALL, EITHER.

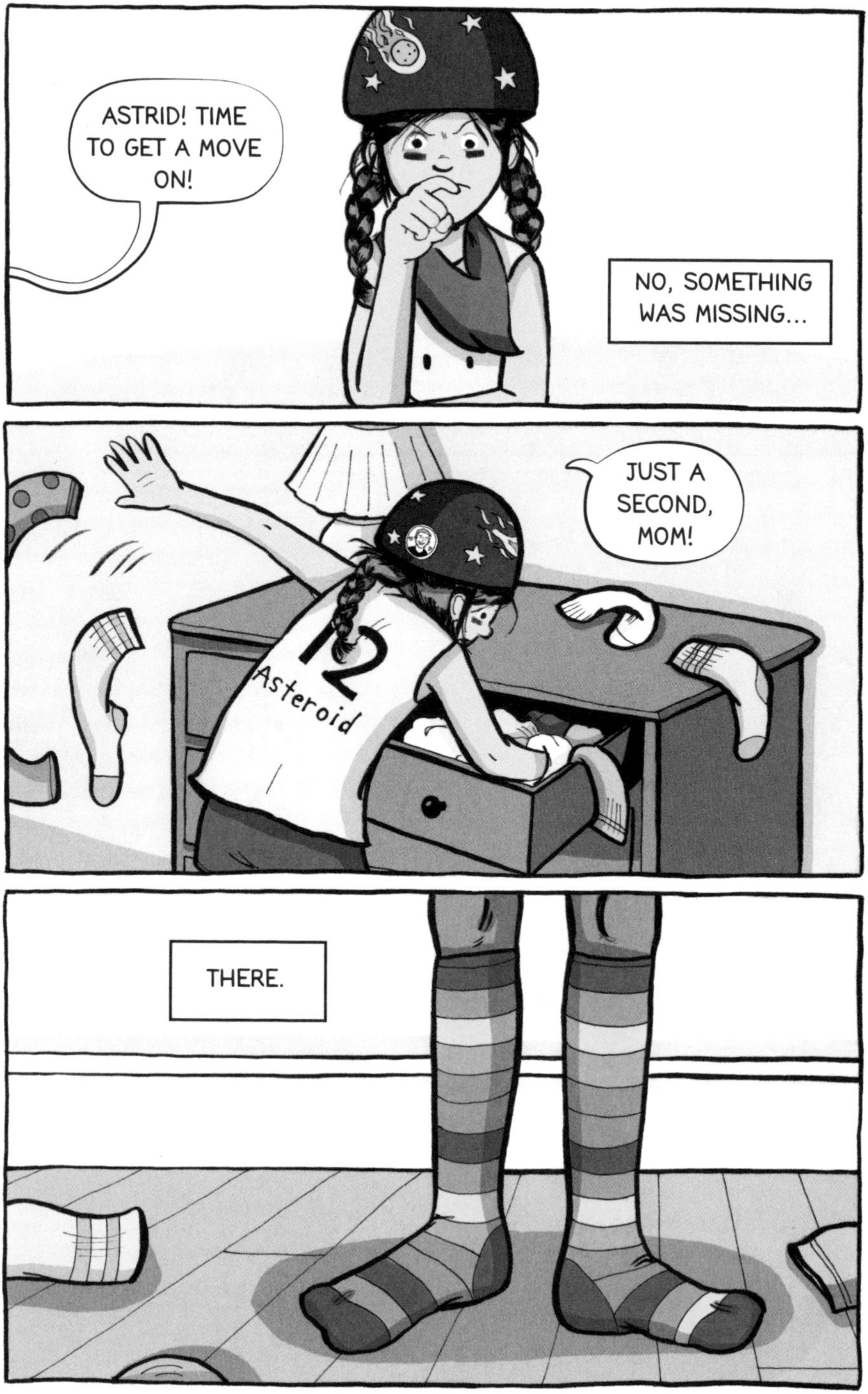
ASTRID! TIME TO GET A MOVE ON!
NO, SOMETHING WAS MISSING...
JUST A SECOND, MOM!
12
Asteroid
THERE.

WHEN WE GOT TO THE HANGAR, I STARTED TO GET REALLY, REALLY NERVOUS. I'D NEVER SEEN IT SO CROWDED BEFORE.

I SAW VOLUNTEERS, ANNOUNCERS, ADULT SKATERS...

... BUT NO ZOEY.

WE'RE MEETING OUTSIDE IN 15 MINUTES! SPREAD THE WORD.

HEY! AND NICE NAME... ASTEROID.

15 MINUTES. THAT SHOULD BE JUST ENOUGH TIME TO ACTIVATE MY SECRET PLAN.

I HAD TO DO IT NOW, BEFORE SOMEONE NOTICED AND ASKED WHAT I WAS DOING.

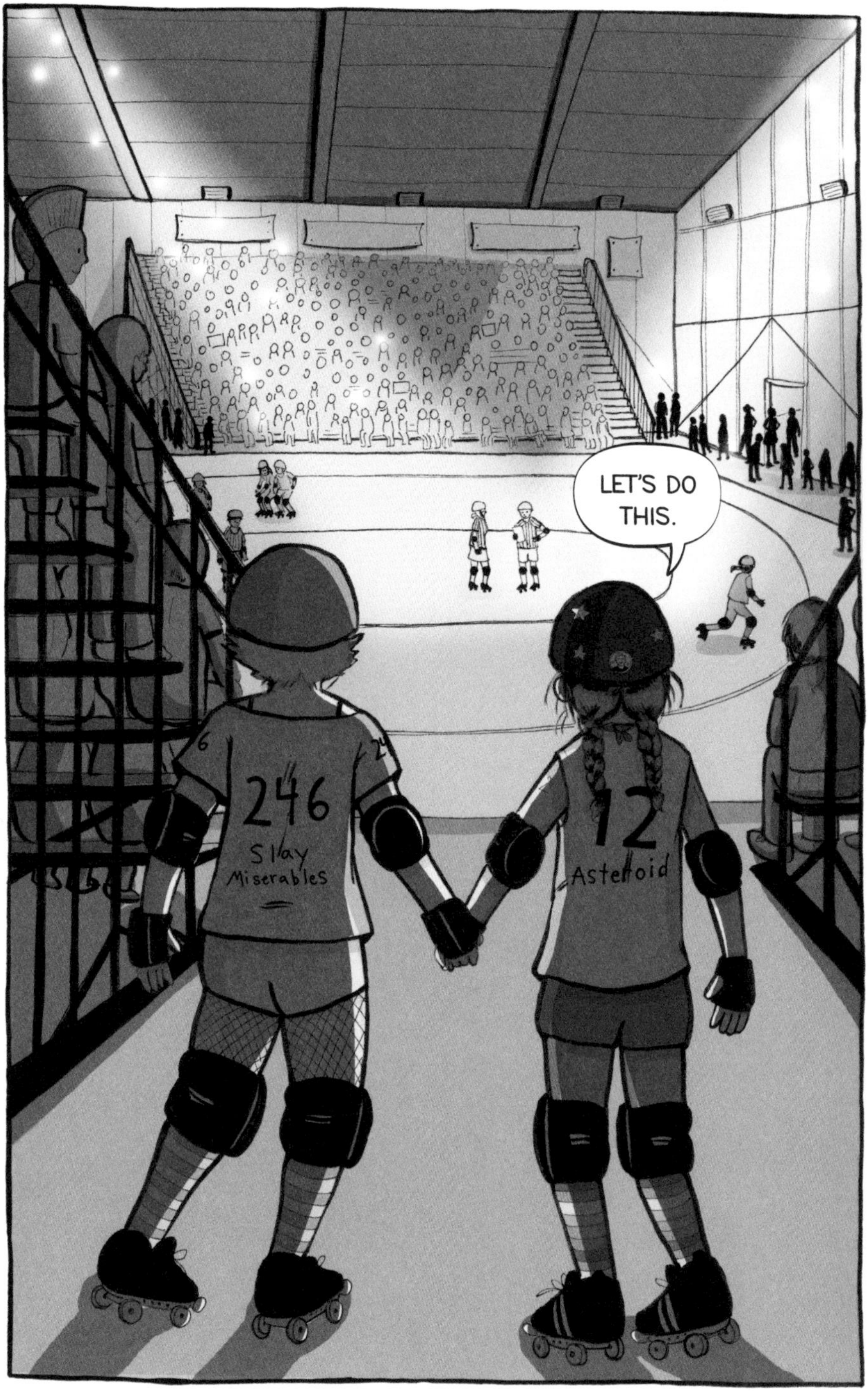
LET'S DO THIS.
246
Slay Miserables
12
Asteroid

CHAPTER 16

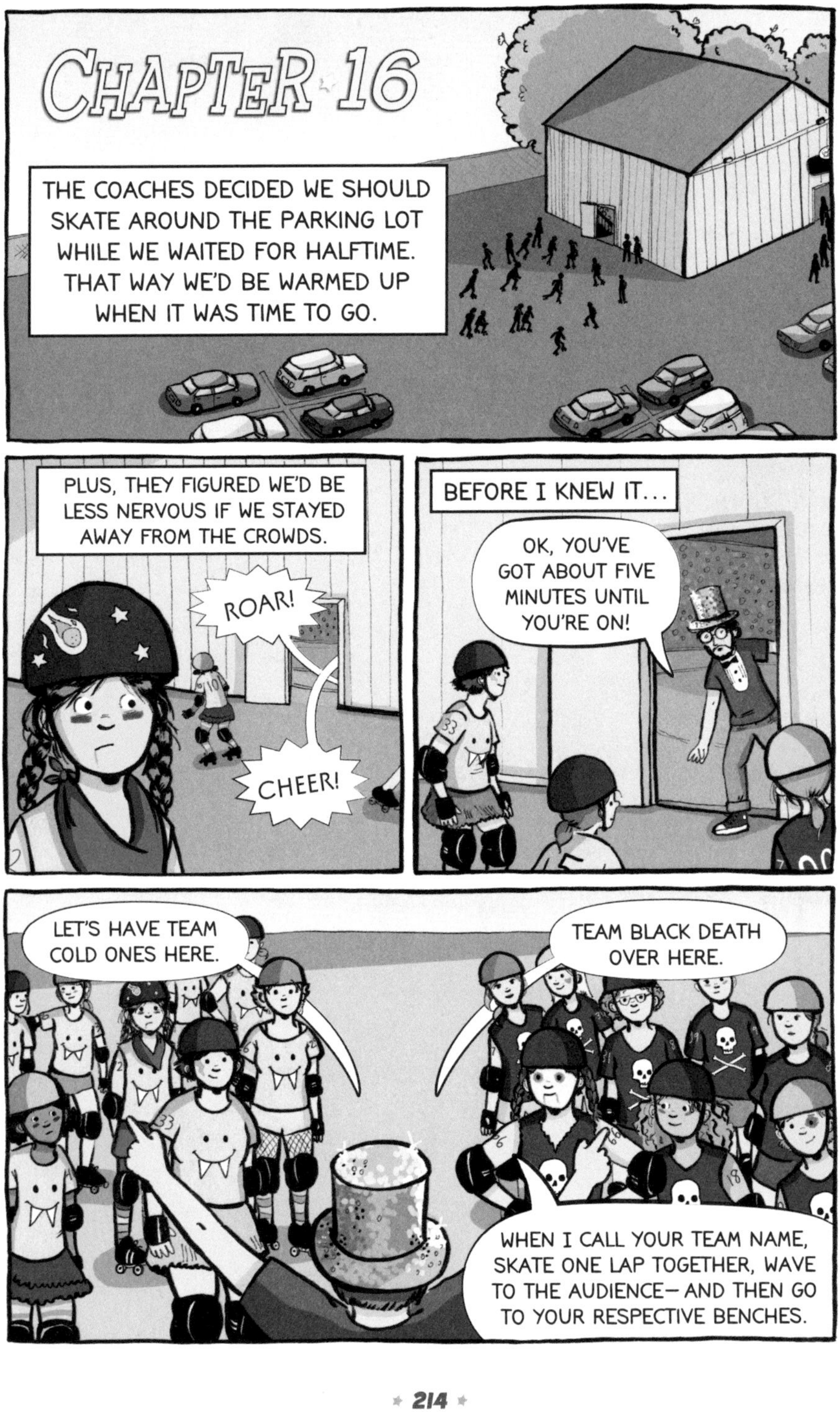
THE COACHES DECIDED WE SHOULD SKATE AROUND THE PARKING LOT WHILE WE WAITED FOR HALFTIME. THAT WAY WE'D BE WARMED UP WHEN IT WAS TIME TO GO.
PLUS, THEY FIGURED WE'D BE LESS NERVOUS IF WE STAYED AWAY FROM THE CROWDS.
ROAR!
CHEER!
BEFORE I KNEW IT...
OK, YOU'VE GOT ABOUT FIVE MINUTES UNTIL YOU'RE ON!
LET'S HAVE TEAM COLD ONES HERE.
TEAM BLACK DEATH OVER HERE.
WHEN I CALL YOUR TEAM NAME, SKATE ONE LAP TOGETHER, WAVE TO THE AUDIENCE— AND THEN GO TO YOUR RESPECTIVE BENCHES.

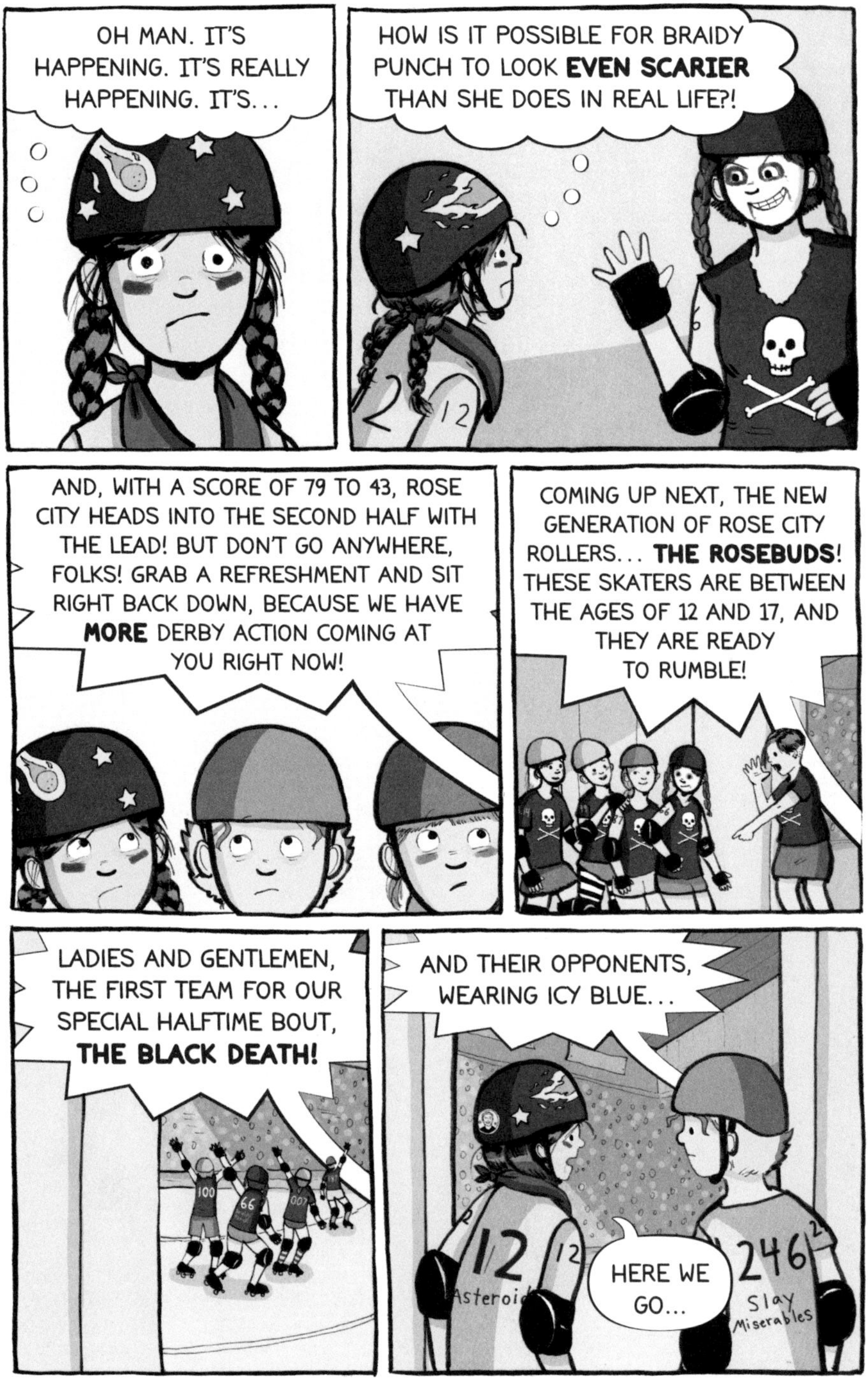
OH MAN. IT'S HAPPENING. IT'S REALLY HAPPENING. IT'S...
HOW IS IT POSSIBLE FOR BRAIDY PUNCH TO LOOK **EVEN SCARIER** THAN SHE DOES IN REAL LIFE?!
AND, WITH A SCORE OF 79 TO 43, ROSE CITY HEADS INTO THE SECOND HALF WITH THE LEAD! BUT DON'T GO ANYWHERE, FOLKS! GRAB A REFRESHMENT AND SIT RIGHT BACK DOWN, BECAUSE WE HAVE **MORE** DERBY ACTION COMING AT YOU RIGHT NOW!
COMING UP NEXT, THE NEW GENERATION OF ROSE CITY ROLLERS... **THE ROSEBUDS**! THESE SKATERS ARE BETWEEN THE AGES OF 12 AND 17, AND THEY ARE READY TO RUMBLE!
LADIES AND GENTLEMEN, THE FIRST TEAM FOR OUR SPECIAL HALFTIME BOUT, **THE BLACK DEATH!**
AND THEIR OPPONENTS, WEARING ICY BLUE...
12
Asteroid
246
Slay Miserables
HERE WE GO...

THE FLASHES OF THE CAMERAS LOOKED LIKE STARS. IT WAS HANDS DOWN ONE OF THE BEST MOMENTS OF MY LIFE...

... SO FAR.

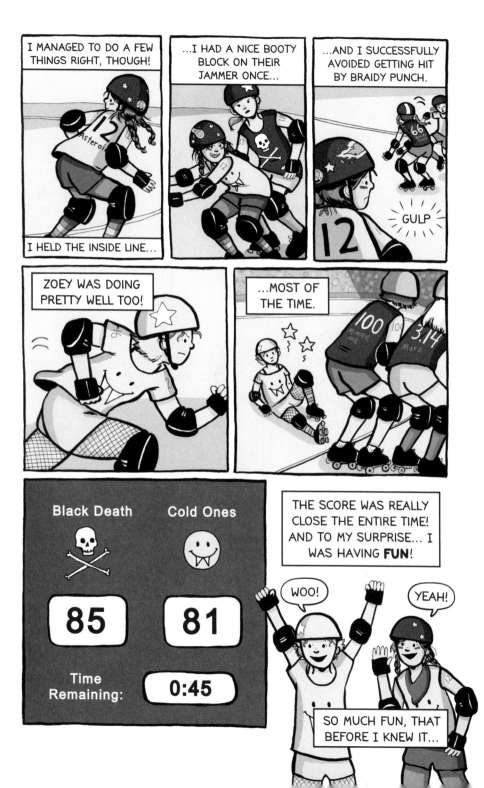

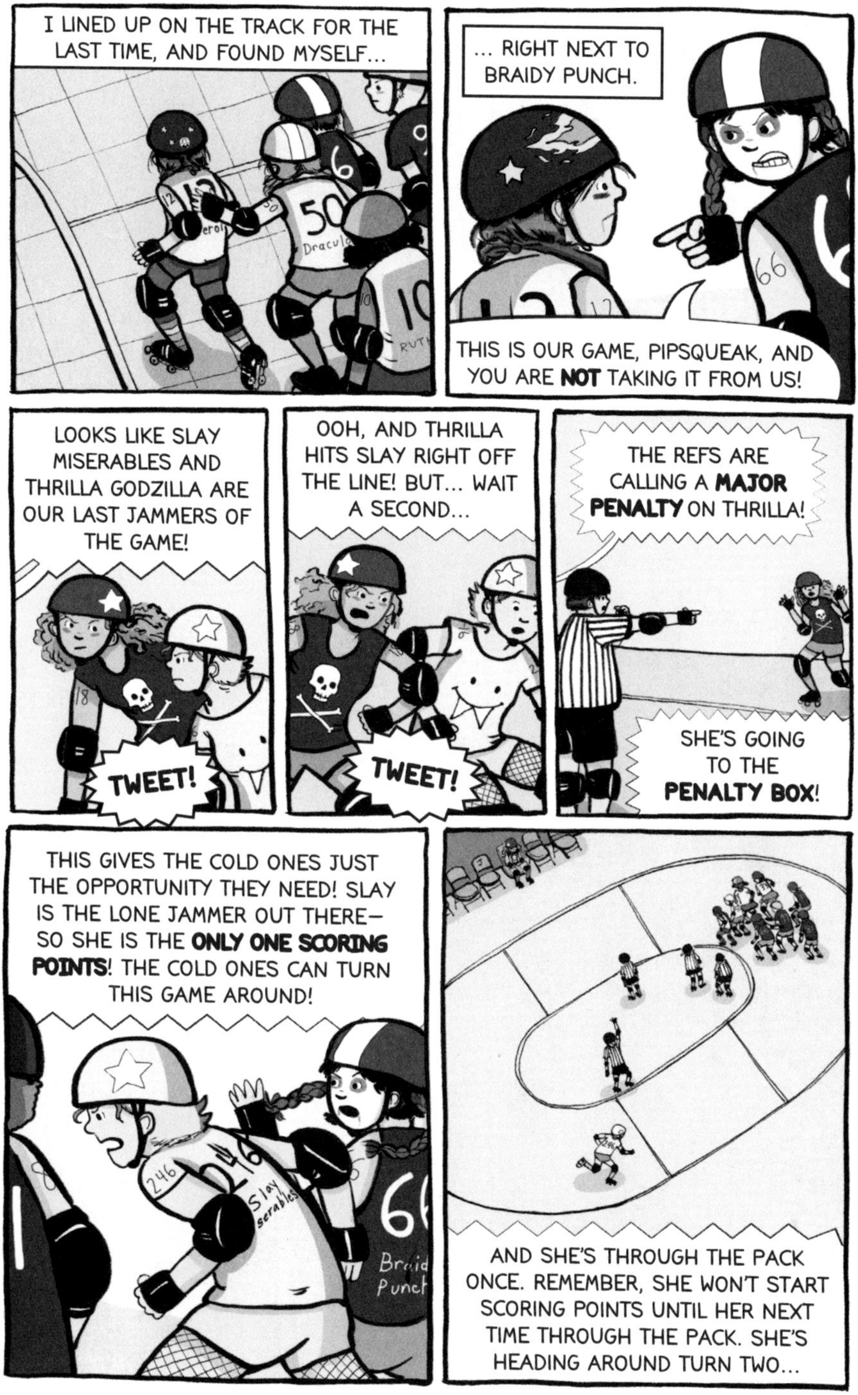
I LINED UP ON THE TRACK FOR THE LAST TIME, AND FOUND MYSELF...
... RIGHT NEXT TO BRAIDY PUNCH.
THIS IS OUR GAME, PIPSQUEAK, AND YOU ARE **NOT** TAKING IT FROM US!
LOOKS LIKE SLAY MISERABLES AND THRILLA GODZILLA ARE OUR LAST JAMMERS OF THE GAME!
TWEET!
OOH, AND THRILLA HITS SLAY RIGHT OFF THE LINE! BUT... WAIT A SECOND...
TWEET!
THE REFS ARE CALLING A **MAJOR PENALTY** ON THRILLA!
SHE'S GOING TO THE **PENALTY BOX**!
THIS GIVES THE COLD ONES JUST THE OPPORTUNITY THEY NEED! SLAY IS THE LONE JAMMER OUT THERE—SO SHE IS THE **ONLY ONE SCORING POINTS**! THE COLD ONES CAN TURN THIS GAME AROUND!
AND SHE'S THROUGH THE PACK ONCE. REMEMBER, SHE WON'T START SCORING POINTS UNTIL HER NEXT TIME THROUGH THE PACK. SHE'S HEADING AROUND TURN TWO...

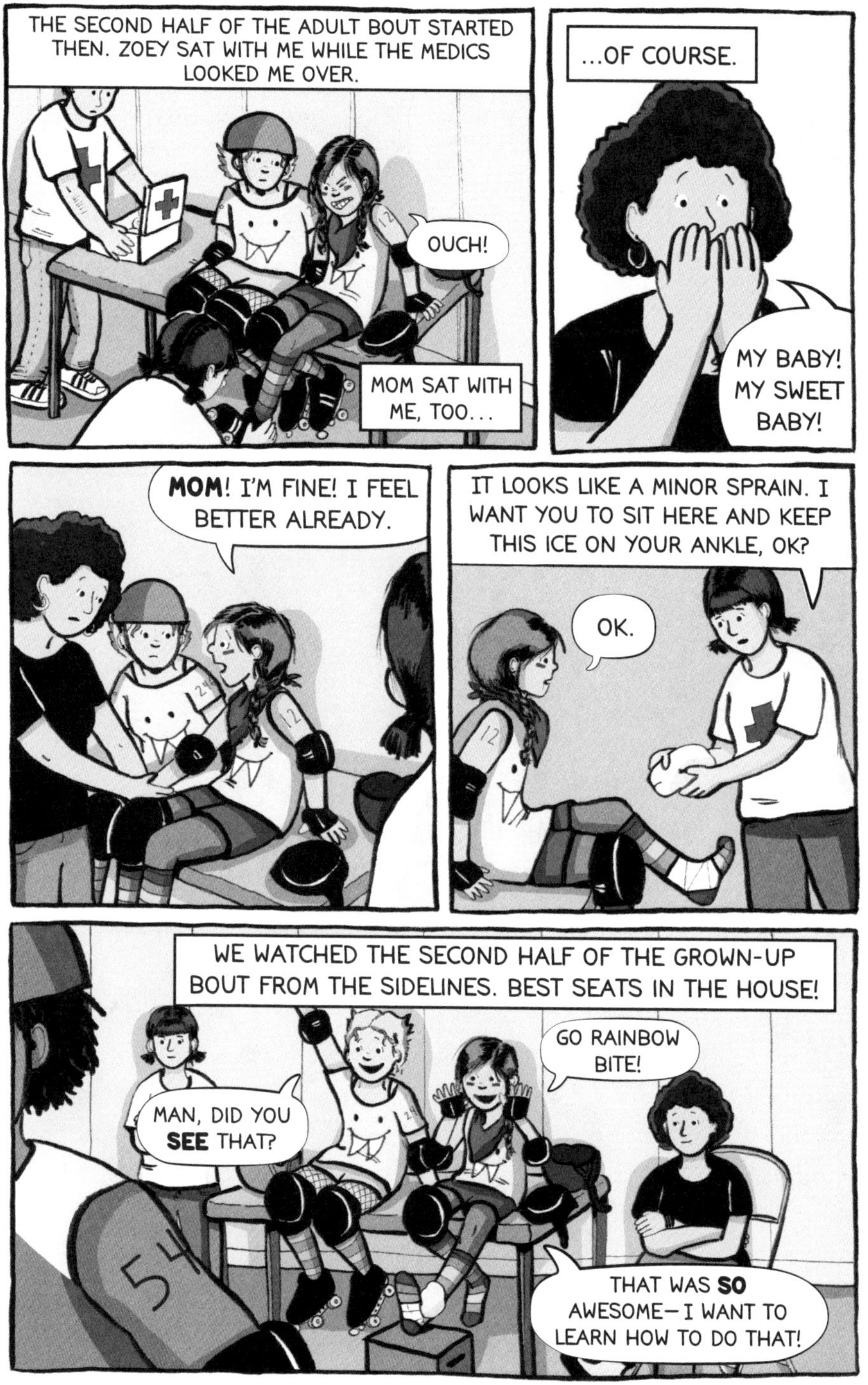
THE SECOND HALF OF THE ADULT BOUT STARTED THEN. ZOEY SAT WITH ME WHILE THE MEDICS LOOKED ME OVER.
OUCH!
MOM SAT WITH ME, TOO...
...OF COURSE.
MY BABY! MY SWEET BABY!
MOM! I'M FINE! I FEEL BETTER ALREADY.
IT LOOKS LIKE A MINOR SPRAIN. I WANT YOU TO SIT HERE AND KEEP THIS ICE ON YOUR ANKLE, OK?
OK.
WE WATCHED THE SECOND HALF OF THE GROWN-UP BOUT FROM THE SIDELINES. BEST SEATS IN THE HOUSE!
GO RAINBOW BITE!
MAN, DID YOU SEE THAT?
THAT WAS SO AWESOME—I WANT TO LEARN HOW TO DO THAT!

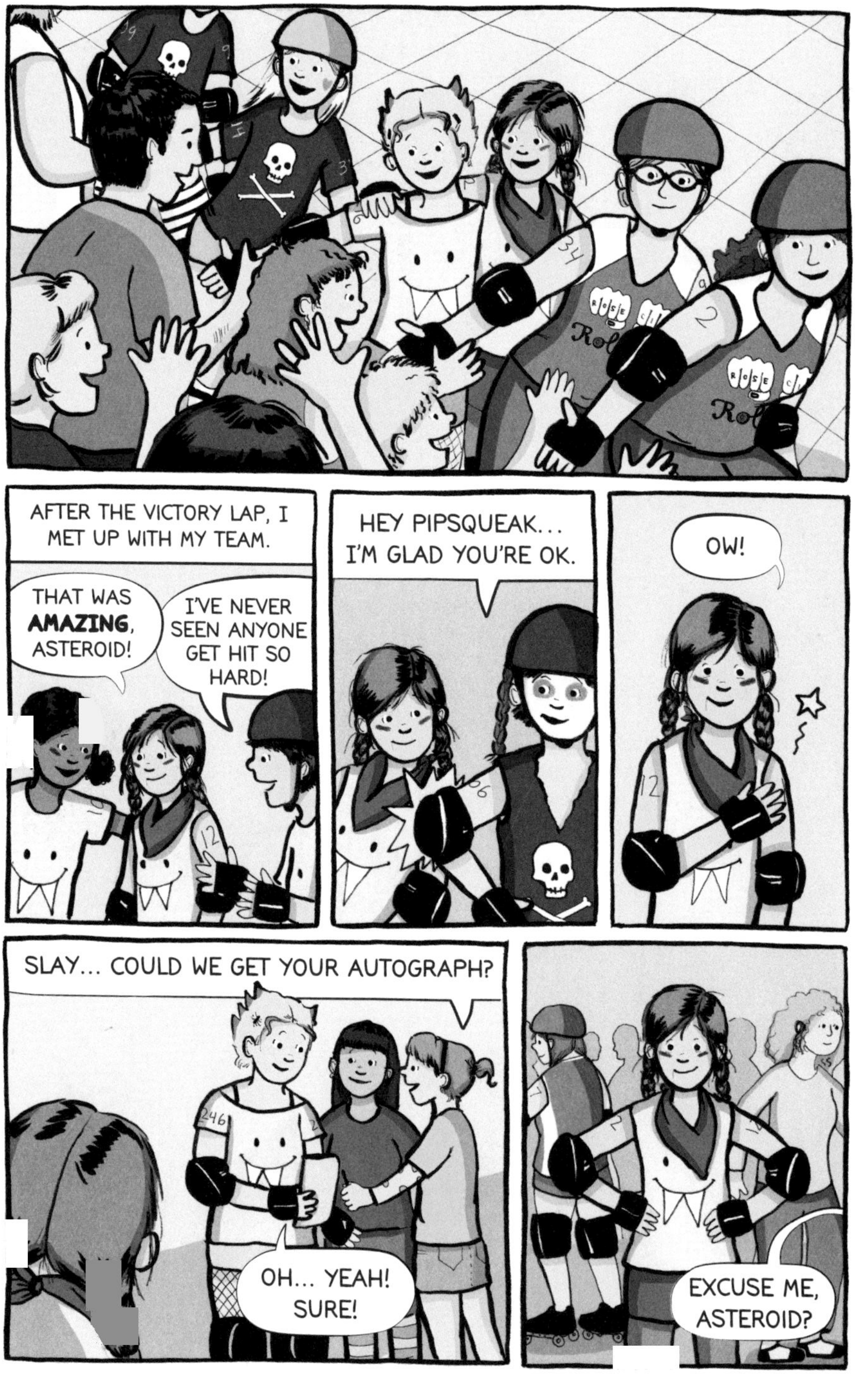
AFTER THE VICTORY LAP, I MET UP WITH MY TEAM.
THAT WAS **AMAZING**, ASTEROID!
I'VE NEVER SEEN ANYONE GET HIT SO HARD!
HEY PIPSQUEAK... I'M GLAD YOU'RE OK.
OW!
SLAY... COULD WE GET YOUR AUTOGRAPH?
OH... YEAH! SURE!
EXCUSE ME, ASTEROID?

IT'S FUNNY, HOW MUCH HAS CHANGED THIS SUMMER.

EVERYTHING USED TO BE SO SIMPLE.
BLACK AND WHITE.
HAPPY. SAD.
BEST FRIENDS. WORST ENEMIES.

NOW EVERYTHING SEEMED SO... COMPLEX. I WAS IN A NO-MAN'S-LAND OF UNCHARTERED TERRITORIES.

MAYBE I HAD TO FIND MY OWN PATH THROUGH IT.

SUDDENLY, I LOOKED AT THE CROWD AROUND ME AND FELT... LOST. IT SOUNDS BABYISH, BUT I GOT A LITTLE PANICKED.

GASP!

MOM? ZOEY?

THEY WERE HERE JUST A MINUTE AGO...

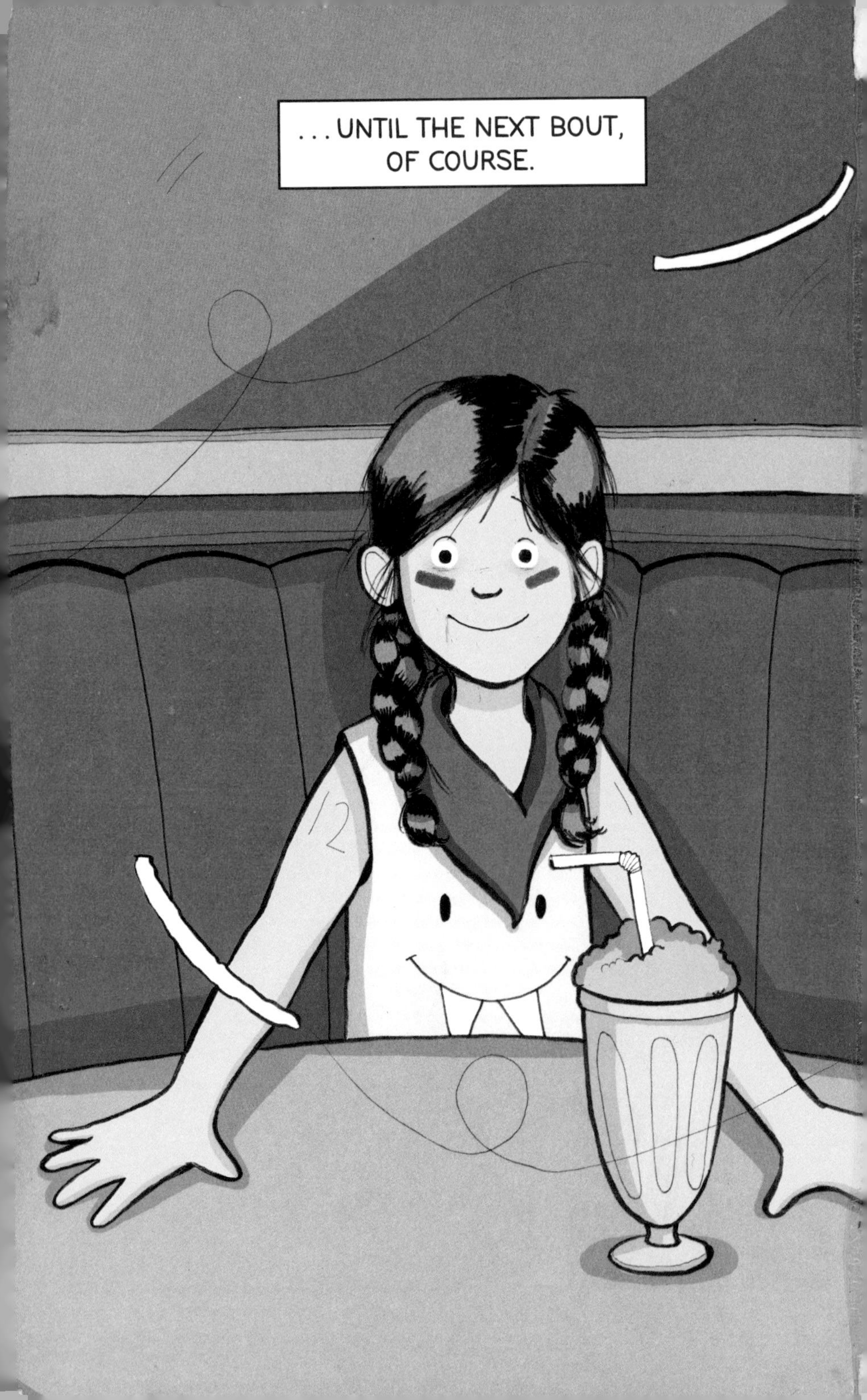
. . . UNTIL THE NEXT BOUT, OF COURSE.